MIRRORS IN THE SKY

GRAHAM ZIMMATORE

*To Calvence
all the best
Graham*

TL Publishers
tlpubsorg@aol.com

Published in the UK by TL Publishers, 2007

Proof read and edited by Tony Brown

Cover by Rick Hayden

Copyright Graham Zimmatore, 2007

This book is copyright under the Berne Convention.
No reproduction without permission.
All rights reserved.

The right of Graham Zimmatore to be identified as the author of this work has been asserted by him in accordance with sections 77 and 78 of the Copyright, Designs and Patents Act, 1988.

ISBN 978-0-9555222-0-8

grahamzimmatore@aol.com

This book is a work of fiction. Names, characters, places and incidents are either a product of the authors imagination or are used fictitiously. Any resemblance to actual people, living or dead is entirely coincidental. However, from time to time coincidences *have* been known to happen.

For Tina.

NEWS BRIEF:

In 1975 the Providence Journal Bulletin ran an editorial by Senator Claiborne Pell, D-Rhode Island. In it he was quoted as saying:

"The U.S. and other world powers should sign a treaty to outlaw the tampering with weather as an instrument of war. It may seem farfetched to think of using weather as a weapon -- but I'm convinced that the U.S. did, in fact, use rainmaking techniques as a weapon of war in South East Asia................"

He also went on to state:

"We need a treaty now to prevent such actions -- before the military leaders of the world start directing storms, manipulating climates, and inducing earthquakes against their enemies. The basic idea of environmental warfare is simple -- if a nation can learn to trigger natural events it can inflict terrible damage on an enemy through rainfall, flooding, tidal waves, earthquakes, and even climate changes that could devastate an enemy nation's agriculture........"

Then there's this - excerpted from an article by Dr Michael Persinger, Professor of Psychology and Neuroscience at Laurentian University, Ontario, Canada, titled "On the Possibility of Directly Accessing Every Human Brain by Electromagnetic Induction of Fundamental Algorithms".

"Within the last two decades a potential has emerged which was improbable, but which is now marginally feasible. This potential is the technical capability to influence directly the major portion of the approximately six billion brains of the human species......

"A process which is coupled to the narrow band of brain temperature could allow all normal human brains to be affected by a sub-harmonic whose frequency range at about 10 Hz would only vary by 0.1 Hz......

"Temporal lobe stimulation can evoke the feeling of a presence, disorientation, and perceptual irregularities. It can activate images stored in the subject's memory, including nightmares and monsters that are normally suppressed......"

For many, these statements would seem to be in the realms of science fiction, but then in the 1990's, the High-frequency Active Auroral Research Program (HAARP) began transmitting high powered, Extra Low Frequency (ELF) micro-waves up into the ionosphere.

Then, in the fall of 2005 something went very wrong.............

PROLOGUE

England. Late Autumn, 2005:

The old man sat hunched over his desk unable to comprehend what he was seeing. He peered through tired and bloodshot eyes, and in abject horror at the information being relayed to him from the monitor.

Through the window, the last rays of the late autumn sun filtered in through the dusty net curtains, casting shadows across the floor of his small apartment, while above him, a myriad of dust motes swirled around as if they had been bottled in the beam of weak sunlight from the window. He watched, mesmerised by their seemingly endless, frantic movements as they whirled around one another, almost as if they were fighting amongst themselves to remain in the rapidly diminishing beam of light. Then they were gone, blanked out forever, as the sleeping sun sank behind the rooftops across the street.

He looked back at the monitor, shaking his head in disbelief. For forty years he had watched and waited for this moment.

For more than 4 decades he had kept this terrible secret, while it burned a hole in his soul. And now, he realised it could not remain hidden any longer.

Since that fateful day, so many years ago, he had remained silent, watching, and waiting for any kind of news on the TV or in the newspapers. But it had never come – until now.

Could it be, he wondered, that he was the only one left alive who knew?

Was it possible that the secret had been so well hidden that no one else was aware of it; even today?

He recalled the sketchy details of the earthquake that had rocked the Kola Peninsular in 1972. Was it possible that all other persons privy to what he knew were killed in that debacle, when that terrible place was swallowed up into the bowels of the earth? If that were the case, then they took this secret with them – to hell.

And if that was so, then it was he, and he alone, who bore the full responsibility of what was to come.

The old man carefully checked the data one more time. It was just possible he could be mistaken.

But there was no mistake!

He knew what he had to do now and yet it filled him with dread.

He reached for the phone, and punched in the number for international directories.

"Yes, hello! Give me the number for the International Atomic Energy Agency Secretariat, in Austria, please."

Graham Zimmatore

Chapter 1

North West Atlantic Ocean, March, 1965

Deep beneath the green-grey surface of a bitterly cold ocean, a dark and menacing silhouette glided effortlessly to a stop. Five metres above the seabed it hung there motionless; like a giant phantom shark waiting silently for its prey.

But this was no hybrid aquatic, mammalian creature. Its skin was made of hard cold metal; a November Class Soviet nuclear submarine, no less. The name emblazoned along its bulbous hull in Cyrillic letters read, "CCCP - K15 – Kosmolov."

From beneath its massive hull, two doors swung slowly open, while inside, standing on the control deck and bent over a panel of blinking lights and monitors, Dimitri Yaetsin, chief Ex-O and second in command turned to face his captain.

"Outer doors open, captain. We are ready to deploy the final payload."

Captain Boris Slatovsky, a veteran submariner, despite the fact that he was yet to reach the tender age of 35, looked up and issued his orders.

"Very good Dimitri, let her go."

From the bowels of the sub a spherical object dropped silently to the seabed and embedded itself in a murky swirl of silt. It settled down with its stubby antenna pointing straight up.

"Mission accomplished, Captain. Everything is in order," confirmed Yaetsin.

With a sigh of relief Slatovski issued instructions to close the bay doors and head north east, at cruising speed, towards Iceland.

It was over. This was the last mission of its kind that he would have to undertake. He had carried out eleven similar missions over the past few months and was now due for retirement. What had just occurred would never be logged; all records of it would, he knew, be destroyed.

His orders, as with all previous missions had been clear and concise:

"Proceed to the Eastern Seaboard, exactly 200 nautical miles from the American coastline. Deposit the cargo and return to base."

Only he was aware of the true nature of this mission. The other 87 crew members on board carried on about their duties content in the knowledge that this, as far as they were concerned, was simply another deployment of a sea bed seismic sensor, just as it had been with all the others.

Slatovski handed over the con to his second in command and made his way aft to his cabin. With the final payload deposited it was as if a huge burden had been lifted from his shoulders. Weary from the stress and worry of the past months he decided to take a well earned nap.

Once inside, he slumped down heavily on his bunk and immediately reached up to the shelf above, gently grasping the monochrome photograph of a pretty girl. He lay back and looked at the gentle face, smiling back at him. It had been almost five months since he had last seen his beloved wife, Chiara. Now that this was all over perhaps they could look at raising a family on the substantial pension which would be awarded him on his return. Resting the framed photograph close to his chest he tried to doze off into a peaceful slumber, aided by the muted hum of the submarine's reactor, below decks.

His consciousness drifted in and out of the twilight zone. Unable to rest fully, the tension not yet released from his limbs, he was finding it hard to unwind.

Eventually he nodded off……..

He was fishing on Lake Bakal. A young boy sat close to him, reverently studying the ripples in the water. In the distance, his wife waved from the shoreline. She was calling to tell them that lunch was ready. It was a picture of calm and tranquillity.

The rod twitched, and the float bobbed once, twice then it disappeared under the water.

"Papa, you've caught something, look!" the boy shrieked, excitedly, peering over the side of the boat.

He tugged at the rod.

It tugged back.

His arms tensed as the fish tried to escape. The tugging became more intense......

Then he looked up.

Yaetsin was standing over him, shaking him vigorously by the arm, a look of grim resolve on his young face.

"Captain, captain, wake up! We need you in the control room immediately. We have a breach in the reactor chamber. An explosion has compromised the nuclear power rods!"

Slatovski woke with a start, looking around him to find he was still in his cabin. He could hardly believe what he was hearing.

"Is the hull damaged?"

"Yes sir, chambers three and four are filling with seawater," replied the young Ex-O. "We are in grave danger Captain. What do we do?"

In a flash, he was up and heading for the door.

As the two men exited the cabin they were met with a scene of utter pandemonium. Warning claxons blared and men were running back and forth, not sure what was going on.

The two of them had to literally fight to get to the control deck as crew members rushed past them in blind panic.

Assuming control of the con, he issued instructions to the helmsman to surface immediately.

The ballast tanks filled with air and the submarine began to ascend to the surface.

He shouted across to the radio operator.

"Launch the distress buoy!"

"It is already done sir," the young technician replied without hesitation.

Grabbing the internal PA microphone, he clicked the transmit switch.

"All hands, hear this. This is your Captain speaking. We have a radioactive breach. I repeat - a radioactive breach. You are instructed to abandon ship upon surfacing. All crew are to immediately make their way onto the foredeck. That is all."

Seconds later the submarine lurched out of the water nose first then crashed down with a mighty splash on the surface as it righted itself.

A mad scramble ensued as the gravity of their Captain's words sunk in. A radioactive breach! They could all be above toxic levels right now. Without further need for instructions 85 men scrambled up the ladder, through the conning tower hatch and out to the foredeck into the freezing arctic air above.

The Captain and Yaetsin came up last.

As his head poked out of the conning tower's hatch, he heard one of the crew shout and saw him point towards the horizon.

"Look comrades, rescue planes are already here!" the man exclaimed.

A loud cheer went up from the others.

No one questioned the odds of search and rescue planes appearing only minutes after being ordered to abandon ship, especially as they were so far out from any Soviet land base. The relief of seeing friendly rescuers at such a life or death moment put paid to any suspicion that something was awry.

But as the aircraft drew nearer Slatovski's eyes narrowed as he began to realise that something was not right. For one thing they were *not* rescue planes. They appeared to be fighter jets, MiG 21's, if he was not mistaken and they were approaching fast. As he watched, the two MiGs fanned out, one going to starboard, the other to port.

"Something is wrong, Dimitri!" he warned. "How could fighter jets be this far out from land?"

But his Executive Officer didn't hear him, he was staring upwards, captivated by the aerobatics show above.

Another loud cheer went up from the crew as they waved with delight; but their high spirits were cut short in a second.

Slatovski realised what was going to happen next and his mouth opened to shout a warning – but it was too late!

The first MiG came hurtling down out of the sky, its jet engines blasting out a ferocious, ear shattering roar that stunned the cheering, jubilant crew, first into silence, then awe, and finally - fear!

Without warning, a hail of bullets exploded from the first MiG's guns and tore into the defenceless men. Blood and flesh splattered across the foredeck as the high velocity shells smashed into their lifejackets and ripped through them. Exposed on the foredeck of the submarine they didn't stand a chance. Seconds later, the second MiG opened fire, blasting into the remaining crew cowering on the deck, amidst their terrified screams and cries for help. He ducked as a volley smashed into the conning tower.

Yaetsin was not so lucky. His head exploded right next to Slatovski, splattering blood and brains over his shoulder. The decapitated body shot backwards with the force of the impact and fell like a stone from the conning tower. It hit the foredeck and slid over the edge into the churning sea, like offal ejected from the galley. It was a scene of utter carnage and horror as the fighter planes screamed past overhead and accelerated upwards.

Numb with shock, Slatovski looked around him. From what he could see, only he and one other wounded crew member remained alive after the second attack. The rest had been blown to pieces, their torn bodies littering the foredeck or floating on the sea swell beside the submarine, having either fallen or been propelled over the side by the force of the bullets.

The only one moving was young Alexei Petrov, the sonar technician. He was sprawled out on the deck, clutching his right leg which had been torn open in the upper thigh section. Blood was spurting from the wound like a small geyser. He was writhing around and screaming in agony.

With no heed for his own safety, Slatovski jumped over the bridge parapet, virtually slid down the conning tower ladder and rushed over to Petrov, quickly assessing the extent of the wound. It wasn't good. The boys face was deathly pale. He'd lost a lot of blood and was going into shock.

"I'll get you inside Alexei. Hold on."

Grabbing him from behind, he wrapped his arms around the sonar man's torso and dragged his shivering body back across the blood stained foredeck towards the conning tower.

Petrov's cries were weaker now. He was fast losing consciousness.

Slatovski looked upwards at the two jets as they circled around the sub, like vultures, in readiness for another attack.

It was only then the realisation of what was happening finally hit home. He had completed his last assignment. With him and his crew lost at sea, only two other people would ever know the whole truth. They had become expendable. The explosion in the reactor room must have been an act of sabotage, most likely triggered by a timer or possibly remote detonation. It was unlikely there was a suicidal traitor amongst his crew. It must have been done during their last refit. He concluded that they were never supposed to have reached the surface. Having done so, by some miracle, they now had to be summarily dealt with.

"You bastards," he shouted, shaking his fist in the air at the circling jets. "You total bastards!"

But there was no time for anger. The pilot of the first MIG had obviously spied movement on the deck and was coming back in to finish the job.

He realised his only hope of survival, at least temporarily, was to get back inside. Even if the submarine was sinking it would allow him and Alexei a few more minutes of safety.

Shielding himself and his wounded comrade behind the conning tower, away from the view of the MiGs, he waited to see what would happen.

The first jet screamed overhead without firing, obviously unable to see or get a clear shot at them. It banked steeply to starboard and circled round. In doing so, he realised the pilot would probably have spotted them cowering behind the bulkhead and would be radioing their position to the other plane.

Slatovski looked down at the boy cradled in his arms.

"We have to get back inside through the hatch Alexei. Do you think you can make it up the steps?"

But the young man didn't hear him. The severed artery in his leg had emptied his veins. Petrov's lifeless body hung limp, the unseeing eyes staring blankly into the void of death.

Slatovski laid him down on the deck and closed the eyelids. He only had himself to save now.

The second MiG had turned and was coming in again, this time from the other direction.

Realising that in his current position he was totally exposed, he darted around the bulkhead to avoid being seen.

Bullets rained down once more, tearing into the deck and ricocheting off the metal bulkhead.

By some miracle he avoided being hit. He leaped up the metal rung steps to the hatch door and reached the top. Just as he was about to enter the hatch, he spied what he thought to be a large ship on the horizon. It looked like an aircraft carrier – and it looked like a *Russian* one!

What the hell is going on here?

But there was no time to think, the plane was almost on him. He dived inside the open hatch just as the jet roared overhead spewing fire and lead from its guns. The bullets ricocheted harmlessly off the outer skin of the tower, clanging like a Chinese dinner gong inside it.

For now, he was safe but what next? The vessel was taking in water from the aft compartments and would surely sink within the next few minutes. He would drown if he stayed inside. Outside, he was cannon fodder. He had to think fast or the next few minutes were going to be his last. Adrenaline surged through his veins as he racked his brains for a solution. Then it came to him in a flash - *the diving suits!*

He ran towards the aft section, remembering that the emergency inflatable life-rafts and diving gear were in a cabin just off the control deck. Like a man possessed he ripped the door open and pulled out a set of oxygen tanks, diver's suit, mask and goggles and a packaged inflatable survival raft.

As he donned the rubberised suit, he felt the sub sway and the angle of tilt increase. Ice cold water began to lap under his feet. There were only minutes, maybe seconds left before the control deck would be completely submerged.

Hastily clad in the clammy rubber suit, he made his way up to the control deck and stood directly under the conning tower tunnel, figuring that it would be the last section of the ship to go under. Checking the tanks were supplying air, he fixed the goggle mask on and waited for the inevitable.

Though the moments spent waiting for the water to fill the final sections of the control deck were measured in seconds, to him it felt like eons.

In the sky above the two MiGs circled the stricken vessel, watching and waiting as the submarine slowly sank beneath the icy sea, leaving only the conning tower visible.

Slatovski braced himself for the deluge of water to flood through the hatch door above. It was up to his waist now but mercifully the rubberised thermal material of the diver's suit kept the icy chill from his flesh.

The deck was now listing at approximately 40 degrees and it was all he could do to stop himself from sliding forward into the already submerged section of the con.

Then it came! Like a floodgate opening in a dam, swathes of water gushed in from above as the conning tower's hatch submerged beneath the surface. He felt the sub sway to port and was immediately enveloped in a powerful surge of dark, freezing sea water. The force of the deluge pushed him backwards, smashing him into a solid object behind him and nearly dislodging his goggle mask. But within a few seconds the gushing and swirling had lessened, the room now being completely filled.

As he looked upwards he saw the light through the hatch was growing dimmer. The lurching feeling in his gut told him the sub was now sinking fast.

It was now or never!

Clutching the inflatable raft with his left arm he pushed with all his might towards the rapidly receding small circle of light. He reckoned the sub must be at least 10 metres below the surface by now. Reaching the hatch he squirmed through it, pulling the packaged life raft after him. With the oxygen tanks strapped to his back it was hard going. Then he was through! But just as he thought he'd made it the straps binding the life raft together caught on something and wouldn't budge. He tugged at it with all his might, stretching every muscle and sinew in his body to breaking point, but it wouldn't come loose. Panic set in. Even if he managed to get out, without the raft he was doomed. He desperately pulled on the snagged line but it was no use.

The light from the surface was getting darker now. He realised that due to the increase of pressure on his eardrums he must be at least 30 metres or more down. Time was running out!

Slatovski struggled frantically with the snagged strap, all the time aware that the huge vessel was pulling him downwards at an alarming rate. Just at the point where he was about to abandon all hope of releasing it, the strap came loose. He immediately pushed himself upwards, dragging the life raft behind him. But he knew it wasn't over yet.

How long had the sub been submerged - three, maybe four minutes perhaps. The burning question was – how long would those vultures stay circling above?

Reaching what he guessed was an approximate depth of 10 metres or so below the surface, he remained motionless, uncertain of when he could safely surface. The tanks, he knew, held enough air for up to thirty minutes and he decided it would be wise to use the maximum amount of time before he broke the surface. If they were still up there and saw him he was surely doomed.

For what seemed like an eternity he maintained his depth, regularly checking the air tank gauge as he floated listlessly in the murky swirl of the North Atlantic Sea. He was all too well aware that above and below, death awaited him in one form or another.

When the gauge indicated the tanks were almost empty, he resolved to surface. There was no way of telling if the planes were still circling above. He would have to risk it or drown. Pushing upwards, he broke the surface as gently as possible and looked all around him, expecting a volley of bullets in the head any minute. He lifted the goggle mask over his head to see more clearly. Nothing - they were gone! No planes, no ship on the horizon. He was alone.

Wasting no time, he un-strapped the cord that bound the inflatable life raft and yanked on the yellow inflator tag. It billowed out with a loud hiss and bobbed around on the sea swell, but then came his next problem. He was so cold his arms didn't have the strength to pull him up and into it. The diving suit had saved him from freezing to death but he'd been in the water for over half an hour now. Hypothermia was taking hold. Another few minutes and he'd go into shock and drown. With one last effort he wrenched himself upwards and was inside, sprawled across the base of the raft like a prostrate crab, shivering and gasping for breath.

For the next hour or so he lay there, savouring the welcome swell of the sea and the cold crisp air. Despite everything that had happened he was, by some miracle, still alive; the sole survivor of a heinous act of savage treachery.

*

Two weeks after the "tragic accident" involving the Kosmolov that apparently claimed the lives of all on board, Captain Boris Slatovski's grieving wife, now five months pregnant and expecting twins, attended a memorial service in his honour. He was posthumously awarded the order of Lenin for bravery and services to his country.

Chapter 2

Oct 5th 2005. Gakona, Alaska.

A full moon shone brightly in the Arctic sky, illuminating the snow clad landscape of Alaska's wilderness. On this particular night the temperature outside was just below minus 15 degrees Celsius and dropping fast.

Inside the warm control room that occupied most of the top floor of the administration building, the young man dressed in a white coat carried out the final checks for the booster test of the transmitters. Barely able to turn his gaze away from the digital screen, even for a moment, he spoke excitedly to the young woman sitting next to him.

"This is gonna be something. All antennae are online. Guinness book of records, here we come!"

The pretty girl grinned and nodded in approval.

Andrew Boetto, otherwise known simply as "Bo" to his friends, had just celebrated his 24th birthday and unlike many of his buddies, who had graduated from University at the same time as himself, he was in full time employment, at the top of his game and had a glowing future ahead of him. For this young man had carved himself a niche as an indispensable member of an elite team of research technicians, carrying out a groundbreaking study into the understanding and manipulation of the ionosphere - the upper portion of the atmosphere that extends from between 35 to 500 miles above the earth's surface.

In the fall of 2003, during his final semester at North Bay's Nippissing University, in Ontario, he had been approached by head hunters from the Raytherm Corporation, a multi billion dollar Research and Development conglomerate and a civil defence contractor to the U.S. Government's Department of Defence. They were keen to recruit new blood into a research program they were undertaking, and Bo's credentials seemed to fit the bill.

To those in the know, this research program was called the "High–frequency Active Auroral Research Program", or HAARP, for short. Tucked away from prying eyes, within a thirty acre plot of land in the backwoods of Alaska's Copper Valley, it was equipped with the very latest, high tech equipment available and was hailed as *the* cutting edge research observatory for exploring the parameters of the upper atmosphere.

His assistant's name was Karen Miller. For some reason she had acquired the nickname of simply

"Miller", and was, as far as Bo was concerned, the best assistant a chief technician could hope for - utterly dependable, quick of intellect, lithe of body and rampant of mind.

She was his latest conquest, or was it the other way round. He could never quite work that one out, though it didn't bother him in the slightest. She was a welcome respite from the rigorous schedule of research and development at HAARP.

The nearest settlement was a sleepy little place called Gakona, some eight miles to the west, while the nearest major town was Fairbanks, over a hundred miles away. In essence, it was a long way from civilisation. From the ground, all you could see of HAARP was a small sign outside the main entrance, just off Alaska's Highway One, that simply said "Ionospheric Research Observatory". Closer inspection would reveal a gravel driveway leading up a slight incline to seemingly nowhere.

From the air though, it was a different story, for carved out of a forest of densely packed conifer trees lay a vast concrete pad, on which were fixed a myriad of antennae, connected together by a grid of steel mesh the size of four football pitches. In total, there were 180 of these antennae, spread out across a quarter mile square of snow laden concrete.

Situated nearby, was a power station, crammed full of powerful diesel generators which supplied the antennae with huge amounts of electricity, whilst several hundred yards further on sat an ugly cubic concrete block which served as the main administration building.

The theory behind HAARP was simple, but radical. Extra Low Frequency microwaves, transmitted from the phased array antennae on the ground could be beamed up and steered to an exact spot in the ionosphere and then reflected downwards again, deep into the earths crust. This steering ability is what set HAARP apart from other electromagnetic transmitters in existence around the world. One commercial use this could be put to, was the locating and imaging of extremely deep subterranean deposits, such as oil and minerals, undetectable by other means.

Previous success with this concept had paved the way for several lucrative contracts being put Raytherm Corporation's way from major players in the oil exploration field; all of them eager to bid for the sole rights to tap into this new way of detecting further deposits of the rapidly diminishing black gold that the planet so desperately needed.

It wasn't long after Bo's arrival at HAARP that the Director soon realised he'd hit pay dirt. Despite his youth and unfamiliarity with this new technology, Bo was to prove himself a genius in this field of science. Within a few months, he had solved one of the most baffling problems the research personnel there had encountered; i.e. how to successfully create what had come to be known as an "Artificial Ionospheric Mirror," or "AIM", for short.

In essence, this was a large section of the ionosphere, fused together to form a reflective surface. To do this, the vast expanse of transmitters spread out on the ground, were used as a kind of inverted magnifying glass, pinpointing the huge amounts of electromagnetic energy they produced into a small area of the ionosphere. This effectively "heats up" the ionosphere, forming a temporary sheet of glowing plasma, hundreds of miles above the surface of the earth. Thereafter, it is possible to reflect Extra Low Frequency (ELF) waves that are subsequently beamed up at it and send them back to earth into locations thousands of miles from the source transmission. These ELF micro-waves can literally "see through" the earth to very great depths.

Bo's knowledge of frequency variations and wave forms, necessary to change the electromagnetic structure of the chemicals and conditions within the ionosphere, knew no bounds, apparently. His ability to steer and focus the immensely powerful electromagnetic transmissions that HAARP produced astounded everyone who worked on the project.

But HAARP was an enigma and was surrounded by controversy. The official blurb promoted by the Raytherm Corporation alluded to the fact that it was nothing more than a scientific project to research and expand knowledge about the nature of long range radio communications and surveillance, using the ionosphere. While this explanation seemed innocuous enough, several eco friendly organisations weren't happy. They believed that the super powerful ELF transmissions it put out were highly dangerous, and that playing around with the fragile ionosphere, mankind's only protection from the deadly Ultra Violet rays that bombarded earth from space, was irresponsible in the extreme. Not only that, Extra Low Frequency microwaves had long been cited as causing illnesses in biological organisms. They had even been linked with cancers and genetic mutations, though there was no official "proof" to further corroborate these allegations. Nevertheless, due to massive commercial interest in the program, research had carried on at a rapid pace, and it had developed into much, much more as work had progressed. This was in no small part due to the aptitude, skill and persistence of its chief technician, Andrew Boetto.

Previous experiments carried out, using only a quarter of the transmitter array, indicated the possibility of moving a 1,000 mile diameter section of the ionosphere upwards by at least half a mile, and creating an Artificial Ionospheric Mirror that could reflect ELF waves back down to the earth's surface to depths of up to three kilometres without fragmenting, a significant achievement in itself. But this wasn't enough for the Raytherm Corporation. They wanted more – much more and had apparently poured millions of R&D dollars into the project in an attempt to get it.

The fact that HAARP was located in a remote region of Alaska, cut off from virtually any form of civilisation or nightlife, didn't seem to bother Bo nor Miller. The challenges they faced on a daily basis kept their active minds buzzing, and anyway, they always had each other for company during their limited amount of time off.

As a rule of thumb, under normal circumstances, personal relationships between key personnel were officially frowned upon at HAARP, but Bo and Miller had somehow circumnavigated base protocol and, so far, the Director had turned a blind eye to it, probably due to their astounding work and results. Though they lived in separate lodgings in the small village of Gakona, they would somehow find their way into one or the other's bed each night. Miller, to Bo's delight had an appetite for carnal pleasures that knew no bounds. It was all he could do to just hang on as she ravaged him on a regular basis.

As far as he was concerned he was living the dream - being paid a handsome salary, doing a job he loved and at which he excelled. The hours were long but fulfilling, and to cap it off he had a girl who wouldn't leave him alone under the sheets, always on tap and ready for action. Not only that, she shared his work and leisure interests. For a young guy in his prime it didn't get any better than this.

Up till now, only segments of the transmitter array had been used to create AIMs. Tonight's test however, would be the most powerful ever undertaken. This was going to shake and rattle the rafters of the global scientific community if it all went to plan. Bo and Miller knew they were making history, right here, right now and the atmosphere in the control room that evening was as electrified as the pulsating antennae, spread out in the forest clearing, several hundred metres away.

"Ten seconds to final boost, Miller. Auxiliary generators coming on line, now," Bo informed Miller, pressing a keypad on his laptop.

Inside the control room a barely noticeable hum vibrated through the floor as the backup generators supplied additional power to the antennae grid.

Bo counted down the final seconds.

"Five - four - three - two - one - zapmeister!"

Portrayed on the screen in front of him was a semicircle, depicting the earth's northern hemisphere. At the very top of this semicircle was a digital graphic of an antenna, indicating the position of the HAARP research facility. To the left of this was the Asian continent, comprised mainly of Siberia. To the right, lay Canada and the Northern states of the USA. Above this were two diffused coloured bands, one showing the troposphere, (the section of atmosphere that stretches from the earth's surface to approximately 35 miles above the ground) which showed up as yellow. Just above this was the ionosphere, depicted as blue.

As he watched the screen, a thick, vertical white line emanated from the small tower, moving ever upwards. As it progressed, it thinned out, till it was almost invisible. This was a digital rendition of the microwave transmissions emanating from the antennae on the ground.

To the uninitiated it would have looked like a video game in progress. To those in the know however, it signified the culmination of several years of work on one of the 21st century's greatest technical advances in electro magnetic field technology, as billions of watts of raw energy soared into the skies above.

"Ho-wee! Look at that baby go!" Miller whooped.

Bo sat motionless, watching the screen as the white arc reached the blue semicircle.

"Initiating artificial ionospheric mirror - now!" he announced, pressing another key.

The white beam began to oscillate, slowly at first. Then it speeded up. After a few minutes it appeared to fill a large section of the screen. As he watched, the blue band of light began to rise upwards, pulling the yellow band with it. A large section of the ionosphere was now being heated and bent out of shape to form a reflective plasma mirror in the sky.

Outside, approximately four hundred metres from where they sat, the symmetrical spread of 180 phased array dipole antennae, their tips pointed hopefully towards the stars, hummed and vibrated in the freezing air. Nestled amidst the vast expanse of evergreen forest, they pulsed out the highest concentration of electromagnetic microwaves ever to leave the planet.

Directly above the antennae, many miles up, the starlit sky transformed from jet black into a radiant display of weaving light. Rivulets of colour, depicting every hue of the spectrum danced across the heavens. Anyone looking up within a hundred and fifty mile radius would have witnessed what they believed to be the Northern Lights, otherwise known as the Aurora Borealis. But tonight was different. *This* display was not a natural phenomenon caused by cosmic occurrences; it was man made.

Miller peered out of the observation window and up at the night sky.

"Jeez, take a look at that, Bo!"

But he was too engrossed with his work to look up. He tapped the keyboard once more. The thicker arc began to shimmer on the screen. Satisfied everything was as it should be, Bo turned to her with a smug grin on his face.

"All set, over to you," he announced.

Miller rubbed her hands together in anticipation.

"Okay, here we go."

She positioned herself in front of the control panel and checked the settings once more, psyching herself up for the next phase of the operation. She pressed a button on the central console, informing Bo of her actions.

"ELF transmission activated."

On Bo's screen, a red line zig-zagged upwards, towards the ionospheric mirror. It reached the concave section and reflected back down again, hitting the surface of the earth some three thousand miles away, in Siberia. The red line continued on its journey, down through the earth's surface. Then it began to fade. Eventually it stopped.

"Depth 3.2 kilometres," announced Bo.

Miller turned a dial on her console to the right, reading off the results as she did so.

"1.2 gigawatts and holding."

After exactly sixty seconds she turned off the ELF transmission.

The two of them sat quietly, watching and waiting to see what happened. After a minute or so, Bo broke the tense silence.

"No change."

The picture on the screen remained the same, indicating that the ionosphere had been heated, and stretched, and was remaining stably in that condition, due to the immense power being focused on it from the transmitters. The previously perfect semicircle of coloured bands was now elongated, resembling a shimmering, digital Easter egg.

Beneath their feet the barely perceptible hum of the generators continued on, unabated.

"Look! Co2 readings are dropping in the atmosphere directly below the mirror," exclaimed Bo, pointing at one of the digital readouts.

Miller followed his gaze. The Co2 monitor indicated a one percent drop in the atmosphere over Siberia, in only the last five minutes. She checked the digital chronometer. It had been almost ten minutes since the initial transmission phase had begun. She counted down the final seconds.

"Four, three, two, one, okay, times up, powering down," she said, slowly reducing the dial to the left until it read zero.

Following the exact procedure he'd rehearsed a thousand times previously, Bo also powered down the electrical feed to the antennae.

The slight humming beneath their feet faded to nothing.

Checking his screen, Bo nodded his head slowly with a broad grin on his face. The Easter egg apparition on his monitor was beginning to return to its previous form of a perfect circle.

"Serweet!" he crooned.

Miller glanced out through the window. The luminous multi coloured light show that had entranced her minutes earlier was gone, replaced by a glittering array of stars in a jet black sky.

Chapter 3

Qinghai Lake, China

The pretty young girl let out a sigh of amazement as she surveyed the beautiful scene through her binoculars.
Tens of thousands of birds littered the shore that encircled the world's largest saltwater lake. The sun was low in the sky to the west. Its golden rays sparkled off the still water, glittering like a thousand Christmas trees. But she wasn't here to admire the scenery. Something was wrong here – very wrong.
Jodi Vanderwal was 23 years old. She worked for the Canadian National Research Centre, and was here in Qinghai Province officially to investigate an anomaly regarding the health and migratory patterns observed in the birds that originated from this region.
It had been *her* idea to come here. Initially her employers were reluctant to send her to China due

to funding shortages in the external research coffers. But she was adamant and after many pleas and several letters to the powers-that-be, her persistence paid off and they had finally acceded to her request.

A few months ago, several thousand birds had been washed up dead on the shore of the lake. Cursory tests had indicated the cause of deaths to be a viral influenza. More detailed lab tests indicated the disease was caused by a DNA mutation, later classified as H5N1 Avian bird flu. But that wasn't what Jodi was here to investigate. Bird Flu was already well known about, and a worldwide operation was already underway to contain it, coordinated by the World Health Organisation.

What she was more interested in was the cause of the strange migratory patterns of these birds which had been observed over the past few months.

Thousands of them were apparently setting off in different directions instead of the standard time honoured migration to the south-west. Some had flown east and others had even headed north-west. It was as if their inherent sense of direction had been tampered with and they didn't know where they were going anymore.

Reports from as far north as Central Siberia had mentioned a flock of geese falling out of the sky over Novosibirsk, frozen solid by the time they reached the ground. Geese never flew that way, ever. They always flew west or south west to escape the colder climes.

She once more peered through her binoculars and observed another vast flock of birds rise upwards in unison and head north-eastwards when they should be heading south.

Jodi's thoughts drifted back to the thing that had initially piqued her interest.

Back in Toronto at the Canadian Research Centre, she had stumbled upon a series of documents in the basement archives. These documents had been filed several years ago by a retired Royal Canadian Navy Officer named Larry Blackhall. The content of the documents fired her imagination because they dealt with his research into what he outlined as the actual cause of bird flu, and several other interesting technical facts.

Blackhall had specialised in advanced electronic warfare apparently. As long ago as the early sixties he was researching ways and means to prevent flocks of birds flying directly into planes, causing immense damage to propellers and engines. He found that by beaming electromagnetic microwaves directly at them, it caused flocks of birds to scatter from the path of the oncoming aircraft. He had even documented several in-flight test studies that appeared to vindicate this theory.

After he retired he had carried out several more experiments, proving that too much background electromagnetic radiation in the vicinity of birds, particularly their eggs and young, could not only radically alter their sense of direction but also mutate their DNA structure. He believed that the H5N1 avian bird flu was directly connected to birds having been exposed to such radiation via microwave and ELF waves, transmitted through the atmosphere over a long period of time. Being that it altered DNA, this mutation further propagated itself in future generations......

Her thoughts were disturbed by a noise in the distance. Some way behind her she heard the revving motor of a vehicle. It grew louder as it neared the lake shore, disturbing several hundred birds closest to it. They swarmed into the sky like rising snow.

The vehicle skidded to a halt about fifty feet away from her, its engine still running. Two military personnel had exited the vehicle and were now making their way hurriedly towards her with purposeful strides. As they got nearer she could see they were Chinese, and by the looks of it not too happy either.

She turned towards them as they approached.

Only a few yards from where she stood they stopped abruptly.

The tallest one spoke in broken English.

"What are you doing here, please?" he enquired. His high pitched voice and haughty demeanour spelt trouble.

His slightly smaller, swarthier partner said nothing, but she noticed his eyes were fixed on the camera hanging around her neck.

"I'm studying the migratory patterns of the geese here," she said, calmly.

"Not allowed Missy. This area is out of bound to foreign tourists, so sorry," he said.

"Why, what's wrong? I've got a permit to be here," she protested.

"Sorry Missy, you have to leave please, now!" The last syllable indicated that this was not a request, it was an order.

Jodi began to get annoyed.

"Hey hold on! I'm doing nothing wrong here, it's perfectly ..."

The smaller man moved menacingly forward, cutting her last sentence.

"You leave now!" he barked.

"Says who?"

"No argue miss, you come with us please," said the taller man, reaching out for her arm.

"I'm not going anywhere. I have every right to be here," Jodi countered, shrugging off his advances and pulling away from him. She was defiant but her voice betrayed an inner fear.

The two mens' slanted and menacing eyes creased even tighter. Like vipers attacking their prey they simultaneously lunged forward and grabbed her by each arm.

"You come with us now, no arguments!" ordered the smaller man.

She struggled to release herself from their grip but it was no use, they were too strong.

The two men then frogmarched her towards the waiting Land Rover, whereupon another man, also dressed in military garb, got out of the back door and stood waiting to receive the three of them. Several exchanges of Chinese sing song syllables were uttered between the three men, almost as if they were arguing with each other.

Her fear turned to terror as she suddenly realised how vulnerable she was. There was no one else around. The thought of being raped and murdered crossed her mind briefly. Perspiration beads began to form on her forehead. A strange tingling sensation coursed through her body as adrenaline pumped into her bloodstream. She found herself trembling involuntarily.

Then, the third man, obviously the one in charge, issued what sounded like an order to her two assailants and she was thrust into the back seat. The third man got in immediately after her and sat silent, staring at her through inscrutable eyes.

She shuffled over to the other side of the seat to get as much distance from him as possible.

"Camera, please," he said, holding out his hand.

"Why, why d-do you want my camera?" she stuttered.

"Give camera now!" he shouted. He was obviously in no mood for chit chat.

She lifted the strap over her head and reluctantly handed the camera to him.

He grabbed it from her, gave it a cursory once over and placed it in his lap. Then, without acknowledgement of any kind, he leaned forward uttering something unintelligible to the driver.

The vehicle surged forward and headed off down the dusty track at a rapid pace.

"Where are you taking me?" asked Jodi.

"You go home now," said the man with the camera.

"But I'm not scheduled to go back for two weeks!"

"You go now, we take you to airport."

Though she was slightly relieved that she was not going to be assaulted or raped, she was still terrified but decided the best course of action would be to remain quiet from that point on.

After fifteen minutes or so they entered a more densely populated area. The driver traversed the bicycles and rickshaws so prevalent in rural China, honking the horn incessantly and swearing at the local peasants as he sped along.

Inside, the Land Rover the atmosphere was heavy and constrained. Conversation between the three men was minimal. The purposeful looks on their faces showed they knew exactly what they were doing and Jodi realised they certainly had no desire to converse with her.

She was driven straight to her hotel where she found her bags were packed and waiting in the lobby, obviously by prior arrangement. She wondered how they knew where she was staying but wasn't given an opportunity to enquire.

As she was escorted out of the hotel entrance she noticed the straight faced manager staring obliquely at her. The look on his face conveyed fear and pity at the same time.

Bundled back into the rear seat of the waiting Land Rover, she was driven straight to Xining airport and quickly ushered through the security barricades onto a waiting twin-turbo-prop aeroplane. A surly Chinese woman, dressed in the same military garb as the three men, appeared by her side and accompanied her up the steps whereupon she indicated for Jodi to sit next to the window. Jodi did as she was told and the woman took up the aisle seat next to her. The plane taxied up the runway, took off and banked sharply to the left on a heading due East to Beijing.

The woman assigned as her minder said nothing the entire trip, which lasted almost two hours.

So much for in-flight entertainment, she thought to herself, for the cabin service was minimal, consisting of a warm glass of water and a spicy spring roll that had obviously passed its sell by date.

After a bumpy landing at Beijing's International airport, she waited while the rest of the passengers alighted and was then quickly ushered out. Two armed security personnel met them at the bottom of the plane's boarding steps and walked ahead of her while her mute minder remained firmly at her side. A few minutes later, Jodi found herself in the bustling International Departures area. She felt like a prisoner as she was escorted through the terminal; her pleas to return her camera and other belongings falling on deaf ears.

After what seemed like hours waiting in a locked observation room, with nothing to read but Chinese language newspapers and magazines, she was marched up to the Air Transet ticketing desk and told to wait while another Chinese official oversaw the ticketing and the issuance of her boarding pass. After several minutes of haggling, the ticket was produced by the worried looking Air Transet desk clerk and handed to her minder.

The Chinese woman stayed on the plane till it was ready to leave. Then with a final smile that was devoid of humour, she left.

As the Boeing 737 took off she gazed blankly out of the window, wondering what the hell she'd done to deserve such treatment and, more importantly, what she was going to tell her boss.

The seat belt sign switched off and the flight attendant, who had watched her incongruous entrance onto the plane, accompanied by her stern faced military escort, came up to her. She was Canadian and her smile was warm and genuine.

"Upset the commies honey?" she asked.

Jodi couldn't talk. The shock of the whole episode had finally sunk in and she began to cry.

The flight attendant gently patted her on the shoulder and walked back down the aisle, returning soon after with a glass of sparkling water.

"You're not the first person I've seen who's had that treatment, if it's any consolation," she said.

Jodi was grateful for small mercies. At least she was safe, on her way home, back to familiar faces she could at least talk to. After an hour or so she settled down for a nap and dozed off.

But her troubles weren't over yet. As if to compound the agony, the plane encountered a freak weather front and heavy turbulence over the Bering Straits. The strength of the storm was such that the pilot was forced to land in Fairbanks, Alaska.

After a night of broken sleep in the airport terminal, stretched out on a row of bony ribbed chairs, she re boarded the following morning and the flight took off again, bound for home. It touched down in Toronto's Lester B. Pearson International airport, without further incident, at 2.30 pm Ontario time.

Chapter 4

Lester B. Pearson International airport, Toronto:

The young man sitting in the departures lounge looked up as he heard the message being broadcast across the public information system.
"Attention, please. Would all passengers travelling on flight AT 273 to London Gatwick please proceed to the Air Transet desk to receive further instructions, thank you."
It was not what he wanted to hear.
"Oh God, not again!" he muttered to himself, shaking his head from side to side in apathetic disbelief.
He'd been waiting almost six hours for his flight which had been indefinitely delayed due to freak weather conditions over the Atlantic. Now it sounded like he wasn't even going to fly at all. Lethargically picking up his holdall he made his way to the information desk.

Rick Hayden was 24 years old and currently unemployed. He'd spent four years at Nippissing University in North Bay, Ontario, studying for a degree in geology and had finally graduated with honours. Yet, since that time, despite his glowing resume, he'd found it difficult to land a job that fitted his skills. Apparently, he was "over qualified". How that could be the case when he'd had no real experience of actually doing anything useful was still a mystery to him. After several abortive job interviews with no prospects of gainful employment in sight, he'd decided to take a break and visit his mother's brother, uncle Tod, in England.

Uncle Tod was always good for a laugh. He lived in a quaint little place called East Grinstead, a small Market town nestled in between the rolling Sussex downs, about thirty miles from the South coast. He ran a successful construction company in the South West of London, sub contracting the work out to a seemingly never ending supply of Polish workers who worked day and night, apparently for peanuts. That is, when he wasn't riding his dirt bikes on his brother in law's farm, racing around the Sussex roads on his supped-up motorcycle, or flying light aircraft. Rick chuckled to himself as he thought about his uncle. For a guy approaching 50 he sure liked to live life to the full. There was never a dull moment with him around that was for sure.

A couple of years ago Rick and his friend Bo from University, had been invited to go over and work for Uncle Tod, during their summer break from Uni.

They both needed to earn some money to pay for their tuition fees. After Rick received the invitation, Bo didn't need much coaxing to go. London was a place he had wanted to visit for as long as he could remember and he'd jumped at the opportunity, having been told about it by Rick after his last visit there as a kid.

They'd had a ball and between them earned over $20,000, painting the outside of peoples houses in the suburbs of London. They also helped his uncle construct an attic conversion in his house - well, not helped really; in actual fact they did all the hard graft work while Uncle Tod stood and bawled instructions at them. Still, overall it had been a fun summer.

They'd both learned how to ride motorcycles for the first time in their lives and figured out how to traverse the crazy London traffic whilst driving on the wrong side of the road in an old Ford Fiesta that Uncle Tod had bought for them for a few hundred quid, (which he'd duly made them pay back out of their wages, mind you!)

They'd even gotten into a few fights in the local nightclubs and to top it all off, they'd gone back home with a whole bundle of dosh - the English colloquialism for hard cash!

Rick would have liked to have taken Bo with him again this time, but he'd gone and landed himself a top job in Alaska someplace, working for some high tech radiography corporation, researching the ionosphere or something like that. Last he'd heard from Bo, he was getting it on with a girl who worked there with him.

"Lucky bastard," he thought to himself. "Maybe I should have majored in that field; at least he's getting paid – and laid!"

After a long wait in the queue at the Air Transet information desk, Rick eventually got to speak to the overwhelmed desk clerk. The poor guy was trying to deal with a posse of irate would-be travellers who had all waited as long as him. The flight had now apparently been cancelled and none of them were very happy about it.

"I'm sorry sir. Flight 273 has been cancelled due to a freak storm over the Atlantic. Please check back tomorrow morning. Thank you sir - next please!"

Rick shrugged. There was nothing he could do about that. He turned round to walk away.

The girl directly behind him in the queue was not so laid back however. She was extremely agitated about something and not in the mood to wait any longer. She barged past Rick, nearly knocking him over and demanded to talk to the man behind the desk.

"Hey! Watch where ya going miss," Rick exclaimed, regaining his balance.

The girl just glared at him and immediately began laying into the rather surprised Air Transet employee, about lost baggage or something.

Rick overheard part of the conversation.

"......If you don't calm down miss I'll have to call security and have you ejected from the terminal," said the rather irritated Indian man, wincing at the barrage of abuse he'd just received from the irate female in front of him.

But the girl was having none of it apparently. Rick wasn't near enough to hear all of it, but he did catch snippets of her remonstrations. The girl was really going for it.

"......no idea what I've been through the last few days...... deported from China for no reason......belongings stolen...... lost all my baggage!"

The desk clerk appeared very flustered.

"I'm sorry Miss......nothing I can do...... we'll do our best......"

Rick could see the girl was getting more agitated by the second. She was relentless with rage.

"......and you work for Air Transet don't you...?"

"Yes Miss, but........"

"......do something about it, you idiot!"

The desk clerk, now apparently at his wits end replied. "I will Miss, one moment please," he said and went to the end of the desk, picked up the phone and talked rapidly into it, his eyes darting intermittently up at the girl as he spoke. Then he put the phone down and returned to face her again.

"So! Who did you phone?" the girl demanded to know, still fuming.

Unbeknownst to her, just across the terminal floor, two armed policemen had received a radio call and were making their way briskly towards the Air Transet desk.

Rick watched as they came up behind the unsuspecting girl. He moved closer, to see what was going to happen.

The little desk clerk motioned behind the girl with a nod of his head. He had a smug grin on his face.

"That man there, Miss."

She looked around and was confronted by two very tall and very big armed policemen staring down at her with glum expressions. The first one was fingering the sub machine gun draped over his shoulder.

"Would you come this way please Miss?" he politely requested.

The girl's irate demeanour seemed to soften to despair. "Oh god, not again," Rick heard her mutter to herself.

The policemen led her off to a quiet spot near the escalators.

Rick was fascinated by the scene evolving before him. This chick was really in hot water now. He sat down on one of the rows of chairs in the central concourse and leaned over the back of it, watching intently.

The girl looked terrified and very small compared to the two burly armed men in flak jackets. From what he could make out they were apparently giving her a right ticking off.

Rick sat there watching as they finished their admonishment of her unruly behaviour, but then instead of taking her away, simply gave her a friendly wave and went on about their business patrolling the terminal.

The girl didn't move from where the policemen left her. She just hung her head and appeared to be crying.

Rick decided to go talk to her. He got up and walked over to where she stood.

"Hi there miss. Hey, sorry about barging into you back there," he said. He knew he hadn't been at fault; she had barged into *him* but he figured another grilling wasn't going to do her any good. She looked like she needed a friendly face to talk to.

The girl peered up at him through moist eyes. She looked despondent.

"It's okay," she said. "It's just that I've had a gutful of bad luck the last twenty four hours and this was the last straw. I'm sorry for being rude back there."

Rick noticed she was very pretty, her high cheekbones accentuating the dark eyes and pert lips.

"That's okay. Say, listen, can I buy you a coffee or something?" he ventured.

"No, thanks all the same. I need to get back home. I'll probably be in trouble there as well."

"Well before you face the firing squad, you look like you could do with a nice cappuccino," Rick suggested, trying to keep upbeat.

She eyed him apathetically with a "oh what the hell" look.

"Oh, okay. I guess so," she said.

Rick smiled, then picked up her holdall and led the way to the shopping area. He soon found them a table at a Garfunkels restaurant where he ordered two coffees.

"I'm Rick Hayden by the way," he said, holding out his hand.

"Jodi VanderWal. Pleased to meet you," the pretty girl replied. "By the way, you'll have to pay I'm afraid. I lost my purse with all my money, credit cards, the lot, somewhere, can't remember where exactly. It could have been in the truck those Chinese police drove me to the airport in."

"The *Chinese* police!" said Rick. "Do you have an attraction with men in uniforms, or something?"

"Very funny," she said, but she wasn't laughing.

"What do you do when you're not flying around the world being picked up by cops, anyway?" asked Rick, trying to keep the conversation on a flippant note and for the first time, he noticed the faint trace of a smile cross her lips.

"I work for the Canadian National Research Centre in Toronto. They sent me on a fact finding mission to Qinghai province to check out a possible connection with bird flu that apparently originated from there. Well, it was my idea actually. After what happened though, I probably won't have a job to go back to. It seems I've ruffled a few feathers in the upper hierarchy. Excuse the pun – "feathers" - Get it?"

Rick chuckled. She had a sense of humour as well as a pretty face; things were looking up!

"It's kinda weird really," she continued. "They just kicked me out for bird watching. That's it! I wasn't doing anything wrong at all. They confiscated my camera too."

Rick noticed her mood darken again and her eyes glaze over, as if she were recalling something unpleasant.

"I was thrust into the back seat of a Land Rover by three antagonistic men, at a place called Qinghai Lake, not knowing what was going to happen next, fearing for my own personal safety."

"Sounds intense," said Rick. "Maybe you saw something you shouldn't have? Those chinks are pretty secretive about what they get up to, so I've heard."

"What could be secretive about a lake full of wildfowl?" Jodi retorted. "It's funny though, I was researching erratic migratory patterns of birds from Qinghai Lake. There's definitely something strange going on over there."

"Huh, sound interesting," Rick said, fearful that she was going to launch into some boring ornithological diatribe of some kind. He decided to change the subject.

"I'm a geologist myself; got an honours degree from Nippissing University in North Bay. Spent most of the time drinking and partying though!"

Suddenly, the girl's mood changed and she seemed to perk up a little.

"Hey! I have a few friends who went to Nippissing. I've heard about the wild parties up there. Do you know a girl called.......?"

From that point on the conversation went from good to better. They talked for hours and found they had a lot in common - music, TV programs, hobbies, even mutual acquaintances, etc. By the time they'd finished they'd consumed several cups of coffee each. Rick noticed that Jodi had transformed from an introverted, moist eyed victim of circumstance into a bright, witty, and very interesting person.

He looked down at his watch. It was now late in the afternoon, almost 6pm and the time had literally flown by.

It was then that Rick popped the question that had been formulating in his head.

"Hey, how about coming out with me some time!"

Jodi appeared a bit taken aback.

"Well, I'm not sure, I mean, I hardly know you," she replied, stroking her hair back, looking a little nervous. Then she smiled again, that pretty, captivating smile that made the back of Rick's neck break out in goose pimples.

"Alright then, why not?" she said.

Chapter 5

Canadian Research Centre - Toronto

On Monday morning, Jodi arrived back at work. She was still smiling, remembering the great time she'd had with Rick on Saturday night. He'd really turned out to be just the tonic she needed and had completely shaken her out of her doldrums from that messy incident in China. As she made her way up to the first floor and entered her office, she realised that she was looking forward to meeting him again tonight.

The sight that met her eyes soon dampened her spirits though. Her desk had been cleared.

At that moment, a familiar head poked around the door. It was Lyndsay Briggs, the Director of Field Operations' communicator.

Hi Jodi! Nice time in China?" she chirped.

Jodi looked up with a frown.

"Oh! er, hi Lyndsay. Yeah! I mean no, not really. It wasn't exactly what I'd call a *pleasant* trip. Say, do you know what's happened to all my stuff?"

Lyndsay rolled her eyes, and her voice reduced to a barely discernable whisper as she spoke.

"Between me and you, Jodi, I think you're in for a bit of trouble. The Director's not very happy with you. He wants to see you in his office right away."

Jodi was under no illusion as to what it might be for. A lump formed in her throat as she acknowledged Lyndsay's warning and made her way out the door and up to the top floor.

Standing outside the Director's door, she steeled herself for what might be coming and knocked.

"Come!" said a deep, commanding voice.

She timidly entered and shut the door behind her.

"Good morning sir. You wanted to see me?"

"Ah! Miss VanderWal, said the Director. "Come in. I've just been on the phone with the Canadian Embassy. I think you've got a bit of explaining to do."

It wasn't a pleasant meeting. After suffering a severe reprimand for the fracas in China, Jodi managed to hold on to her job, but only because of her previous unblemished record and good work, she was told. No one thereafter, including the Director, wanted to hear her side of the story. Apparently the Chinese authorities had made a big deal of her having to be "deported" and had decided to waive a charge of "international espionage" against her so long as she never attempted to come back to China again. It had flapped as high as the Canadian Embassy in Beijing, apparently.

Despite her pleas of innocence, which as far as she was concerned were totally valid, Jodi was told, in no uncertain terms that she'd damaged the Research Centre's reputation no end and had narrowly avoided being incarcerated in a Chinese prison. She was lucky to still have a job and would be relegated to an admin desk until further notice. Deciding that it was pointless to argue further, she ungraciously accepted her penance.

Though she was assigned menial gofer jobs, she still managed to continue to collect data coming in to the Field Operations Bureau regarding the Avian Bird Flu pandemic, which by now was apparently spreading across Asia and Europe at an alarming rate. It wasn't that hard to do. The media wires were abuzz with the subject since infected poultry had turned up in Turkey, then Germany and even in several swans in Scotland!

Apparently, all fingers were pointing to China as the source of the disease but the Chinese authorities were being extremely uncooperative in accepting outside help. Making matters more difficult, details of illnesses amongst humans had to be leaked out of there as they had chosen to make the truth about more recent developments "a state secret", according to a Chinese news service.

Well, she had first hand knowledge of how difficult they could be, that's for sure!

It also began to dawn on her that there was quite possibly an ulterior motive as to why she had been so rudely extricated from Qinghai Lake.

China was ignoring the World Health Organization's pleas for more information about reported illness and death amongst not only wildfowl but humans too, in regions surrounding Qinghai Lake where a dangerous new influenza "A" subtype had apparently appeared.

She knew that ferreting out the truth about the nature and extent of an epidemic, with the potential to decimate human and animal populations around the world, was critical. It would take enormous cooperation and coordinated global pressure and effort to prevent an all-out human survival catastrophe of historically unprecedented proportion. Unfortunately, they weren't playing ball.

Before the media clampdown, local officials and state media said the geese had been dying since May 6 at the Qinghai Lake Nature Reserve, in the northwest province of Qinghai. An official at the Qinghai provincial administration for wild animals and plants, who refused to be named, had been quoted as saying; "I can confirm these birds have died but it is not bird flu. They died of disease but we don't know what it is. We are still investigating. There are no results yet, but no bird flu virus has been found."

The failure of the major organisations to find bird flu was also not very reassuring. The World Health Organisation had been trying to detect WSN/33 human flu in Korean swine for the past 5 months and had failed to do so.

Migrating birds were transporting a new form of virus, known as H5N1 sequences each season. Since birds from the south would be migrating north at this time of the year, transmission of H5N1 to various points in China was a distinct possibility.

Moreover, there had been reports of dying wildfowl in Fujian province. These farms being restocked with geese from Jiangsu and Jiangxi Provinces.

It was also evident that the monitoring of bird flu in Asia had, up to this point, been scandalously poor. In fact, it seemed at this moment in time, the most imminent threat to human survival was not war or suicide bombers, not a nuclear attack, but this fistful of frighteningly effective and adaptable viral agents. Minute "genetic geniuses" capable of morphing to evade immunity, break species barriers, and outsmart man's best efforts to control them.

They were currently multiplying in animals and people in at least 12 countries. No respecters of borders, they had invaded Russia and were now in Europe. Within weeks, many experts believed, they would be spreading to other countries and communities along flyways taken by infected migrating birds, or in the lungs of a human passenger on the next flight from China to Seattle to Toronto, with a stop-over in Washington.

A myriad of questions began to manifest themselves in her inquisitive mind.

Was there a connection between the altered migratory patterns and the bird flu?

Why did the Chinese authorities not want anyone to go near the dead birds found washed up in Qinghai Lake?

Was it possible they were being poisoned in some way or perhaps irradiated with toxic compounds?

Although she attempted to alert her superiors, it seemed they just didn't want to know.

"Keep you head down and ride it out," she'd been told by Lyndsay. In other words – shut up and stay low if you want your pay cheque at the end of the month, thought Jodi. She realised she had reached an impasse and needed more data.

It was then that she recalled Kwan Yo, an old Chinese architect who had helped design houses for her father several years ago in his capacity as a consultant structural engineer. Kwan Yo had apparently lived in the Tibetan regions of China and had come to Canada in the seventies as a refugee, not long after the Chinese military had invaded his homeland of Tibet. He had applied for political asylum which had been granted and had subsequently become a successful and reputable architect. But where was he now? He hadn't worked for her father for some years. The last time she met him he was already very old. Perhaps he had died?

The next day she phoned her father and enquired after Kwan Yo.

To her delight he told her that old Kwan had retired and was living in downtown Toronto. After a lot of pestering he dug out an old telephone number, warning her that it may not be current.

Jodi resolved to look him up and found he was still alive and well. He even vaguely remembered her as a small child and would be overjoyed to have her visit him.

For the next few days she laboured on at work, doing nothing in particular. She acted as the coffee maker, bin emptier and general dog's body. It was soul destroying, but at least, she thought, she still had a job. Friday afternoon came and went. At 5pm she couldn't get out the door fast enough. The relief she felt as she walked out the front entrance was amazing.

On Saturday morning, she took the Go-train into central Toronto. Old Kwan lived in an apartment on Yonge Street, the longest street in the world.

On her arrival he welcomed her effusively into his apartment and immediately set about preparing some Ginseng tea and rice crackers. He was a wizened and wrinkly but still very alert and lively individual. At the grand old age of 89 he still held a valid drivers licence and kept a neat and orderly house, even though he lived alone with no domestic help.

After the obligatory pleasantries and enquiries as to the wellbeing and health of her father and everyone else Kwan had anything else to do with in her family, they settled themselves down in two ornate wicker chairs on the balcony, overlooking the main road.

Jodi lost no time in explaining the reason for her visit.

The old man listened intently as she relayed the sequence of events leading up to her expulsion from Qinghai Lake and her subsequent research which had drawn a blank. When she was finished there was a long silence.

Kwan closed his eyes as if he were taking an afternoon nap.

After what seemed to her several minutes, Jodi began to feel a little uncomfortable. She wasn't sure if she'd bored him so much that he'd nodded off.

Then he opened his eyes and looked at her.

"Let me tell you a story," he said. "Since I left my homeland and came to your wonderful, free country I have maintained a constant vigil on events as they have unfolded in my home country of Tibet. The Internet has become one of my greatest mediums through which I have kept abreast of ongoing events. You see, once, long ago, I was a political prisoner of the glorious People's Republic of China, taken away from my family and forced into hard labour because of my views on the so called liberation of my country.

"For several years I toiled under the yoke of tyranny propagated by our aggressors. Because I was educated I became what was known as a "useful prisoner" and was put to work as a laboratory assistant at the Jiuquan Atomic Energy Complex. This was otherwise known as Plant 404 and is situated in the Kansu Province.

"It was only due to a serious explosion there, which caused immense confusion and loss of life that I managed to escape. With the help of several of my countrymen I made it safely across the forbidding Tibetan plateau to Nepal. From there I travelled to India and was lucky enough to find a place on a merchant shipping boat bound for Canada. I paid for my passage by working in the engine room as a stoker."

Jodi was impressed.

"A political prisoner! Wow, I had no idea."

"Why would you?" he said, matter of factly. "I never spoke of it to anyone – until now."

Kwan continued.

"There is a great deal that has been, as you Canadians say "brushed under the carpet" regarding the plight of my people. In 1949, People's Liberation Army soldiers entered Eastern Tibet. Not long after this, in the spring of 1950, China's 18th Army invaded Tibet through Dartsedo in the east and through Amdo in the northeast. The 14th Division entered through Dechen in southeast Tibet. After occupying Kham and Amdo, the advance party of the 18th Army reached Lhasa in September 1951, followed by the unit's main force. This was only the beginning of the vast Chinese military build up in Tibet, which continues to this day."

Jodi interrupted him.

"I'm sorry Kwan but what exactly are you trying to tell me?" She didn't quite get where this conversation was heading.

Mirrors In The Sky

Kwan looked at Jodi through his beady old eyes.

"I am telling you this, my dear, because I believe the source of your Avian bird flu stems from background cumulative radiation of some kind. In other words - radioactive poisoning!"

Chapter 6

HAARP

In the control room, on the 4th floor of the administration building, Bo and Miller sat back in their chairs, feet on the desk, swigging a bottle of Coors beer each. The look on their faces told it all. They were saturated with accomplishment. The experiment had worked!
For the first time ever, the ionosphere had been manipulated, under controlled conditions, and moved upwards to almost half a mile above its natural level without a glitch. Then, it had returned to normal within a couple of hours. An ELF transmission had been bounced off the Artificial Ionospheric Mirror and had travelled down through the Siberian substrate to a depth of 3.2 kilometres. The subterranean spectrometer was still reeling off data and images coming in from it. What they had found really interesting though was that the $Co2$

readings in the lower atmosphere, directly below the mirror, had reduced significantly.

Another interesting phenomenon was a sudden drop in temperature over Siberia, of almost 3 degrees Celsius! Bo had made a note to investigate these weird anomalies during future tests.

Sitting there, relaxing, Bo reflected on his tenure at HAARP. He'd been interested in radiography from a very early age. As a kid he'd always been fascinated by the ionosphere, ever since he'd learned that radio waves could be bounced off it. Landing a position like this, with all the advanced technology at his disposal, was like a young child being given the keys to a candy store.

"So, ya think we're up for a bonus?" asked Bo, taking another swig from the half empty bottle.

"A vacation would be more like it," Miller replied. "I haven't seen the outside of this wretched place for almost six months."

"I know what ya mean," said Bo, a wry smirk creasing his beer moistened lips. "Still, at least I've had other things to keep me occupied on cold nights!"

Miller gave him a sly wink. She knew *exactly* what he meant.

"Just out of interest, do you ever sleep?" enquired Bo, jokingly.

"Not if I can help it," she beamed. "I'll sleep when I'm dead."

Bo grinned. He really liked this girl. That was one or her clichés and it fitted her character to a tee.

They both burst out laughing.

Their merriment was cut short by the abrupt opening of the control room door, and the entrance of the Director's personal secretary. There was no humour in *her* cold grey eyes.

Bo instinctively lowered the beer bottle and eyed her up and down. She was 27 years old, slim and reasonably attractive in a curt sort of way; not dissimilar to Miller in physique and stature, but that's where the similarities ended.

Miller on the other hand was full of life and oozing with sex appeal.

This girl was as cold as ice. Her name was Coleen Jones. She had a lack of personality and an apparent zero interest in the opposite sex. Prior to Miller's arrival at HAARP, Bo had tried several times in the dim and distant past to engage Coleen in chit chat with him but with little success. What little she did divulge indicated that she was from a broken home and had spent most of her young life in and out of foster homes. She had no immediate family to speak of and was somewhat of a loner.

Bo had taken pity on her at first. Her distant and elusive character had initially attracted him, like an insect to a Venus flytrap, but he had long since decided that getting into her pants would require more effort than he could muster. He had given up attempting any kind of extra curricular activities with her.

When Miller turned up all bright eyed and full of bounce, Bo thereafter avoided Coleen like the plague.

The woman's dark eyes bore into the two of them.

"Good evening," she rasped.

Her voice was hard and impersonal, like a drill sergeant's.

"Working hard again I see, Andrew!"

"All work and no play ma'am. It's a hard life." Bo quipped.

"You should try getting more sleep; it'll give you more energy," she replied.

Bo immediately got a mental image picture of her standing over him, butt naked with a whip in her hand. He shook his head to clear the thought. This chick had that effect on him whenever she was around. It was spooky. Was it her, or him? He could never quite work it out.

Miller immediately jumped to her feet.

"Hi Miss Jones, what's up?" she asked, purposely putting herself between this unwelcome female and Bo.

"Nothing is *up*, Miss Miller!" Jones replied, with a disdainful emphasis on the word *up*.

Miller just stared at the prim, poised, but rather strange female standing in front of her.

Bo knew that Miller didn't like this chick. Every time she was around him, Miller went all weird. She was always asking him if something had gone on between the two of them before she'd arrived and he had always adamantly refuted any such thing.

Anyway, it was true, nothing had! But despite his vehement denials, he knew Miller still harboured nagging suspicions.

"Director wants you two in his office right away," Jones barked. She turned to leave. "And, by the way, that means now, not tomorrow!"

Bo turned to Miller and smiled wanly.

"Sounds serious, Miller. Let's go see what the old boy wants, eh," and up he got.

Miss Jones led the way with Bo in tow. Miller lagged behind, cringing as she watched Bo following hot on her heels, looking like a scolded schoolboy being taken to the principal's office for a caning.

The Director's office was on the third floor at the back of the administration building.

Jones stopped in front of the door.

"Wait here," she ordered, and went inside.

"Do you think she talks to her boyfriend like that?" said Miller, pulling a face.

Bo raised his eyebrows.

"Boyfriend! I doubt if she could get a randy racoon to take her on a date, let alone a ....."

Jones poked her head around the door, cutting his last comment in mid flight.

"Director Heckler will see you now. Come in please," she announced, now in her best secretarial voice.

John Lee Heckler, the Director of HAARP was sitting at his desk, reading a memo when they entered.

"Miss Miller and Mr Boetto are here to see you sir," said Jones, her tone now helpful and friendly, which Bo knew was reserved only for her peers.

Heckler looked up, "Yes, bring them in Miss Jones. Thank you."

As they entered, they noticed there was another man in the room. He was sitting in Heckler's armchair facing away from them.

"Thank you. That'll be all, Miss Jones," said the Director.

Jones shot Bo a serious look, sneered at Miller and with a haughty cock of her head, left the room.

"Come in Karen - you too Andrew," said Heckler, motioning with his hands for the two of them to enter. "Sorry about Miss Jones, she can be a little cold and impersonal at times. Now, I have someone here who'd like to meet you."

As they neared the desk, the stranger rose from his seat and turned to greet them. He was impeccably dressed in a hand tailored suit that disguised a bulging torso and physique, indicating a career in bodybuilding or the armed forces. The top of his head was bald and by the looks of it had been polished with a buffer. A long, once - graceful nose hinted at having been broken and repaired with plastic surgery at some time in the past. His leather shoes shone almost as brightly as his head. He could have been anywhere between 45 and 60.

"This is Mr Clavell from the Pentagon's Scientific Operations Bureau," said Heckler.

The powerful man strode across to Miller first and shook her hand, then did the same with Bo. The official aura he exuded was palpable. When he spoke, it was with the purposeful dialogue of a senior executive, with clout.

"Well ladies and gentlemen, seems you've cut the mustard. Congratulations! I've just been informed by your Director that HAARP has been classified as fully operational as of tonight."

Miller and Bo looked at each other slightly bemused. "Accolades indeed!" Bo thought to himself, but he knew immediately that there was more to this meeting than met the eye.

"Thanks Mr Clavell but we've only just done our first test with the full array of transmitters earlier this evening, and anyway, what's the Pentagon got to do with it?"

"Sit down please, the both of you," said Heckler, hastily taking over the conversation and motioning to the two chairs in front of his desk.

"Now, I know something's not right," thought Bo. If there was one thing that wasn't in the Director's makeup, it was congeniality.

They cautiously settled themselves in front of the desk to the left of the government man.

Clavell did likewise, seating himself in the armchair opposite them.

Heckler cleared his throat.

"There's been a change of plan. Our testing schedule has been brought forward," he announced.

Mirrors In The Sky

It was obvious to Bo that the old boy wasn't happy with what he was about to say next.

"I have been instructed to begin testing at full power the minute the transmitters are operational."

Bo exchanged worried glances with Miller.

"But sir, the potential energy output of all the antennae online at any one time is approximately 3.7 giga-watts. That's a lotta juice; enough to push the ionosphere up at least 3 miles!" explained Bo.

"We're well aware of that Andrew, but there are a few things you need to be made aware of. I'll let Mr Clavell brief you on the situation."

With a slight jut of his chin upwards, Heckler's gaze passed from them to his guest.

Clavell sat back and clasped his hands together as if he were about to say a prayer.

"What I am about to tell you is highly classified information. As with all technical data you are privy to at HAARP, this will remain within the confines of this facility. I trust we are clear on that?"

He definitely had the attention of both of them now.

"Up till now HAARP has been a joint venture between Raytherm Corporation and the Department of Defence. From this moment on however, all civilian research has been postponed indefinitely and all non military personnel on the base relocated to other lower priority facilities - except yourselves."

Bo and Miller looked at each other, slightly bemused.

"Why us?" Bo asked.

"I'll get right to the point," said Clavell. "Over the past few years, several rogue nations and terrorist breakaway groups have acquired the ability to produce nuclear weapons, mainly due to the influx of old Soviet warheads being smuggled out on the black market. In fact, this has been going on since the fall of the iron curtain in the late eighties. Not only that, our intelligence network in Iraq has discovered that weapons of mass destruction were successfully removed prior to the Allied forces invasion of that country and relocated elsewhere. Recent intelligence we've received indicates that these WMD's have been placed in underground bunkers. These bunkers are extremely deep and incredibly well concealed. We know that they exist but we don't know where."

Bo was confused.

"What's this got to do with us?"

"A great deal, as you will soon discover, if you'll let me continue," said Clavell. "Microwave energy, when used to form Artificial Ionospheric Mirrors can, as you both know assist with earth-penetrating tomography. Beaming radio energy into the Auroral Electrojet is the way forward, I'm sure you'll agree with that?"

Bo nodded. This guy knew his stuff!

Clavell continued.

"Traditional ELF antennae systems can emit waves that penetrate into the ground, depending on the geological makeup in the targeted area. Our aircraft or satellites, stationed overhead, collect the reflected ELF waves and relay them to computers at a processing station. The US Navy already uses this technology to communicate with their fleet of deep sea submarines via the Ground Wave Emergency Network in Wisconsin, otherwise referred to as GWEN.

"With HAARP's upgraded array of ground based transmitters however, we can dispense with aircraft or satellite relays and utilise the ionosphere to locate subsurface structures, such as underground weapons facilities which could be buried as deep as several kilometres under the ground."

Bo sat mesmerised at the technical proficiency of Clavell's dialogue. This was no run of the mill government pen pusher. This guy knew his onions. He also began to get an inkling of where this was headed.

"And you want me to help you do that with my expertise in forming Ionospheric Mirrors, right?" Bo enquired.

"Got it in one, young man!" Clavell exclaimed.

"That would require immense output, sir", said Bo. "And it's not as easy as you might think. It could also be extremely dangerous to organic life on the surface. If you direct almost 4 Giga-watts of microwave beams into a specific area at extra low frequencies, you could possibly even mess with peoples' brainwave patterns, or fry an organism's DNA if it were exposed to it for any length of time!"

Bo didn't like the way this conversation was going. This guy was a skilled specialist in their field, but why was he giving them all this so called classified information? He couldn't fathom it at all.

Miller had her piece to say as well.

"Look sir, we don't know anything about nuclear warheads and atomic arsenals, or ferreting out terrorists. We enrolled in HAARP because we were told we could use the research instruments to research the ionosphere; to work out ways of controlling it for the benefit of everyone; even learn ways of preventing adverse weather conditions and prevent global warming. Its purpose is to bring greater understanding of the ionosphere's impact on...."

"Its purpose has changed," announced Clavell.

Bo involuntarily gripped the side of his chair with both hands.

"Wha...Hold on a mo. Whaddya mean – changed, exactly?" he challenged, a deep frown creasing his forehead. He shot a glance at Heckler, as if to garner some support, but the Director said nothing.

"I mean your project orders have been, shall we say, modified," said Clavell. There was a hint of menace in the Government man's voice. It was hardly perceptible but it was there, none the less.

Alarm bells began ringing in Bo's head.

He glanced sideways at Miller, then at Heckler, questioningly but the old boy just sat there, stone faced, as if he were powerless to intercede.

"Modified to what, exactly?" asked Bo. This conversation had him worried, yet despite his scepticism and concerns, he was inwardly intrigued.

Clavell's tone relaxed slightly. He gave them both a smile, but it was devoid of warmth. It was the smile of a man in control; one with the upper hand. When he spoke his tone was friendly but his eyes were cold and calculating. His next comment was right on the money.

"Now come on you two. Why, do you suppose I let you in on all this classified material?" he asked.

"Good question! Why did you?" challenged Bo.

"Because you two are key to our efforts, and your expertise is invaluable to this project. Why, without both your genius and ability to improvise, this facility would be way behind its current state of research and development.

"We at the Pentagon have been keeping a close eye on your endeavours and so far what we've seen has been impressive. In essence, we need your input and experience. As you know, the military has use of HAARP at certain times and has been conducting its own research here. The fact of the matter is that you two have excelled yourselves to such a degree in your capacity as civilian research technicians that we would like you to come on board with us, to assist in one or two projects of our own.

"This country and probably the majority of the Western World, if not the entire planet is in greater danger than you could ever contemplate. If these underground weapons facilities do in fact exist, to the extent we believe they do, then they have to be located and neutralised.

"Understanding how the ionosphere interacts with radio signals is, I agree, an important issue and we mustn't lose sight of the fact that we are, no, *you* are making great inroads on that subject. However, they come low on the list of priorities compared to the possibility of a bunch of rogue nuclear missiles shooting out of some subterranean silo, (from we know not where), aimed at Israel, Europe, or even, god forbid, the United States, without warning."

Bo didn't know whether to be flattered or alarmed. This could be the opportunity of a lifetime. On the other hand he still couldn't quite get to grips with what Clavell was saying.

"Do you mean to tell us that the entire network of the United States intelligence forces dotted around the world, have absolutely no idea where they are?" he asked.

"Not exactly, no. We know they are somewhere in the Middle East, the Caucuses, or possibly even as far east as China," answered Clavell.

"That's pretty much the entire continent of Asia – a pretty big area if my geography classes serve me right," said Bo, stunned at the scope of it.

"Exactly, it's not much to go on, which is why we need HAARP, and, to put it more succinctly, you to help us find them, and fast," urged Clavell.

At this point Heckler broke into the conversation.

"This is a big deal Andrew, Karen. We need to locate these subterranean arsenals without delay. Since the invasion of Iraq by allied forces the terrorist factions, who have possession of these

WMDs have gone to ground, literally. It's our duty to assist the Government to find them. HAARP has the infrastructure and equipment to do just that. That's why Mr Clavell is here."

"Okay, I get the point, but there are complications with setting up an ionospheric lens sufficiently large enough to penetrate several kilometres underground." said Bo.

"Go on," urged Clavell, crossing his arms.

"Well firstly, transmitting almost 4 Gigawatts of radiated power from the ionospheric research instruments, up into the earth's upper atmosphere might cause lasting damage to it. That would amount to over a twenty thousand times the power of the biggest commercial AM radio transmitters in use today. We have no idea what will happen.

"Secondly, the effects on organic life, when the reflected beams hit the surface in the targeted areas could be catastrophic. There's a possibility they could alter DNA structure, cause cancers etc. So far, we've kept our ELF transmissions isolated to remote areas of Siberia and Northern Canada, where we know there are almost no human inhabitants. What you're asking, would almost certainly involve irradiating populated areas. We can't ethically do that. It's too risky. We've already had several cases of brain tumours reported in the local area amongst the Ahtna Indians. Only a few weeks ago we set off three fires in cars that were parked too near the transmitter masts, and they were only pushing out less than one giga-watt at the time."

Clavell just nodded, but Bo could see that his eyes betrayed a hidden agenda. He got the idea somehow that this man was fully aware of everything he was saying, even before he said it. But he pressed on, labouring the point, regardless.

"It's not just that either. If we don't know exactly where to look we'll have to scan vast areas of the earth's surface. Like I said, the intensity of the beams could endanger life."

Clavell was quick to counter.

"Well, that's where you two come in. You have more experience with this kind of thing than anyone else on the planet, from what I've seen and heard. I'm sure you'll come up with a safe way of doing it. We can start with a lower power output, if that's what you believe is best, but we still desperately need your assistance to help us locate those underground weapons facilities as quickly as possible."

"This is quite a responsibility you're asking us to take on, sir," Bo asserted, shifting uneasily in his chair.

"Of course it is," agreed Clavell. "And one which will not go unnoticed on your résumé's in the future. This could be the making of your careers! Why, who knows what doors a successful conclusion to a project such as this could open, for you both."

Clavell was not just a technically savvy individual, he was the quintessential salesman, and he was doing a good job.

Bo and Miller exchanged glances. They knew exactly what he meant.

Before either of them could reply, Clavell delivered his coup-de-grace.

"There will of course be a few perks, such as an increase in pay for you both, to the tune of *twice* your annual salaries!"

Bo moved back in his chair slightly.

Did he say twice?'

He looked across at Miller, who also appeared to be in a state of shock. That would amount to almost $80,000 for her and over $100,000 per annum for him!

But Clavell hadn't finished. His piece de resistance was yet to come.

"Not only that. There will be a bonus of $250,000 for the both of you - upon a successful conclusion to the project, of course."

Bo shook his head, aghast at the figures being thrown at him.

Two hundred and fifty thousand dollars – each!

He was still reeling from Clavell's earlier comments, but now the concept of this unheard of amount of money was making his head spin.

Despite this however, he felt he was being asked to cross a bridge that might not be there when he looked back. What Clavell was asking was totally new territory and as yet untested, but the lure of the financial rewards and career opportunities it promised were just too tempting to pass up.

A quarter of a million dollars - each. Jesus!

He let out a long sigh.

"We could try it sir. Given time, I guess it's possible."

"Can I take that as a yes then?" Clavell enquired, eagerly leaning forward in his chair.

"Bo and Miller looked again at each other and then back at Clavell. Though no words had passed between them, they'd made their minds up. Both of them nodded in agreement.

Clavell clapped his hands together.

"Excellent! Congratulations, the two of you. I think this will be the beginning of a very fruitful relationship between us all."

Chapter 7

Yonge Street, Toronto

Jodi was still trying to get to grips with Kwan's last statement.

"Radioactive poisoning! From where?" she asked.

The old man chuckled to himself.

"So impatient, young people these days," he sighed, nodding his head from side to side. "There is no quick answer to that question but if you let me finish, young lady, I'll tell you."

Jodi apologised and sat back, suitably admonished.

Kwan continued.

"The first Chinese nuclear weapon to be brought onto the Tibetan Plateau was installed in the Tsaidam Basin in northern Amdo. The Northwest Nuclear Weapons Research and Design Academy, known as the Ninth Academy, or Factory 211, was built by the Ninth Bureau of the Chinese Nuclear Production Establishment in the early 1960s to produce China's early nuclear bomb designs. It is China's top secret nuclear city, located in Haibei, Tibetan Autonomous Prefecture in Amdo, about one hundred kilometres west of Xining. The Ninth Academy is situated 10,000 ft above sea level, 10 miles east of Lake Kokonor, or Qinghai Lake as it's otherwise known."

Jodi's ears pricked up. "Qinghai Lake!" she exclaimed. "But that's where........."

The old man raised his hand to stop her and smiled knowingly, nodding his small head as he continued.

"During the 1960s and 1970s, political prisoners like myself, were used to build China's nuclear infrastructures. Huge prison labour camps, called laogai, were consistently placed next to nuclear missile sites. Next to the Terlingkha silos, for instance, is the "Delingha Farm", which is one of the three largest labour camps in China with a prison population estimated at 100,000. The two nuclear missile sites in central Amdo, Large Tsaidam and Small Tsaidam also have sizeable labour camps alongside them. Labour reform camps in Amdo use prisoners to excavate radioactive ore. Prisoners were, and probably still are forced to enter nuclear test sites in order to perform dangerous work."

"But surely, that's illegal, Kwan! Jodi exclaimed. "What about health and safety procedures?"

Kwan stifled a cough at that innocent remark.

"I'm afraid they hadn't quite got round to that, my dear. At least, not while I was there," he chuckled.

"In the late 1970s, the Ninth Academy further established a chemical industry institute to conduct experiments on reprocessing highly enriched uranium fuels. Throughout the 1960s and 1970s, the Ninth Academy operated under emergency conditions to build China's nuclear weapons capability. This facility was supposedly decommissioned in the late eighties, and the base moved to sites in Sichuan Province in Eastern Tibet. However, Chinese security personnel still secretly guard the Ninth Academy around the clock and a direct railway line connects the Academy with Lake Kokonor where they dumped the radioactive waste."

"So, you mean they've been filling the lake up with radioactive waste for decades then?" Jodi said.

"That's exactly what I mean. An unknown quantity of radioactive waste, in the form of liquid slurry, as well as solid and gaseous waste, was dumped there by the Academy. How much exactly, we may never know because the disposal of waste was haphazard and their record-keeping dismal.

"In Haibei Tibetan Autonomous Prefecture, near the shores of Lake Kokonor, there is a 20 square meter dump for radioactive pollutants. The Ninth Academy is located on marshy land allowing polluted water and radioactive particles to easily seep into the groundwater which flows into the Lake. Initially, it was dumped in shallow and unlined landfills, but it was also dumped into the lake. Accidents, leading to nuclear pollution of the lake occurred frequently, but they were, and still are kept very secret."

Jodi was reeling from the data she was being given. This was the first time she'd ever heard of anything like this.

"So, what are the potential effects of something like this?" she enquired.

"Radioactive wastes are chemical wastes which are highly toxic," replied Kwan. "They can cause cancer and other diseases in human beings, animals and birds. Most frightening of all, radiation emitted by radioactive wastes can cause genetic mutation resulting in birth defects in human babies."

"Oh my god, that's awful!" Jodi exclaimed.

"It gets worse, I'm afraid, my dear. Scientists have not discovered any foolproof way to permanently contain radioactive wastes, and currently spent fuels from these power plants, are stored in dry castes, which must be kept cool. One spoonful of plutonium powder, by the way, is enough to destroy the population of a large city."

Jodi gasped, but let him continue.

"As I mentioned earlier, China's record of waste disposal on the Tibetan Plateau is dismal, to say the least. Shallow land burial techniques for nuclear waste, considered obsolete in the West, have unfortunately, been deemed "sufficiently safe" for implementation in China.

"Since Tibet is sparsely populated by what are known as "minority nationalities" and is far removed from Beijing, the Chinese consider it as a perfect site to dump poisonous nuclear wastes. However, this will directly affect the lives of people and the health of the environment in both the short-term and over millions of years.

"For example, the half life of uranium - the time it takes to lose half of its radioactivity - is 4,500 million years. Therefore, harmful radiation emitted is a health hazard for millions of years to come and can lead to a number of deadly diseases including cancer and leukaemia."

Jodi took another sip of Ginseng tea. It suddenly tasted sour.

"If what you are saying is true, Kwan, and I have no reason to doubt you, how come the millions of wildfowl that live and breed there don't just up and die?" she asked.

"I am not a nuclear physicist, my dear. Nor am I a biologist. I can only assume that the sheer size of the Lake dissipates the radioactivity, somewhat. It *does* require quite a lot of radiation to kill, however. That I *do* know. Smaller, more diluted doses of radioactivity don't always kill organisms immediately, but it can still have adverse effects, long into the future. Radiation doesn't just go away. It sits in the fatty tissues and cells of an organism for a long time. The DNA of living cells can be mutated by it, causing genetic disorders and deformities that can be passed from generation to generation in humans, animals, birds, and even plants."

Jodi was all ears. This was interesting stuff.

"What about humans. Have *people* in the area died from this?" she asked.

"The effects of the experiments and waste in the Tibetan regions have been devastating," Kwan replied. "The crop yield has shrunk and, yes, people and animals are dying mysteriously, and in increasing numbers. Abnormally high rates of diseases occurred in the nearby towns of Reshui and Ganzihe, particularly amongst children of nomads, who grazed their animals adjacent to one such nuclear base, several of whom died of cancer within five years. There has also been a sharp rise in the number of deaths of domestic animals, and fish have all but vanished."

"This is unbelievable, Kwan. I had no idea."

"You are not the only one my dear."

Jodi sat there, spellbound. This wizened old man was a virtual hive of information. She realised that if what Kwan was saying was true, the radioactive dump sites in and around Qinghai Lake could very possibly account for genetic mutations in the birds that watered there and could even be the cause of the H5N1 pathogenic virus. It would explain why she was so abruptly removed from the area.

But what about the migration anomalies?

The research papers filed by that guy Blackwell came to mind. Radiation and electromagnetic radiation go hand in hand apparently, and from what Kwan had just told her, there was radiation aplenty in that area. Her mind was awhirl with possibilities. She felt she was on the brink of something important. But there was one more piece missing in the jigsaw puzzle.

"May I use your computer for a while, to check a few things on the internet? There's something I want to look up," she asked, politely.

The old man agreed, but only on the proviso that she stayed for dinner. After all, he reasoned, it wasn't every day he received a visit from such a young and beautiful visitor.

Jodi accepted his generous offer, so Kwan settled her in front of his PC and shuffled off to the kitchen.

While Kwan was talking earlier, she'd recalled a subject she'd come across at university, (known as bio-electromagnetism), and looked it up on the browser. There was quite a bit of data on it.

Reports on the behaviour of some fish and birds, for instance, suggested that these animals had some kind of magnetic detector in their bodies. During the past decade, researchers had discovered a magnetic substance, called magnetite, in the brain cells of some species. Magnetite is a black mineral form of iron oxide.

Years of experiments with released birds had proved that they use sun compasses on sunny days but have magnetic backups for cloudy days.

Jodi then found something that got her really interested.

Several investigations into bird orientation had been undertaken. In pilot studies it was observed that the headings of homing pigeons were slightly altered in the vicinity of a buried electromagnetic transmission antenna.

In more detailed studies, they constructed cages on the ground, directly over the buried antenna to explore the effects. When the antenna was energized the birds dispersed randomly and exhibited no mean bearing.

Radar tracking of individual migrating birds, flying over the antenna, at altitudes from 80 to 300 metres, revealed that when the antenna was activated, departures from straight and level flight occurred significantly more often than when the antenna was shut down. In other words, these electro-magnetic transmissions were screwing up their natural ability to fly in the right direction! Not only that, electromagnetic beams, if they were transmitted with enough power were in essence a form of radioactivity in themselves.

Jodi looked up to see Kwan was returning from the kitchen with several sweet smelling, mouth watering dishes of food on a tray.

She realised she was onto something here. Pieces of the jigsaw puzzle were fitting into place. Tired and exhilarated at the same time, she logged off the internet. She could research more some other time.

"Dinner is served my dear," he said, motioning for her to join him.

The meal was delicious and she was hungry, but she found it hard to concentrate on it. Too many thoughts were still spinning around inside her head.

Jodi excitedly recited the data she's found on the internet to Kwan, in between mouthfuls.

The old man listened intently, devouring each bit of information as carefully as the food on his plate.

When they were finished it was almost 10.30pm. and Jodi realised she should go.

"Kwan, you've been so helpful to me. How can I ever repay you?" she asked.

"You have done so already my dear, by listening. I can see that you have a good heart, are extremely intelligent, and have an inquisitive mind. I only hope that you and your generation may one day expose the situation fully for what it really is.

"The Avian bird flu pandemic is a real and present danger; illegal dumping of radioactive waste, no less so. But people have become blind to its menace. Perhaps now, with this Bird Flu pandemic, you can use the situation most prevalent in peoples' minds, and perhaps expose the true source of the evil."

Jodi bade old Kwan farewell and made her way back home to Ajax on the Go-train. The meeting with this fascinating and knowledgeable old man had left an indelible impression on her.

She had a lot of work to do.

Chapter 8

HAARP

It was 6.30am. Miller and Bo sat bleary eyed in the operations room. Neither of them had slept a wink. They had stayed up all night, going through the possible scenarios and implications of Clavell's unreal demands.

"This is crazy," Bo exclaimed. "Did you see those engineers out there all night, in minus zero temperatures, putting the finishing touches to the new transmitter arrays. Does he have any idea what he's asking us to do?"

"We don't have a choice now Bo, we agreed to do it," said Miller. "This guy Clavell means business and he's got the savvy and clout to back it up. You heard him talking about the technical details, he knows what he's talking about. Besides, think of all the things we could do with that kind of money."

Bo had thought about it alright, no doubt about that. But the lure of an inflated salary with even bigger bonuses still couldn't deter him from the technical and ecological questions that it posed. What they were being asked to do was extremely difficult and quite possibly highly dangerous.

Just then Clavell breezed into the room.

"Good morning one and all!" he chirped.

His face was pink and flushed from the cold.

They didn't know it, but he'd been up all night as well, overseeing the final hook-ups to ensure everything was on target.

Not only that, all the other non military technicians and radio operators at HAARP had already gone, hurriedly packed up and driven off into the night by army personnel, their positions replaced by just two Department of Defence technicians.

Bo and Miller were the only civilians left on the base now.

Over the next few days they worked on calibrating the phased transmitter arrays so as to get them working in unison with each other. This was a vital task and one which required intense technical skill.

When this task was completed, a series of tests were carried out, with gradually increasing amounts of power, to set up ionospheric mirrors over the coordinates specified by Clavell. Particular emphasis was put on Indonesia, China, South East Asia, the Caucuses and the Middle East regions.

The Ionospheric Research Instruments (IRIs) are capable of temporarily modifying 30-mile diameter patches of the upper atmosphere by exciting, or "heating" it with focused beams of powerful, high-frequency radio energy. A household analogy would be a microwave oven, which heats dinner by exciting the food's water molecules with microwave energy. The radio energy then disperses over large areas through duct-like regions of the ionosphere, forming a virtual antenna that can be thousands of miles in length. They are effectively, virtual mirrors in the sky. These transmitters can then emit powerful Extra Low Frequency (ELF) waves, that when reflected back to earth, are capable of penetrating several hundred metres into the ground, on land or sea bed.

HAARP's power output is staggering. A bank of thirty 2.5megawatt, 3,600-horsepower diesel generators powers it, while the rest of the facility taps electricity from a nearby power line.

With the process of creating the virtual mirrors pretty much taped, Bo's next step was to somehow beam increasingly powerful bursts of ELF waves into the earth's crust, to search for traces of fissionable material buried underground, that would show up on the geo-spectrometer.

During the month of November a full scan was done of all the designated areas, at half power.

All known, official radioactive material storage sites in the target areas had previously been meticulously logged into the database so as not to confuse them with any unofficial ones.

As the days turned into weeks, further scans were carried out at gradually increased power outputs, turning up no real results. It began to dawn on Bo that either these rogue weapons facilities were buried incredibly deep, or they didn't exist at all. The chance of them being protected by some form of shielding was a possibility, but highly unlikely to pose a problem. ELF waves, at the frequency and power being transmitted would go through anything - rock, lead, you name it; they were unstoppable.

The thing that worried him most though, was that they went through living organisms too, like a hot knife through butter. Because of this he was reluctant to increase power beyond 2.5 giga-watts for fear of causing disturbances in the climate, and more importantly to organic life, both on land and in the oceans.

Even now, he already felt that what he was doing was, from an ethical standpoint, borderline.

Chapter 9

Canadian Research Centre, Toronto.

Back at work on Monday morning, Jodi found an unmanned workstation and logged on to the internet again. What she had discovered at Kwan's home was mind blowing, but she was sure that wasn't all there was to it. There was something else nagging at her inquisitive mind. For some reason she felt that a key piece of the puzzle was missing. The migration anomalies weren't isolated to just Qinghai province. Thousands of birds as far north as Western Siberia were also affected. She needed to isolate some kind of common denominator.

It was then she had a hunch. All the birds were waterfowl. That meant they frequented lakes and rivers.

Water! That was it - rivers, lakes and even oceans. If Qinghai Lake was irradiated, it was possible other waterways and lakes were too. But surely, not just from illegal nuclear dump sites in Tibet?

After surfing the net for half an hour or so, systematically narrowing down the target, she opened up another can of worms: Russia's history of radioactive waste dumping!

It wasn't pleasant reading. There were radioactive dumps, filled to overflowing, at a number of different locations. These included the Kola Nuclear Power Plant, Murmansk Shipping Company's nuclear icebreaker base, Atomflot, the civilian Radon storage facility, and most of the naval bases and shipyards of the Northern Fleet. Radioactive waste and spent nuclear fuel were also stored at the naval yards in Severodvinsk outside of Archangelsk.

She also discovered, to her horror that until recently, most of the solid and liquid radioactive waste had been dumped in the Barents Sea. Sixteen reactors, some with, and some without spent nuclear fuel were also dumped into the Kara Sea.

Oh my god. The oceans as well! How much of this stuff is floating around in the water up there?

She looked up the location of the Kara Sea in her computers atlas.

'Hmm! nicely tucked away in the Arctic Circle. No one's going to notice up there, are they.

The last records showed that a total of 19,307 tons of solid radioactive waste was stored at the Kola Nuclear Power Plant.

Tons! They're not talking about a few bucketfuls of the stuff. They're talking about thousands of tons of it!

Horrified, and yet fascinated at the same time, she read on.

She discovered that the liquid radioactive waste at the Kola nuclear power plant is in the form of saline concentrate and ion exchange resin. Low level liquid waste and 5,612 m^3 of medium level liquid waste was stored there. Most worrying of all was that the available storage for medium level liquid waste was already completely full.

So where was it being dumped now?

The figures being quoted were mind boggling.

Her cell-phone rang. She checked the digital caller ID and saw it was Rick.

"Hi Rick," she purred.

"Hi Jodi, what you doin'?" he enquired.

"Not a lot. They won't let me do anything interesting so I'm surfing the net."

"Aren't you supposed to be working?"

"Doing what? I told you, no one trusts me to do anything useful around here anymore. Not since I created an "international incident." I'm persona-non-grata," she chuckled. "And you? What you up to, lover boy?"

"Whaddya think? Looking for a job. Duh!"

"Any luck?"

There was a disgruntled noise from the earpiece.

"I guess that means "no" then."

"You got it. At this rate I'll be thirty years old before I get something."

You could always try McDonalds," she joked. "They're always looking for over qualified geologists, so I'm told."

"Hah, funny! So, what you surfin' for on the net? handbags?"

"No. Nuclear waste sites, actually."

She could hear him chuckling to himself on the other end of the line.

"Yeah right, nuclear waste sites," Rick scoffed.

"No really. The stuff that's coming up is mind blowing, Rick. You wouldn't believe it, there's so much......"

"Jodi! You really should get back to work. I think you ate too many magic mushrooms in your noodle soup in China."

Jodi let out a sigh of exasperation.

"I told you already, Rick. There's nothing for me to do! The only reason they haven't fired me is they'd have to pay me severance. It's cheaper for them to just leave me to my own devices." She realised, that she was whispering as she spoke.

"Okay Jodi. Whatever. At least you've got a job. Hey! By the way, what ya doin' tonight? We could catch a movie or something, maybe," Rick enquired, hopefully.

"Sounds good to me. Come and pick me up at seven at my house then?"

"You got it, see ya."

"Bye lover boy."

She blew him a kiss over the phone.

Rick's such a sweetie, but he's got no imagination. Now, let's see. Where was I? Ah, that's right - tons of the stuff!

The document went on and on, revealing ships in poor condition, overflowing with spent radioactive waste because there was nowhere to send it; solid radioactive waste, stored in open air containers with no form of protection. Most of the storage tanks being full, and a number of them in very poor condition.

She discovered that the Russian Navy had taken more than 130 nuclear submarines out of active service. The greatest safety risk was presented by the 69 submarines which had not yet been defuelled due to lack of funds.

Jodi mulled over the figures for a moment.

Nigh on seventy rusty submarines, full of radioactive waste and no money. Great!

Then there was the corrosion and heat generated in the nuclear fuel and lack of monitoring equipment, making it difficult to evaluate the condition of the fuel assemblies prior to opening the reactors. Apparently, damaged fuel assemblies and the pressure inside the reactor vessel can lead to the release of radioactivity, or at worst, to a pressure explosion when the reactor lid is removed.

Jodi recalled the images of the Chernobyl disaster she'd seen on TV as a kid. It made her shudder just to think about it.

The horrific tally of statistics continued, like a nightmare that had no end:

It was then, that she found what she was looking for. Apparently, as much as 26 metric tons of radioactive waste materiel was being released into Lake Karachay each year as a result of reprocessing activities. This lake already contains 4,400 metric tons. Radioactivity had been detected in the lake sediments, and radioactive contamination was spreading in the ground water at a rate of 80 metres per year.

Eighty metres per year! So, Qinghai Lake wasn't the only one affected then.

Jodi rubbed her eyes and took a break. Either this was a scam, some sick joke posted on the internet to spook the living daylights out of people, or it was factual.

She found it all a bit much to absorb.

Was it possible that this vast amount of radioactive waste was simply sitting around in rusty tins, waiting to unleash its lethal cocktail of isotope thingies, or whatever they were called, on an unsuspecting world? And what about the stuff already disgorged into the Arctic Oceans, Lakes, and rivers? How come she'd never heard of this before?

Jodi clicked off the net, having seen enough to keep her awake at night for a year.

She looked at her watch. It was almost noon. She'd realised she'd been engrossed for almost three hours!

Jodi summarised the data she'd discovered. The illegal radiation dumps, electro-magnetism, and magnetite. It all added up.

The continent of Asia alone was a radioactive time bomb, leaking deadly gases and liquids from every orifice. It was a wonder, to her, that any living organism was still alive at all!

Kwan was probably right. Radioactive poisoning could well be responsible for the HN51 bird flu. And somehow, someway, electromagnetic waves had some part in it too. But how? And from where?

Chapter 10

HAARP

It was 7.30 in the evening. After a long day that had begun at 8.00am, Bo was ready for a shower and some relaxation. He grabbed his coat and called over to his assistant-cum-girlfriend.

"Come on Miller, let's go."

Miller eagerly followed him down the steps to the basement garage and jumped into the Jeep beside him.

"Fancy a game of pool at old Jim's?" Bo asked, as he started the motor.

"Sounds like a plan, Bo." she replied, stretching her left arm around his shoulder.

As they reached the corner and turned onto the driveway that led to the main road, they noticed something unusual up ahead. Where there was previously nothing, now there was a sentry box and a bright yellow drop barrier across the driveway, blocking the exit.

Bo pulled up to a halt in front of it and half lowered the window. He shouted across to a guy who had just come out of the small hut.

The guy walked slowly over to them. He was dressed in battle fatigues and khaki camouflage gear.

"Who the hell is this joker?" Bo quipped.

"Hey pal! What's going on here? Open up will ya!" he demanded.

The man walked right up to him and nonchalantly peered in the window. Then he looked in the back seat area. He appeared to be checking to see if anyone else was inside, all the time saying nothing. He returned to the driver's side window and looked directly at their faces, then down at his clipboard.

"Sorry Mr Boetto, Miss Miller, no one can leave the premises from now on without a permit; Mr Clavell's orders."

Bo turned to Miller, a look of confusion on his face.

She just shrugged her shoulders, signifying she knew as much as he did.

"Since when does Clavell tell me where and how I conduct my private life?" Bo rasped.

"Sorry sir, those are my orders. If you have any queries please take them up with Mr Clavell," suggested the man.

Bo looked at the guy in disbelief. Was this some kind of Joke? He was just about to jump out and open the barrier himself, when he noticed the guy was holding his left hand on a holster, attached to his belt.

Is that a gun?
Bo did a double take.
Yes, it was definitely a gun.
He decided against his first plan of action. Eyeing the man warily, Bo took another despairing look at the drop barrier in front of him. He looked across at Miller and felt his heart rate increasing.
What the hell's going on here?
Deciding it would not be a good idea to argue further, not with someone with his hand on a gun, he just nodded blankly.
"We'll see about this," Bo retorted.
He gently pulled the stick shift into reverse and drove slowly backwards up the driveway. When he was at what he felt was a safe distance from the gun toting sentry, he yanked the handbrake violently upwards and spun the jeep round to face the way he'd come.
"I've got some queries all right! Let's go see Mr fucking Clavell, shall we," he cursed, accelerating forward towards the main building at full lick.
They found him in Heckler's office, deep in conversation with the Director.
"What the hell is this?" Bo screamed. "Why can't we leave the grounds?"
Clavell swivelled round in his chair and looked up at the two of them. His face was calm and unfazed.
"There have been developments in the last few days Andrew, security issues. I have taken the necessary steps to ensure the safety of all the research facility personnel by ordering a curfew."

"A curfew! Look, Mr Clavell we are civilians, if you hadn't noticed," Bo asserted. He was beginning to feel decidedly claustrophobic.

"Quite so, but you are civilians with a unique aptitude for this particular kind of work. You two have years on anyone else on how exactly to go about doing it."

After a few seconds silence, Bo responded, angrily. "Well, if this is the way we're going to be treated I don't want any part of it. Count me out."

"Me too," added Miller.

By the look on Clavell's face, it obviously wasn't the response he wanted to hear.

"I was hoping it wouldn't get to this," said Clavell. "You see, I must insist on your cooperation in these matters as this is now a matter of National security."

"Ha, that's a rich one!" Bo exclaimed, but his smile was waning as he spoke.

The Government man's impassive features hardened. He reached down and pulled out a sheaf of papers from his briefcase.

"If you look carefully at the small print on your contracts with Raytherm Corporation, you'll see that clause 53E, pertaining to the official secrets act, states quite clearly that, "in the event of a national emergency, a state of Martial law may be enforced at all Government run research facilities." You both signed it."

"Let me see that!" Bo demanded, reaching out for the thick wad of papers.

Clavell handed the contracts to the two of them.

"Of course these are only photo-copies of the originals."

The manner in which he uttered the last word sent a shiver down Bo's spine.

Bo and Miller nervously scanned the small print of the contracts. Sure enough, that's what it said.

The two of them then simultaneously shuffled the wad of papers to the back page to see their signatures, bold as brass at the bottom.

"But – but we didn't agree to being cooped up here all day and night. This might be a matter of state security but we have our own lives to lead. And anyway, we don't work for the U.S. fucking Government," Bo protested.

"You do now!" countered Clavell. "And you'd better get used to it. You have both been privy to extremely sensitive technical data that could be of great value to terrorist factions. I can't risk the possibility of yourselves being abducted or worse, killed by external factors outside of my zone of control."

Bo's hands were shaking. He suddenly felt completely trapped! That Bridge he'd walked across when he agreed to Clavell's offer had just burned down. It wasn't a nice feeling. He fixed Clavell with a determined stare.

"Look, we didn't check out all the small print when we signed this; it would have taken days!" he protested. "You tricked us, you creeps! We were so excited at getting the chance to work here we just signed it. No one told us about being banged up in the slammer, goddammit!"

Clavell was impassive.

Heckler remained silent.

"I hear your concerns and they are duly noted," said Clavell. "However, you and Miss Miller did sign it, and this *is* a state of emergency, albeit not BPI. That means Broad Public Issue in military speak, by the way. You are by no means being 'banged up in any slammer', as you so eloquently put it. It's simply that I have deemed it necessary to initiate and enforce a no go zone outside this facility for the both of you, for your own good, until further notice."

Bo sat motionless. He looked across at Miller. He could tell she was nervous as evidenced by her biting her fingernails, but she said nothing.

A tense moment of silence ensued.

Clavell could see that they were both overwhelmed and he attempted to diffuse the situation.

"Now look here, it's not as bad as you might think. In essence this is just a security measure so that we can control the situation more easily."

Bo wasn't buying it.

"You mean so you can control *us* more easily, sounds more like!"

"I would advise you Mr Boetto to watch your tongue. You are talking to a senior Pentagon official at this moment. I wouldn't want us to get off on the wrong foot."

"The wrong foot!" Bo exclaimed. "For fuck's sake, I don't want to be cooped up here for god knows how long and nor does Miller."

"I'm afraid I'm going to have to insist that you cooperate for as long as is necessary," Clavell replied. "Alternative on site accommodation has been arranged for you on the 4th floor. It's not the Hilton but it's got everything you need to make your stay as comfortable as possible, under the current circumstances."

"What about our things at our digs in Gakona?" Miller said

"That's all been taken care of. I took the liberty of having everything brought here," replied Clavell.

"Fuck this!" said Bo. He got up to leave.

Miller said nothing. She just followed Bo as he headed for the door.

Clavell and Heckler remained seated.

"It won't do you any good to attempt to leave, either of you," Clavell added. "Since 5pm this evening, armed guards have been posted at the main entrance, as you are well aware and around the perimeter of the grounds. There are no physical fences as you know, however, a network of laser trip parameter beams have also been installed in the past week and are now operational around the 30 acre perimeter. They are powerful enough to detect and repel any unauthorised movement and are capable of inducing a severe electric shock which could be quite unpleasant, so please, don't venture near them. This is simply a precautionary measure to keep people out as well as in. Only personnel cleared by myself may enter or leave HAARP and neither of you now fit into that category."

"You can't do this!" shouted Miller, for the first time showing her emotions.

"I just did Miss Miller, and I suggest you both calm down and get used to it. We have a lot of work ahead of us and I'd prefer it if it were done in a professional and mutually cooperative manner."

The two of them stood there, speechless, trying to think of something else to say but then, realising there was no point in arguing further, they both left. Miller slammed the door behind her.

Outside in the corridor they walked silently to – they didn't know really, they just walked, lost in their own thoughts.

Miller broke the silence "What we gonna do Bo?"

"We're going to get the hell outa this place, that's what."

"But he said there are armed sentries at the exit. You saw them yourself!"

Bo knew she was right. There was no way out except through the main entrance. He wondered if Clavell had been bluffing about the laser fences, though he doubted it.

"Where are we going?" asked Miller, seeing that they were heading to a corridor that dead ended.

Realising that they were going in the wrong direction, the two of them returned the way they had come. As they rounded the corner to the corridor that led past Heckler's office they were confronted by Clavell coming the other way.

"As I said earlier, your new accommodations are on the 4th floor," he repeated, all smiles again. "All exits are cordoned off. You can't leave the grounds without a pass, which neither of you have. Best you go and get a good night's sleep. We've got a busy day ahead of us tomorrow."

With those final words, he walked past them and sauntered off down the corridor. He reached the end of the corridor, whistling to himself as if he were going for a stroll in the park, turned left, and was gone.

When he was out of sight they looked at each other.

"Heckler!" they both said, in unison.

The Director of HAARP was still sitting at his desk when they burst through the door. He looked up at them with an air of feigned indifference.

"I'm sorry, there's nothing I can do. We've been taken over by the Government. I'm not running the show anymore. Clavell is in charge now."

"They can't do this!" Bo exclaimed. "This is a free country and we're not even Americans. We're Canadian citizens. He can't hold us prisoner like this."

"Well, he just did." Heckler's tone was deadly serious. "I don't like it any more than you do Andrew but that's the way it is right now. Don't try to disobey the curfew either. I've seen the contingent of men Clavell brought with him. You wouldn't make it past the perimeter fences, even if you did manage to get through them. You can't communicate with the outside world either as they've set up a transmission scrambler that prevents any outgoing cell-phones from working. They've also disconnected the land phones and broadband internet connections."

Despite Heckler's despondent manner, Bo couldn't help feeling that he wasn't telling him everything. The disinterested tone of Heckler's voice betrayed hidden shadows that danced across his eyes.

"What about you?" Bo asked.

"We're all in the same boat I'm afraid, me included. These are delicate matters we're dealing with here Andrew; matters of state security. I'm sure you understand."

Bo was stumped. There was no answer to that. He studied Heckler's features. There it was again - that look. This guy wasn't telling them the whole story, he was sure of it.

After carefully considering his and Miller's options Bo replied, "Okay sir, we'll play ball but something stinks about all this."

Heckler just dismissed the comment with a sigh and a shake of his head.

Realising that further discussion would be pointless, the two of them left the room and made their way up to the 4th floor.

Mirrors In The Sky

Chapter 11

Twickenham, England:

The old man sat alone in his small apartment, checking the many radio transmissions broadcast from around the world on his battery of makeshift receivers. This was his daily ritual in the dimly lit lounge above the shop each night, before he went to bed.

Yegor Asimov was 76 years old, and proprietor of "Yegor's Eatery" a small delicatessen, situated on the main thoroughfare of the town. He had been a working installation there for as long as the locals could remember.

But life had not always been so uneventful for this seemingly simple and unassuming old man, for deep in his past lurked a secret so malign, so potentially deadly, that even to this day it still posed a potential threat to the lives of billions of people.

He'd buried it away in his subconscious so well that now, in his twilight years, he was sometimes unsure that it was ever true at all. It *was* possible, he had reasoned to himself, that over time, the terrible series of events that had occurred over four decades ago would be forgotten. It was possible, except......

......Except at night, when the shadows crept in through the window and the weariness of old age enveloped his weary bones in restless slumber.

In reality he knew, deep down, that he would never be able to forget.

For almost forty years he had occupied himself with his little shop, serving up coffee and snacks, bothering no one and now, in his seventies, was apparently living out his twilight years in peaceful anonymity.

He tuned in to a Russian broadcast on the long wave frequency, and listened in for a while. The inflections of the Russian dialogue reminded him of his past. Distracted for a moment by mental image pictures that flashed before his eyes his mind reeled back to the harsh winter of early 1965; to that fateful day, when two KGB officers came to collect him from his small apartment in Murmansk. He clearly recalled the uncomfortable flight, huddled in the fuselage of a Tupolev cargo plane, and arriving several hours later at the Zhukovski aerodrome, just outside Moscow. Then the long drive to the city centre in a large black Chaika, through the deserted, grey streets in the early hours of the morning. And finally, his secretive entrance through the back entrance of the Soviet State Committee for Sciences and Technologies, where he was ushered into a stark, windowless room and made to wait

He could still smell the disinfectant, so common to military briefing rooms of that era, as he sat there pondering his fate But his name was not Yegor Asimov any more. It was Boris Slatovski, a seasoned sub mariner with the rank of captain, technical specialist to the KGB for electromagnetic warfare.

The door opened, revealing a large silhouette of a man, outlined by the stark light of the corridor lights behind him. Slatovski recognised him immediately. It was none other than Sergei Brikhalov, director general of the Soviet State Committee for Sciences and Technologies. The huge brute of a man stood before him, stiff, resolute, and overpowering. His rhetoric was, as always, direct and purposeful:

"Good evening, Comrade Slatovski. I trust you had a pleasant trip?"

"As pleasant as can be expected, Comrade Brikhalov. Thank you."

"Excellent! Now comrade, you are about to briefed on something that you have unwittingly been a part of for the past six months. Please sit down."

Slatovski did as he was told, still none the wiser as to the purpose of his being called out at such short notice.

Brikhalov got right down to business.

"I am about to describe to you the kinds of weapons that fall under the heading of 'psychotronic weapons'. These devices are truly phenomenal. Through their use, a human being becomes a silent cog in a hellish machine of all-devouring fear. An individual's brain can be suppressed, his activities curtailed to the point where he is forced to submit to any wish of the operator.

"There are several types of psychotronic weapons: The first, most effective and destructive type tortures the victim and then kills him. It is based on very low frequency radiation. The human brain and peripheral nervous system cannot withstand such directed radiation. The secret of putting it to proper use is finding the right screening emitter, which we are working on as I speak."

Brikhalov was visibly in a state of heightened elation as he continued......

"Application of directed, high power microwave and ultrasound radiation is the principle factor in the second type of psi-weapon. Although these are two separate concepts, each one affects the nervous system equally effectively, wherein humans lose sleep and insomnia wrecks their ability to function properly. Such weapons can be made portable.

"The third type are known as chronal guns. The destructive effect here is achieved by creation of chronal beams. Such beams are all-penetrating, and their velocity allows the beams to disperse in space instantaneously.

"After a volley from a chronal gun, the human aura is torn to pieces and the victim's bio-energy defence is gone. Should the energy circle around an individual's head be hit, the mental abilities of the targeted person will be affected. Such weapon's do not kill, but do maim the psyche. Prolonged exposure to bullets from such weapons systems can affect the urinary system, sexual organs, the cranial brain, and the spinal cord. Leukaemia and malignant brain tumours are the result.

"But by far the most dangerous for human targets is the psi-generator. It is also known as a psi-amplifier, or psi-data unit; and generators they truly are!

"These devices produce electromagnetic radiation that conforms to brain frequencies. Such radiation, when directed at the target, can be used to suggest and transmit anything, any feeling; love, hate, euphoria, anger, anguish, and suicidal thoughts. The psi-generators have now been modified by our engineers for remote transmission.

"If hit directly, the victim loses his will power, and should the person be excited or think intensely about something at the time of the attack, he will suffer cerebral thrombosis.

"Are you following me, Slatovski?" boomed the big man

"Yes sir!"

"Excellent. In a psychotronic attack, using microwaves modulated by ELF waves, it would no longer be necessary to kill whole armies by inducing cardiac or respiratory irregular signals. The enemy can simply be incapacitated by disturbing their states of balance, or confusing the ability to think logically.

"In essence, the manipulation of human beings, by means of ELF waves is relatively easy to perform.

"Our military would have to overcome no insurmountable difficulties to modulate carrier frequencies with ELF signals. An army of occupation could then manipulate a nation's ability to make decisions in confusing political situations, or disable the militias of their loyal resistance forces. Once any kind of desire to defend or capacity to resist has been dispelled, political activities by negotiation are sufficient to incorporate into one's power a nation subjugated in this way."

Slatovski had sufficient security clearance regarding the technical aspects of Brikhalov's speech but was completely unaware, until now, of the political side of it. However, he kept his thoughts to himself.

Brikhalov was obviously leading up to something major here.

"As you are probably aware comrade, the Americans have been experimenting with drug induced mind control for some time now. Their so called "project paperclip" netted them several key Nazi scientists who have been assisting their efforts in this technique since the end of world war two. We of course couldn't care less about that. Chemical, drug induced control of the enemy has been disregarded by us for some time now as a time consuming and relatively useless method.

"It is with the technology of electromagnetic radiation and, more specifically, extra low frequency transmissions where the future of mind control lies. In regard to this technology we are superior in the extreme."

Brikhalov stepped forward and stood over him. He fixed Slatovski with a steely glare.

"This project is a culmination of ten years work comrade Slatovski. The Americans are decades behind us in this field. The information you are about to see is highly classified."

He then reached up and pulled down a large map of the North American continent. Dotted along the East and West coasts of Canada and North America were a dozen red flags, located about 200 nautical miles out to sea.

"Our scientists have developed a unique means of swathing the entire continent of North America with sufficiently powerful ELF waves, so as to render the entire population of that capitalist regime totally powerless to resist us."

The old man pulled down another screen which covered the first.

"Behold the USSR's ultimate weapon, the photon psi-generator, which has now been modified for remote transmission, as you can see here."

Brikhalov pointed his finger to the schematics on the canvas.

"Inside these vacuum-filled, pressure-resistant, stainless steel chambers are highly complex ELF transmitters and receivers that, when activated, will criss-cross the land mass in between them, creating an extremely powerful and more importantly, untraceable grid of pulsed, electromagnetic ELF signals.

"This diagram shows one of several deep sea devices, that you and your crew, comrade, are going to drop into the oceans off the East and West coast of the United States. You will be using a deep sea, nuclear powered submarine specially modified for this purpose. These devices will be fixed inside the belly of your vessel, using electromagnetic solenoid latches. Once in position, you will deposit the device on the sea bed by simply disengaging the latches, much the same way that a bomb is released from an aircraft."

As he spoke, Brikhalov pointed to the red flags on the map.

"You will repeat this procedure in these twelve exact locations."

"Correct me if I'm wrong comrade Brikhalov, but don't these devices require immense power to create that kind of effect over long distances? The North American continent is approximately 3,000 miles across!"

"Quite correct, they do. That is why these devices contain, within their core, a fission reactor, capable of producing up to 100 giga-watts of electro magnetic energy each. Because the power source is nuclear they can remain active for as long as we wish, without need for fuel replenishment."

"How are they activated at such depths?"

"As you know, we have for some time now been able to communicate with our fleet of nuclear submarines, using ELF ground wave transmissions from Kiev. This system uses a similar method but is much more powerful. The nuclear fusion cores and transmitter units remain dormant until activated by a specific extra low frequency transmission beamed from our new transmitter, located on the Kola Peninsular.

"This technology has been secretly progressed by our technical staff to a standard that the Americans could not yet even contemplate. The generators require a signal with a power output of over 3.5 giga-watts to activate them. Should they be tampered with in any way, subsequent to them being armed, they will self destruct. It is a foolproof system. Can you imagine the devastation that would cause to the coastlines of North America, comrade?"

He couldn't. It was unimaginable. The tidal surges would reach inland for miles, probably as far as the federal capital, Washington, itself.

Brikhalov continued.

"The Americans, as far as we are aware, do not possess this technology or even anything remotely like it. Without a transmitter system such as ours, it is unlikely they will ever get the point where they could emulate such powerful frequencies."

"No disrespect comrade director but while the Americans are inferior in technical intellect, compared to our own glorious Soviet technicians, they are still not fools. Suppose that in the future they do invent or, god forbid, manage to steal the plans for such a transmitter; what then?"

The old man laughed.

"If that ever occurs they will find they have bitten off more than they can chew. Look here at the intended locations where they will be placed."

Brikhalov pointed to the dots on the first map.

"The devices are strategically located, so as to affect only their own air space and land mass, as you can see from this map. If they ever do somehow manage to produce the correct frequencies, at the right power output, they will effectively bring about their own demise!"

"I am doubly impressed comrade director; a significant achievement I must admit."

The old man puffed his chest out.

"Indeed, but there is another more important factor you must be made aware of. Whilst several thousand scientists and technicians have been involved in the implementation of this project, due to compartmentalisation of the design and manufacturing of the devices, only three people in the entire world, you included, know of this information in its entirety, and that is the way it will stay. Is that clear?"

"Yes, comrade Brikhalov!"

"Good. You have been chosen for such a task because of your impeccable record in the service of your country, comrade Slatovski. It requires the skills of a master sub-mariner, with intimate knowledge of the coastal waters surrounding the North American Continent. It was I who put forward your name. Successful completion of this mission will earn you the order of Lenin, a hero of the Soviet Union!"

"I am honoured that you have entrusted me with such a responsibility comrade, thank you sir. May I ask, apart from ourselves, who the other knowledgeable comrade is?"

"You may not. That is something you should never know, for security reasons," asserted Brikhalov.

A brief silence ensued. Matters of high security were always handled this way. Should he be captured by the enemy, he would only be able to divulge so much, even if he were subjected to the most strenuous torture methods, mental or physical. That is the way it was in the clandestine world of Soviet politics.

"Your wife and immediate family members will be well looked after during the tenure of your mission, also for security purposes. You understand what I mean of course?"

He understood alright. Any mishap or breach of security and he would never see them again and he would end his days in the Siberian salt mines, *if* he was lucky.

"Very well comrade Slatovski, you are to commence your mission immediately. That is all............"

"Commence your mission immediately, – commence your mission – commen..........." Yegor found himself mumbling as he came out of his reverie. He stared into space, through vacant and bloodshot eyes. A cold sweat palled on his forehead and his breathing was erratic.

He tried to expel his recollections from his mind, wishing they were just a fantasy and wishing he were once again with his wife Chiara, in their small apartment in Murmansk, hoping against hope, as he had done for so many years, that it would all go away. But he knew deep down in his burnt out soul that it wouldn't.

He may yet still live to see it happen!

He clicked off and powered down his computer, then wearily slumped down on his bed. Eventually, he dozed off into a restless sleep, filled with dreams of his youth, his secret past, so long, long ago........

Chapter 12

HAARP

Bo and Miller had both decided to buckle down to the task at hand. They weren't going to get off the base in a hurry and had come to the conclusion that there was no point in arguing with Clavell any further. They were trapped by their own written agreements, and that was that. Further resistance would, they were certain, do nothing more than aggravate the situation.

They decided between them, that the best plan of action was to work hard and fast on locating those secret weapons facilities, if indeed they did exist.

Over the next few weeks they completed two thorough scans of the entire Asian continent, stretching from Eastern China to the Mediterranean Sea, which to their chagrin, turned up nothing out of the ordinary.

On the evening of October 20th they were visited by Clavell in the operations room. He was not a happy man. Time was running out apparently, and from the tone of his voice, they assumed he was probably getting it in the neck from his superiors, due to lack of results.

Clavell ordered them to increase the output of the transmitters to 3 giga-watts, almost full power, which would enable the ELF waves to penetrate the earth's crust to far greater depths than previously. His reason being, that if the first scans had turned up nothing, then the concealed weapons facilities were buried deeper, or were protected by some kind of wave barrier material that he was unaware of.

Bo and Miller were not happy with this. They both knew that injecting the Auroral Electrojet with such immensely powerful ELF waves could possibly cause irreparable damage to the ionosphere as well as the fragile ozone layer within it. Not only that, beaming them down into the earth's crust and sea beds, by reflecting them off the virtual mirrors in the upper atmosphere, was going beyond being extremely dangerous to living organisms. In this seemingly futile quest to locate underground weapon storage facilities and production plants, Clavell was effectively putting millions of lives at risk.

From what Bo understood of high powered ELF rays (and he understood plenty), it was tantamount to placing every living thing under the path of the scan into a microwave oven and cooking them slowly, from the inside out.

However, despite severe misgivings, and with no way to verify his fears, he had little choice but to comply with Clavell's orders.

Only Bo had the expertise and dexterity to control the ever increasingly powerful wave bands that surged upwards into the upper atmosphere. His skill at creating electrostatic plasma mirrors, and the way he reflected the ELF waves down onto the earth's surface with pinpoint accuracy, was a source of amazement to Clavell and the two military technicians who had been assigned to "oversee" their progress - in other words, to watch them.

Bo knew however that there was much more work to be done on this procedure. Several times the plasma mirrors had broken up, causing the ELF transmissions to scatter over wide areas. He had no way of knowing what this was doing to the atmosphere or organic life on the surface, only that he was sure it wasn't going to be beneficial to either.

Though their involuntary confinement to the inner perimeter of the HAARP grounds was not to their liking, the concept of earning twice as much salary was. There were no real expenses to incur whilst on the base. Their food was supplied from the staff canteen and all the hygiene basics they needed were issued free of charge. With little else to do in the evenings, they spent a great deal of time contemplating what they'd do with all that hard cash they were earning. Not to mention the possible bonus they would both receive if they came up with the goods Clavell was looking for.

They really only had each other for company. There were several other military personnel around but they kept pretty much to themselves. During their time off the two of them would sometimes take walks around the grounds and through the woods to get some exercise. They were repeatedly warned however, not to approach the laser fences. Perimeter markers had been set up with fluorescent tape, 3 metres from the poles that formed the terminals for these invisible barriers. The space between the tape and the barriers themselves was considered no man's land. It was forbidden to pass into this area for fear of possibly tripping over and falling into the laser beams which were capable of causing severe discomfort and burns.

Over time, Bo and Miller got to walk around the entire perimeter several times and duly noted the location of each and every terminal pole.

Bo had befriended the site electrical engineer, a young guy called Jake. He was responsible for ensuring the main electricity sub station, which also housed the emergency and main bank of generators feeding the antennae, was always functional and in good repair. He found out from Jake that the laser fences were powered directly from the mains supply, *not* the generators. If this was disconnected for any reason, the emergency generator would cut in immediately, reducing down time to a maximum of three seconds. A fact he noted with great interest.

Their only form of off duty entertainment was a TV in their makeshift quarters. Bo and Miller would watch the news quite regularly to keep abreast of the goings-on in the "outside world"; a place which they were not otherwise privy to. Bo was especially interested in the vast number of freak weather storms that had been crashing into the Southern states of America and other places around the world.

It seemed that every time they checked the weather channels, another record velocity storm or earthquake had occurred somewhere on the planet, causing massive devastation and loss of life. He wondered if it were possible that these were somehow connected to the transmissions that HAARP was putting out. After all, it wasn't inconceivable that manipulation of the ionosphere, on the scale they were doing it, could possibly alter the weather as well as other things. It was a hunch he'd had for a long time, based on his earlier experiments.

That Saturday afternoon, Bo was walking back through the building by himself. He passed by Clavell's office on the third floor and noticed the door ajar. A burning desire to take a look inside overcame him.

Peeping round the door, without knocking, he found the room empty. The big man was nowhere to be seen. On the desk sat Clavell's personal laptop. The impulse to check it out was irresistible.

Perhaps he had access to the internet? He thought.

He desperately craved communication from outside.

To his amazement, the computer was still turned on! He couldn't believe his luck! Now he wouldn't even need a password. But where was Clavell? He knew that if he was caught in here he would be toast. He'd better be quick!

There were several icons on the desktop but no visible internet connection. Dismayed, he clicked on a few of the icons to see what they contained. One of them was full of technical data; boring stuff that he was already acquainted with. Another listed several memos, again not very interesting. Another icon read 'ELFSTORM.'

Bo opened the document. It read so:

TOP SECRET
PROJECT "ELFSTORM"
Extra Low Frequency Specific Targeting Orographic Radiation Module.

A brief technical outline:
"Non-lethal weapons" is a broad category which includes devices for beaming various kinds of energy at human targets in order to temporarily incapacitate them, or to control or affect their behaviour. Non-lethal weapons research has been conducted at universities on contract to the CIA and has overlapped with research on hallucinogens and brain electrode implants......

Mirrors In The Sky

Bo was a bit confused as to what he was reading, but he carried on anyway.

> ......US Special Operations Command already have a portable microwave weapon with which US Special Forces can cook internal organs......

He squinted at the monitor, perplexed.
What the hell is this?

> ......Another concept is "Infrasound" using acoustic beams. Our laboratories have developed a high powered, very low frequency acoustic beam weapon, projecting non-penetrating acoustic bullets. Already some governments have used infrasound as a means of crowd control. The British have made the greatest inroads with this. Very low frequency (VLF) sound, or low frequency RF modulations can cause nausea, vomiting and abdominal pains. Some very low frequency sound generators can cause the disruption of human organs and, at high power levels, can crumble masonry......

Bo figured he must be reading a script from a science fiction movie, but something about the way it was written made him think otherwise. He read on.

......Funding of these experiments began in MKULTRA. It has been found that certain kinds of radio frequency energy have been found to effect reversible neurological changes in chimpanzees. Studies of how to produce concussions from a distance, using mechanical blast waves propagated through the air, have had a modicum of success. Such a concussion is always followed by amnesia for the actual moment of the accident. The blast duration would be in the order of a tenth of a second. Masking of a noise of this duration should not be difficult. It would be advantageous to establish the effectiveness of both of the above methods as a tool in brainwash therapy......

Brainwashing!

......As early as 1969 we have detailed the effect an infra-sonic system would have on humans. These effects range from disruption of nervous systems to death. That such weapons have far reaching possibilities in controlling dissidents can be in little doubt. When the deployment of Cruise missiles at American bases in the UK was at its height, women peace campaigners staged a series of highly publicized peaceful protests outside the perimeter wires......

> ......A prototype infra-sonic weapon was deployed, wherein the women in the peace camps at Greenham Common began to experience unusual patterns of illness, ranging from severe headaches, drowsiness, menstrual bleeding at abnormal times or after the onset of menopause, to bouts of temporary paralysis and faulty speech coordination......

Suddenly, he realised this was no science fiction script. This was the real thing! He actually remembered watching the Greenham Common demonstrations on TV when he was a kid; something to do with nuclear missile sites.

He began to take a closer interest in what the document said.

> ......The evidence to hand suggests that the technology to produce "voices in the head" is feasible. The Department of Defence has already acquired the technology to alter consciousness through previous projects and programs. We have also devised a variety of systems for stimulating the brain to exhibit specific brain wave rhythms and thereby alter the state of consciousness of the individual subject. It should be noted that silent subliminal messages were used quite successfully throughout Operation Desert Storm in Iraq.

Desert Storm! Wasn't that the Gulf war conflict?

> By 1974, Stanford Research Institute had developed a computer system capable of reading a person's mind by correlating the brain waves of subjects on an electroencephalograph with specific commands. In essence, the concept of mind-reading computers is no longer science fiction. We now have an electronic device which can implant thoughts in people.

Oh – my – god!
He was getting worried now. What he was reading didn't sound good at all. However, he was captivated and couldn't take his eyes off it. He read on.

> ......The latest development in the technology of induced fear and mind control is the cloning of the human EEG, or brain waves of any targeted victim, or indeed groups. With the use of powerful computers, segments of human emotions (which include anger, anxiety, sadness, fear, embarrassment, jealousy, resentment, shame, and terror) have been identified and isolated within the EEG signals as 'emotion signature clusters.' Their relevant frequencies and amplitudes have been measured......

......Then the very frequency/amplitude cluster is synthesized and stored on another computer. Each one of these negative emotions is separately tagged. They are then placed on the Silent Sound carrier frequencies and could silently trigger the occurrence of the same basic emotion in another human being.

The potential applications of artificial electromagnetic fields are wide-ranging and can be used in many military or quasi-military situations. Some of these potential uses include dealing with terrorist groups, crowd control, controlling breaches of security at military installations, and antipersonnel techniques in tactical warfare. In all of these cases the EM (electromagnetic) systems would be used to produce mild to severe physiological disruption or perceptual distortion or disorientation. In addition, the ability of individuals to function could be degraded to such a point that they would be rendered combat ineffective.

Another advantage of electromagnetic systems is that they can provide coverage over large areas, with a single system. They are silent, and countermeasures to them may be difficult to develop.

They're talking about mind fucking people here. On a BIG scale!

But if that wasn't enough to get him spooked, it was what came next that floored him......

......The main stumbling block to the systems outlined above is lack of sufficient electrical power to attain global capabilities. Completion of the HAARP phased antenna array in Gakona, Alaska, the most powerful of its kind ever built, should overcome this shortfall......

Hold on a minute – did that just mention HAARP?

......HAARP will complete the network of all the necessary high frequency transmitters in key locations around the world, including Dushanbe-Tadzhikistan, Arecibo, HIPAS, the British run Akrotiri Salt Lake in Cyprus, and the EISCAT transmitter in Tromso.

The purpose being: To set up a "global shield" powerful enough to specifically target and counteract terrorist individuals and their organisations with impunity, and on a planet-wide scale......

Bo was really getting scared now. He looked down to find his hands were shaking involuntarily. This was getting too close to home.

......It should also be noted that experiments so far, with other high yield antennae have produced marked changes in weather patterns around the globe. Great inroads have also been made with earthquake causation and there is great interest in further refining this, as a possible weapon.

However, it has been decided that the emphasis should be placed on using the full network of ionospheric heaters for mind control, a far more precise and directable weapon against the threat of global terrorism......

Earthquake causation, weather pattern, MIND CONTROL! Fuck me. This is intense!

Summary:
1. HAARP has, up to this point in time, been publicly operated as a civilian research module under the official guise of "researching the ionosphere to understand its impact on radio waves". This however is no longer workable......

What was that Clavell said? "Its purpose has changed."

Bo kept reading. He was entranced.

> 2. During the past several months, HAARP's activities have become a matter of public concern, creating negative media. Environmental group activities and security breaches have reached a critical point. It will therefore be necessary to close down HAARP as a civilian research facility while "necessary repairs and testing" are carried out. In the meantime, the facility should be made off limits to all visitors in as innocuous a way as possible so as not to arouse suspicion. Its true purpose however, which is to remain completely secret at all times, will be to locate and render harmless individual terrorist factions and organisations around the world who have been deemed legitimate targets through the use of electromagnetic mind control, as outlined in the protocols of project 'ELFSTORM'.........

Bo could hardly believe what he'd just read. The heading at the top pretty much summed it up, "Project ELFSTORM - Extra Low Frequency Specific Targeting Orbital Radiation Module".

Here, in no uncertain terms was a strategic plan to use the full battery of the HAARP ionospheric phased array antennae for a full power ELF wave scan of pretty much the entire planet, its primary purpose being to subjugate dissident individuals and groups.

Then what - entire populations? And what was all that about the other transmitter stations?

He knew there were other ionospheric heater arrays and ELF transmitters around the world but had no idea there was any intention to network them in any way.

He quickly re-read the tech specs one more time. There was no doubt about it, Clavell and his cronies were using him and Miller to fine-tune a mind control weapon, the final one and the most powerful. Connected up and transmitting in a coordinated fashion, they could cause serious harm to billions of people. Not only that, no one would ever know they were being used!

In one fell swoop, the enormity of it hit him. The locating of subterranean weapons facilities was just a hoax, to gain his and Miller's cooperation, while the true purpose remained hidden. Global mind control! It was so simple it could work.

He'd once heard the saying that the best way of keeping something hidden was to exhibit it in plain view. Well, so far, they'd succeeded. With his and Miller's work on deep tomography wave injection perfected, the next step would be this!

The ramifications of a global network of transmitters similar to HAARP, operating at one time was beyond anything he could envisage. There was no way that multiple ELF waves could be safely pinpointed for use in this way. Inject the kind of power that HAARP put out and then multiply that by six, and you could fry the DNA of any living organism it came into contact with. Not only that, there would be no clue as to its source. This wasn't just dangerous, it was utterly mad.

These idiots didn't know what they were doing. Their manic obsession with global population control would be the downfall of them, as well as their "terrorist" enemies. Once you started a thing like this national boundaries ceased to exist; everyone would suffer.

There was more, pages and pages of it; but he'd seen enough. Clavell, and whoever he was working for were madmen, hell bent on accomplishing their mission of locating and neutralising the "axis of evil," as Clavell put it. In doing so, he and his cronies were about to unleash a power so great, it could lead to the suffering and quite possibly, the annihilation of millions of innocent people.

He realised he had to get out and blow the whistle on what was going on here.

It occurred to him however, that they would need him to complete the final calibration tests and set ups for this. Without his expertise the project could be set back weeks, even months. Miller was the only other person sufficiently experienced enough to carry on the work. It was now imperative they *both* get out of here, and fast!

He was about to leave when he heard a toilet flush. Clavell had an en-suite washroom. He was on the can!

Galvanised into action by the sound of the flushing toilet, Bo quickly exited the document and rushed for the door. By some miracle, he made it out into the corridor unnoticed. Once outside, he made sure to leave the door slightly ajar, just as he'd found it. With his back pressed against the corridor wall, he strained his ears, listening for any sign that he'd been rumbled.

Inside, he heard Clavell clear his throat and pull back his chair. There was no startled concern. Nothing!

Bo let out a sigh of relief and quietly sloped off down the corridor. Cold sweat beads had formed on his forehead and his breathing was erratic. He felt his heart pummelling away inside his chest as he walked on tip toes towards the stairs, hoping against hope that he didn't hear – "Hey, you!"

But the call never came. Clavell was none the wiser!

As he crept along the corridor, his pulse was pounding so hard it sounded like a loud drum in his ears. He kicked himself for not having a disk to download the documents; but then, he wouldn't have had time anyway. It would require him coming back again, a thought he didn't relish. And anyway, he wasn't a spy! He was a technician, caught up in a horrible sequence of events and he was way out of his depth. Nevertheless, he knew those documents had to be retrieved and somehow smuggled out with the two of them.

Bo made it back up to the fourth floor without running into anyone else. When he entered the temporary accommodations room, Miller was sitting on the bed watching TV.

"What's up?" she asked, with an enquiring look.

"It's not good Miller." Bo replied. The look on his face would have told her that anyway.

"What is it, what's wrong?"

Bo fixed her with a determined stare.

"We're in deep shit, Miller. Those freak weather conditions I've been going on about - the one's we've seen on TV - we're responsible for them."

Bo was so shocked by what he'd seen, he couldn't think straight.

"Not only that, they intend to use the HAARP transmitters to zap half of Asia and the Middle East with enough ELF to fry the brains of anyone unlucky enough to be in the way. These guys are crazy, Miller! If we carry on with this it could... could be...., who knows what could happen!"

Miller eventually calmed him down and got him to relay to her what he'd spied on Clavell's computer.

When he'd finished telling her, she sat quiet for a few moments, deep in thought.

"So we've been conned, big time," she said.

"It sure looks that way. Clavell's been using us for this; using our expertise to prime the transmitters for this one purpose, without letting us in on it. What idiots!" he cursed.

Miller was scared by the tone of his voice.

"What do we do then?"

Bo sat next to her on the makeshift bed with his head cupped in his hands, looking down at the floor. "I, I don't know yet. I'll have to think."

Miller wrapped her arm around his bent over shoulders.

"We could always sabotage the project, Bo. You know, a little mistake here and there, so no one will notice. That way we could slow it down; at least, stop it from coming on line, while we figure out what to do next, maybe."

But Bo wasn't so certain.

"Nah, they'd suss it out in no time. Then we'd really be for it. It's an idea but it won't work, not for long enough, anyway. The only solution is to make out we know nothing while I figure out a way to get a copy of that document on Clavell's computer. After that, we need get the hell out of here."

The two of them sat silent for a while, both wrapped in their own thoughts.

After throwing around a few more ideas, they came to the conclusion, that whatever they did, it wasn't going to be easy.

That night sleep evaded them. External assistance was out of the question. All communication to the outside world had been cut. Both their mobile phones had mysteriously disappeared, soon after Clavells's announcement of his curfew. The internet didn't function any more and all land lines were disconnected. The planar laser trip beams encircling the grounds would alert the guards to any movement; and anyway, trying to pass through them would knock out a full grown moose for hours, let alone what they would do to a human being. It wasn't worth thinking about.

Bo knew a little about these high-tech barriers. The powerful and yet invisible field between each pole created an impenetrable force field, comprised of criss-crossed electromagnetic microwave beams. They were capable of disorientating any living organism, by scrambling the neuron receptors in the brain and nervous system; basically, an advanced form of stun gun. He came to the conclusion that if they were going to get away, he would have to disable them, somehow.

Over the next few days, Bo and Miller continued as if everything was normal, while they tried to devise a means of escape. They also needed to get back into Clavell's office without being seen and download those secret files.

They slowed down the progress as much as possible, without arousing suspicion. But there was only so much they could do before someone figured out what they were up to.

On two occasions, Bo managed to sneak into Clavell's office, in a vain attempt to download the documents he had spied earlier. On the first occasion the computer was there but it was turned off. Despite several attempts at guessing the password he couldn't get into it.

On the second attempt, he found that the computer wasn't there at all, nor was it anywhere in his office, in the drawers or cabinets. He assumed that Clavell kept it somewhere else on the premises, but could never work out where.

He and Miller eventually formulated a possible plan of escape. Because the perimeter laser barriers were powered from the mains electrical grid, if that power source could be shut down and the emergency generator disabled, even for a few minutes, they could escape through the woods. What they would do after that they had no idea but at least the door was open, if only a crack. They decided the best time to escape would be when there was no moon, which would be a week from now.

The next day, Bo took a trip to the first aid room on the ground floor. There, he purloined a bottle of chloroform he'd spied earlier.

He was going to have to take care of Jake, the electrical engineer, if he was going to cut the mains power to the facility. The thought of knocking the little guy out didn't fill him with joy but he had no choice. It was either that or crack him over the head with a crowbar. Jake didn't deserve that.

On the evening of October 30th they were called to Clavell's office. Bo and Miller knew something was definitely awry because Clavell always made it his business to come up to see *them* in the past. He never invited them into his inner sanctum.

"I'm instructing you to commence a full power scan of all areas." Clavell informed them.

Bo hesitated for a moment before he spoke.

"I think I've made my views pretty clear on that sir. A full power......."

"This is not a request Andrew. The current situation in the Middle East requires that we do our utmost to bring these fission jockeys to heel and shut them down. Our intelligence warns us that a nuclear strike from rogue factions affiliated to Al-Quaida is imminent. I fully appreciate the dangers, however we have no choice. If you won't cooperate you'll be removed from your posts and replaced by my own staff technicians, who have assured me, are up to speed on how to run the operation."

That raised Miller's heckles.

"No one can operate that glorified ray gun like Bo sir," she asserted. "It'd be like giving a bazooka to a bunch of monkeys; they're not up to it."

"No one is indispensable, Miss Miller. We have a job to do and I'm afraid I don't have the time or the patience to pander to prima-donnas with queasy stomachs. If you refuse to cooperate, I'm afraid I'll have to......"

"I'll do it," Bo chimed in, before Clavell could finish.

Miller looked at him aghast.

Bo knew that to refuse would be pointless. Clavell was not the kind of guy to make hollow threats, even though he must know that without their expertise the progress would be slowed. Their only course of action was to comply.

Miller was right though. No one else could steer the beams as deftly as he could. Those two bozos

Clavell had watching him wouldn't have a clue; he was sure of that.

He figured that they could sabotage the computers before they made a run for it. In the meantime however, they had to play ball, otherwise Clavell would have them confined to their quarters, or worse!

"I'll do it sir," he repeated.

Clavell stood up, clinically surveying Bo's taught features.

"Very well, I'm glad you've come round to your senses. We'll commence a full power scan tomorrow morning. Thank you, that's all."

Bo grabbed Miller's arm and walked her to the door. As he left, he noticed Clavell giving him a suspicious glance.

Does he know?

On the way back up to the operations room Bo kept his voice low as he spoke to Miller.

"We go tonight. I'll short circuit the mains breaker and disable the emergency generator links in the power station control room. You rig the computers so they overload, using the virus program I made. It won't stop them for long but it'll give us some time, a few days maybe while they figure out how to fix it."

Now that the moment was here, Miller began to get cold feet.

"I don't know about this, Bo. What if it all goes wrong and we get caught? Those guards out there have guns. They could shoot us!"

"It's a chance we're going to have to take. We have to get out of here. I'm not gonna run the transmitters at full power; its insanity."

Miller just nodded at him blankly. They'd been over this a dozen times. Even so, as they began the preparations for their escape, she found herself shaking like a leaf. She was scared out of her wits.

Chapter 13

At 10.30pm on the dot, Bo put on his coat and handed the virus CD to Miller. Then he went through the final points with her, one last time.

"Now remember, at 11pm you feed this virus program into the computer. You'll have ten minutes before it goes to work. Then, fast as you can, without anyone seeing you, meet me down at the power station. After that there's no going back."

He gave her a final hug.

"Be careful Bo," she pleaded.

With that, he was gone. He made his way down the stairs and out into the freezing night air. The power station was a hundred metres or so from the main building and he walked with purposeful strides towards it.

Where are the armed guards?

He'd never seen more than one at any time. Because of the dense forest and their camouflaged uniforms, they were hard to spot but he knew they were out there, somewhere. He'd made a note of at least a dozen faces over the past couple of weeks, having spied them in various places around the grounds, as they changed shifts and came into the canteen area to eat.

Reaching the power station entrance, he opened the door just a crack and peered inside.

Jake was sitting at his desk with his back to him. The young technician was preoccupied with his equipment, checking the bank of dials and gauges that monitored the flow of current from the generators and mains supply.

The cacophony of noise from the bank of generators was almost overwhelming. As it happened, this went to Bo's advantage.

Jake was wearing a set of sound deadening headphones, and was totally oblivious to him entering.

Reaching into his pocket, Bo felt for the chloroform bottle and the wad. He unscrewed the bottle's top and soaked the wad with the greasy, pungent liquid. Even in the fuel and oil soaked air that permeated the space, it was an overpowering odour. He'd better work fast!

Jake still hadn't noticed him as he moved closer.

With great stealth, Bo crept up behind him, but as he did so, he saw Jake's face reflected in the glass dials.

And that meant only one thing - Jake could see him! The young engineer whirled round in surprise.

Before Jake had time to react, Bo lunged forward and slapped the chloroform pad over his mouth and nose.

Jake fell backwards with Bo on top of him. The two men crashed to the floor, Bo landing with both knees on Jakes chest, knocking the wind out of him. But the little guy wasn't going to give up without a fight. He managed to shake the chloroform wad off his face and landed a lucky punch into the side of Bo's head.

Bo lurched sideways from the impact, giving Jake just enough leeway to slide out from under him. Bo was seeing stars from the punch, but a surge of adrenaline spurred him on. He knew that if Jake got the better of him, it was all over!

He reached out and grabbed a handful of Jake's hair with his left hand, yanked it hard towards him and smashed his head down hard on the concrete floor, almost knocking him out. With his right hand, he pushed the wad down over the half-conscious man's nose and mouth once more and held on for grim death.

After a few tense moments, Jake stopped struggling and was still.

Bo pulled himself up and stood over Jake's body, rubbing his jawbone. It ached something rotten. He checked his watch; it was 10.53pm.

Realising there was no time to lose he quickly located the main breakers. Further over in the back corner of the room was the emergency generator. He had to somehow prevent it coming on line the second the mains electricity was cut, and he knew just how to do it.

Being a diesel, it required an uninterrupted, air free supply of fuel. If the fuel feed to the injectors was cut, it wouldn't fire up. The most expedient way of ensuring this occurred was to unscrew and disconnect the fuel filter. When the fuel pump engaged, the fuel would spew out onto the floor causing the pistons to suck in air. The starter motor would just spin and spin but the engine wouldn't fire up. At least that was the theory.

He located the fuel lines and traced them round the huge crankcase of the generator housing, till he had his hand on the glass filter body. Then he unscrewed the knurled release nut and prised the wire clip out from under the glass bowl. The filter housing was full of fuel. He pulled on it and it came loose with a loud pop, as the rubber seal broke, spilling pungent smelling diesel fuel all over his hand. About a gallon of fuel seeped out onto the floor, before it slowed down to a trickle.

He knew that when the mains power was shut off and the generator began to turn over, that small puddle would become a river as the fuel pump went to work.

He checked his watch again. It was 10.59pm.

Everything was set. As the final seconds ticked by, Bo tried to ascertain how long it would take for him and Miller to get through the woods and then, from there, to Gakona. He reckoned at least an hour, on foot.

Another three minutes went by.

Miller would have installed the virus and would be making her way down the stairs by now. A few more minutes and the program would activate. He waited, hardly able to breathe.

Jake lay sprawled across the floor, sound asleep.

He won't be a happy boy when he comes round.

The minutes ticked by as if they were days.

It was now 11.17pm.

Where the hell is she?

Bo made his way to the entrance door.

She should be here by now.

He began to panic.

Then, just as he was about to rush out the door to find her, Miller's head popped round the door.

"Jesus! I thought you'd been nabbed. Everything okay?" he asked.

"The virus is installed and running, if that's what you mean. Oh boy, we've done it now!" said Miller.

She was still trying to keep herself from hyperventilating with fear. Then she saw Jake's body lying on the floor.

"Oh my god, what did you do, Bo!" she exclaimed, cupping her hands over her mouth.

Bo placed his hands on her shoulders and looked into her eyes.

"It's okay. He's not dead, if that's what you mean. He's just unconscious, that's all. Everything's gonna work out, don't worry."

Directing her attention off Jake's prostrate body, he pointed to the electrical isolator switch.

"Now listen, when I pull this breaker down, I reckon we'll have about two minutes to get through the perimeter barriers before they figure what's happened and try to turn the mains on again. When I say so, run like hell and don't lose sight of me, got it?"

Miller just gulped and nodded that she understood. The look in her eyes conveyed real fear as she gazed down at the unconscious man on the floor.

Bo held on to her and grabbed the breaker bar with his other hand.

"When I pull this down the lights will go out. Don't panic. Just follow me and do as I say," he said.

He yanked on the breaker and the interior of the building was immediately plunged into inky blackness.

Almost instantaneously, the battery operated emergency lights flickered on. In the corner of the room, the emergency generator's starter solenoid clicked, followed by a whirring noise as the starter motors' gears engaged.

"Let's go!" yelled Bo.

He yanked on Miller's arm and together they ran for the door. As they ran, they could hear the emergency generator rumbling and coughing as its cylinders gasped for fuel. The engine almost caught then it spluttered and whirred again, the greasy diesel fuel spewing out of the empty filter housing, onto the floor beneath it.

Mirrors In The Sky

They were outside now and running as fast as their legs could carry them, Bo in the lead, firmly grasping Miller's hand as he guided her towards the total dark of the surrounding forest.

The ground was thick with snow and they tripped over branches and bracken in a frenzied attempt to find their way to where Bo guessed the barrier fences were. They couldn't see a thing. It was like blind man's buff, except the stakes were a lot higher.

At one point, Miller tripped and landed face first in the snow, letting out a squeal as she fell.

Bo literally hauled her to her feet and pulled her on behind him. In these dark conditions they would only know if they'd reached the perimeter fences if they ran into the fluorescent tape. He wished now that he'd brought a torch, but had decided against it for fear it would give away their position to anyone pursuing them.

As they trampled through the snow-laden brushwood, Bo heard shouting for the first time, way back in the distance. Seconds later he ran straight into a springy barrier that stopped him in his tracks.

The tape!

"Miller, we're here. Come on quick; let's get through," he gasped.

They fumbled their way under the thin plastic line of tape and carried on. There were no visible signs depicting the barrier fences but he knew they were turned off, because of the intense quiet. If they were active they would be emitting an audible, electrostatic hum.

Hauling Miller behind him again, he stumbled over the brushwood and stopped after going another twenty or so steps, figuring that they must have passed the laser poles by now. He wiped his brow. Despite the freezing temperature, the sweat was pouring off him.

Miller was in worse shape than he was though. She was wheezing and shaking from the heavy going through the thick snow.

"We made it!" he exclaimed, stooping over for a moment to catch his breath.

But it wasn't just the running that was tiring them out, it was the not knowing what lay ahead or where they were going, that exhausted them. It was mentally, as well as physically, draining.

Bo knew that the Tok highway lay to his left and the Richardson highway to the right. They needed to get to the road and then make it to Gakona or the next nearest settlement, Christochina, if they were to have any chance of escaping for good. From either one of those towns they would be able to elicit help or transport and get well away.

They pressed on through the pitch black woods, hoping they were going in the right direction.

Behind them, in the distance, the lights went on at the research centre. Bo could see them flickering through the trees. He also thought he heard a muted buzzing noise behind him and realised the barriers were probably alive once more. If they were lucky their pursuers would have to turn off the power again, so as to get through the laser fences. That would slow them down a bit. But he knew it would only be a matter of time now before a search party found them. They had to keep going. They heard men shouting in the distance, and the voices appeared to be getting closer. Someone must have spotted their tracks in the snow!

Spurred on by a surge of adrenaline, Bo ran as fast as he could manage, pulling Miller behind. She was doing her best but it soon became apparent to him that she was finding it hard going.

Then the unimaginable happened. Miller screamed and fell down.

"My ankle!" she yelled out.

Bo knelt down beside her.

"What's up?"

"My ankle Bo, I think I've broken it."

She screamed again, as she tried to move it.

The shouting was getting nearer now. Bo figured that their pursuers couldn't be more than a few hundred metres away.

"I'll carry you Miller; hold on," he groaned as he tried to lift her up, but as he moved her she let out another howling scream of pain.

"I can't Bo. I can't move my foot; it's too painful." Tears streamed down her face from the agony and the irony of it.

Bo realised he would never be able to carry her in her condition. He had only moments to decide what to do. If he left her here they would find her. If he tried to carry her they would *both* be caught. But what fate would befall them if they were apprehended? His mind reeled at the possibilities.

Miller made the decision for him.

"Get going, leave me here. I'll be fine. You have to get away and get help. I'll be okay, believe me. Now go!"

Bo was stunned. The thought of leaving her in the snow, crippled and alone and at the mercy of these people, was not an option he'd even considered. But it looked like he had no choice. No matter which way he looked at it, she was right. Better that one of them made it. At least, if he successfully got away, he could get help. After all, Clavell wouldn't let her come to harm. Whatever happened, he wouldn't do that. Despite every instinct prompting him to stay, he knew their only hope now was for him to make a run for it.

Biting his upper lip, he pulled her contorted face close to his.

"I'll be back for you Miller, I will, I promise."

She looked up into his anguished eyes, kissed him on the lips and pushed him away.

"Get going, you idiot. Go!" she cried.

He pulled his hand away and ran, swallowed up in the darkness in an instant. He ran like the wind, but tears were streaming down his face, as the enormity of what he'd just done began to sink in.

Oh God, what have I done? I have to make it. I have to!

Mirrors In The Sky

The further he ran the more determined he became.

After another several hundred yards he broke out of the forest, but to his instant dismay, found he was nowhere near any roads. Instead he was confronted by an impassable barrier - the river! He looked right and left. The river stretched into the darkness as far as he could see either way. There was no way he could cross it; it was too wide. One thing he knew for sure, he'd freeze to death if he tried to wade or swim across.

Clouds of steam pulsed rapidly from his mouth as he crouched down to catch his breath but the sound of excited shouts in the woods from behind him put paid to any chance of resting up. They must have found Miller and that meant they would be on him in minutes.

Then, something moved in the bushes behind him!

Chapter 14

A dark figure emerged into the clearing, as if from nowhere.

Bo swirled round, reactively raising his arm in fright but instead of being confronted by an armed assailant, he was amazed to see a young boy standing there, probably no more than twelve or thirteen years old. By the dishevelled look of him he was an Indian, probably one of the local Ahtna tribes that lived in the Copper Valley Basin, he thought.

"You from the sky devil, mister?" asked the small scruffily dressed boy.

Bo was too shaken to comprehend what he meant.

"The what?"

"Sky devil, over there," explained the boy, pointing towards where Bo had just run from.

"You mean HAARP. Is that what you mean?" Bo asked, still not fully understanding what the boy was talking about.

"That bad place man, bad vibrations, kill my friends, take their spirits away," the boy muttered.

Bo figured that whoever or whatever he was, this kid was no fan of HAARP, though at the moment he had no idea why. Then suddenly an idea occurred to him. If this little guy didn't like it, then they both had something in common. Perhaps he could help.

"Listen pal, I need help to get away from here. That place is bad, you're right. You hear those people shouting? They want to hurt me!" he explained.

"I know. I watch you run, see woman fall," the boy replied.

Bo was aghast, "You know? You saw?"

"You need help? Mahgee help you. Your spirit not the same as them, I feel it. Come with me, whitey," ordered the boy.

With that, he ran off along the shoreline of the river, disappearing quickly into the darkness.

Bo guessed that Mahgee must be his name. He ran headlong into the dark after him but he couldn't see anything.

Where'd he go?

A voice came out of the darkness and something tugged at his sleeve.

"Follow me whitey, this way."

The boy led Bo down to the bank of the river, where, nestled in between the ice was a small boat tethered to a tree. The boy got in and beckoned Bo to follow.

Gingerly edging his way into the small boat, Bo carefully tried not to tip it over. No sooner was he in than the boy pushed off and began rowing silently out into the river.

Bo could clearly hear his pursuers now. They were almost at the river shoreline, probably no more than fifty metres away but they were obscured by an outcrop of trees on the river bank that jutted out into the water.

The young Indian paddled silently away from the location of the voices, keeping the outcrop between them and the boat so as not to be seen.

Bo sat silently, watching him paddle and couldn't help but admire the little guy's expert rowing. The single oar made almost no sound as it entered and exited the water, yet the little boat was moving fast across the river, rapidly approaching the bank on the other side. A minute or so later, it hit ice and ground to a halt.

The boy jabbed at the shore ice with the oar blade, breaking it up, then paddled the boat the final few metres till it hit the bank. Quick as a flash he was out and onto dry land, securing the rope to a snow laden bushel.

"Come on whitey, follow me," the boy whispered, disappearing once more into the coarse undergrowth with the agility of a monkey.

Bo jumped out and clambered clumsily onto the bank, splashing his right foot into the freezing water as he did so. It was so cold it felt like fire burning his skin.

Following the young Indian in the dark was hard going, especially with his right foot beginning to go numb with cold. After another minute or so however, they came to what looked like a small cabin with smoke rising from above it. The cabin seemed to be wedged against a hillside and had a door that couldn't have been more than three feet in height, and only about eighteen inches wide.

Mahgee didn't knock, for a buckskin latch-string was hanging outside, which he gave a vigorous pull.

Immediately the door opened and the boy stooped down and went inside.

Bo got down upon all fours and crawled in after him.

There was very little light illuminating the interior of the abode, save for an oil lamp hanging against the far wall and the burning embers of a log fire in the centre, obviously the source of the smoke he'd seen outside. As his eyes adjusted to the meagre light the fire and lamp gave off, he took stock of his surroundings.

The cabin appeared to be built of logs, one story high, and about twenty feet across. It had no windows. There was an opening in the centre of the roof about three feet square, through which smoke exited from the fire.

Upon each side and running the entire length, was an elevation, a wide shelf, about four feet from the ground and about the same in width. Upon this, sat what Bo figured must be the members of the household. He counted about fifteen in number, ranging from a grey-haired grandsire of seventy or more, to a wee baby of perhaps a month old. This baby was placed in a little wooden tray hammock just the length of its body, and kept swinging by an old woman.

Upon his entering, the woman immediately moved away and huddled in the corner, taking the sleeping baby out of its hammock with her.

The men eyed Bo with suspicion and then cast their eyes on the bringer of this white stranger into their domain - the young boy.

Mahgee ignored them. He immediately went to the old man and whispered something in his ear.

The old man looked up at Bo as he listened. His face was wrinkled beyond recognition. The intense gaze of his wisdom-filled eyes was impassive, like that of a professional poker player.

When Mahgee had finished his whispering, the old man nodded and beckoned Bo over.

With fifteen pairs of eyes watching his every move, Bo shuffled slowly over to him.

The old man held out his withered hand.

"Grandfather says to take his hand," explained Mahgee.

Bo cautiously extended his hand and put it in the old man's wrinkled palm.

The old man closed his eyes and clasped the top of Bo's hand with his other equally wrinkled hand and sat there for a moment, his eyes closed, as if he were asleep.

The silence in the room was such that Bo could clearly hear his pulse. Then something strange occurred. Flashes of memory from the past few days materialised in his mind, as if out of nowhere. It was as if they were being summoned up and purged from his soul.

Suddenly the old man let go of his hand and spoke again to Mahgee. He talked in a sing song dialect that Bo couldn't understand a word of.

Mahgee seemed to understand him okay though. He turned to Bo and smiled.

"Grandfather says you have a good spirit. He says you are welcome here," said the boy.

The tense atmosphere in the small enclosed space suddenly lifted, as if broken by a magic spell. One of the women offered Bo some bread and soup that was simmering in the pot over the fire, which he gratefully accepted and ate ravenously. The exertions of the last few hours and the intense cold had burned him out.

"You stay here tonight," said Mahgee. "You safe here. Tomorrow we talk."

Bo didn't argue. He realised this was probably the best hiding place anyone could find in his situation. The guys at HAARP would probably have no knowledge of it.

After consuming the soup and bread, which tasted incredibly good, he was led into another area which he assumed was the sleeping quarters for the male members of the household. Their beds were of coarse blankets and the skins of wild animals, arranged in a row upon the ground. At the rear end of the room was a small door, which Mahgee told him was used by the family as a wash-room.

"You sleep now, need rest for tomorrow," Mahgee said, carefully laying out an animal skin on the hard floor.

Bo lay down on a thick fur skin spread out on the clay floor. It wasn't much, but it would do and despite his heightened sense of awareness, he slept almost as soon as his head hit the fur. He drifted off into a restless slumber, filled with dreams of Miller being dragged away, lightning bolts flashing and people screaming with pain......

......The next thing he knew, someone was calling to him to open his eyes.

"Wake up whitey, wake up now!"

The voice was insistent and urgent.

Bo opened his eyes to see young Mahgee teetering over him, tugging at his coat.

"Sky Devil men coming, you have to hide, quickly!"

Bo came round in an instant. Outside he could hear English voices, speaking in angry tones.

"This way," said the boy, making his way to the back of the room.

Bo followed him through the door, ducking as he went.

Mahgee led him to what looked like a hatch in the ceiling and pushed it open, adroitly clambering through it with the agility of a chimpanzee. His head popped back down through it and nodded, indicating to Bo to do the same.

The hatch led into a tunnel about a metre high, through which Mahgee was scrambling along at a rapid pace.

Bo followed him for about ten metres, till he came to an opening covered by brushwood. Pushing through the leafy barrier he found himself outside in the open air, looking up at the mountain ranges to the North.

"We sit here for a while. Safe here," explained the boy.

Bo popped the obvious question, "How do they know I'm here, Mahgee?"

"They not know. They looking for you. Tell my father to report to them if they see bad whitey running away down river," he replied.

Bo looked down at the small native boy sitting cross legged next to him.

"You saved my ass, Mahgee - twice!"

Mahgee looked up at Bo. He was only young, but his eyes shone with the wisdom and experience of someone much older. When he spoke again it was with a melancholy lilt.

"Maybe your coming meant to happen," he said. "Maybe the gods send you, to stop the bad magic from the sky devil."

Before Bo could formulate a reply, another head popped out of the bushes that covered the opening of the tunnel. It was Mahgee's older brother, signifying it was safe to come back. The white men had gone.

They shuffled back into the tunnel and soon found themselves back in the main living area again.

That evening Bo was treated to the same level of hospitality as the night before. He ate grilled fish and afterwards was offered a bath which he declined. It was too cold to bathe, and besides, he needed to work out his plan of what to do next.

He discovered that Mahgee and his brother were the only ones who spoke English in the entire household. They were taught it from a very early age at the local school in Gakona. They had left school last year to come and help the family to make ends meet.

Mahgee acted as translator between him and the others. They discussed his predicament and Bo soon discovered that his situation was not so different from theirs. He began to realise that HAARP was intimately connected with these simple peoples' lives. They were incredibly perceptive, intelligent, and spiritual, and although they didn't know how, they were aware of the electromagnetic pulses that HAARP emitted, and they knew that somehow they were the cause of several deaths in the local Indian community too.

In the past year, seven members of local Ahtna families had fallen ill with a mysterious malady the white doctors called "tumours." Not only that, two men had committed suicide. Apparently they had gone mad, rambling on about strange voices in their heads, before hanging themselves. This had never occurred before, never in living memory. Ahtna Indians loved life, despite the hardships they endured. Taking his own life was a sure way to never let a man's spirit rise to the stars when he left this mortal world. No, something was wrong and they knew the cause. Before HAARP was built, nothing of this kind had ever occurred before. That's why they called it the "Sky Devil."

While they talked, Bo cringed. He knew exactly what they were talking about. It was one thing to know about it from a distance, from behind closed doors. It was another to be directly involved with the victims; people who had helped him without thought for themselves. If they were suffering so badly, what was happening elsewhere across Alaska, even Canada and beyond? It didn't bear thinking about; especially as he had played a major part in its development. He came to the conclusion that his mission was, without a doubt, to expose what HAARP was doing.

During the day however, life went on as usual around him. One thing that amazed him was the hygiene levels of these simple people. In a little underground room they would take a sweat bath every day. They built a fire around large stones, heating them very hot. When sufficiently heated, two Indians generally entered, and took their baths together. Pouring water on the stones created swathes of steam, which very soon started a copious sweating.

Then they would switch each other with small switches made of a handful of small boughs of some tree, until the bath was considered finished. This usually lasted about fifteen minutes, until perspiration was coming from every pore. They then would come out from their bathroom, rush down to the banks of the river, stop a moment to cross themselves, and take a headlong plunge into the freezing water. After a moment or two of this cold plunge bath, they'd come out and sit on a log, or stand around talking for ten or fifteen minutes, before returning for their clothes.

Bo watched, utterly amazed, as they stood entirely naked, when the weather was so cold that he wore a fur skin over his own coat and was still cold even then! And this he was told was their daily practice.

Later that day, Mahgee showed him how to hunt wildfowl using only a home made catapult. Wild birds were a delicacy but hard to catch. Mahgee and his brother however were expert marksmen, able to knock a bird off at 50 yards.

That night they dined on roast arctic cormorant. It was delicious, but Bo was getting restless, expressing his concerns about getting back to civilisation. He had told them all about his work at HAARP and how and what he intended to do. He went into detail about how he and Miller had escaped; believing as they did that the dangerous transmissions it put out had to be stopped.

Maghgee had already explained to the others what had happened to Bo's "Dutchman", the Ahtna definition for "girlfriend."

After much debate, they decided his best plan of action was for him to get back to Ajax, his home town, in Ontario, via the Alaskan Highway. From there he could contact his friends and family who would hopefully, be able to help him. It was unanimously agreed however, that he would need their assistance to get to the border. If he was caught on US soil he would surely be in danger. In Canada he had a better chance.

They hatched up a plan to disguise him as one of them, daubing his face with brown stain from tree bark and dressing him in old scruffy clothes and a wide brimmed hat. From here they could make it by boat, up the Copper River to a small settlement called Slana where they could enlist the help of a distant cousin, who owned an old pickup truck. He would take Bo and Mahgee to Tok, the next largest town. After that, they would arrange, through a contact they had there, to stow him away on a long distance truck bound for Winnipeg or Whitehorse. From that point on, he would have to make it on his own.

At approximately 4am the next morning, long before dawn, Bo said his farewells to the family. They had shown him incredible hospitality and courtesy. He was determined now, that his journey would not only result in getting his girlfriend back safe and sound, but also enhance the lives of these wonderful people.

Sitting in the little boat as it sped effortlessly up river, Bo reflected on the plight of Miller and what she might be doing right now. He hoped to God that she was alright.

They reached Slana just as the sun began to rise. This is where the Copper River becomes the Slana River and forks off to the left, about a mile past the sleepy settlement.

Mahgee's cousin was waiting for them on the riverbank.

"How did he know we were coming?" Bo asked.

Mahgee smiled, that wise smile he had that belied his youth.

"Don't worry Bo, we have our ways," he grinned.

Bo didn't pursue the matter. He made a mental note that there was more to these natives than met the eye.

After several minutes of obligatory welcomes, hugs and greetings, Bo was directed towards an old beat-up Ford Ranger pick up truck and told to sit in the middle.

Mahgee sat to his right, while his cousin took up his place at the wheel. After three attempts at starting the engine the motor spluttered into smoky life. First gear went in with a resounding graunch and a few moments later they were bumping off down Highway one, otherwise known as the Tok cut-off.

The next stop, Mahgee informed him, would be the town of Tok itself.

Mahgee made conversation with his cousin along the way in the local dialect, which Bo couldn't understand a word of. The two of them appeared to know each other well though, he thought, judging by their friendly tone and copious bouts of laughter.

The journey to Tok lasted no more than an hour and a half, during which time Mahgee told Bo that he was explaining Bo's situation with his cousin, about the sky devil and the illnesses in the local area amongst the local population of Indians.

"They have the same problem here," explained Mahgee. "Many people sick. We tell doctors why we think reason is, but they not listen. They say Indians get sick because we no take their useless medicine. They don't care for us, we not important people to them."

Bo thought about that one for a while. He could just see the local doctors pushing off a few pills on them and leaving them to their own devices. These Indians were generally viewed as vagrants and drunks; worthless flotsam and jetsam that had to be tolerated. It was the same back home.

Ontario's Indian reservations were full of listless, out of work, or rather "unemployable" people, who were looked down on by the majority of white middle class Canadians. They were that way because they were segregated and forced to fend for themselves. Once proud and handsome warriors and huntsmen, they had been reduced to the status of non-people, due to their colour and creed.

Even *he* had thought that way when he was younger. Peer pressure amongst his friends at high school decreed that native Indians were to be made fun of and ridiculed. It was bred into the white children at school from an early age.

Then he thought back to the succour and friendship he'd received from Mahgee and his family. One thing was for certain. He would never think that way again. These people were his friends now. At the present moment they were the best friends he had.

They were coming up on Tok now and Mahgee's cousin pulled into an industrial complex on the outskirts of the town that looked like it had seen better days. He traversed a few tight bends and headed for an old disused warehouse.

"My cousin says you can stay here for tonight," explained Mahgee, pointing to two huge doors at the front of the badly dilapidated building.

Bo didn't like the look of it at all.

Mahgee sensed Bo's concern.

"It's okay Bo, my cousin friend live here. Nice place at back of building - TV, shower - you like it. Just like back home." He was smiling as he said it.

Despite Bo's misgivings, Mahgee was good to his word. Secreted away from prying eyes in the back of the warehouse was a relatively comfortable pad, complete with all mod-cons, though they looked like they'd been borrowed at some time or other.

The owner was not there to greet them, however. Apparently, he worked as a long distance truck driver and would be back tomorrow afternoon. In the meantime, Bo was to have the keys to his kingdom and allowed free rein in his disused warehouse des-res.

"When friend come back, he hide you in his truck and take you to Canada. No one see you cross border; very secret." Mahgee explained. "I go home now with my cousin. Our friend, he knows you are here. He good guy, hate sky devil too."

Bo was reluctant to stay here on his own, but nevertheless, he said his farewells to Mahgee and his cousin and watched them leave.

As they were pulling out of the compound he had to ask one last question.

"Hey Mahgee, how *did* your cousin know we were coming to Slana?"

Mahgee cracked a wide grin and pulled a mobile phone from his pocket.

"We have our ways," he said, and he laughed.

Bo shook his head.

"Jeezus, and I thought...." He couldn't suppress a chuckle though.

Then a sudden thought crossed his mind. He could maybe call home and get help from his parents. Even better, he could call his old pal Rick. No – his parents would probably freak out and cause a scene. Rick would be more discreet.

He went to raise his hand to stop the truck, but then had second thoughts.

Suppose Clavell has connections to the mobile phone cell network?

He couldn't discount the guy's capabilities, not after what he'd seen. His indecision cost him the opportunity to try.

Mahgee gave one last wave as the old pickup exited the gates of the compound. Then they were gone.

Bo was alone once more.

Again he reflected on the incredible trust and friendship these guys extended to him, a total stranger. He reckoned his tale of plight and the fact that he was an avowed protagonist of HAARP, had carried some weight. For sure, it had motivated these Indians to help him. They seemed to know that place was up to no good but they couldn't do anything about it, because of who they were. He figured one white man on their side was a bonus to them. He wondered though, just how much did they know?

The larder in the makeshift apartment was full of tinned fish and meats. There was plenty to drink and there was even a TV and stereo. He wondered how come this place never got looted, but figured that it was so well concealed that no one would ever find it. Anyway, he would wait here till Mahgee's truck driving pal turned up and take it from there.

He spent that evening watching TV.

At around 9pm he realised he was flaked, having been on the go since before dawn. He settled down to rest, dozing off into a restless slumber, with the TV still on.

Chapter 15

Gakona

County Sheriff, Steve Lake, received the call from his deputy at 11pm, just as he was going off shift.

"Control to Sheriff Lake, come in Steve."

The radio crackled again.

"Sheriff, come in please!" There was a hint of tension in the voice this time.

"Probably Pete wanting someone to talk to," Steve figured. Nothing much ever happened in Copper Valley on the night shift.

Picking the handset up, he clicked the receiver to transmit and spoke into it, with an air of disinterest.

"Steve here. What's up Pete?"

The reply focused his attention immediately.

"We got a corpse washed up on the Christochina river banks, near ol' Jim's community centre. Need ya down there pronto!"

"Shit, just my luck." Lake cursed under his breath. He'd just been about to sign off and head home for a nightcap, a quick shuffle under the sheets with Mrs Lake and then a good sleep. Still muttering obscenities to himself, he scanned the rear view mirror for any vehicles behind. Seeing none, he slewed the car around. The tyres spun on the icy tarmac and the car skidded left to right as he executed a less than perfect U turn on Alaska's Highway 1.

"Okay, on my way. This better not be a crank call or someone's gonna know about it," he barked into the radio handset, as he floored the accelerator pedal and accelerated westward, towards the river.

The crackly reply echoed around the car's interior.

"Seems it's a bloater Sheriff; been in the water a few days by the sounds of it. A young Injun, who was out on his canoe fishing, reported it to ol' Jim a few hours ago; one of the Ahtna tribe. That's all I know right now."

"Another Injun suicide, I'll bet," Steve muttered to himself.

There had been two suicides amongst the small community of Ahtna Indians in as many weeks. Young un's too, which he'd found unusual.

The natives were a weird bunch, but they weren't usually in the habit of taking their own lives. Suicide was not a natural thing for an Injun to do. In fact it was a big taboo, as far as their beliefs went, and the last victim couldn't have been more than eighteen years old.

Mirrors In The Sky

He reflected on the fact that the Injuns been acting up strangely of late. It didn't come as much of a surprise to him though. There were no real prospects for them in Copper Valley. They lived out their miserable lives in run-down shacks, eking out a living from fur trading and selling fish. It was a hard existence. The life expectancy of the average native was around 50 years. At this rate though, the entire community would be gone in a couple of years!

The car's headlights picked out an ice laden sign coming up on the left. Though the white painted words on the dark blue background were partially covered, he knew what it said.

"IONOSPHERIC RESEARCH OBSERVATORY."

He'd driven past here several times and often wondered what went on in that place. A bunch of moon watching geeks with beards and cardigans no doubt; wasting the taxpayer's hard earned money and talking techno gobbledegook till they were blue in the face. But this time he noticed something was different. Now there was a barrier across the entrance and a guard post hut.

He slowed down to get a better look.

Never seen that before?

There was a guy in the hut who was peering through the small window, watching him intently as he cruised past.

Strange?

Still, it was none of his business what those nancy boys did. He pressed the accelerator and sped on.

A little further on, he slowed down as he saw the sign for the community centre appear in the distance. He swerved off the highway and taking care not to veer off the track, turned left into the woods, where he could now see lights flickering through the pine trees, down in the direction of the river bank.

Deciding it would be unwise to drive any further, in case he got stuck in the snow, he parked the car and reached into the back seat for his flashlight.

Leaving the engine running, with heater blower at full blast, he hauled his burly frame out of the seat.

This wasn't going to take long, not if he had any say in it. Another dead injun who'd lost the will to live wasn't going to cause him to lose too much beauty sleep.

It was well below freezing and his breath turned to white mist as he begrudgingly slammed the car door shut. Tugging his coat around his swarthy neck, to stave off the cold, he trudged off through the crunchy snow towards the lights.

Two figures, silhouetted by the flash lamp, were bending over a dark mound on the river's edge.

He made out the spindly frame of ol' Jim and a smaller figure standing next to him.

"That you Jim?" he shouted.

The spindly figure's head bobbed upwards.

"It be me Sheriff. Over here," came the reply.

Careful not to slip on the icy coating of the sloping bank, he edged his way forward till he was standing next to the two of them.

"What we got here then?" he asked.

Jim's next words were not what he was expecting to hear, not by a long shot.

"It's no Injun Sheriff, if that's what yer getting at. This here's a whitey, and a woman at that!"

It took a few seconds for the old man's words to register. He stood motionless digesting the consequences of what this meant.

Firstly, the chances of him getting his welcome nightcap, sitting by the fire with a hot cup of cocoa, were now fast diminishing.

Secondly, there would be endless paperwork to fill out, a detailed autopsy, and newspaper reporters to fend off. The body would have to be identified. It could even be a homicide and if the corpse was from out of state that meant the FBI would have to be involved, which meant even more paperwork!

"She's been in the water a few days, bloated like a suckling pig. Take a look fer yerself," suggested Jim.

Lake flashed his torch onto the hump at Jim's feet. It looked like a dead seal at first glance. As he moved round to the left though, it became clear that this was definitely a human cadaver. The face was bloated to twice its normal size but still recognisable as a homo-sapien. She definitely appeared to be Caucasian and not native, that was certain. Her matted blonde / brown hair lay straggled across her face and shoulders. He could also see that this was no local girl either; her clothes were too businesslike.

He picked up a stick and poked at the middle section of the corpse, attempting to pick away some of the slime and weeds, to get a better look.

"Young Mahgee here found her floating under the jetty and we pulled her onto the bank," ol' Jim explained, patting the small boy standing next to him on the shoulder.

Lake cast a glare down at the boy.

"What you doing out here at this time of night son?"

Mahgee looked up at the burly sheriff, the whites of his slant eyes barely discernable in the darkness.

"I out fishing, sheriff. Good time for fish now; nice and quiet. My hook catch something big and I pull it out, thinking it seal, or something."

Lake suppressed a chuckle.

"Well you netted a big one this time, son."

He turned his gaze on the old man.

"Don't touch anything else, Jim. I'll call it in and have the coroner hauled outa bed. He's gonna love me!"

Then he looked up into the sky.

The Northern lights or Aurora Borealis, as they are otherwise known, lit up the horizon with amazing clarity.

Jim followed his gaze.

"I never seen them so bright, Sheriff. Been like it for the last few nights, but tonight they're brighter than ever. Never seen it like that, never in all my years."

Gakona didn't possess a coroner. The nearest one available had to be called in from Christochina and Lake, to his chagrin had had to wait almost two hours for him to turn up.

The coroner, an old man called Jacob Dwight was not in a good mood when he arrived, but with the help of 'ol Jim, the three of them eventually wrapped the body in a zip up body bag and bundled it into his station wagon. Dwight then followed the sheriff to the police station which was situated in the middle of the small town of Gakona.

There was also no morgue per-se, in these parts. The nearest official one was in Fairbanks, over a hundred miles away. When someone died in this neck of the woods the body was temporarily stored in what was known as the "cool box" which was in essence, a "portakabin", or mobile workman's hut situated round the back of the small police station. Although it had a refrigeration unit attached to it, there was no call for it right now. The temperature rarely rose above freezing, even on a sunny day at this time of the year.

Upon their arrival, Lake and Dwight laid the bloated corpse on the floor of the hut and stepped back outside. Lake locked the door.

"She'll be safe there for a while, sheriff. I'll be back tomorrow morning, to pick her up and take her to Fairbanks for an autopsy," Dwight explained. "Any idea who she is?"

Lake just shook his head.

"Never seen her before. She's from out of town though. I'm sure of that."

"Well, I'll leave that part of it up to you, Sheriff. You can go home and enjoy your nightcap now," Dwight said, smirking.

Lake wasn't amused. It was now almost 6 a.m. and he'd need to be back on shift by noon. It didn't seem worth the while even going home. Still, he was bushed, and a few hours sleep wouldn't do any harm.

Thanking the old man for coming out at this ungodly hour, he set off for home in his car. As he drove, he pondered on the identity of the corpse. He knew pretty much everyone in Gakona and the surrounding areas but he was sure he didn't recognise the dead girls face, bloated though it was. This had definitely been a night for surprises.

But he got a further surprise when he tried to park in his driveway. Another vehicle was already parked there, blocking the entrance. It was a dark blue Ford Ranger pickup truck, with a hardtop rear canopy. The windows were tinted.

Lake was incensed.

What the fuck is this?

As he pulled up behind it, he could just see through the black tint of the truck's windows that there were two men in the car. On his arrival they both got out. They looked official, and by the looks on their faces, they weren't here for a social visit.

The larger one of them walked purposefully up to the driver's side of his car and tapped on the window.

Lake wound it down.

"Sheriff Lake?" asked the man.

"That's me, pal. Who the hell are you?"

"FBI," said the man, quickly flashing his ID card.

Lake's already weary shoulders sank even lower.

Oh no! Not now for Christ's sake!

"We need you to drive back to your office and show us the body of the girl you found in the river," demanded the FBI agent.

"Now! Can't it wait till morning?"

"It *is* the morning and we need to see the body now!" asserted the man. He wasn't asking, he was telling.

Lake could sense urgency in the man's strained voice.

"Shit! I've been up all night!"

"Sorry Sheriff, this is Federal business and we need to see that body immediately," repeated the man.

He could see it would be pointless to argue. He figured that the Fed's would be involved but not for at least a day or so. Still, shrugging his weary shoulders, he shifted his car into reverse and turned around.

The two FBI guys got back in their vehicle and followed him. But as Lake drove, he had the sudden realisation that apart from himself, ol' Jim, the coroner, the Indian boy, and Pete, no one else knew about this incident. So how come the FBI did? He figured Pete must have alerted them. He'd have a few words to say to *him* when he next saw him.

Ten minutes later, the three men stood huddled outside the "cooler" in the freezing cold, while Lake fumbled with the keys to the padlock. He unclipped the hasp and swung the door wide open, then stepped inside and turned the single light bulb on. The zipped up cadaver lay dead central on the floor, exactly where he and the coroner had placed it.

"There she is boys," announced Lake, motioning with disinterest at the black lump at his feet. "Say, how come the FBI knew about this, anyway? Who told *you* about it?" he asked.

"Neither of them answered. In fact they just ignored his question altogether. They were more interested in the body. The big guy immediately knelt down and unzipped the body bag to reveal the puffy, bloated face of the dead woman.

"That's her alright, Karen Miller," he said to his partner.

The other man nodded sagely, as if he knew exactly what his partner was talking about.

Captivated by the conversation between the two FBI agents, Lake forgot about his original question.

"You know who she is!" he asked.

The first guy looked up at him, and grinned, but his eyes were cold and vacant. "Yep! Karen Miller. She worked at the Ionospheric Research Observatory down the road."

"Jeez! So that's where she's from. I figured she wasn't a local," said Lake, genuinely surprised.

"Nope! Canadian. This is a Federal matter now Sheriff, and a homicide. That's why we're here. We'll be taking over the case from here on."

The bulky FBI agent held out his hand expectantly as he spoke.

"Give me the keys to this place," he demanded.

Lake frowned and stood back a pace. "Hey! Hold on a minute. I'm the local law enforcement around here. This is *my* body until the coroner's done an autopsy. I can handle this," Lake asserted.

"Not any more Sheriff," said the second FBI man. "Like my pal here just said, this is a Federal investigation now. You can go home and get some rest. We'll take a statement and your report from you tomorrow. Now give us the keys."

Lake faltered for a moment. He wasn't expecting this.

The two FBI men stood up. They turned their attention on the Sheriff. It was almost as if they grew a couple of inches taller as they encroached on him and in the enclosed, claustrophobic space of the little makeshift morgue, Lake suddenly felt vulnerable and alone. He didn't really know why, but there was something not right about these two characters.

"The keys!" demanded the big guy.

For a second, Lake thought about going for his gun but then decided against it. He was exhausted, alone, outnumbered, and outranked. And anyway, these two guys were bigger than him and the big one's right hand was hidden inside his coat. Not very good odds! He handed the keys over with an apathetic sigh.

The big guy took them from him, and smiled. "Thanks Sheriff. You can leave now," he ordered.

"What about her?" Lake asked, nodding his head towards the body.

"We're taking the body to Anchorage for forensic testing."

"Anchorage! That's a long way."

"So – you did you're geography at school. Big deal! We know it's a long way, bud. That's why we aint got time to stand around in this shit hole talkin' to you! Now let us do our jobs, and fuck off!"

Lake had had enough of this. He just wanted to get home and get some sleep. Let the FBI sort it out if they wanted to, he thought. At least they didn't want him to drive with them to goddamn Anchorage! He stepped outside and started off towards his car. Then he realised something.

"Hey! Who do I give my report to?" he asked.

"We'll contact you tomorrow," replied the big guy. "Goodnight Sheriff," he remarked. The tone of his voice, suggesting he wasn't in the mood for further dialogue on the matter.

Lake turned and left. On the drive home, he remembered that he'd forgotten to ask again, how come the FBI knew about all this when no one had called them. Still, that could wait till tomorrow now. Right now he needed some shut eye.

Chapter 16

Tok

Bo lay sprawled out across the threadbare sofa, half asleep and mumbling incoherently.

He thought he heard someone calling his name.

He turned restlessly on the sofa for the thousandth time.

There it was again!

He turned over once more and opened his right eye. It was daylight outside. He could see light seeping through the warehouse doors in the dim distance.

The TV was playing the local news channel. Then he heard his name a further time. It was coming from the TV! He realised he must have fallen asleep, with it still on. But then he thought he saw his own face looking back at him from the screen. He opened the other eye. It was his face, staring back at him from the flickering monitor! The picture panned out to a newsreader and the words being spoken hit him like a blow to the head.

"...The fugitive's name is Andrew Boetto. Police have issued a broad public announcement to not approach this man as he is most likely armed and extremely dangerous. Anyone having any information as to his whereabouts is to contact the Alaskan Federal State Police immediately, on this number......"

Bo sat transfixed, his eyes glued to the screen, not quite comprehending what was going on.
There, now, on the TV, filling the screen was a picture of Miller, his girl! But what was this the announcer was saying?

"......Miss Karen Miller came from Ontario, Canada, to work at the Ionospheric Research Observatory last year. It's believed she was stabbed to death during an argument with Boetto that got out of control.

Her body was found washed up on the banks of the Copper River last night, at 11p.m. by local County Sheriff, Steve Lake.

Miss Miller's family have been notified of this tragedy and it is believed her parents are being flown to Alaska by federal Agents, to identify the body as I speak.

Other news just in............"

Bo just sat there, unable to move, unable to grasp the situation at all.

No! No way! She can't be – be dead?

He slapped himself on the cheeks. Was he seeing things? Was this just a bad dream? He stood up and paced around.

No, no it can't be. It's impossible, they would never go that far, not Miller. Oh god no. Please no!

The next few hours came and went, but Bo didn't notice. He came out of his depression once or twice only to found himself pacing backwards and forwards across the small space, almost in a trance.

He sat on the floor and cried, he didn't know for how long, till his tears wouldn't come any more. Then he began to blame himself. He'd left her there, knowing she was in danger. It was his fault. He felt ashamed. He was a coward, and because of that, she was gone. Then regret reared its ugly head, reminding him that it was his idea to run for it. If he hadn't come up with that crazy idea they'd still be together – she'd still be alive!

His world was one of deep loss and despair now. With no one to turn to that he knew, Miller dead, and with him now being hunted as a runaway murderer, things didn't look the same to him anymore. It was as if everything was happening in slow motion; as if he were in a dream - a very, very bad dream. He had no idea how long he'd sat there. It was only when he heard the powerful rumble of a diesel engine and headlights flickering through the cracks in the main doors of the warehouse that he came out of it.

When Benji Hal, Mahgee's cousin's friend, stepped inside his makeshift apartment, he found two vacant, lost eyes peering back at him through the gloom.

"You must be Bo?" he said, sporting a wide grin that showed off his tobacco stained teeth.

Bo just nodded.

"Seems you be in a lot of trouble, man. I been listening to the radio on the way here. You hot property right now," said Benji.

Bo didn't even acknowledge him. He didn't care. Nothing mattered anymore.

But Benji had his instructions from Mahgee and was intent on carrying them out. Inside the refrigeration unit of his truck, which sat above the cab, he had created a secret compartment. He'd used it on several occasions to smuggle contraband across the border with great success. It could be accessed by a panel cut into the roof of the cab. It was small and cramped, but just big enough for a grown man to lie down in.

Benji managed to shuffle Bo up and into it, despite the fact that the guy seemed totally disinterested in doing anything at all.

"Sorry about this, man. It's not very comfy but it'll get you across the border undetected. You'll be right above the cab, so it'll be warm enough in there. Just stay totally quiet if I tap on the roof, okay?" he explained.

Bo just shrugged and lay down in the secret recess. He went through the motions, as instructed by Benji, like a robot.

Once Benji was sure Bo was comfortably ensconced in the secret compartment, he pushed the panel door shut and covered the roof over with a large poster of Pamela Anderson - topless of course. Then he set off for his next stop at the Costco warehouse on the outskirts of Tok. He had a shipment of groceries to load, bound for Whitehorse in Canada. It would be a two day trip.

Chapter 17

Ajax, Ontario (several days later)

It was a Saturday evening and Rick was watching TV, with a half downed bottle of Coors in one hand, while the other fiddled with the TV's remote control.

Jodi was upstairs, getting dressed and taking her time about it too, thought Rick. They were going out tonight to watch the Toronto Maple-Leafs play Chicago in the semi finals of the NHL Stanley cup and Rick was really keen to get going. This was going to be one hell of a game. But, as usual, he was waiting patiently for Jodi to get ready.

Rick and Jodi had been seeing each other now for a few weeks. They had definitely become an item. Rick's sense of humour and laid back attitude to life endeared Jodi to him, while Rick found his new girlfriend exciting beyond compare, in every aspect.

They had become pretty much inseparable in the short time they'd known each other and spent pretty much every spare moment together. If they didn't have any money between them, which was quite often, due to the fact that Rick still hadn't managed to get a job, and Jodi only had her basic pay to rely on, they'd still always find something interesting to do, in or out of the sack.

After several minutes of flicking through the live coverage of the commentators preambles, he was impatient to get going. He was just about to shout upstairs for her to get a move on, when the phone rang.

"I'll get it Jodi. Hurry up will ya!" he called out, picking up the receiver.

"Hello, Rick Hayden speaking," he said.

The voice on the other end of the line was low and hurried.

"Rick, it's me!"

For a couple of seconds Rick was confused. He didn't recognise the voice, then, suddenly his eyes widened.

"Bo! Where the hell...."

The caller cut him short in an instant.

"Sshhh for Christ's sake, will ya! I guess you've probably already heard about me on the news."

"Well, yeah but......"

"Listen, Rick, I can't talk on the phone. I'm in a call box just down the street. You know the place; where we used to slide down the bank when we were kids. Meet me here in ten minutes and bring some food. I'm starving, and hurry up!"

The phone went dead.

"Hello, hello! Rick repeated, but Bo had rung off.

"Holy smoke," he muttered under his breath, still clasping the telephone handset still in his right hand.

Jodi had just come downstairs and entered the room.

"Who was that?" she asked, innocently.

Rick looked like he'd seen a ghost.

She walked over to him and gently shook his arm.

"Rick, what's up? What's the matter?"

"That was Bo. He's here in Ajax," he muttered, still unable to comprehend what had just happened. His eyes were glazed, as if he were looking through a fog.

"Bo!" exclaimed Jodi. "What, you mean Andrew Boetto, your friend, the murderer?"

"Yep and he's in trouble. Come on Jodi, we've got to go see him."

He reached for his jacket but Jodi grabbed him by the arm.

"Trouble! You're damned right he's in trouble, and you're doing no such thing, Rick Hayden. That guy is being hunted by every law enforcement official in Canada and the United States. He's a wanted felon. You're going to call the police right now and turn him in."

Rick could see Jodi's bottom lip was trembling.

"Listen Jodi, Bo may be on the run but there's no way he killed his girlfriend. Something stinks about this whole thing. I've known Bo since we were in first grade. He's no murderer."

"Oh yeah, well try telling that to the Mounties and the FBI *and* CNN," she protested. "If you go and meet him you'll become an accessory to murder. I won't allow it!"

"You'll shut it!" Rick screamed. "Bo's my friend and he needs help."

It was the first time Rick had lost his temper with her. The effect was no less than if he'd punched her in the face. She just stood there, stunned into silence and tears began to well up in her eyes. Rick could see he'd overdone it.

"Look Jodi, I'm sorry for shouting. I don't believe Bo killed that girl, whatever anyone says. He's out there alone and frightened and the only person he can trust right now is me. That's why he phoned here. Would you turn in your best friend?"

"I don't, I don't know what I'd do. I guess not, but what can you do for him?" said Jodi, still smarting from Rick's last outburst.

"That's exactly what I'm gonna find out, right now. So, you coming or not?" he asked as he hastily packaged together some food from the fridge. He was going, with or without her.

Jodi nodded soundlessly, shrugged her shoulders, and without another word spoken between them, they donned their coats and headed out the door.

"Where is he?" asked Jodi, keeping pace with Rick, who was now walking at a brisk pace towards Finley Avenue, the main road that led down to the Lake Ontario shoreline.

"Down by the lake. We used to slide down the embankment there when we were kids. Come on, we can walk it in ten minutes. It's not far."

They walked hurriedly along Finley, Jodi with her arm clutching Rick's.

It was early November and the air had a severe chill to it that made them both shiver. They carried on, past the school where Rick and Bo had played as children and before long they could smell the algae from the Lake shore.

"Damn, it's cold out tonight," winced Rick. "Bo must be freezing out here."

A few minutes later they reached Lake Driveway, the road that ran parallel to the shoreline. In the moonlit night sky the surface water of the lake glittered like a million stars.

"That's where Bo must have called from," said Rick, pointing to a phone box a hundred or so metres away.

They walked towards it.

"The embankment slopes down just after it, over there," he said, with a slight nod of his head towards a break in the wall, about thirty feet past the phone box.

"Where is he?" she asked.

"He'll be down by the lake shoreline. There's a cave there where we used to play. The slope will be icy so watch you don't slip."

Reaching the break in the wall, Rick looked down into the murky darkness.

"I can't see much. Mind your step," he warned, motioning her towards the opening.

"Wait!" said Jodi, grabbing Rick by the arm. "There's a guy coming, walking his dog. We better not let him see us go down there."

Rick looked up and saw the man Jodi was talking about, walking their way. He was restraining an eager German shepherd dog on a sprung leash.

Jodi was right. The guy might think something strange about two people disappearing down towards the lake in the darkness, especially at this time of night.

The man and his dog were fast approaching now.

"Give me a kiss," said Rick, wrapping his arms around her.

As the dog drew closer to them it barked and became excited, then it scuttled towards the opening in the wall. The owner pulled on the leash, violently restraining the powerful beast.

"Whoa there boy; nuthin down there fer ya. What ya looking fer?" he said, gruffly.

Rick placed his accent as a Newfy, (Newfoundland.) He looked over Jodi's shoulder at the burly figure.

"Evening, sir," he said.

"Evening folks. Bit cold fer that koinda carry on aint it?"

"Oh love finds a way sir," said Rick, faking a weak smile.

The dog was insistent about getting through the break in the wall and down to the shoreline. It barked loudly and reared up as the man pulled it back.

"Git down Bruno. Down boy! What's the matter with yer?" the Newfy rasped.

Rick realised that the dog had probably smelled Bo's scent and was intent on sniffing him out. The Newfy was having trouble controlling the powerful beast and cursed loudly at it.

"Damn dog, got a moind of it's own he has. Come here boy. Heel!"

The man grabbed the dog by the collar and pulled it away from the opening. Finally, he got it under control and led it off down the pathway, still barking.

Rick and Jodi remained as they were, holding on to each other until the dog and his handler were way in the distance.

"Phew! That was a close one. Okay, let's go," said Rick.

Checking once more around them for anyone else in the vicinity and seeing no one, Rick went first, holding Jodi's arm.

The slope was pure ice in the middle. Either side of it were rocks and boulders. It was difficult to see in the dark but Rick guided Jodi down to the flat section at the bottom, without too much trouble. Turning right he followed an outcrop of rocks that obscured the walkway above for about twenty metres. Suddenly, he stopped, dead in his tracks.

"What's up?" said Jodi.

A whispered voice emanated from the darkness.

"Rick! I'm in here."

Jody gasped and froze to the spot. She clung onto Rick's arm, her hands trembling.

A figure emerged from a dark recess to their right.

"Did you bring me some food?" asked the voice.

"Right here, Bo. Long time no see eh?" said Rick, offering over the small package he'd put together back at the house.

"No kidding Rick. Thanks pal. I'm starving."

Jodi watched, transfixed as the shadowy figure ripped open the package, and hastily began to consume the first of the contents, a pork pie.

As Bo munched away on the food, Rick looked his old friend over. He had grown a thin beard and his eyes were hollow, indicating lack of sleep or just plain exhaustion.

"What the hell happened?" asked Rick.

"I got fucked with the rough end of a pineapple, that's what happened, Rick," Bo replied, now munching ravenously on the next item, a smoked sausage.

"What's the deal with this murder rap? Did you......"

"No! You think I'd kill my girl? Those bastards did it. She was alive when I last saw her, she, she...." His eyes were moist and his voice faltered as he remembered what had happened. "She's dead Rick. They killed her and dumped her in the river, then pinned it on me."

"Who? Why? The TV reports said *you* killed her!" said Rick.

"The fucking Government guys where we were working must have done it. I found out about something I shouldn't have, and we tried to escape. They bribed me and Miller to work on their shitty project and wouldn't let us out; something to do with official secrets act. It's all bullshit. They were going to bang us up for twenty years if we didn't cooperate."

"Are you kidding!" exclaimed Rick.

"No I'm not. The place was cordoned off like a concentration camp; electrified fences, and guards everywhere. We managed to get through the electronic barriers they'd put up and nearly got away but she broke her ankle and they caught her before we even got to the main road. I managed to escape but I had to leave her there. I never thought they'd *kill* her, for Christ's sake. God! What am I gonna do?"

Rick tried to calm his friend down. He could see Bo was almost hysterical.

"It's okay, Bo. Let's take it one thing at a time. How did you get here? Alaska's over three thousand miles away!"

"I was helped by a local Indian boy who lives near the place. His family took me in; great guys; saved my life. They hid me for a few days and disguised me to look like one of them. Then they drove me to Tok, a small town north-east of there. That's where I heard the news that Miller was dead. It was all over the local news broadcasts. They even had pictures of me and her on the TV, for Christ's sake!

Mirrors In The Sky

They stowed me away on a long distance truck that was bound for Winnipeg. That got me through the border control on the Alaskan highway, undetected. At Winnipeg I stole a car and made it all the way to here."

"You stole a car! Where's the car now?"

"I dumped it not far from here in the back lot of the old disused mall, off highway 44. You know the one."

Rick looked at his old friend. Bo looked wiped out. He could only imagine what he'd been through the past few weeks.

"We gotta get you somewhere safe, Bo. You can't stay here."

Jodi, who till now had remained silent, listening to the two of them, finally plucked up the courage to speak.

"You mean this is a set up of some kind? Why would they do that? It doesn't make sense."

Bo suddenly became aware of the girl standing next to Rick.

"Who's this?" Bo asked, in a guarded tone.

"Oh! Sorry. This is Jodi, my girlfriend," explained Rick, realising that Bo had no idea who she was.

Bo glared at her with caution then turned back to his friend.

Rick knew immediately what was on his mind.

"Its okay Bo, we're on your side. If you say you didn't do it, I believe you. So does Jodi." He turned to look at his girl. "Don't ya?"

Jodi sighed. "I don't know what to believe, but he's your friend and as of right now, if we don't turn him in we're all in it up to our necks."

Bo recoiled abruptly at that remark.

"Turn me in!"

Rick acted quickly to pacify him. "No! No, we wouldn't do that, Bo." He said, turning to Jodi and giving her a reprimanding look.

"Sorry," said Jodi.

But Bo was visibly shaking.

Then Rick had an idea. "We could hide him in the cottage on Lake Argyle, Jodi. No one will ever find him there; at least while we figure out what to do next".

Bo appeared to breathe a little easier.

"Look you guys, I've got to somehow prove my innocence. I don't know how though. They've got it all sewn up but that's not all of it. There's another problem, a bigger problem," Bo said.

"What could be bigger than being hunted down by a thousand cops for a murder rap?" queried Jodi.

"I can't explain it here; it's too complex. Can you get me to this lake cottage you're talking about? On the way I'll give you all the gory details".

Rick and Jodi looked at each other. A myriad of things ran through each of their minds, not least *how* they were going to do it.

Then Jodi had an idea.

"We could take my car, I guess. I could go and get it from my house and meet you back here. I'll bring some food and drink too, so we won't have to make any stops. We could drive there tonight."

Then she appeared to be having second thoughts.

"But what if we we're stopped by the police and they find Bo in the car? We'll *all* be put in prison!"

Bo was looking increasingly agitated. He looked pleadingly at Rick to say something – so Rick did.

"Jodi. I don't care what he's done. He's my best friend and I'm not leaving him at the mercy of some Government spooks, so they can kill him too. Look at him, for Christ's sake. Does he look like a murderer to you?"

Jodi looked at Bo, then at Rick and for a moment, there was a tense silence.

"No. No he doesn't," she said. "Okay, I'll go get the car. Whatever we do, we can't leave him here. I'll fill up the gas tank before I come back. You two stay here. I'll be back within an hour."

"Attagirl! Go for it." Rick urged. "We'll listen out for you."

Jodi turned and made her way back along the rocky shorefront, leaving Rick and Bo in the dark recess of the cave.

When she was gone, Bo looked pensively at Rick.

"Do you trust her, Rick?" he asked.

"Yep! I trust her," replied Rick, without hesitation.

It took Jodi less than forty minutes to get back to the house. Her parents weren't home yet fortunately. They were still out visiting friends and wouldn't be back till midnight, which made things a bit less complicated.

She went inside, grabbed a few things, and threw them in her car, an old Honda Civic. Then she went straight to the gas station to fill up and get some provisions. As she drove back towards the Lake front road, she was constantly nagged by the thought that this was a bad idea.

Jodi pulled over, exactly opposite where she and Rick had gone down to the shoreline earlier, and waited.

Out of the darkness, two furtive figures emerged from the break in the wall and ran across the road. Rick jumped in the front and Bo sprawled himself across the back seat. Seconds later they were on their way.

None of them spoke as Jodi traversed the relatively clear back streets of South Ajax. Bo stayed low, lying across the back seat, out of sight.

Jodi turned left and made her way to the Interstate but as she rounded the next corner she checked the rear view mirror. There was a car following her - a police car!

It was all Jodi could do to keep the wheel straight as her shoulders tensed in fear.

The cop car followed them for a minute or so, then began to overtake them, slowing down as it came up alongside the old Honda. The officer was checking the car out, peering suspiciously through his window at them.

Jodi was having kittens but Rick just smiled and gave him a friendly wave.

Rick's ploy worked. The policeman smiled back, and, satisfied there was nothing wrong, he too gave a friendly wave, and accelerated off up the road. A minute or so later his tail lights turned left and he was gone.

"Oh God! That was too close," said Jodi, as she exhaled a long, deep breath.

"You're not kidding," replied Rick.

A few miles further on, she turned north on the Interstate and headed for Barrie. From there they'd need to continue northwards to Huntsville, then North Bay and on to New Liskeard. It was going to be a long drive.

Once they were on the main highway they all began to relax a little.

"Okay Bo, you gonna tell us now?" asked Rick, turning his head to peer over his seat.

Bo sat upright on the back seat.

"Guess so," He said. "Okay, you've heard all about those hurricanes they've been having down south and the earthquakes in Asia, right?"

"Yeah," Rick replied, a little puzzled.

"Well, I think I had something to do with them; some of 'em anyway," said Bo.

Rick looked across to Jodi with a worried look on his face.

Jodi knew what that looked conveyed. Bo had gone nuts! He must be hallucinating or worse than that, he was mentally unbalanced. She lost control of the wheel for a second and the car veered to the right onto the hard shoulder, throwing up gravel under the wheel arch. She had visions of the guy in the back pulling out a gun and shooting them both in the head. A cold sweat formed on her brow. Her vision became blurred. It took all her mental willpower to just stay on the road and steer in a straight line.

"Wha-what are you talking about Bo?" Rick asked.

Bo shook his head. "I know you guys think I'm nuts. I can see it in your faces but you have to hear me out on this, okay?"

Rick looked at his friend's face in the rear view mirror. He'd known Bo since they were small kids; they'd grown up together. He decided he had to at least let him have his say, whether it sounded crazy or not.

"Okay Bo, shoot," he urged.

As Rick uttered that last word, Jodi involuntarily gripped the steering wheel tight, stifling a frightened yelp, but she managed to keep her eyes on the road. Any more of this and she was afraid she'd tip them all over the embankment!

Bo began.

"For the last couple of years I've been working at a research facility called HAARP - that's an abbreviation for High-frequency Active Auroral Research Program. It's located a few kilometres from a little town called Gakona, tucked away in the Alaskan backwoods........."

For the next half hour or so, Bo relayed the whole story, from his initial work at HAARP and how he met, worked with, and eventually fell in love with his assistant, Miller, (he winced as he outlined the details of their meeting with Clavell), to his discovery of top secret documents pertaining to something called project E.L.F.S.T.O.R.M, the mind control program that he and Miller had unwittingly helped to bring about. He told them of the untold damage he thought it could cause to millions of unsuspecting, innocent people, if it were implemented; how they went along with it for a while, not knowing what else to do and how they carefully planned their escape together, by shutting down the mains electricity supply and getting through the electrified barriers, only for Miller to break her ankle in the process, forcing him to leave her stranded in the snow bound woods.

He told of her cries, as she pleaded for him to run for it and leave her there; then, how he ran, pursued by Clavell's guards and how he was befriended and taken to safety by the young Ahtna Indian, Mahgee, how he and his family disguised him to look like one of them; the journey down river and then being driven in Mahgee's cousin's pickup to Tok.

Bo's eyes misted over as he told them how he discovered Miller was dead, supposedly murdered by him and the realisation that now he wasn't just an escapee with top secret information any more, he was a fugitive, wanted for the murder of the sweetest girl he'd ever known. He explained in detail how he had been stowed away on a truck by another of Mahgee's connections, another native Indian called Benji; then, the hazardous journey back home, through Northern Canada to find someone he trusted - someone he knew - right up to their rendezvous by the lake.

Rick and Jodi sat silent and spellbound throughout the whole story.

When Bo was finished, Rick let out a long, slow whistle.

"Holy kaschmoly, this is intense!" He hadn't understood everything about all the technical stuff but he'd got the general gist of it.

"How the hell do we do anything about that?" he asked.

"We don't!" Jodi intervened. "We tell the authorities, someone higher up than the guys Bo was working for and let *them* deal with it. When they find out what really went on there, Bo will be in the clear."

Bo let out a deep sigh and shook his head in denial. "You don't get it," he asserted. "These guys I was working for, whoever they are, they *are* the top of the food chain. If I let myself get into their hands I'll probably never be seen again. That guy Clavell was from the Pentagon for Christ's sake. That's pretty high level, if you ask me.

"Anyway, there's no way that they'll let me get away with knowing what I know and they almost certainly won't admit to it. Even if I did survive, I'd still probably be sectioned under the Mental Health

Act and end up in a loony-bin on a diet of prozak and valium for the rest of my life. No thanks very much! It's not just that, either; they don't know what they're doing with those transmitters. If they do what I *think* they're going to do, pretty soon there's going to be a lot of very mad Arabs running around with steam coming out of their ears, and no one will know why."

"I feel sick," said Jodi.

"I feel like a beer," said Rick. "A crate of beer!"

A period of silence ensued as the little Honda ate up the miles on the freeway.

Eventually, Bo crashed out in the back seat, enjoying his first night of relatively safe sleep for weeks.

Rick took over the driving after they'd reached Huntsville, while Jodi attempted to catch forty winks. She couldn't relax though. She was anxious and not a little afraid. Her and Rick were now harbouring a felon on the run. She knew there was no going back from this.

Rick wound the window down a little and turned on the radio to prevent him from nodding off and found a station that played all night rock. At 4am the news came on. The newscaster's voice was the usual polished anchorman style rhetoric, prevalent throughout Canada and the United States.

He almost lost control of the wheel when he heard the name in the first bulletin:

"... Police are still hunting Andrew Boetto from Ajax, Ontario, for the murder of his girlfriend Karen Miller, also from the State of Ontario who was stabbed to death and her body dumped in the Gakona river, South Central Alaska, three weeks ago...

Jodi and Rick sat bolt upright, their senses honed to the broadcasters' monotone voice as he continued.

Bo slumbered on in the back seat, unaware of anything.

The bulletin continued:

"...Boetto and Miss Miller were employees at the Ionospheric Research Observatory in Gakona which is apparently run by the Raytherm Corporation, to research ways of improving radio signals in the upper atmosphere. Per reports received from HAARP director, Mr John Heckler, Boetto attacked Miss Miller after an argument one night and fled the scene, but not before tying her body to some rocks and dumping it in the icy water, in a failed attempt to conceal the crime.

The felon has still not been apprehended, despite a massive manhunt by federal US Marshall's, the Alaskan National Guard and Canadian Mounties, which is still underway.

People are warned not to approach this man if they see him as he is extremely dangerous and could kill again.

Other breaking news this morning, the Prime Minister said........."

Rick turned the radio off. He and Jodi looked at each other, eyes wide, mouths open.

"Holy Christ Jodi, this is one hell of a mess," he said, adjusting the rear view mirror to catch a glimpse of Bo, who was still sleeping, blissfully unaware of what had just transpired.

"I'm scared Rick; I've never been in a situation like this. Suppose he did do it - what then?" Jodi asked.

"I'm not exactly over the moon about it myself; this is way over my head. Do you really believe a guy like Bo could do a thing like that and lie through his teeth, to his best friend?"

"I don't know. I don't want to know and I wish I never had known. This is too much for me, Rick. We're in big trouble and it isn't going to go away fast."

Jodi began to cry. The strain was showing.

"If my father finds out what we're doing in his Lake cottage... Oh my god!"

Tears were streaming down her face now and she began to sob quietly.

Rick looked despairingly at his girlfriend. This *was* too much for her. She'd put her neck on the line for a guy she didn't even know, just because he was his friend. He felt guilty but at the same time, focused.

"It's okay Jodi, we'll get it sorted out. Something stinks about this whole shabbang and I'm gonna get to the bottom of it," he said.

But she couldn't hear him. She was lost in a nightmare from which it seemed there was no awakening.

The little Honda droned on into the night. It may have been an old banger but it had never missed a beat yet. Rick thanked the stars for little mercies. That would have been the icing on the cake if the car had broken down on the journey, with Bo still in it. He shuddered at the thought.

They entered the outskirts of New Liskeard just as the sun was rising. Rick turned off and took Highway 65 West, through Elk Lake and headed West on Highway 66, then on through Matachewan and over the Montreal River Bridge to Highway 566. Fifteen miles further on, he saw the signs for Lake Argyle.

Bo was just coming round. He'd slept solidly for almost five hours. He stretched his arms out and leaned forward, looking unshaven and every bit like an escaped fugitive on the run.

Jodi had finally fallen asleep, slumped up against the passenger door at an awkward angle. Her mascara had run down her cheeks from the tears during the night.

"Where are we Rick?" asked Bo.

"Almost there, pal. The cottage is about three miles away. Keep your head down. I don't want anyone to see you," Rick warned.

After a few more minutes, Rick spotted the sign he was looking for – "VanderWal Cottage." He'd only been up here once before. That time it was for pleasure. He recalled that last trip up here with Jodi only a couple of weeks earlier. The fishing was the greatest. He and Jodi would stroll along the river banks, canoodling, hand in hand. And the nights, yo the nights! But now he was here for a different reason, to do...... do what? He didn't know right now, only that he had to keep his friend out of harm's way until they came up with a plan.

Rick slowed the car down and indicated left, turning sharply off the road onto an unmade track. They bumped down it for another hundred metres or so till they came to the cottage, which lay nestled in a small clearing just back from the lake. It was made of redwood logs criss-crossed together with three front windows and a door. A brick chimney protruded from the side, capped with two china man's hats, conical metal caps, to prevent snow and rain getting down the chimney. Startled by the car's motor, a racoon scurried away from under the porch as they pulled up outside.

"Is this is the place?" asked Bo, looking out through the car's grimy windows.

"Yep, you'll be safe here, for now anyway. No one's gonna be here until the New Year, so Jodi says, anyway," Rick explained, as he opened the door and eased his aching bones out of the driver's seat.

Jodi was still asleep and she looked a mess. Her hair was matted and strung across her shoulders.

The mascara-stained tear streaks seemed more pronounced in the daylight and her head was still cricked at an awkward angle.

They left her in the car rather than disturb her. Rick managed to find the keys to the front door after rummaging around in her handbag and the two of them went inside.

It was a pleasant little place. The smell of natural wood permeated the air, though it felt a little stuffy. Bo took a look around while Rick busied himself opening a couple of windows to let the air circulate better.

As he was fumbling with the opening mechanism on the second window, he looked outside and his heart skipped a beat. Coming up the driveway, between the trees, was a woman he'd never seen before! She was making straight for the open door.

"Jesus Bo, hide, quick!" he warned.

Bo looked at him confused. "Wha........"

"Someone's coming. Quick, get out of sight, now!" Rick urged, flapping his left arm indicating to Bo to hide, pronto.

The tension in Rick's voice put paid to any further discussion and Bo quickly slipped out of sight into the kitchen area, wedging himself behind the door.

Rick quickly ran to the front door and stood on the porch, blocking any entrance into the cabin. The woman was peering inside the car at Jodi, who was still fast asleep in the passenger seat.

"Hi there, ma'am. Can I help you?" asked Rick.

The stranger turned round and faced him. "Good morning there," she said, slightly suspicious in tone. "You must be related to Mr and Mrs VanderWal." It was a statement rather than a question.

"Uh, yes in a way ma'am. I'm Jodi VanderWal's boyfriend, and that's her in the car," Rick replied, still a little in shock at the sudden emergence of this strange woman from out of nowhere.

The woman eyed Rick up for a moment, hands on hips. Then she broke out into a friendly, neighbourly grin.

"Well I never. That's Jodi? My, she's grown a might since I saw her last. I'm sorry, er, what was your name again?"

"Oh, er, yeah, Rick's my name. And you are?"

"Why, I'm Cindy from over the way, on the other side of the Lake. I saw the car pull up and just had to come and say hello. We don't have many visitors to this neck of the woods you know," she said, craning her neck past Rick's shoulder to get a look inside. "Just the two of ya then? Lovebirds nest is it?" she gestured, a crinkly smile creasing her lips.

Rick realised she must not have seen Bo get out of the car.

All the better she didn't!

"Tha-that's right Cindy, just the two of us," Rick lied. "Jodi's catching a nap; she drove most of the way. It's quite a haul from Ajax to here. Anyhow, pleased to meet you. Maybe we'll catch up with you when we've got settled in."

Cindy either had a strain in her neck or she was definitely interested in what was behind Rick - in other words, the inside of the Cabin. She kept trying to get a glimpse inside, probably because subconsciously he was trying to prevent her from doing so, by keeping his frame squarely in the doorway.

"Uh-huh; well, nice to meet you, Rick. Now, you and Jodi be sure to come over and see me and Art, soon as you can, okay?"

"Yes ma'am, I'll tell Jodi, that you called by, er, when she wakes up. Thank you."

"Bye for now then," said Cindy, gesturing a wave and walking back the way she came.

Rick watched her walk back up the driveway and when she had turned out of sight, he let out a sigh of relief.

"Jesus, that's all we need; a nosy neighbour," he muttered under his breath.

Jodi slumbered on in the car, dead to the world.

He raced back inside and found Bo cringing behind the kitchen door.

"Has she gone, Rick?"

"Yep, but she'll be back, you can be sure of that, and she thinks there's just me and Jodi here. That means you have to stay out of sight at all times."

"Great!" moaned Bo, "I can't even go for a piss in the bushes without looking over my shoulder."

"Think yourself lucky pal. You could be in Pentonville right now, or worse!"

Bo thought about that for a second and realised Rick was right. He *was* fortunate to be here at all.

"You're right. Sorry pal, and thanks for all your help so far. You're a lifesaver."

Chapter 18

Bo, Rick and Jodi sat around the fire they'd eventually managed to get going in the lounge, trying to get to grips with what they were going to do next.

Both Rick and Jodi couldn't help but notice that Bo was an emotional wreck. If they left him to his own devices for more than a few minutes, he'd sink into a deep depression which was hard to snap him out of. Obviously, Miller's death was not something he could easily come to terms with, which was understandable. Not only that, he was supposed to have done it, which made it even worse. Neither Rick nor Jodi were counsellors and they were finding it hard going just trying to keep him from caving in.

Rick decided to try and engage Bo in some kind of activity, in an attempt to try and snap the poor guy out of it. He set up his laptop and connected the modem to the phone socket.

"I'm gonna do some net surfing, Bo. I've got a hunch, about what you were saying regarding those ELF waves, and there are a few other things I want to check out as well," he said.

Bo just nodded. He wasn't interested.

Jodi had the same idea as Rick. She'd been thinking again about her trip to China. Not about the incident with the police, or whatever they were, but her reasons for being there in the first place - the weird migratory patterns of the birds from Qinghai Lake. After hearing Bo's story something had clicked in the back of her mind.

She recalled the research papers she'd found in the archives at the Canadian Research Centre; that old ex navy guy Blackwell and his reasoning for the cause of avian bird flu. She wondered if there really *was* any connection. After mulling it over she decided to get Bo's opinion.

"Bo, you said that the weird weather we've been having recently is probably something to do with HAARP, right?"

Bo mumbled an acknowledgement that sounded like a yes.

"Did you transmit those ELF waves, or whatever you call them, anywhere near China by any chance?"

Jodi could see that question had made him think for a moment.

"Yeah. Why?" replied Bo.

"And those transmissions are dangerous to organisms, right?"

"They can be, if the power output was too high, which it definitely was," he muttered.

"How would it do that?" she asked.

Bo suddenly became more animated.

"The microwaves it emits could be harmful to any form of life and could cause cancers, mutations; you name it. That's the reason I got in Clavell's black book in the first place. I kept telling him it was highly dangerous but he just ignored me. Of course, now I know why. We were doing direct scans over China for some time at fairly high power outputs and Qinghai Province is virtually right in the beam path trajectory we were covering."

Jodi was getting somewhere now - on both counts.

"Then this guy Blackwell's research could have been right," she said.

Bo wasn't following. "Blackwell? Who's Blackwell?"

Jodi explained to him the details of her trip to Qinghai Lake and the reason she'd gone there in the first place - the archives she'd found back at the research centre in Toronto.

"Those ELF waves *could* have messed with their DNA. Blackwell said in his research papers that birds are extremely susceptible to microwave beams, even in flight. It would explain why their migratory patterns were screwed up."

"How's that?" asked Bo.

"Well, I learned that birds, amongst many other mammals and organisms, have a substance called magnetite secreted in their brains. Humans have it too, apparently. No one really knows how or why but a lot of theories have been bandied around about the possibility that birds, turtles, whales etc. somehow use it to locate the earth's natural magnetic fields, to find their way and migrate. If the electromagnetic ELF waves coming from HAARP are as powerful as you say, that could be why. Not only that, many of these birds have been exposed to radiation, which would make them even *more* susceptible."

"Radiation! From where?" asked Bo.

"From nuclear reactors, mainly. The Chinese and Russians have been dumping it secretly for decades into lakes and oceans. There's so much of the stuff that they don't know what to do with it, so they dump it wherever they can. Qinghai Lake, for instance, where millions of waterfowl live and breed is awash with it. I did a lot of research on this a few weeks back and what I found was pretty scary stuff."

Bo shrugged.

"So what's that got to do with bird flu?"

"Plenty! Radiation, along with exposure to high intensity microwaves can mutate DNA. That's all viruses are really, mutated DNA and bird flu is just one form of it."

"Huh! That's pretty interesting stuff. You could be right," said Bo.

At that moment, Rick who had been engrossed for some time with his laptop, called them over.

"Hey you two take a look at this!" he yelled.

His research was apparently coming up with some mind numbing facts as well.

"Look, I've found some really interesting stuff connecting all these weird weather conditions, to guess what? HAARP! Seems you were right, Bo. See for yourself."

Bo and Jodi stood behind him so they could observe the screen.

"There's tons of stuff here from all kinds of scientists and action groups ranting on about the place. Several links indicate that the transmissions from HAARP may possibly have caused freak storms, earthquakes etc. It's only conjecture and some of it comes from the usual UFO and conspiracy nuts, but there's a lot of technical data here you just can't ignore."

He scrolled down the page culling items of interest, then copied and pasted a collection of data into a separate file he'd named "weather research." It comprised a list of the most damaging natural disasters that had occurred in the past year.

"Okay, take a look at this and let's see what the official records show."

The list was extensive......

> ......Australia's hottest year: Australia's Bureau of Meteorology says that 2005 was the country's hottest year since records began in 1910, with temperatures, on average, 1.09°C higher than normal......

Mirrors In The Sky

> ......Second year of drought in Spain. The drought in Spain in 2005 was the worst the country has ever experienced. As the drought enters its second year, the National Meteorological Institute (NMI) says there are no signs of relief and new water management mechanisms have been put in place.
> Hurricane names exhausted: For the first time since Atlantic hurricanes were given names in 1953, all 21 names were used up in 2005......

"And that's just the headlines," explained Rick. "Here's the breakdown of individual disasters by month, starting from February 2005."

> ......Freak storms lashed eastern Australia. Melbourne received more rain in 24 hours than since records began in 1856, leaving the city's rivers and waterways swollen to bursting point.
> March
> Two tornadoes tore through Northern Bangladesh, killing at least 37 people, injuring nearly 1,000 and leaving thousands homeless.
> That same month witnessed Cuba's worst drought in a century.
> A severe drought that stretched from China to India damaged crops and left millions of people struggling to find water.
> Cyclone Percy was the fourth such storm in the South Pacific Cook Islands in as many weeks, with winds packing gusts of 255km/h......

......In Algeria, the heaviest rain in decades hit the Sahara desert killing dozens of people. Floods and landslides destroyed many houses and blocked roads for days.

April
Up to 66cm of snow buried parts of Wyoming and Montana. Logan was swollen by snowmelt and a heavy rainstorm.

Streams in northern Utah overflowed their banks.

Freak flooding in New Jersey cost millions of dollars in damage.

In Pennsylvania, the Delaware River surged out of its banks.

In Serbia and Montenegro hundreds of homes were flooded and livestock drowned in what is thought to be the worst flooding in the area ever.

In Australia, after no proper rain for months, it looked as if the drought that hit in 2002 – the worst on record- was returning.

In China, more than nine million people faced drinking water shortages after the worst drought ever to strike the country in half a century.

May
Freak storms lashed Bangladesh with lightning and rain, killing at least 21 people. The dead were all struck by lightning.

In China, 2,000 reservoirs spilled over in flash floods......

......In Ethiopia, floods afflicted more than 100,000 people in the eastern Somali region as torrential rains continually pounded the region for days.

In Romania, heavy rains in the western region of the country were the worst in living memory.

In Saudi Arabia, a normally dry country, flash floods swept cars off roads.

Spain suffered its driest winter and earliest spring, since records began. Rainfall from November to the end of March in that country was 37 percent below average for the period and the lowest since records started.

Australia is experiencing the worst drought in its history.

Hurricane Adrian slammed into El Salvador and broke up over Honduras.

June

Heat-waves seared Bangladesh, France, Italy and Pakistan. The temperature in Chuadanga reached 43 degrees Celsius.

Europe suffered a heat-wave on the first day of summer. Near Paris, a temperature of 35.7 degrees Celsius was recorded.

Heat related casualties in Italy were double the normal level.

A heat-wave in Punjab killed approximately 175 people in eight days......

......Drinking water in cities and towns across Australia dried up. Worst hit was the aptly named town of Goulburn.

In China over 300 million people were without potable water.

Typhoon Dante brought heavy rains and floods in the Philippines.

<u>July</u>
Hurricane Dennis caused $1.4 billion in damage.

A deadly heat-wave killed at least 24 people in the Phoenix, Arizona area during temperatures that soared past 38 Celsius.

One of the strangest freak weather phenomenon recorded was a tornado in Birmingham - not the one in the US but in Great Britain which ripped through the city, uprooting trees and tearing chimneys from the top of buildings!

<u>August</u>
There were a spate of unprecedented thunderstorms, lightning, heavy rain, floods, and landslides in regions as diverse as Austria, Bulgaria, China, India, Iran, Mexico and Korea.

More than a quarter of Bulgaria's 7.4 million people were affected by severe flooding, which killed approximately 20 people and caused $633 million worth of damage in the wake of heavy rainfall.

Hurricane Katrina caused a death toll in New Orleans that has still to be established, but over 1,000 people are thought to have been killed after it lashed the US coast, causing the levees which were supposed to protect the city, from the Mississippi river, and Lake Pontchartrain to give way.

The storm was one of the strongest ever to have hit the USA.

September

China, Thailand, the Phillippines, and Vietnam fell victims to Typhoon Kanun and Damrey in short succession, the strongest storms to hit those regions in decades.

In Japan, Typhoons Nabi and Songda pummelled the south western regions causing floods and landslides.

In the USA, Hurricane's Ophelia and Rita followed in the wake of Katrina.

Thirty people died in Mongolia when temperatures suddenly and inexplicably plummeted to record lows.

October

A blitz of hurricanes and tropical cyclones caused mayhem in the USA and Central America causing huge waves in Cuba which flooded the capital, Havana.

In Guatemala, over 1,400 people were buried in a huge mudslide as a result of heavy rain occasioned by Tropical Storm Stan.

Hurricane Wilma, was the most powerful ever recorded with winds of up to 175mph as it lashed the Gulf coast of Mexico……

> ......Tropical storm Vince was the first of its kind on record to make landfall in Iberia.
> Severe drought continued to ravage South-East Australia as a result of rainfall deficiencies.
> In Bazil, the worst drought in 40 years struck the world's largest rainforest, plaguing the Amazon basin with wildfires.

The list read like a prelude to Armageddon.

"That's a hell of a lot of freak weather patterns, Bo, a lot more than you'd expect in any one year," Rick said.

"You're not kidding," agreed Bo. "The thing I don't get though is that they're scattered all over the planet. I can't see any pattern to them at all?"

"That's because you're a radio man and not a geologist," explained Rick.

"Howdya mean?"

"It's simple. If you alter the weather in one part of the world you'll cause imbalances somewhere else. The geophysical makeup of the planet works on balances of atmospheric pressure. Drop the millibars in one region dramatically and you'll create an increase elsewhere, possibly on the other side of the planet. From what you've told me, the HAARP transmitters heat up areas of the ionosphere, right?"

"That's a pretty simplified explanation of it. They do a lot of other things too, but that's about the gist of it, yeah."

"Okay! Do that too often and you'll create all kinds of imbalances in the denser atmosphere beneath it, which could result in the freak weather patterns, just like the ones on this list."

"Huh, it's possible, I guess," Bo mused. "We were just discovering that exact thing before Clavell came along but what has that got to do with earthquakes, like the one in Indonesia last year, or the one in Pakistan?"

"Plenty! I remember a course I did a few years ago, where I learned about how ELF waves were being used to predict movements under the surface of the earth; in other words, to predict seismic movements as precursors to the earthquakes themselves; but that was only being done using orbiting satellites and a small amount of power.

"HAARP, on the other hand, if what you're saying is true, kicks out thousands of times the power of those satellites. I reckon the ELF waves they are transmitting from HAARP into the upper atmosphere and at the frequencies they put out, are doing the opposite of predicting earthquakes. I think they're *causing* them!"

"How the hell would they do that?" Bo asked, now intrigued by Rick's train of thought.

"Well, it's only a gut feeling and it would need to be verified using extremely sensitive seismic equipment to make certain, but here goes:

"The earth's core apparently causes the crust surrounding it to vibrate at a very low frequency, a kind of humming sound, which is more like shadows of a sound really. Researchers, who've investigated this phenomenon, call them "background free oscillations". This hum is not one note but as many as fifty, crammed into less than two octaves. They're not perceptible to humans because the pitch is too high. Even if you speeded it up and amplified it so you could hear it, the result would just be a random blast of noise.

"To give you an idea of what I mean, imagine sitting down at a piano and slamming down every note within reach, while somebody next to you does the same thing on another piano, a quarter tone out of tune. It would be like banging a trash can with a baseball bat. What's peculiar about the notes in the hum is that they have no obvious source; not earthquakes, not nuclear explosions - nothing. The vibrations triggered by cataclysmic events fade away to nothing, but the hum continues, regardless.

"They've been called many things by many people. Another definition by mystics is the 'Taos Hum.' This humming starts with a kind of drumming, the constant throb of fluctuating atmospheric pressure all over the Earth. When air pressure rises, the atmosphere presses down slightly harder on the ground or sea beneath it. When the pressure drops, the surface gently rebounds. In other words, the world is like a gong being constantly buffeted by countless soft rubber mallets and at any given moment, some of them will be tapping at the right frequencies to excite the modes that make up the hum.

"Now, if something like a heated up ionosphere dramatically increases or decreases the pressures in the atmosphere below it, the soft rubber mallets turn into sledgehammers, metaphorically speaking.

"The result is that the earth's crust comes under unnatural pressure over a very wide area. The weakest links in the chain are the fault lines between the tectonic plates, in the earths crust. If these get battered in this way, enough times, it doesn't take much to figure out what's going to happen next!"

Bo scratched his head.

"Sounds pretty far fetched Rick. I mean, where did you come up with that idea?"

"I studied it in my geology classes, back at Nippissing; well not officially. My tutor wouldn't accept stuff that far fetched but it really interested me, so I researched it in my own time. The thing that brought it all together though, was completely unrelated."

"What was that?" Bo asked.

"Believe it or not, it was riding my uncle's classic motorcycle over in England! You remember the one Bo - his old 650 Triumph Bonneville."

Bo smiled. He remembered it alright. He also remembered that crazy uncle of Rick's. The guy was a motorcycle fanatic.

"Anyway," Rick continued. "He let me take it out for a spin down to Brighton one day and he raced me pretty much all the way. That old bike really tore up the tarmac but it was prone to a thing called "speed wobble', something that sometimes occurs on high performance bikes, especially older ones. Usually, they're fitted with a steering damper that's connected between the front forks and the frame, but this didn't have one. I found out about it first hand when I nearly high-sided the bike on the dual carriageway, doing almost a hundred miles an hour. I was trying to keep up with the mad son-of-a-bitch! He told me afterwards that it needed a steering damper but he hadn't yet got round to fitting one!"

Bo still wasn't tracking with him.

"What's that got to do with all this?" Bo enquired, scratching his head again.

Rick expanded on his theory.

"Well, speed wobble occurs when the vibrations created by the engine exactly match the vibrations from the road. The vibration travels up through the front forks to the handlebars. It only occurs rarely but boy, when it does, you better watch out! The handlebars start to vibrate and wobble uncontrollably and if you don't shut the throttle off pronto, you're off! It's the weirdest sensation and it can take you completely by surprise. Because the pitch of the vibrations is identical, it sets up a resonance in the frame which manifests itself in the handlebars as a wobble that, if uncorrected, literally shakes the bike to bits; not too funny when you're hacking along at almost twice the legal speed limit. I managed to control it but it put the willies up me. Uncle Tod was impressed though. He said he'd seen better riders than me sliding down the road on their butts after something like that had occurred.

"Anyway, I got to thinking, after you told me about the ELF waves that HAARP produces and realised there might be a connection between them and the atmospheric pressure changes. When I read this stuff about the possible connection between HAARP and earthquakes, it kind of came to me, just like that! Weird huh?"

"Weird? It's pretty clever, if you ask me! said Bo, having finally clicked on Rick's idea.

"I can think of another simple analogy; the feedback you get from speakers when the mike gets too near them!" he added, suddenly realising the possibilities. "That too, is just another type of vibration, caused by equal frequencies in close proximity to one another!"

Bo was lost in his own thoughts for a moment.

"You know, I think I know why you could never get a job in your major, Rick."

Rick gave Bo a wary look.

"Oh yeah, why's that then?"

"Because you're over qualified!" said Bo, the faint trace of a grin showing for the first time in a while.

"You have *no* idea!" Rick grunted.

"I mean, who else could come up with something like that? It could just be plausible," Bo remarked.

Rick's face broke into a wide smile.

"Nice to know someone appreciates my talents."

Suddenly it was as if a light bulb had lit up inside Bo's head, as another realisation hit him. "So it wouldn't really matter where the ionosphere was heated up then. The fluctuations in the troposphere below it could cause vibrations above and below ground, anywhere on the planet! We were altering the conditions in the Ionosphere over Asia and the Middle East and were probably causing effects on the other side of the planet as well, like in America, without realising it. It makes perfect sense. Rick, you're a genius!"

"I know, don't rub it in," Rick replied mockingly, yet at the same time, he was obviously chuffed with himself.

"I won't, don't worry. But it sure pans out, whichever way you look at it," said Bo. "We were playing the piano without any sheet music, metaphorically speaking, and we couldn't even hear it."

Jodi, who had been sitting quietly in the background, listening in awe at the techno speak of these two guys, finally managed to butt in to the conversation.

"So, Chopin and Valentino Rossi, what exactly *are* we going to do about this then? If you haven't already forgotten, Bo, you are still a wanted by the Fed's and the police. The weather isn't getting any better by the sounds of it. Bird flu is about to mutate into a form that can be passed between humans at any moment, heralding a pandemic the likes of which has never been seen before and the boys at HAARP are merrily attempting to warp the mindset of over a billion human beings in the

Middle East, with their new toy ray gun. They might even succeed, that is if they don't crack the planet in half beforehand! We may think we have all the answers but there's damn little we can do about it sitting here talking and patting each other on the back."

Jodi's matter of fact statement brought them back down to earth. Rick and Bo looked at each other.

"She's got a point, Bo," Rick agreed. "We have to do *something*."

Bo couldn't argue with that.

"Anyone got any ideas?" he asked, looking pensively at Rick and Jodi.

The three of them sat silent for a while, contemplating the enormity of the situation. There didn't seem to be any answer to that question. After all, what *could* they do?

Rick broke the silence.

"Fuck this, I need a beer!" he exclaimed.

"That's the best idea you've had today," Bo concurred.

Jodi sat back in her chair and put her hand on her forehead in a gesture of exasperation.

"Jeezus," she exclaimed. "Old habits die hard eh?" Then, realising she was just as stumped as they were, she too, gave in.

"Okay, you guys win. There's always a few crates of Coors out back in the woodshed, Rick. Crack one open for me too," she said.

The last few days had been exhausting and the good tasting beer was a welcome respite. For the next couple of hours they relaxed. But all the while, Bo had been formulating an idea in his head. A new look of determination - one neither Rick nor Jodi had seen before, seemed to have gripped him. After his third beer, he began frantically scribbling some calculations on his notepad. After a while there were sheets of paper strewn all over the floor. Rick and Jodi watched in mild amusement as he sat there, beavering away with his pencil. Then, suddenly, he banged his fists on the table.

"Yes!" he yelled. "I've got it. I know how to take the bastards down."

Rick and Jodi nearly jumped out of their skins at Bo's sudden outburst.

"Got what? asked Rick.

Bo sidled up to the two of them and tearing a clean sheet of paper from the pad, he began to draw a diagram.

"I've figured out a way to do something about it. Take a look at this," he said, sketching as he spoke. "HAARP's transmitters run off huge amounts of electricity. This is supplied by several generators as well as the mains supply. They beam high energy radio frequencies upwards into the ionosphere, just like a high pressure water jet emits H_2O. These beams excite the electrons in the ionosphere which, geologically, must be causing massive dips and peaks in pressures and electrifying the area beneath it. This, like you said, Rick, is probably the cause of all those wild, random electrical storms that turn into hurricanes etc.

"Well, electricity flow can be reversed, simply by changing the polarities around. If the transmitters were used in a controlled manner to create a huge electrical storm directly overhead and then suddenly the polarities were switched in the middle of it - guess what would happen?"

Rick got it straight away.

"The transmitters would act like a superconductor. The full force of that electricity generated in the upper atmosphere would be immediately attracted to its source. It'd be the biggest lightning bolt in history!" Rick exclaimed.

"Exactly," agreed Bo. "Within a few seconds of the polarity switch, the force exerted upwards would reverse downwards. The whole place would be blasted to dust in a second, by a godzillion volt lightning strike."

"Mother earth getting her own back," Rick mused, realising the potential of Bo's idea.

"More like Andrew Boetto getting his own back!" Bo added.

"But how would we ever be able to do that?" Rick asked, suddenly realising that coming up with the idea was a lot easier than putting it into practice.

"By getting back in there somehow and reconfiguring the trajectories and power outputs of the phased antenna array," explained Bo, still beaming.

"Er, you mean us?" Rick enquired, not quite getting Bo's drift.

"Not you. Me," said Bo.

Rick and Jodi just looked at him, perplexed.

"And how do you reckon on doing that, exactly?" Jodi asked.

"I dunno yet, but I reckon if we have a few more beers we'll come up with something."

Jodi and Rick both shook their heads.

Rick could see that Bo was coming back to his old self. At least he was smiling again. Nevertheless, this idea of Bo's had him spooked.

They all fell silent again and downed the remainder of the crate of Coors.

It was then, that Rick suddenly had an idea.

"Hey Bo! You remember my uncle had a friend who was a karate sensei, or something?"

Bo thought back.

"Yeah I remember. Paul was his name, wasn't it?"

"That's it, Paul Perry. You never met him but I remember him from when I was a kid – a real big powerful guy. He taught me a few moves."

"So? What about him?"

"So, he said if I ever needed anything, to look him up. Uncle Tod said he lives in Colorado nowadays, on a big ranch near Denver. Said he'd made millions of dollars in stocks and bonds or something like that. I don't know all the details because I wasn't listening properly but he said something about how the guy runs a kind of super sleuth ninja outfit in the States, called Jin Sei Kai. It's a bit like a SWAT team or Special Forces shit. God! I wish I'd taken more notice. You know what? I'm gonna look him up."

"And do what?" Bo asked.

"And get him to help us get back in there," Rick explained.

"Are you serious?"

"I guess. Let's face it right now we don't have a lot of options, do we."

Bo and Jodi shrugged their shoulders.

"I guess not," they both agreed, simultaneously.

It was late in the evening, so it would be late afternoon in England. Rick lost no time in phoning his uncle, to ask him for Paul Perry's number. He didn't go into why he wanted it, saying simply that he intended to go to Denver for a job interview and that he'd like to look him up while he was there. There was no way he was going to involve his uncle in something like this. The less people that knew, the better, he reasoned.

This time however, he got more background data on his Uncle's friend. And what he heard made him smile.

Thanking his uncle for the data, he put the phone down and looked at the notes he'd made during the call.

There was no time to waste.

Nevertheless, he hesitated as he picked the phone up a second time. He realised he could be putting Paul in a compromising situation. What would he say to him?

Deciding that there was no point in procrastinating, he dialled the number. His fingers tapped nervously on the receiver as he heard it ringing on the other end.

"Hello, Paul Perry speaking."

Rick recognised the British voice immediately.

"Hi there, Paul! This is Rick, Rick Hayden – remember me?"

The voice on the end of the line hesitated for a moment.

"Rick, Rick?"

He seemed to be trying to remember him.

"Oh yeah, Rick me old mucker! Tod's sister's kid, right?" came the friendly reply. "How the hell are you?"

"Er, not so good Paul," said Rick, wondering how to best put the reason for his call. "Paul, um, I'm in a bit of trouble, I need your help."

The voice became serious and concerned in an instant.

"Uh-huh. What's up Rick?"

"It's not really something I can go over on the phone. Can I come see you?"

Paul's reply was instantaneous and Rick sensed concern in his voice.

"Of course mate; when?"

"Er, like tomorrow."

"Where are you?" Paul asked.

"Um, I'd rather not say over the phone, Paul. But I can get a flight to Denver tomorrow, if that's okay."

"That's fine with me. Call me from the airport. I'll pick you up."

"Okay Paul, got ya," and with that, he hung up.

Chapter 19

Early the next morning, Jodi drove Rick to the bus station in New Liskeard. They had decided that she should keep the car at the cottage in case there was, god forbid, an emergency and they had to make a quick getaway or something.

Bo had been instructed to keep out of sight inside the cottage while she was gone.

After a long drawn-out farewell, Rick boarded his bus and was on his way to Toronto's Lester B. Pearson International airport. The journey took the most part of the day but he made it without incident. Upon his arrival, he bought a one way ticket to Denver and then made a call to Paul to pick him up. They agreed to meet in the Arrivals hall.

The flight from Toronto to Denver took two hours and landed right on time.

Paul, true to his word was waiting for him when he came through the arrivals concourse and Rick recognised the guy easily. His tall, muscular frame stood him apart from the rest of the crowd and Paul didn't look any different than the last time he saw him back in the UK. It had been several years since they'd last met. Rick was just in his early teens then. He waved to him, but the big man just squinted, unsure, who he was, obviously.

Then Paul suddenly recognised Rick, and pushed through the waiting crowd, extending his arms and embracing him with that customary bear hug of his that Rick well remembered.

After having all the wind crushed out of him, Rick managed a greeting.

"Hey Paul, how's things with you?" he gasped, trying to get his breath back.

"Better than you, Rick; by the sounds of it. Christ almighty I hardly recognised you. You're ten feet taller than the last time I saw you," Paul replied, slapping Rick on the back again and knocking the rest of the air out of his already bruised lungs.

"Come on mate, the car's parked outside. Let's go. You can tell me all about it on the way back to the ranch."

Outside, Paul opened the trunk of a gleaming black Range Rover and threw Rick's bags in.

"Range Rover Sport!" Paul beamed with pride. "I only picked it up last week; one of the first in the country, and fully loaded. This is the Bentley of four wheel drive vehicles, mate."

Rick was impressed. He got in and ran his hand over the soft Connolly hide, leather seats.

"She's a beaut!" he crooned.

The big Land Rover purred like a cat as Paul cruised out of the airport and on to the highway.

"So, come on, out with it then!" Paul urged.

Rick knew there was no point in beating around the bush.

"I need your help on something Paul. My friend Bo is in shit up to his neck. He's on the run from the cops for a murder he didn't commit and he's currently holed up in a lake cottage in North Ontario, with my girlfriend; but that's not even the half of it."

Paul gave Rick a curious, sideways glance. "Murder! And you left him in a cabin in the woods with your girlfriend. Are you nuts? Who did he kill or rather not kill, as you say?"

"His girlfriend; she was his assistant where he worked," replied Rick. "He didn't do it, Paul. I'm certain of that."

"Huh, sounds bad. What's the other half?" Paul enquired, now captivated by his young passenger's tale.

"He was working for a U.S. government research facility in Alaska, called HAARP - that's an abbreviation for High-Frequency Active Auroral Research Program."

"What the fuck's that when it's at home?" Paul asked. "Sounds like a bloody musical instrument to me!"

"No. It's a powerful transmitter station that bounces huge amounts of microwave and extra low frequency waves, off the upper atmosphere and then down into the earth."

"Microwaves! I've got one of them in my kitchen," Paul quipped.

Rick suddenly remembered that Paul had a weird sense of humour.

"It's no joke Paul. They're intending to use it to fry peoples' brains out." Rick explained.

"Well then, me and that mad uncle of yours shouldn't need to worry too much then," Paul joked, with a loud cackle.

Rick just shook his head and chuckled to himself. Paul Perry's sense of humour could be hard to understand, he reminded himself, but that's the way he was - take it or leave it.

He recalled the time back in England when he, Paul and his Uncle used to shoot the shit together.

Nothing could faze this guy. He was built like a brick shithouse and could tear a thick telephone directory in half with his bare hands, as a party piece, just for fun. He appeared to be a bit crude and basic in intellect but that was only to people who didn't know him.

Rick knew him much better than that. The rough edged characterisation was just a social façade; probably a leftover from his basic working class upbringing in England. He also knew that Paul had an intellect quicker than a speeding bullet and a physical aptitude exceeding even that.

From what he could remember, from the stories Paul and his uncle had told him as a kid, Paul grew up on a farm in Hertfordshire, England, next door to his uncle. He was a normal, active, fun loving youngster. He and his older brother loved taunting the family bull and they played games, daring each other to stand in the path of this charging beast, only leaping out of its way at the final moment!

School hadn't been the most interesting place for him however, more because at a young age he had a sense of inner freedom and personal growth rather than a disinterest in learning. But also he was a big kid and an obvious target for teachers looking for a scapegoat.

He started practicing karate at the age of 17 and loved it. He practised constantly, either at classes or with a friend or on his own and moved quickly through the grading syllabus.

In 1968, at the age of 18, he emigrated to Australia. While there he had the opportunity of training with Japanese masters, as well as teaching others. He trained with Yamaguchi (The Cat), the bare-handed tiger killer. He also travelled to Japan on many occasions, training with Hirokazu Kanazawa, whose style and grace of movement grounded Paul in his love of the art. Kanazawa Sensei was his main influence and teacher, making Paul a 3rd generation Karateka, with direct lineage from the main introduction into the west, via Gichin Funakoshi.

An accomplished Tai Chi Master, Paul had studied with Yang Ming Shih while in Japan, training in as many different martial art and yoga dojo's as he could.

Returning to England a few years later, Paul continued practicing and teaching while perfecting and deepening his art.

Rick recalled a story Paul had told him. It was while nursing an injury that Paul had made a breakthrough. Because of his injury, he couldn't practice as hard as he normally would have but went to the dojo anyway. While practicing kumite (hand to hand combat) with a partner, he discovered that his blocks, punches, and kicks were faster and more powerful by not trying so hard. He loved the way that his body felt when he moved and so he studied body mechanics, reading and talking to professionals and experts in the field.

He began picking apart every karate stance and movement; making them bio-mechanically perfect. In so doing he developed the Jin Sei Kai style of "perfect movement and exact placement." The power and accuracy of this style was fantastic. Once thoroughly learned, the body recognizes and knows where it is supposed to be, comfortably falling into the same position time after time. The body, the feeling, becomes the conscious element, and not the mind. This feeling generated by "perfect movement and exact placement" plus soft flowing movements ending in muscle contraction (called kime), releases built up tension or energy and frees the self. It is a primary element of the practice but very hard to master. 'Perfect movement and exact placement' was the key to the Jin Sei Kai style of karate.

Another little ditty Rick recalled was when Paul had been invited by DERA, the research centre of the Ministry of Defence, to help in their research of energy transmission. During experiments there, he'd been tested on the speed and strength of his punch, and to the amazement of the observers, they discovered that it put out as many kilojoules of energy as a 9mm bullet!

But now apparently, so Paul had told him on the journey from the airport, he was an 8th degree black belt and Founder, Director and Sensei Master of an organisation called Jin Sei Kai Corporate Services. He'd lived in America for several years now and was a multi millionaire, having done pretty well for himself in the heady world of international bank debentures and Medium Term Note trading. But, as always, his real passion was his martial arts training doctrine.

He now had a huge empire of clubs, dotted around the globe that operated under the Jin Sei Kai corporate banner. Tens of thousands of people had learned the advanced techniques he had developed to reduce stress, increase concentration, and perfect body movement. His organisation had developed into a multi faceted conglomerate and continued to grow on a daily basis.

The sun was low in the sky as the Land Rover Sport chewed up the miles on the Freeway. In the distance, the Colorado Mountains reared up on the horizon, growing ever higher, as they neared their destination. The place they were headed for was Jin Sei Kai's central organisation, based on Paul's ranch in the foothills of the mountains. It was comprised of a hundred or so individuals, hand picked by Paul himself. They live on campus in wood cabins dotted around the vast estate. Paul was really proud of them by the way he talked, thought Rick. These were the best of his best students, trained in martial arts, stealth gliding, mountaineering, long distance underwater swimming etc. And like a feudal chief of old, Paul still presides over his empire, constantly perfecting his art and expanding his organisation.

As the Land Rover cruised effortlessly down the highway, Rick and Paul were once more deep in conversation about Rick's predicament.

"So what do you want me to do about it?" Paul asked.

"Help us to knock out HAARP at its source. We can't go public with this; they'd shut us down in a second. The only way to clear Bo's name and prevent a global catastrophe in the making is to infiltrate the place and put it out of commission, for keeps. I don't know anyone else who could pull it off. That's why I'm here Paul."

"Oh, you don't want much then!"

"Paul, you told me when I was a kid, if I ever needed anything, to come to you. Well, I'm here and I'm going to take you up on your offer. I know you have the skill and expertise to do it. I've seen you in action. This'd be a walk in the park for you."

"Keep talking," Paul urged, smiling and flexing his shoulders up and down as if he were enjoying the flattery from his younger friend.

Rick knew he was getting somewhere. Paul did indeed have the wherewithal, expertise and personnel to carry out a dangerous mission like this and from what he could remember of this guy, he couldn't resist a challenge. He had every intention of closing him to do it.

He also knew, from what his uncle had told him, that Paul had been approached many times in the past by the SAS, Delta Force, CIA, Mossad etc. in a bid to get him to assist them in their war games but he'd always declined their requests. Apparently his name and his organisation were well known and admired in the Special Forces community around the world.

Uncle Tod had informed Rick that Paul was a pacifist, first and foremost. He had many friends in the SAS back in Hereford, England, apparently and had trained them on many occasions in the art of self defence, but that he was not interested in the activity of killing and sabotaging in the name of "freedom," which was always the lip service attached to such ventures.

Paul, so his uncle had told him, was adamant that the so called "war on terror" was nothing more than a façade, drummed up by incompetent politicians and diplomats to keep the planet in a constant state of attrition.

As they drove up the dusty track that led to the ranch, Rick noticed a landing strip in the field, over to the right. There were a couple of planes and a helicopter parked near a hangar.

As they got nearer, Rick noticed that the big plane wasn't like anything he'd ever seen before. It looked like a cross between a helicopter and a cargo plane.

"What the hell's that thing over there?" he asked, pointing to it.

"That's the Osprey. A V-22 Osprey tilt-rotor, to be precise," replied Paul. "It's the only one in service outside of the US military. I had to do some serious ass licking to get that baby, let me tell you."

"All the toys, eh Paul?"

"Of course mate. We use the Osprey for parachute jumps. The Lear Jet's mine and the chopper is Michelle's little baby - comes in useful for popping out to the shops."

"Who's Michelle?"

"The wife!" replied Paul, grinning.

"Oh, that's right. Uncle Tod said you'd got married. Neat!"

Rick peered further out across the landing strip and noticed two dots in the sky, coming towards them over the runway.

"Stealth gliders," explained Paul, following his gaze. "We launch off an escarpment halfway up the Mountains and glide down to the ranch. It's about a ten mile trip."

"What's a stealth glider?" asked Rick.

"A bit like a hang glider except it's attached to the person; a kind of webbed cape," explained Paul. "In flight, they make you look like a huge bat but they're incredibly light and very manoeuvrable in the air. Not only that, they're virtually invisible to radar because of their size and the material they're made up of. I designed them myself."

The two dots were getting bigger as they approached the ranch house. Rick could make out what did indeed seem to be two bats in flight, just like Paul had said, their outstretched wings silhouetted against the backdrop of the evening sky. They swooped over the top of the Range Rover and landed in the paddock to the left of the house, just as Paul pulled up outside.

Rick got out and noticed a woman coming out of the front door and walking towards them. She was tall and slim with dark hair, probably in her thirties. The manner in which she moved indicated she was as fit as a fiddle.

"Who's the babe?" Rick said, admiring the curves.

"That's Michelle, my wife mate, otherwise affectionately known as Bogwitch," Paul replied, leaning out the window and giving her a friendly wave.

"Bogwitch! How does she take that?"

"With a pinch of salt, like everything else I say!"

Rick suppressed a chuckle and gently nodded in disbelief. "I gotta remember his sense of humour is weird!" he thought to himself.

Michelle gave Paul a hug and then turned to Rick. "So you're Rick. I've heard a lot about you," she said.
"Oh-oh, that sounds ominous!" Rick replied.
"No, no, it was all good. Come on in. Make yourself at home," she said, grabbing his bag from the trunk.

The outside of the house belied its internal grandeur. Inside, it was like walking into a time machine. The lobby opened out into a huge lounge area, complete with solid stone pillars and a massive granite stone clad fireplace. Towards the back, several glass doors opened out onto a patio, with a large swimming pool beyond that. The view was spectacular, outlining the distant mountains against a red sunset.

"Wow, you sure know how to live!" Rick exclaimed. "Who built this place?"

"We did!" Paul said, wrapping his arm around Michelle. "It took two years. I used to be a brickie back in England; came in handy."

Brickie is a slang term for bricklayer in the UK, though Paul's skills extended far beyond that one craft. He could turn his hand to pretty much any construction technique and the structure Rick was standing in paid testament to that fact.

Michelle served up filtered coffee and cakes and laid them out in the lower area of the lounge, on a solid redwood table that looked like it would have required a crane to move it.

Paul seated himself in one of the sumptuous cowhide armchairs and beckoned Rick to do the same.

"Okay Rick, lets have the full monte. I want to know all about you and your pal's little problem, and what exactly you want me to do about it?"

Chapter 20

For the next hour or so, Rick ran through every detail of Bo's escape from HAARP, exactly as Bo had relayed it to him; how they had found him shivering in the shoreline caves of Lake Ontario; then, the long drive to New Liskeard, where they'd secreted him away in an empty cottage that belonged to Jodi's father.

He explained that Jodi was looking after Bo, ensuring he had enough provisions and, more importantly, to keep the nosey neighbour at bay. He spoke of the tropical storms and earthquakes that he now believed were caused by the HAARP transmitters.

And finally he detailed the secret project known as Project ELFSTORM, designed to use specific frequencies and immense power outputs to mind-fuck billions of people.

Paul and Michelle listened without interrupting him.

When he'd finished, Rick could see they were impressed by what he was saying, though they appeared to be a little sceptical.

"Let's get this straight," said Paul. "The mind control stuff is way over my head, so to begin with let's stick with something I *can* understand. You're telling me that all these tropical storms, earthquakes and other natural disasters are being created by the energy beams this place puts out, right?"

"Not all of them, Paul. The earth is a pretty unstable place climate-wise, always has been. But there's something going on that indicates an *increase* in climate abnormalities and they're date coincident with what Bo told me. I've done my own research on this and it definitely pans out. I'm not saying HAARP is responsible for all of these abnormalities. Like I said, they happen all the time. I *do* think though, that it's responsible for the increase in *intensity* and *amount* of them."

"How do you mean?" Paul asked.

"Well, for instance, in 2005, there have been *twenty eight* tropical storms. Fifteen of these were hurricanes; in just *one* year alone! In fact, there were so many that they ran out of names for them. Hurricanes are assigned names based on alphabetical order. Because there were so many they had to start using the Greek alphabet, just so they could keep the names going. That's never happened before. It's unprecedented.

"2005 has also produced the most category five Hurricanes since records began; four in total. These were Emily, Katrina, Rita and Wilma.

"There was also the highest ever Accumulated Cyclone Energy - 245 units in total. The normal average for a season is 93.

"Hurricane Wilma was the strongest ever on record with 882mb central pressure. Not only that, it produced the fastest intensification ever by an Atlantic Hurricane, dropping 97 millibars in only 24 hours.

"Then there's Hurricane Vince, which was the first tropical cyclone in recorded history to strike the Iberian Peninsular.

"I could go on, but you get the point.

"The other weird thing is that these storms are still raging into the winter; they're usually a summer phenomenon. And *that's* just hurricanes.

"Earthquakes appear to be on the increase too. There are thousands of earthquakes around the world every year, and statistically, only a tenth or so of those were big ones; by that, I mean over 6.0 on the Richter scale. For instance, in 2001, just on a hundred of these big ones were recorded, but in 2005 there have been 150!

"Now, seismic shifts are not uncommon. The tectonic plates in the earths crust are always shifting. They always will but I strongly believe that these powerful ELF waves are amplifying the current trend. If you remember what happened in Indonesia and Pakistan last winter you'll get some idea of what's in store if something isn't done to stop this uptrend."

"What! You mean the tsunami?" asked Paul, remembering the devastation and loss of life that caused.

"That's exactly what I mean; but many times more destructive. If that happens, you'll probably be swimming in your front garden as well as the back, even way up here in the mountains."

Rick could see that both Paul and Michelle were having a hard time assimilating all the data he was giving them. He realised he had to find some common ground; something that would be real to them.

He thought about it for a moment, then he had it.

"Paul, you're acquainted with the Taoist philosophy, right?"

Paul perked up a bit.

"Yeah. It's a Chinese philosophy founded by Lao-Tzu. It advocates a simple life and a policy of non-interference with the natural course of things. Why?"

Rick explained his theory regarding the Taoist hum and the analogy with the speed wobble on Uncle Tod's Bonneville that he and Bo had theorised about in the cottage at Lake Agyle.

When he'd finished Paul sat back in his chair and let out a long sigh.

"Blimey! You've done your homework alright," he exclaimed.

Rick just nodded and continued.

"The other problem is, no one else, including the International Data Centre, has any idea that HAARP is possibly the source of the problem. They think it's down to global warming - too many hydrocarbons in the atmosphere or something else like that. They're just running around like chickens with their heads cut off, looking in all the wrong places for the cause of it."

"Jeezus!" said Paul, rubbing his chin.

Michelle, who was listening intently, just sat there, her face ashen.

"And talking about chickens," Rick continued, "the H5N1Avian Bird Flu pandemic, which is just on the cusp of mutating across to humans, was most likely caused by - guess what? You got it - good old HAARP. Believe it or not, it's a definite possibility.

"How did you come by that one? Paul enquired, incredulously.

Rick explained.

"There's a Canadian guy, a retired Navy warfare technician called Blackwell who discovered, years ago, that microwave beams were the cause of the bird flu. He even wrote a research paper on it and presented it to several government agencies as well as a Federal Investigative Commission but did anyone listen? Did they hell! They just whitewashed his findings and threw them in a dusty vault.

"The reason I know this is because my girlfriend Jodi works at the Canadian Research Centre and she found his research papers by chance, archived, in the basement. That's how it came to her attention. She even went off to China to investigate and got thrown out on her ear for poking around there.

"I won't go into all the technical details of it right now. To be honest with you, I don't understand it all myself. Jodi's the expert on the biology stuff. But, be that as it may, the fact is, we know he was onto something there and we need to do something about it. My friend Bo's false murder rap pales into insignificance compared to this stuff but all these things are all connected, just the same."

Paul shifted in his chair.

"Why don't you just go public with it then? If you have the documents and all this data about the secret agenda at HAARP, why not just go to the newspapers?" he asked.

Rick sighed and took a deep breath.

"Well, for one thing, because no one will listen. Look, many people have tried to alert the public to the dangers of messing with the ionosphere, many times in the past. Books have been written about it, by accredited and knowledgeable people and the internet is awash with data about it. But it just gets brushed under the carpet and explained away, probably due to vested interests. The corporation that employed Bo, for instance, is a multi billion dollar enterprise connected to the U.S. Government. They do research and development for the arms industry, for Christ's sake. That's *big* money!"

"And let's face it, who's going to take any notice of us anyway? I'm an unemployed geologist, fresh out of Uni and Jodi's on her organisation's black list for causing an international PR flap with the chinks; albeit not her fault. As for Bo, look at what happened to his girl when he twigged what was going on up there! Besides, Bo is the only one who's seen the secret plans but he has no hard proof. On top of that he's a felon who supposedly ran from the scene of a murder. Do you think anyone would listen to him? No way. Whoever's running that joint up there wants to keep this under wraps and will do anything, including kill innocent people, to keep it that way."

"I get your point," said Paul. "So, you want me to help you put this place out of commission, on the sly. Is that right?"

"I need you to help us get in there, yes," Rick replied.

"And then what?"

Rick quickly pulled out his laptop and placed it on the table. Paul hadn't said "no" yet and he wanted to keep it that way.

"Here's a layout of the grounds and buildings at HAARP."

Paul took a cursory look over it.

"Where are the fences? I don't see any."

"That's because there aren't any, except for the ones around the phased antenna arrays which keep big animals out," replied Rick.

"Well, these characters can't be too worried about intruders then, can they? Paul scoffed.

Rick was quick to reply.

"Just because you can't see 'em doesn't mean they're not there. Hidden amongst all those trees are a series of planar laser trip beams. Stick your toe in the beams transmitted between the poles and you'll see why no one gets in, or out, in a hurry.

"Patrolling around these fences are several camouflaged sentries, armed with sub-automatic machine guns. The idea, apparently, is to not attract attention to the site and, if you think about it, that's a pretty clever way of going about it. Bo mentioned to me that they're very hard to spot in amongst the forest that surrounds the place.

"Our objective is simple. We need to get inside that perimeter laser barrier fence and infiltrate the facility without being seen. That will almost certainly mean neutralising the guards.

"Once inside, we need to do two things. Firstly, we need to locate Clavell's computer and steal it. Hopefully, it still contains the secret files, outlining the intention to use HAARP as a glorified global ray gun for global mind control.

"Secondly, and this is where we step into the unknown, Bo will reconfigure the computers to initiate an electrical storm right above the place. He reckons that he can generate enough electrical energy in the sky above, to fry everything within a quarter mile radius."

Paul and Michelle looked at Rick in utter amazement, both wordlessly shaking their heads from side to side in disbelief.

Rick held both hands up in front of him.

"Hey! He says he can do it and who am I to argue?"

"How?" Paul asked

"Well, that's where we get to the interesting bit."

"Go on," urged Paul, now utterly intrigued.

"I don't profess to know all the technical details but I'll try to explain it the way Bo explained it to me, as best I can. These phased array transmitters output a tremendously powerful beam of high frequency radio waves; billions of watts of raw energy, apparently. The HAARP transmitters are unique, in that they can condense this power into a precise spot and even steer it to wherever the operator decides it should go. This condensed beam literally heats up the electrons in the ionosphere, producing drastic changes in the atmosphere below it. In other words, it can create an electronic storm which will continue to build in ever increasing intensity the longer the transmission lasts.

"When the storm has reached a certain critical point, we reverse the polarities of the current feeding the transmitters. If what he says is correct, the transmitters will suddenly become conductors. Instead of pushing power out, they will create an electrostatic vacuum on the ground, and pull it in on themselves. The immense electrical charge created in the atmosphere above, will be attracted to them like Clinton's dick to Monica Lewinsky. Kapow! No more HAARP. We'll have to be well out of there before the polarities are reversed, before it turns into a cinder pot. We then have to get away from the place and, using the information contained in that computer, blow the whistle on the whole thing."

Paul and Michelle just sat there, amazed at Rick's technical grasp of a subject that he initially said he knew little about.

But Rick wasn't finished yet.

"This is the only way we can clear Bo's name and bring his girlfriend's killers to justice, as well as prevent any further damage through the use of those transmitters. They've done enough already and we have no way of knowing how far along they are with their plans in achieving their ultimate goal. Every time they go pot shooting for Arabs, to zap their brains out, they exacerbate the situation. Much more of this and it won't be worth doing. So we have to get cracking."

He let that last bit sink in before he continued.

"I've got all the data we should need here from Bo, including what I could pull off the internet. Fantastic thing the net isn't it?"

"Never used it myself," Paul replied. "I've got better things to do than dick about with computers and keyboards. I leave that up to Michelle; she's the expert in that field."

"You've never used the internet?"

Rick was aghast. He'd never imagined there was anyone who *didn't* use it. Still, Paul was from the old school and his expertise lay in martial arts and organising groups. In that respect he had no peers. Though, how he'd done that without ever punching in a website address had him flummoxed. Rick had grown up with this technological marvel. Paul had never needed it.

"Bo couldn't come with me, for obvious reasons." Rick went on. "It would have been too risky getting him across the border, for one thing." "But he will need to come with us, for the reasons I just stated, if we're to pull this off successfully. That is, of course, if I can persuade you to help us."

Paul just smiled.

"Those armed guards, how many are there?"

"Bo reckons about a dozen but that was a while ago. There could be more or less. He doesn't know right now."

"What about the big cheese, this guy Clavell, will he be there too?" said Paul.

"If what Bo tells me is correct about this guy, he'll be there all right and so will that computer of his. I bet Bo would like to get his hands round his neck too, though by the sounds of it, he can take care of himself. Bo reckons he's built like the back end of a ferry. It's almost a certainty that he engineered the killing of his girlfriend, to keep Bo from going public. Like I just said, who's going to believe a murderer who ran from the scene of the crime?"

"Makes sense; pretty clever too, in a perverted kind of way. I'd like to meet this guy sometime," Paul savoured, cracking his knuckles.

"It may be that you will," said Rick. "If we do get him cornered it would be useful to extract a taped confession. Perhaps a Samoan back crick to loosen him up a bit, eh Paul?"

Paul chuckled at that. He'd demonstrated this technique to Rick when he was a teenager. By exerting just the right amount of pressure to the spine, whilst holding the victims legs and neck in a certain position, you could render them helpless and get them to do or say pretty much anything you wanted.

"You remember that one, eh Rick? That may be an idea but the name of the game here will need to be stealth. Ideally, the guards should be taken out without a sound. Once that's done, the next step would be to get hold of that computer. After that, we can tackle the next step of getting your mate in to stir up a few storm-clouds. Man! Now that is something I've just got to see. If we can do all that without alerting anyone outside the place, we're on the home run. When it goes up it'll probably be visible from Mars, so we'll need a fool proof escape plan."

"Good point, Rick concurred. "How *would* you plan to get everyone out?"

"I haven't figured out how to get us *in* yet. Give me a break!" protested Paul.

"So you'll do it then?"

"I didn't say that. One thing at a time, Rick. I need all the data first. Can you print off those plans for me?"

"You bet! How many copies would you like?"

Chapter 21

VanderWal cottage, Lake Argyle.

Jodi and Bo spent the night in the cottage. He slept on the sofa while she used the bedroom.

The next morning, Jodi decided to phone her parents. Better they were aware that she was there, rather than them finding out some other way, such as Cindy phoning them, she figured. As she dialled the number, she was trembling a little. She was going to have to tell a lie, something she wasn't accustomed to. It made her nervous.

Her father answered the call.

"Oh, hi dad," Jodi began. "Rick and I have decided to take a few days off at the cottage."

She obviously didn't mention the little fact that they had brought along a wanted felon with them.

Her father, a hard nosed businessman, made no bones about this turn of events.

"Your mother and I wondered where you'd got to," he replied. "I've no objections with that, though I find it a bit strange you went there without letting us know. I'm also concerned that you've taken time off work at such short notice. Is everything alright at work, Jodi?" he asked.

"Dad, my employers probably won't even miss me very much under the current circumstances, and anyway, I'm due some annual leave," she replied.

She could hear him sigh as he listened to her.

"Young people never take their work seriously these days," he remonstrated.

Jodi relaxed a little. Her father was a bull of an executive, but in essence he was an easy going guy. He had worked hard all his life and had built up a very successful construction company from nothing. Taking time off work at a whim just didn't sit well with him, she knew that. Nevertheless, he didn't sound too concerned. He knew what had happened in China and had taken Jodi's side on the matter, feeling she'd been hard done by.

"Go and see Cindy and Art sometime, to say hello, will you?" he said.

Jodi suddenly realised that might not be as easy as it sounded. Rick was in Denver, plotting to carry out a terrorist act and the guy in the cottage with her was someone else altogether. In fact he was a wanted murderer whose name was all over the papers and the TV, still being hunted down by every law enforcement agent in Canada and the U.S. How was she going to get round that one?

Cindy knew Rick by sight now. There was no way Bo could masquerade as him and, besides, Cindy would almost certainly recognise him, what with all the airing of his photo in the media. This was going to have to be carefully handled.

"Okay dad, I'll make sure we see them but Rick's a bit poorly right now - flu or something. I'll let him rest up a while before we go socialising," she lied.

Her father bought that one.

For now, at least.

"You two have a nice time up there," said her father. "And don't do anything I wouldn't," he joked.

Jodi cringed.

If only you knew, dad.

"Thanks, dad. Bye then."

With those parting words, she ended the call.

Jodi stood for a while, looking blankly at the ceiling.

Oh my God. What am I doing?

Bo, meanwhile, had busied himself with researching the internet for more material regarding ionospheric research, particularly anything to do with HAARP. He used Rick's email address, not wanting to alert anyone to the fact that he might be online.

At 7.45 p.m. that evening, the phone rang.

Jodi and Bo both tensed, unsure whether to answer or not. Unable to contain her curiosity, Jodi picked up the receiver. To her relief it was Rick calling in from Paul Perry's ranch. He told her he'd gone over everything with Paul and that he was waiting for his decision.

They kept the call short and to the point, not mentioning names or locations, just in case.

There was no TV in the cottage. Their only form of entertainment came from the radio, which Bo had been listening to intently throughout the day for any further updates on the manhunt underway for him. At 10 o' clock, the news came on.

He didn't think anything could ever shock him again, until now:

"Breaking news just in. Another bizarre series of events has unfolded in relation to the killing of Miss Karen Miller, the young scientist brutally murdered in Alaska by her estranged boyfriend and co worker, Andrew Boetto.

Unconfirmed reports coming in have suggested that the plane carrying the parents of Miss Miller and federal US agents from Ontario to Fairbanks International airport, apparently disappeared over the North Slope Mountains last night. The aircraft, a Lear jet, leased by the U.S Government, vanished off the radar somewhere over the Alaskan / Canadian border.

No wreckage has yet been found but initial reports say there are unlikely to be any survivors. If this is the case there will be no immediate next of kin to identify Miss Miller's body as her parents were her only surviving relatives.

A rescue mission is currently under way but has been halted due to bad weather.

Mr Boetto's parents have also mysteriously disappeared, believed to have gone into hiding after the media hue and cry regarding their son. No one has seen them since the day after Mr Boetto allegedly killed Miss Miller in Gakona, Alaska over a week ago. Stay tuned for further updates on WKBO........."

Bo looked at Jodi. He couldn't believe what he was hearing.

"No! *Both* our parents missing? I don't believe it!" he exclaimed. He was absolutely beside himself.

Jodi tried to console him but she could see the news had really hit him hard.

Bo was in a desperate state. He rocked back and forth on his knees on the floor, pummelling the wooden boards with clenched fists, cursing under his breath.

But then, Jodi thought for a moment. Something about the newscast didn't make sense.

"This is getting too much, Bo. Something definitely doesn't add up here."

What do you mean?" Bo muttered, still trying to come to terms with everything that was happening.

"I mean, I don't believe that plane went down at all. Think about it for a moment. First Miller gets killed then both hers *and* your parents disappear. Something doesn't ring true here."

Bo perked up a little and looked up at her.

"You know what, you're right! My Dad wouldn't go into hiding. He'd stick up for me; always did. This whole thing must have cut my family to pieces but they'd never run away. It's just not like them at all. None of it makes sense."

"Exactly!" Jodi agreed. "Not only that, the plane carrying Miller's parents just happened to belong to the FBI. Something's weird about all this."

Bo just couldn't figure it out. It was too much of a coincidence. Was this some kind of vindictive, sadistic ploy by Clavell and his cronies to lure him out in the open? Was he holding them hostage or something? He wouldn't put it past the cold hearted, calculating bastard. He recalled how Clavell had cleverly manipulated him and Miller to do his bidding at HAARP, all under false pretences.

For a few minutes, he and Jodi sat there in silence; then it hit him.

"They've been kidnapped!" Bo exclaimed. "I'll bet my bottom dollar they're languishing in a secret location somewhere, hidden away from prying eyes. Clavell knows I know too much. That's why he killed Miller and then made it look like I did it, so the police would get involved and pick me up. He'd be able to get to me through them. After that it'd be a piece of cake for him to have me bumped off too. That way his secret would be safe. He knew I was on to him. I saw it in his eyes that time when I was leaving his office."

At that moment the phone rang. The shrill pitch shook them both out of their wits.

Jodi answered it, thinking it might be Rick again.

"Jodi!" It was her mother's voice.

"Hi Mom, how are y......" She didn't have a chance to finish her sentence.

"Jodi, have you heard that your boyfriend Rick is a close friend of that young guy from Ajax who killed his girlfriend - you know, Andrew Boetto!" Her mother's voice was gushing on the other end of the line.

Oh boy, she knew alright.

"Um yeah, kind of, Mom. Rick did mention something about it. Why, what's up?" she asked, in an attempt to remain blasé.

"Well, his whole family have been arrested and taken into custody by the FBI. That's what's up!"

Jodi's jaw nearly hit the floor. She stood rooted to the spot at what she'd just heard her mother say.

"What! Rick's family?"

"No, no, Andrew Boetto's, not Rick's," her mother replied.

Jodi briefly breathed a sigh of relief, then realised she and Bo had just been discussing that very thing only minutes earlier.

"Why?" she replied, trying to keep her composure, but doing a very bad job of it.

She looked across at Bo, who was listening intently to Jodi's questions and answers, unaware of what was actually going on.

Her mother continued to blurt out the awful news.

"They apparently went missing all of a sudden. Then, Mr Davies from next door came round and told us that Mr Boetto, Bo's father, had been arrested in connection with industrial sabotage;

something to do with the place where his son worked in Alaska. His wife was apparently taken in as well!"

Jodi was in a quandary. She was as shocked as her mother at the news but was trying to downplay her emotions, for fear of alarming Bo before she could tell him.

"Mom, I'm sure this is all a mix up. There must be some mistake."

Her mother was at sixes and sevens.

"I need to speak to Rick right away. Put him on would you? I want to know all about this Andrew Boetto friend of his."

Her mother's words struck her like a sledgehammer. She was flummoxed. She'd never lied to her parents before this. Now she was lying to them every time she opened her mouth.

What do I do?

Bo was looking at her, perplexed. He gestured outwardly with his hands, desperately indicating to Jodi to let him in on it. He couldn't hear the other end of the conversation but he knew something was very wrong.

"Well, where's Rick?" demanded her mother's voice, insistently.

"Um, um, Rick's not h-here right now Mom," she stammered. "He's gone out for some groceries in New Liskeard. He'll, er, be back in about an hour." The sweat on her palms was making the phone feel slippery. This was going from bad to worse.

Her mother, being her mother, knew something wasn't right.

"Jodi, are you okay? Is something wrong?" she asked, suspiciously.

Jodi tried to catch her breath. She was beginning to hyperventilate. This was all too much for her but she was in it up to her neck now and had to handle the situation. If she said the wrong thing it would all be over. The police would be here in minutes. She and Bo would be arrested. How would she explain being alone with him in a lakeside cottage, without another soul around. She had to focus.

"Mom, listen, it's kinda late and I think I've caught the flu from Rick. Can I call you back in the morning after I've had some sleep. I'll be better then."

There was a brief silence on the other end of the line. Then her mother's tone softened slightly and she apologised.

"Of course dear, I'm so sorry. You have a nice sleep and I'll call you in the morning. You look after yourself, okay."

"Yes Mom. Thanks for the call. Goodnight Mom." Jodi replied, and put the phone down.

I really do feel sick now!

Bo was almost falling off his chair to hear what all the fuss was about.

"Jodi, come on, tell me!" he demanded.

"We're in big trouble, Bo. It's just like you said. Your parents have been arrested and taken away by the FBI."

Bo began to shake. He clenched his fists in front of him.

"I knew it! They want me to turn myself in. This is covert blackmail. Clavell knows I won't let my family suffer. It's a ploy; that slimy scumbag!"

He smashed his fist down on the small coffee table, breaking it almost in half.

At that very moment there was a knock at the door!

The two of them froze.

"Hi there, anyone in?" came a female voice. "It's Cindy from over the way. Helloeee!"

Jodi nearly pee'd herself.

"Oh no! Jesus, Bo! Hide, quick!"

Bo dived into the bedroom and turned off the light, crouching behind the door in an effort to conceal himself.

Jodi tried to compose herself. She patted down her cardigan and jeans and attempted to tidy her hair in the mirror.

"Just coming Cindy, won't be a moment," she called out, in as normal a voice as she could muster. Then she noticed the broken coffee table. She quickly picked up the pieces and hid them behind the sofa.

Jodi braced herself, took in a deep breath and cautiously opened the door. She was immediately met with an effusive hug and a kiss from Cindy. Behind her was her husband, Art. They hustled past her, bowling in uninvited. Jodi didn't have time to stop them entering before they were in.

"Jodi VanderWal! Well I never. You've grown; my how you've grown!" blurted the rambunctious woman.

Her much less effusive husband stood behind her, smiling. He didn't say anything.

Jodi didn't have time to speak.

"Well, it's been a while, young Jodi. Now, where's that handsome boy of yours? What's his name, Rick?" Cindy enquired.

Jodi thought fast.

"Erm, well er actually...he's not very well at the moment Cindy, he's got the flu. I've put him to bed with some salts, to rest," she said, the last sentence spoken slightly louder than normal. She hoped to hell that Bo was listening to what she was saying. These guys weren't going to be so easy to get rid of. If they barged in the bedroom, he needed to be under the covers, snoring and pretending to be Rick.

"Aw, that's too bad; poor fella. These men are not as tough as us women, Jodi. You'll learn that in years to come. Art's just the same, aren't you dear?" Cindy crooned, turning her attention to her timid spouse.

Art just stood there, gleefully accepting his wife's patronising statement.

"Now, I brought you some apple pie over. Made it myself this morning," she said, offering Jodi a bundle wrapped in cloth.

Jodi took the package and thanked her.

"You seem a little peeky yourself honey. Best you rest up yourself by the looks of it."

Peeky? More like scared out of my wits!

"Thank you so much, Cindy. It's so nice of you two to look in on us. We'll return the favour, soon as Rick's feeling himself again. I don't want you catching anything you know," Jodi flustered.

She *had* to get rid of them. If they spotted Bo in the bedroom the game would be up!

Slowly and gradually she sidled the two of them towards the front door.

After a few more minutes of idle social chit chat Jodi managed to get them to leave. As she shut the door she turned and slid down it, till she was sitting with her face on her knees.

Oh God! How long can I keep this up?

Bo peeked cautiously around the bedroom door.

"Can I come out now?" he whispered.

Jodi just nodded her head. She didn't have the energy to speak.

"Whoa, I'm getting used to this shit!" Bo exclaimed.

"I'm not, and never will. Oh God, what have I gotten myself into," Jodi whimpered. Then she started to cry.

Chapter 22

Denver, Colorado

The next day, Paul carefully studied the plans Rick had printed off for him, while Michelle took the young buckaroo out for a tour of the ranch.

He had already secretly decided to help his young friend but hadn't let on. As a challenge it was irresistible but it was the tsunami story that had finally hooked him and Michelle. He had lost friends amongst those poor people who had died in their tens of thousands in that debacle. As far as he was concerned, it just wasn't good karma whichever way you looked at it.

As for those tropical storms, ravaging the Gulf Coast, he knew there was no way on God's green earth that there could be that many hurricanes, one after the other. Something was not right and he reckoned that Rick could well be on to something here. Whether he and his pal Bo really knew what they were getting themselves into was another matter but one thing was for sure, he admired his young friend's resolve to sort it out; little Rick had balls. For someone of his tender years, to be able to confront something of this magnitude was, in his estimation, indicative of the character he tried to inspire in all his students.

He had masterminded several operations like this and trained special forces personnel, at their behest, many times in the past. Two of his best kohai's (students) were ex SAS and he had many friends back home in Hereford, still fighting what they called "the good fight" against Her Majesty's foes.

Not for him though; not any more. Although he loved the challenges thrust upon him by such endeavours, he abhorred the wanton violence, death and destruction that so often went along with it. In his opinion there was no real reason for firearms or other weapons, anyway. As far as he was concerned, the true test of any one of his students, was whether he or she could take down one or several opponents, silently and cleanly, using only their perceptions and bare hands, rendering them harmless in the process. Guns, or weapons of any kind, for that matter, were merely instruments used by those who couldn't confront people, or real life situations.

He had developed hand to hand combat to such a fine art that a true Jin Sei Kai exponent should never be the effect of anything that came within his sphere of influence. He called this sphere "his universe."

The ninjas of old practiced this philosophy and were expert in its application. However, over the centuries the true ways of the ninja had become alloyed with the use of weapons, such as the shurikin, (a metallic roundel with spikes protruding from its perimeter). Deadly accurate in the right hands but nevertheless a weapon. No, a true exponent had no real need for weapons. Trained properly and thoroughly to use mind and body, fused together into a fantastically perceptive and powerful tool, that individual could not easily be overcome.

Many people had assumed these training regimens and techniques were the stuff of mind over matter and to the uninitiated it would appear to be so. In essence, a person doesn't think things to happen, he *causes* them to. Total cause is a far cry from thinking. So it was with any new kohai. They had to be untrained out of their slack, lazy mindset, and re educated, often at great pains to themselves, until each realised that it was he himself, the being, not the body, that caused those in their "universe" or zone of control, to succumb.

As for this mission, the only major obstacle would be getting inside the place, undetected. Incapacitating armed guards without a fight would be easy, but how to get inside first, that was another matter

Paul decided that the stealth glider suits were the way to go.

A stealth suit is a very advanced article of clothing that is radar absorbent, a kind of "Chameleon suit" that mimics the colour and appearance of the background. It is neutral grey in colour and is saturated with heat and light conductive fibers that enable the suit to match the ambient thermal and lighting environment. The suit contains its own photometers and heat sensors, which adjust to the environmental conditions around it, automatically.

This doesn't make it invisible to the eye but does help in blending into the background, especially in dark areas. Against a light background, the suit will be light grey, against a dark background, dark. But always grey.

If the ambient temperature is lower than body temperature, the suit will collect body heat in an "ice can". It can only do this for as long as the ice can holds out - the colder it is, the more body heat has to be collected, and the quicker the can will melt its coolant. The temperature over Alaska at this time of year, especially at a jump height of around 10,000 feet would only allow a short time in the air. They would need to jump as close to the target as possible to avoid freezing up before they landed.

Fortunately, the stealth suits would render the team invisible to radar, which, he could see from the plans, was quite evident and active in that area.

They were also deathly silent when operated by skilled fliers and incredibly accurate to land on a pinpoint target.

The stealth gliders were definitely the best option but this then presented another problem - how to get Rick and his friend in? He hadn't yet enquired as to whether Rick intended to go with them, but somehow he knew it wouldn't be necessary. Rick was a true kohai in every respect, even if he didn't know it yet. He would want to be in on it, though. He and his friend had no training in the fine art of expertly gliding down amongst a group of fliers in the dead of night and anyway, there wasn't enough time to train them. From what Rick had told him, neither of them had even jumped out of a plane! They would have to be taken in, attached to one of the fliers by a harness.

Paul decided he would begin a training regimen the next day, to check out the feasibility of this idea. Meanwhile he would decide on the number of operatives and begin selecting those who would be eligible for such a task. One thing was for sure, there would be no shortage of volunteers!

That evening Michelle prepared dinner for Rick, Paul and herself - vegetarian curry.

By the end of the meal Rick couldn't contain himself any longer.

"So, Paul. What about this whole thing then?"

Paul looked up, munching on a piece of Nan bread.

"You ever done any hang gliding before, Rick?" he asked, nonchalantly.

"Er, no. Why?" Rick replied.

"Because mate, you're going to need to know how to do it. If you're coming with us, that is."

Rick's pulse began to rise. He beamed with excitement.

"Yes! When do I start?"

"6a.m. tomorrow morning mate, and don't be late."

"Oh," exclaimed Rick, suddenly realising what he'd let himself in for.

Hang gliding! Sheesh!

After dinner, Paul explained his strategy for the infiltration of HAARP.

"I've decided, on this mission, to take a complement of seven of my guys, plus Michelle, as well as you and your mate Bo. We'll fly to New Liskeard in the Osprey and pick him and your girl up first. The Osprey can land pretty much anywhere where there's a clearing, so you'll need to tell them to be ready for a quick pick-up. After that we'll head for Alaska........."

On into the night they talked. Paul's own research of HAARP and his attention to detail astounded Rick. Calling on vast experience from numerous missions he'd planned for the SAS and other Special Forces, Paul had devised a cunning and clinically precise operation that seemed perfect in every way.

When they were done it was almost 1.30am.

"Better get some kip, Rick. When I said 6.a.m, I meant it." Paul said, in mock authority.

The next morning Rick was up and raring to go. He hadn't slept much but was wide awake and ready for anything.

Paul had already chosen and briefed the members of the assault team the day before and had arranged to meet everyone in the hangar at 6.30 a.m. After a quick breakfast of fruit and cereal, they set off out the door and headed for the aircraft hangar across the field.

A group of people were already waiting for them when they arrived.

There were four young men and three women and if Rick didn't know better, he'd have thought he was going to a fancy dress party. They were all kitted out in the strangest attire he'd had ever seen. The suits they wore resembled capes made of a dark grey, rubbery, leather type material that hung down around them like an ill fitting overcoat. It was a strange sight.

One of the girls, a trim pretty blonde, came over and introduced herself.

"Hi Rick, I'm Chelsea. We've heard a lot about you. Ready for some action?" she challenged.

Rick looked her up and down. She was small and petite, yet poised and confident at the same time. "Guess so," he replied, not all that confident.

Paul then gathered everyone together and introduced them to his young friend.

"Guys, this is Rick Hayden. He's the one I told you about, who's going to get us in a lot of trouble."

Everyone laughed.

"Won't be the first time, Paul!" said a stocky young blond haired guy at the back.

The group laughed again.

Paul introduced each member of the team to him, ladies first.

"Chelsea you've just met. This is Samantha; we just call her Sam. She'll act as co-pilot on the inbound mission and pick us up after we're done."

Rick and Sam shook hands.

"Lynnea is the feisty one, otherwise known as Noogie."

She also shook his hand and smiled.

Then Paul introduced the guys. The tallest one, called Brook, resembled a US Marine, with his muscular build and cropped hair. He had an American accent but was at pains to assure Rick he was British through and through, having been born in the UK but lived most of his life in the States.

The second guy's name was Leigh. He was thin and wiry, but his firm handshake put Rick under no illusion that he could hold his own in any given situation. His eyes pierced deep into Rick's, portraying a keen intellect and wisdom beyond his years.

The third guy resembled a California surfer dude, with his shock of golden hair and tanned complexion. As with the other two young men he was alert and focused, but he had a flippancy about him that set him apart from the other two. His name was Ryan.

The last guy was called Ross or, "Ross the Boss," as he was affectionately known. He was the stockiest of the four men and quieter than the rest. He was also the pilot of the jump plane but would be going in with them on the drop. With the introductions done, Ross and Sam made their way out to do the pre-flight checks on the Osprey.

Rick noticed they were all a pretty up-tone bunch; very friendly and exuberant, though he couldn't help wondering how come the chicks were all in on this. From what Paul had told him, this escapade called for some pretty tough characters and while the men looked like they could hold their own in a fight, these girls didn't seem to fit the bill at all.

Paul spotted his concern immediately and while the others were talking amongst themselves, he took Rick aside.

"If you're wondering about the number of birds in the group, don't worry."

Rick looked at him a bit confused.

"Birds! What dya mean?" he asked.

"Birds. That's British slang for girls, you dimwit. You should know that. You met enough when you were in the UK, so Tod told me, anyway."

Rick smiled and nodded sheepishly.

"Anyway, they're all highly trained and as dangerous as anyone you'll ever have anything to do with. I chose them for this mission because they're light and extremely agile and have plenty of experience flying the stealth suits at night. If they get in a fight on the ground it'll be the opponent who's in trouble, believe me. They're also skilled in various mechanical and technical matters, which will come in useful if the need arises."

Rick just shrugged. Paul obviously knew what he was talking about and he'd learned by now that nothing was normal where this guy was concerned.

Outside, the Osprey's turbo-prop engines fired into life and the group of bat caped men and women started towards the hangar doors.

"Ready for some fun, Rick?" asked Paul, leading him outside.

The Osprey was a sight to behold. Known in military circles as the V-22, it's what's known as a tilt-rotor aircraft, combining the speed and range of fixed wing aircraft with the vertical flight performance of a helicopter. With its engine nacelles and rotors in vertical position, it could take off, land, and hover like a helicopter. However, once airborne, its engine nacelles would rotate to convert the aircraft into a turboprop airplane capable of high-speed, high-altitude flight, and it was capable of transporting 24 personnel or up to 20,000 pounds of internal or external cargo, at twice the speed of a helicopter.

On the ground the rotors can fold and the wing rotates so the aircraft can be stored in extremely small and narrow spaces.

Two Rolls Royce, 6,150 horsepower, turbo-shaft engines each drove a 38 ft diameter, 3-bladed prop-rotor, enabling it to reach a top speed of 483 km/h with an operational range of 1,182 km.

An integrated electronic defensive suite, including a radar warning receiver, a missile warning set and a countermeasures dispensing system had been installed, along with a multitude of other radically advanced techno wizardry.

When they were all safely aboard, the plane lifted off and soared into the sky, with Ross and Sam at the controls.

As they climbed, Paul handed Rick his hang glider backpack.

Rick grabbed it, looking slightly bemused.

"What do I do with this?" he asked.

Strap it on, mate," urged Paul. "It'll come in handy after I push you out of the door. It's an auto opener, which means it'll deploy as soon as you're out of the plane. After that, just hang on and glide down. It's easy."

"Easy! Easy what? I've never done this before in my life! Are you kidding me?" exclaimed Rick.

"Never been more serious, mate," replied Paul. "You'll get the hang of it, don't worry – get it? *Hang* of it, ha ha."

Rick didn't see the funny side of it at all. Nevertheless, he strapped on the backpack with a little help from Paul and nervously stood at the back of the queue of jumpers, awaiting his fate.

"The others will be stealth gliding," explained Paul. "I'll follow after you with a hang glider like yours. If you get into trouble, I'll be right there to help."

Rick found himself unable to reply with words. He just nodded.

At 10,000 feet, Brook slid open the door and a blast of ice cold air surged into the cabin that seemed to suck the air right out of Rick's lungs. The noise was deafening, a mixture of high velocity wind and the roar of the Osprey's two engines and rotor blades above them. Brook shouted a series of commands, and one by one, the team disappeared through the door.

When it came to Rick's turn to jump he couldn't do it. The thought of jumping into empty space from 10,000 feet locked his legs solid.

But that was no problem for Paul who was right behind him.

"Ready, Rick?" Paul yelled.

But the words went in one ear and out the other. Rick couldn't move. Still rigid and screaming in abject terror, he found himself being lifted up and thrown out the hatch. As he fell, swept away in the current of fast moving air, his legs reactively flailed around, desperately trying to locate something solid under them and for a terrifying moment, Rick realised what it must feel like to be hanged. As a kid, he'd watched those old cowboy films and wondered why the cattle rustler's legs flailed wildly around, as the horse pulled away from the doomed man sitting on it. Now he knew! Seconds later, he felt like someone had grabbed him and was pulling him back as the chute pulled open. Hanging helplessly under the billowing canopy, all he could think was – *Shee-it! I'm gonna die!*

But he didn't die. Despite a pretty rough landing and being dragged several yards across the ground by an unrelenting wind, he ended his first jump with success and not a scratch, much to the delight of the others who were waiting for him on the ground.

Then up they went again, and out and down Rick went again – and again – and again, until he was jumping of his own accord, in his own time and of his own volition.

That evening, back on solid ground and seated in front of the huge fireplace of Paul's ranch house, Rick, Paul and Michelle went over that days training routine. Rick was buzzing. He'd never had so much fun his whole life. After several jumps it was easy. His fear of launching himself out of a plane into mid air was now long gone.

"Well Rick, you certainly exceeded my expectations, mate. Tomorrow you can jump with Noogie in the dual harness stealth suit," announced Paul.

Rick had no considerations about that.

"Piece of cake, Paul. I could do it blindfolded!" he boasted.

Paul and Michelle laughed. This young guy had good spirit. He'd do fine.

"I'm going to have to teach you a few key moves as well," explained Paul. "If we run up against any armed guards, you're going to need to know how to handle 'em."

"I can handle myself, Paul," explained Rick. "Back home I played defence for my ice hockey team in the Junior Hockey League. My nickname was "Hammer

Hayden." No one got past me easily without a bruise or two."

Paul just smiled.

"Even so, you'll need technique as well as brute strength, you fucking big head!" he said.

"Sounds good to me!" beamed Rick.

That evening, Paul went through some basic routines with Rick in the dojo. It was simple stuff, well, it looked simple, but then with an 8th Dan Sensei teaching him, Rick realised that everything seemed uncomplicated.

He learned the art of disarming a man by using the assailant's energy against himself. He couldn't believe how effortless it was when Paul demonstrated it to him.

"Basically, the key to the technique is to ensure the guys balance is thrown off by stepping adroitly to the side, so he doesn't have a straight aim at you. Then, twist his wrist at a certain exact point and let his forward motion work to your advantage," Paul instructed, gently manoeuvring Rick's wrist to the left.

"Now, as he lunges forward, out of his own control, turn his force back on himself and disable the wrist so he can't fire his weapon. After that, twist him round, following the flow of his motion, then, knee in his back, twist back the arm, grab the gun, and apply your own weight downwards onto him. He can't resist you or his arm will break. Then a quick chop to the neck and he's out – simple."

And in essence, it was! After several attempts, Rick soon had Paul locked in a compromising position, time after time.

"Well, I think your ready me ol' mucker," affirmed Paul. "We'll leave for New Liskeard tomorrow."

Chapter 23

Lake Argyle

It had been almost two days since Rick had left to meet Paul in Denver.

In that time Bo had busied himself with figuring out exactly how he was going to create an electrical storm of sufficient magnitude, directly above the HAARP facility, to carry out his plan. It wasn't the sequence of actions to do it that bothered him. It was getting far enough away in time, before the lightning bolt struck, that was going to pose the biggest problem.

He was well aware that lightning was really not much more than a very large and powerful spark, caused by a discharge of electrical energy that has built up inside a thundercloud.

Though he was well acquainted with what went on in the *upper* atmosphere, the workings of the troposphere, the area where thunderstorms form, was not so familiar to him. He had to do a fair bit of research to get all the data he needed.

He learned that during a thunderstorm, processes involving things such as vertical winds and different-sized water droplets cause electrical charges to build up in various parts of the cloud. When these charges become powerful enough, they discharge, causing a stroke of lightning. From deep within a mature storm cloud, electrical discharges occur that are caused by negative charges, reacting with positive charges, creating lightning and consequently thunder.

The top of a storm cloud is positively charged, while the middle to lower regions are negatively charged. A small area at the bottom of the storm cloud and the ground beneath it are positively charged, so consequently there is a huge potential for lightning to occur, once the static electricity builds up inside.

The type of lighting that occurs depends on the locations of the opposite electrical charges in and around the cloud. This huge electrical "spark" literally jumps the gap between the opposite charges, causing a swift and intense heating of the air immediately around the lightning bolt. This causes the air to expand and then contract rapidly, creating sound waves, in this case, thunder.

Apparently, the voltage flowing through a lightning bolt can reach 200 million volts and the amperage can be anything from a few thousand to tens of thousands of amps.

Bo calculated that he would need something much more powerful. A couple of trillion volts would be more like it, and at the minimum, at least a million amps.

Some of the data he *was* familiar with. For instance, lightning is, in essence, made of air. The visible forks are actually nitrogen and oxygen which has been converted into plasma. Plasma is a conductor and was something that Bo had thoroughly researched when piloting the creation of The Artificial Ionospheric Mirrors, at HAARP.

He found that there are at least six different forms of lightning, each with their own individual characteristics. Of these, fork lightning was the most spectacular of all. It was also the most destructive. He decided that fork lightning, (but an extremely condensed version of it), was what was needed. To bring this about, he would have to program the phased array antennae to transmit at exactly the right frequencies and power outputs.

Another thing that came up was that the electrons density has great variations during the cycle of night and day, and this causes different behaviours. Because he would be attempting this at night he would have to calibrate the outputs accordingly.

He discovered that lightning generally originates around 15,000, to 25,000 feet above sea level, when raindrops are carried upward until some of them convert to ice. A cloud-to-ground lightning flash originates in this mixed water and ice region. The charge then moves downwards in 50-yard sections called "step leaders". It keeps moving toward the ground in these steps and produces a channel along which charge is deposited. Eventually, it encounters something on the ground that is a good connection, in this case, the connection would be the phased array antennae grids and this would complete the circuit.

The entire event should take less than half a second. The bright light of the lightning flash, caused by the return stroke, would generate a great deal of energy. That amount of energy would heat the air in the channel to above 50,000 degrees Fahrenheit, in only a few millionths of a second!

The air surrounding it would be at such a high temperature it would have no time to expand. It would flow outward into the surrounding air, compressing it, and causing a disturbance that would blast out in all directions.

Bo mulled over this point for quite a while. The safety of everyone in the vicinity was the thing that posed the biggest problem. Normal cloud-to-ground lightning can kill or injure people by indirect as well as direct means. But there wasn't going to be anything normal about this one.

He calculated that even if they were even as much as a kilometre away, the lightning current could branch off to a person from a tree, fence, pole or other tall object. In addition, the current could conduct through the ground to a person, after the flash struck.

Mirrors In The Sky

The best defence against this would be to plan ahead and avoid exposure to the lightning bolt, before it occurred. They would have to leave enough time to reach a safe distance before it struck.

Bo systematically worked through the power to frequency ratios, temperature coefficients, and Ionospheric conditions that were likely to be present in the skies above HAARP at this time of the year. He calculated that if he wanted to totally obliterate the entire antennae array, all one quarter square mile of it, and leave nothing standing, the lightning strike would have to contain approximately 5 trillion volts and at least 1.5 million amperes, in order to gain the necessary destructive power required.

Finally, after several hours, he felt he had it taped. He then ran several digital models on the computer, ironing out any bugs and adjusting the calculations here and there till he was satisfied it would work. Finally, he downloaded the program onto a disc and took a break.

While he'd been at it, the nosey neighbours, Cindy and her husband, had twice come round to visit. Each time Bo had to hide in the bedroom while Jodi managed to keep them at bay, explaining why her boyfriend Rick was still too poorly to accept visitors. So far she'd been successful but they both knew that they weren't going to buy these lame excuses for much longer.

That evening Rick called and informed them that everything was ready to roll. Tomorrow morning, he would be flying back to pick them up, along with Paul and several other people. Then he explained what they should do next. In the morning, they were to drive to the old mining site, which sat in a clearing in the woods, about four miles away from where they were now. He instructed them to hide the car in the woods and cover it with camouflage, then wait there for the plane to pick them up.

Jodi said she knew the place he was talking about. She'd driven past it a few times. Very few people went there, especially in winter. It was an old derelict mine and miles from any habitation. But then, while Rick was talking, she'd suddenly had a horrible thought. It would be impossible to land a plane there. There was no runway!

Rick had to explain to her about the plane they would be using, something called an Osprey tilt-rotor and, though it was in fact a plane, it could land just like a helicopter. He made it crystal clear that they were to be there no later than 9.30a.m.

After saying goodbye, Bo let Jodi talk privately for a few minutes to Rick and went into the kitchen to gather his thoughts. This was it! They were really going to do it.

Mirrors In The Sky

Chapter 24

Perry Ranch, Denver

When everyone was aboard the Osprey, Paul signalled for Ross and Sam to take off.

The twin turbo engine powered tilt-props began to spin faster and soon the inside of the plane was shuddering as the down-draught of air pummelled its fuselage. Then, with a stomach dropping lurch, it soared into the air and headed skyward. Within 15 minutes or so, the sturdy little plane had reached its cruising altitude of 20,000 feet and Ross levelled her out, heading North-west to Canada.

As the plane sped onwards Rick wondered what lay ahead of him, and pondered the bizarre series of events that had led him here. Just over a month ago he had been worrying about whether he'd ever find a new job. Since then he'd fallen in love, been party to concealing a known fugitive and now he was about to take part in what amounted to international terrorism. Blowing up a U.S.

Government research facility, even if the purpose was to prevent a cataclysm of global proportions, definitely wasn't going to go down lightly with the powers that be.

He looked across at Paul and the others, who were sitting, talking, and joking between themselves, as if they were off on a pleasant day trip. These guys were something else, he thought. At the drop of a hat these nine individuals had agreed to put themselves in harm's way to undertake an incredibly dangerous task that could end up with them all going to prison, or much, much worse. Yet it didn't seem to faze them one bit. Their skill in flying those bat capes in the pitch black and their incredibly agile and lethal fighting techniques; those things alone instilled hope and awe in him, but it was their indomitable spirit that struck him the most.

Take Chelsea for instance - she wasn't more than five foot three, yet she could drop a two hundred and fifty pound man like he was a twig that she'd just plucked off a tree.

Then there was Lynnea or "Noogie" as everyone called her. Brook had told him a funny story about how she had earned her nickname. Apparently, there was an incident a year or so ago, on a subway train in New York. Some punk rockers were playing a ghetto blaster at full volume in the carriage, causing real concern to Lynnea and everyone else within earshot. She was about two heads shorter than the smallest of the yobs, yet had told them, in no uncertain terms, to turn it down.

Deciding to be particularly obnoxious they cranked up the volume.

She then went up to the biggest guy and noogie'd him on the top of his head, basically rubbing her fist hard into his scalp.

His reaction was to go berserk and threaten her with a flick knife. Two seconds later he was lying on the floor with a severe headache and a broken wrist, the knife lying next to him on the floor. The other two thugs reacted just as violently but Noogie subdued them with lightning kicks to the groin. She then used their scarves and clothing to tie their hands behind their backs and trussed them together around one of the passenger grab-poles.

When the train stopped at the next station, she was arrested by the somewhat bemused transport police, but then released, after several other passengers gave a detailed description of what had occurred. She'd never lived it down and the nickname had stuck.

Then there was Sam. She was the brainy one, apparently. As well as being a skilled pilot she was also a fully trained nurse.

In fact all the members of the Jin Sei Kai team were just as formidable, mentally as well as physically, though it didn't seem to matter about size or physical power. The techniques Paul had trained into them were enough to make this little group a veritable tour de force. As well as being awesome fighting exponents, each male member of the team had a secondary hat which they would use when the need arose. Leigh was a highly skilled electrician. Brook was an electronics and computer whiz kid. Ryan was adept at any form of mechanics or engineering, and Ross, apart from being an expert pilot, was a mathematical genius apparently.

In the ensuing few hours he got to know each of them pretty well.

Two and a half hours into the flight, Rick checked his watch. It was 7.30a.m. The tone of the engines had decreased a little, as Ross put the Osprey into cruise mode. The talking between the guys had ceased as each member of the team went over the coming sequence of events in their heads.

Rick went through it one more time, himself. Bo and Jodi had been fully briefed to be ready and waiting at the mine, no later than 9.30a.m. The plane would only put down for a few minutes to pick them up. After that they would fly to Yukon Territory where they would refuel in preparation for the assault on HAARP.

As he mulled over it, Rick wondered how Jodi was coping with all this. She was a tough gal that was for sure and she'd gotten herself into ten buckets of shit doing all this for him and Bo. He just hoped it all came off as planned, otherwise...., well, he didn't want to think of the other alternatives. He just hoped it did.

*

Neither Bo nor Jodi had slept much the night before, though Bo had eventually dozed off into a restless slumber for an hour or so.

He awoke to the incessant ringing of the alarm clock that he'd set to go off at 7.30a.m. Quickly splashing some cold water on his face, he went into the bedroom to find Jodi still sound asleep. He shook her vigorously by the shoulders.

She opened her eyes with a start.

"Jodi, wake up, it's time to go," he urged.

She got out of bed and looked at her watch, then bathed her face with water.

Bo, meanwhile, packed Rick's computer into his backpack and waited for her by the door. After days on end being cooped up inside the cottage, he was impatient to get going.

"Wait here till I get the car started Bo," she said, grabbing her belongings, such as they were. "When I say so, jump in and lay on the back seat. I don't want old nosey parker over the way to see you."

Bo nodded in agreement.

Jodi took one last look around the cottage, and slipped outside. A few seconds later the old Honda burbled into life and she motioned to Bo to come out.

Bo shut the front door and scampered towards the waiting car. As he did so, he noticed movement to his left out of the corner of his eye. Before he knew what was happening he was confronted by Cindy.

"Well, well, well! And who are you, young man?" she asked.

Bo stood there, his eyes locked firmly on Cindy's, wondering what to do next.

Cindy looked at him, first with genuine curiosity, then, her eyes narrowed with suspicion.

Bo could almost hear her thoughts. She knew he wasn't Jodi's boyfriend. Rick was much taller and looked completely different to him. There was no way he was going to blag his way out of this one.

Bo was lost for words, not knowing what to do. He cast a glance at Jodi who was sitting in the car, her face as white as a sheet, mouth open in abject horror.

It was then that a look of startled recognition crossed Cindy's face. Suddenly she wasn't the nosey neighbour from hell anymore. She was a frightened, terrified little woman and she started to back slowly away from him, as she realised the man before her was the same guy she'd seen on TV; the murderer!

"Oh my god, it's, it's you. You're that - that Boetto guy!" she stammered.

Before he could react, she was gone, running up the drive and screaming at the top of her voice for help.

Bo's mind went into hyper-drive. It would only be a matter of minutes before she alerted the police. He looked across at Jodi, who was just sitting in the car, totally speechless with her head held in her hands.

All the careful subterfuge and planning had come to nothing. They'd been rumbled!

Bo yanked the door of the car open, jumped in the back seat and screamed at her to get going.

But Jodi just sat there. Her eyes were glazed over, as if she were in a trance.

"Jodi, come on, move it!" Bo yelled.

But Jodi didn't budge.

"It's no good Bo. We'll never get away now. She'll send the Police after us. This old car will never outrun them, and anyhow, what's the point? There's nowhere to run to."

"Just drive for Christ's sake. C'mon! Rick and the others will be here in under an hour!" he urged.

At that moment, a big 4x4 pulled into the driveway and skidded to an abrupt halt, effectively blocking the exit. As Bo watched in horror, Cindy jumped out and locked the door, running away like a scared rabbit as soon as her feet touched the ground. With the exit blocked there was no other way to drive out onto the road. Bo assumed she had already phoned the police and taken it upon herself to make it impossible for the two of them to get away.

But Bo wasn't giving up that easily. He had an idea.

"Jodi, does that quad bike in the shed, out back, work?" he asked.

Jodi didn't answer; she was still in a state of shock.

He reached across and shook her by the shoulder.

"Does the quad bike run?" he screamed.

She just nodded, absently.

Her father used it for fun during the summer months. She'd gone pillion with him a few times, through the woods and across shallow streams. She apathetically reminisced about those happy days when she didn't have a care in the world, when she wasn't party to heinous crimes against the state, when she...... But that was all gone now, forever. Cindy would have phoned her parents and delivered the damning news to them by this time. Their daughter was an accomplice to murder, a liar, and facing years in jail. It was hopeless. She was sure she could hear the telephone ringing inside the cottage. That would be her parents, she thought, frantically trying to contact her.

Bo, however, had different ideas. He and Jodi were getting the hell out of here, with, or without the car. He got out and rushed round the side of the cottage. Reaching the shed, he yanked the door almost off its hinges and tore the protective cover off the quad bike. Grabbing the handlebars with both hands he quickly pulled it forward and out rolled it outside onto the grassy area. He looked it over. It was a big sucker; powered by a Rotax 350cc, single cylinder engine and by the looks of it, had been well cared for. The keys, he knew, were hanging up above the fireplace in the lounge. Without another thought, he ran back to the cabin and slammed his boot into the back door, smashing it open.

Seconds later, he was back outside, keys in hand. He clicked the key into the ignition and turned it. The battery was weak but the engine turned over.

After a few turns however, the battery started to fade.

"Come on you bastard, fire!" he cursed.

On the second attempt the engine spluttered and began to kick into life but the firing sequence was intermittent; not enough to make it run. Bo determinedly continued to hold the key down as black smoke belched out of the exhaust. He knew this was a sign the engine was flooding.

Thinking back to when he rode bikes with Rick's uncle, he remembered that, to get a flooded engine to fire, you had to hold the throttle wide open while turning it over. He yanked the throttle full back and turned the key once more. The engine spluttered and backfired. Then, to Bo's delight, it burst into life with a resounding roar.

Yes!

Wasting no time, he jumped aboard, pulled in the clutch and slammed the gear lever downwards. Feathering the clutch lever and grabbing a fistful of throttle, he lurched forward as the powerful motor transferred its drive to the rear wheels. With grass and dirt spewing from the knobbly tyres, the bike shot forward.

He tore round the side of the cottage and stopped in front of the porch to find Jodi out of the car and sitting on the front porch step, her head in her lap.

"Jodi, come on, we can make it out the back way, and through the forest!" he yelled, blipping the throttle of the bike to keep it running.

Jodi just looked at him through bloodshot eyes.

"What's the point; everyone knows what I've done now," she bleated, apathetically.

At that moment the wailing siren of a police car on the main road, not more than a few hundred yards away, pierced the air.

Bo looked up in fear and desperation. They had to get away now or it'd be too late.

"Jodi, please! Get on!" he screamed at the top of his voice.

But Jodi just looked up at him, unmoving, lost in a deep apathy of blame, shame, and regret. She just shook her head sideways as tears began to drip down her cheeks.

"If you don't get on I'll leave you here," he threatened.

She still wouldn't budge.

Bo grabbed the throttle and spun the quad around in a U turn, spewing up a cloud of snow and gravel as he did so.

The wail of the police car's siren grew ever nearer.

"For Christ's sake, Jodi - please!" Bo urged.

Still she sat there, just looking at him through misty eyes. The poor girl was a pitiful sight, bereft of hope. He felt a pang of pity for her, but there was no way he was going to just sit here and give up, not yet.

"That's it!" screamed Bo. He jumped off the bike and grabbed her by both shoulders. Then with a mighty heave, he lifted her off the ground and over his right shoulder.

Jodi screamed and beat on his back, but Bo took no notice. He thumped her down on the seat of the quad and jumped on the front. Before she could wriggle off, he slammed it into first gear and accelerated off towards the forest at full throttle.

As they careered down through the coarse undergrowth and towards the back woods, Bo looked over his shoulder and caught a glimpse of Cindy crouching down next to the 4x4. She was waving her left hand behind her, directing two cops her way.

Unable to get in past the truck Cindy had placed there, two burly armed officers ran past her towards the cottage, guns raised at the ready. Bo saw the first one aim directly at him. Seconds later, two bullets zinged past his head, one of them so close he heard it hiss past and thunk into a tree to his left. Two more shots rang out across the clearing, narrowly missing the front and back tyres. In a blind panic he wrenched the throttle back and gunned the bike towards the rapidly approaching forest. Shots rang out once more as the first of the dense conifers whizzed past either side of him.

The change from bright daylight to the relative darkness of the forest made Bo reactively shut off the throttle, lest he crash headlong into a tree. After a few moments however, his eyes adjusted to the dim light and he opened her up again.

Perched precariously on the back seat of the quad bike Jodi clung on for dear life as Bo careered through the woods at breakneck speed. She was afraid to open her eyes, clinging around his waist as they bumped up and down, narrowly missing snow laden trees and fallen boughs littering the way. But the quad was the perfect vehicle for this kind of terrain. Its wide knobbly tyres bit into the uneven ground beneath it, propelling the two of them along at over 30mph.

As luck would have it, Bo was no stranger to off road motorcycling. Rick's Uncle Tod, had taught him a great deal about it when he and Rick had gone to work for him, in England. Though he'd never ridden a motorcycle in his life before that time, he had taken to it like a fish to water and Quads were not much different to motocross bikes. They just had an extra pair of wheels, which made them more stable over rough terrain. As he began to get used to the bike, he speeded up. Trees whooshed by like storm clouds as he traversed his way between the conifers and various obstacles along the way.

But Bo soon realised that in the total panic of getting away, he was now totally lost. He'd been thrashing through the woods in any old direction, just to get as far away from the cottage as he could, but now he realised that they had to head for the mine. He slowed down and shouted back over his shoulder to Jodi.

"Am I going the right way?"

All Jodi could manage in response was a weak, "yes."

After another ten minutes or so of playing chicken with tree trunks, they reached a clearing, and Bo stopped to get his bearings.

"Which way now?" he asked, looking at Jodi, over his shoulder again.

Jodi pointed North West.

With another twist of the throttle the bike shot forward with a neck wrenching leap and they were careering off into the thick forest again, he *hoped*, in the right direction.

This next part of the forest was more densely packed with trees than before. The ground was very uneven and the tree trunks thinner and more frequent. He had to slow down a little so as to avoid them.

Then, out of the corner of his eye, while still pounding along at about 20m.p.h, he spied movement off to the left. Something was running between the trees. For a moment he was distracted, but when he looked forward again, it was too late. A tree seemed to rear up out of nowhere, directly in front of him. There wasn't enough time to avoid it. He yanked the handlebars to the right. But the quad skidded and slammed sideways into the base of the trunk. Bo was thrown clear over the front of the handlebars by the sudden impact. He sailed through the air and landed on his back, skidding along the forest floor for a further few metres till he came to an abrupt stop.

Jodi wasn't so lucky. Her left leg bore the full brunt of the impact as it hit.

Bo lay there for a second or so, looking up at the sky, which was just barely visible through the thick foliage. For a moment, it was deathly silent. Then he heard Jodi scream out in pain.

"My leg!"

Bo sat up and looked around. As he did so he saw a large Elk running off through the woods. He realised that must have been what distracted him.

Jodi cried out again.

"Bo, where are you? Help me!"

She was jammed between the tree and the quad bike and she was in terrible pain.

Bo was shaken but otherwise unharmed. He scuttled up off the pine covered ground and rushed over to her.

"It's okay Jodi, I'll get you off," he said.

Bending down, he lifted the back wheels of the quad away from the tree trunk, with Jodi still on it. As he did so she screamed out in agony. She was free but she was in a bad way, and lay back on the seat of the bike, groaning.

Bo leaned over her and touched the injured leg. As he did so she yelped.

"Don't touch it. I think it's broken," she groaned.

"Can you move your foot?" Bo asked.

She could, but only a fraction, and when she did it hurt like hell.

Managing to slide her off the seat, he laid her gently on the ground next to the bike.

"Lay here for a second, Jodi," he said.

He quickly checked the bike over. There was very little damage. It would still run.

He went back to tending to Jodi.

"Do you think you can make it on the back of the bike to the mine, Jodi?"

She reached down and felt her leg. It was numb from the waist down.

"I can't feel anything, Bo. I think it's broken. There's no way I'll be able to get back on that thing."

With those words, Bo was back in the woods surrounding HAARP. Images of Miller, lying on the floor, crying with pain flashed through his mind. The thought of it was too much. He began to panic. If Jodi couldn't even sit on the back of the bike, how were they going to make it?

Somewhere in the distance, he heard the wail of a police car siren, then, above the trees, the thrumming of what sounded to him like helicopter blades.

Chapter 25

The Osprey touched down with a shuddering jolt in the clearing. Strong cross winds forced Ross to slam it down on the ground hard.

Rick peered out of the window for any sign of Jodi and Bo, but he saw no one.

Paul opened the door and jumped down onto the snow covered ground. Rick followed. They searched as far as the eye could see, but there was no sign of life anywhere. The place was totally deserted, as he'd predicted it would be, except that Jodi and Bo should have been here to meet them.

It was really cold outside and the wind chill factor made it even worse, so they got back inside the plane and shut the door.

They waited.

Five minutes later there was still no sign of them.

"I don't like the look of this Paul," Rick said, still peering ruefully out of the porthole.

Paul remained calm.

"Patience Rick, they'll be here," he said.

Another five minutes went by.
Rick checked his watch again.
Something's wrong!
Jodi knew the location of this place; she'd been here several times in the past.
So where the hell are they?
Another ten minutes laboured by.......Fifteen minutes.
There was *still* no sign of them.
Then it all happened at once!
In the distance they heard the muted revving of what sounded like a four stroke motorcycle engine. It seemed to be coming from the forest across the clearing.
Farther in the distance came the ominous wail of a police siren.
"Holy shit!" screamed Rick. "There they are!"
A quad bike came tearing out of the woods. Its powerful motor screaming at full revs as it shot across the clearing and headed straight for the plane. Plumes of fine snow trailed behind it, like the dust from a dozen stampeding buffaloes.
Rick could see Bo, head down across the tank, his arms stretched out on the handlebars. Jodi was on the back, hanging on for dear life behind him. They broadsided to a halt beside the plane, throwing up a swirl of snow and dust.
Paul opened the door and jumped down, followed by Rick and Chelsea.

"We've got to get out of here now!" Bo shouted, pulling the key out of the ignition, his face flushed with fear.

Jodi was still in shock, she just fell off the back of the bike, straight into Rick's arms, her face as white as a sheet. Her leg was useless and she had to be lifted off the bike.

"What the heck happened?" Rick asked.

"The cops are on to us. Come on, get going! We're only about a mile ahead of them," Bo exclaimed.

Without the need of further explanation, they helped the two exhausted escapees into the plane, as Ross began a hasty pre-flight check and prepared to take off.

Rick, aided by Chelsea, tended to Jodi's injured leg.

There was no time for introductions. Bo explained what had occurred, as the others crowded round to hear. His words came in spurts, as he tried to get his breath back.

"The neighbour across the lake ... that chick Cindy ... she must have seen me and recognised me ... she called the police ...shit!"

He was really distraught.

"We got away on the quad; through the woods but....... I think they followed us."

The fuselage began to shudder and vibrate as the plane's tilt-props wrenched it off the ground and into the air at full throttle. Ross piloted the Osprey vertically upwards, banking left into the wind after it had reached three hundred feet.

Meanwhile, after a cursory check of Jodi's injured leg, Chelsea gave her the thumbs up. Luckily, she'd avoided breaking it but it was badly bruised and she wouldn't be walking for a few days.

In the cockpit, Ross peered out of the starboard window and noticed flashing blue lights on the ground - two police cars were turning into the entrance of the clearing beneath them.

Ross looked over to Sam, sitting in the co-pilot's seat next to him. "Phew! That was a close call," he exclaimed.

Jodi overheard him and despite her injury, managed a glimpse out of one of the cabin windows.

"I'm done for now," she said. "My parents are going to find out about all this. I'm done for. They'll probably be arrested too!"

Rick held on to her, saying nothing. What *could* he say? She was probably right!

The plane reached two thousand feet, heading due west and still climbing.

Sam shouted back through the cockpit partition.

"We've got company guys. There's a chopper heading right for us at five-o'clock, to port!"

Paul and the others immediately peered out of the port windows.

It was a helicopter alright, and it was heading directly towards them. It didn't take much imagination to figure out who it belonged to. As it got nearer, it turned to follow and displayed its signage – "POLICE."

Paul called out towards the cockpit.

"Put the pedal to the metal guys; time to cover up!"

The turbo prop engines screamed in unison as Ross pushed the thrust levers fully forward, and the plane soared upwards suddenly, ascending at an alarming rate.

Rick's mind was racing, as he too spied the pursuing helicopter in the distance with its flashing blue lights.

"What we gonna do?" he asked, turning to Paul.

"Improvise, mate," answered Paul. "This little baby's got a few modifications I haven't told you about yet." He was smiling at Rick and Bo with a sly look in his eye as he spoke.

"Hold on to yer horses, cowboys!" Paul whooped.

He ran along the cabin and had a few words with Ross, then returned.

Rick, Bo and Jodi looked around them.

All the others sported the same wry smirk, as if they knew exactly what Paul meant.

In the distance, the police helicopter fell back, unable to match the speed of the Osprey. Soon, it was just a speck far below them.

Rick peered through the cockpit window. Up ahead, a storm was brewing up over the mountains. The dark grey clouds seemed to rise interminably into the sky as the Osprey headed directly towards them.

Paul sat down next to Bo and shook his hand.

"Nice to meet you mate. Rick's told me a lot about you."

Bo couldn't help but notice the vice like grip of this man's hand around his.

"Same here Paul. I remember Rick's uncle talking about you. You're just like I imagined."

Paul grinned and turned his attention to Jodi.

"Pleased to meet you too Jodi. Well done for hanging on the back of that quad bike - no mean feat from what I could see, especially the way this guy rides."

Jodi offered her hand and managed a weak smile but she was in no mood for jest. The last few hours had been even worse than the past few days.

Paul began to outline his plan.

"Okay, listen up you lot. The police know we've got you two now. That means they'll send a posse after us, in short order. Fortunately, we filed a false flight plan to Fort Severn on Hudson Bay, just in case something like this happened. That means they'll initially focus their attention in that direction. It should put them off the scent long enough for us to reach Gakona."

Bo immediately interrupted him.

"No offence Paul but they'll pick this plane up on radar. We'll never evade that. Flight plan or no flight plan, they can see us right now. Believe me, I know."

"Not this plane, mate. It's got a radar cloaking device, courtesy of Leigh and Brook here."

He pointed to the two eager faced members of the team sitting alongside him.

Brook and Leigh raised their hands to him, in greeting.

Paul continued.

"That's what I meant when I told Ross and Sam to "cover up". We kinda borrowed the technology from the RAF, in a roundabout sort of way. I've got a few friends in the SAS who helped out with the acquisition. Right now we're invisible to radar and we're going to hide out above that storm ahead of us for most of the way. Ross informs me that it stretches pretty much right across the Rockies, so we'll be out of physical sight too."

Bo was impressed. Rick's description of Paul didn't do him justice. There was obviously a lot more to this guy than just a karate master.

Soon they were enveloped in thick grey cloud. The plane bucked and weaved as the turbulence of the storm caused the cabin to shudder. But a few minutes later the turbulence abated, as it gained altitude and got above the clouds. Bright sunlight beamed in through the cabin windows.

Paul informed them it would take another four hours to reach their destination. He explained they would head for Carmacks, a small town just north of Whitehorse, where they would refuel. He then revealed that, two days ago, he had despatched a specially converted gas tanker from the Ranch, disguised as a cattle truck, to a predetermined site in a remote area just outside Carmacks. They would refuel there and stay until it got dark, before heading on to Gakona later tonight.

Throughout all the excitement of the last hour or so Bo and Jodi hadn't yet been introduced to the rest of the team. Bo was surprised, just as Rick had been, at the number of females present.

He was even more surprised to learn that he would be jumping out of the plane, attached to the underside of one of the girls. The petite blonde, called Chelsea, sitting next to him, would be gliding the two of them in, using nothing more than a glorified bat suit apparently! Rick was to jump attached to Noogie.

These two girls were chosen because of their light weight, which would offset the additional dead weight of their passengers. The stealth suits they were using were slightly heavier and wider in girth than the single fliers, to allow for greater air resistance.

"What about me?" Jodi asked.

"You stay on the plane with Sam," replied Paul. "She could use a bit of company when we're all gone."

Jodi could see the logic in it. She'd be no use to them anyway. Besides, there was no way she'd jump out of a plane at night, busted leg or no busted leg. She clung on to Rick, tired - injured, and afraid.

Once Bo understood the concept of what he was being asked to do he was pretty put out about it all. He'd never jumped out of a plane in his life, let alone strapped to someone else, and to make it even worse, they weren't even using parachutes!

Chelsea thrust a stealth suit in his face and after a bit of coaxing he reluctantly attempted to slip into it.

The suit was a one piece garment, similar looking to what a scuba diver would wear, but it was made of a silky smooth material, like mohair. Once it was on he began to sweat, it was so warm.

"It'll be fifty below freezing when we jump at that height," Chelsea informed him. "You'll be glad you've got that on, believe me."

......And at that very moment, several thousand miles to the East, inside a small concrete building on the Northernmost tip of the British Isles, a young man sat down at his desk......

Chapter 26

United States Atomic Energy Detection System (USAED.) Shetland Isles station, Scotland

Brandon Oakes-Massar, seismic instruments calibration technician, leaned back in his chair and sighed with contentment. He was engrossed in his latest book "Genetic Meltdown" a blockbuster novel about global conspiracies; his favourite pet subject.

With both feet planted firmly on the table in front of him and a steaming mug of coffee waiting patiently to be consumed on the desk, he settled down for an uneventful shift.

This is the life, he thought to himself. What a doddle this posting is - good books, peace and quiet; lovely!

The Shetland Isles seismic monitoring station was one of many such remote location networks around the globe, set up the by the United States National Data Centre (USNDC), with the cooperation of the British government to report events of interest in monitoring the Comprehensive-Nuclear-Test-Ban-Treaty (CTBT).

It had the ability to acquire, process and archive continuous seismic and hydro-acoustic data, collected by sensors that are part of the United States Atomic Energy Detection System (USAEDS), and the International Monitoring System (IMS).

Linked to the National Data Centre (NDC), in the U.S., it was part of the eyes and ears of a global watchdog network that could detect clandestine usage of nuclear tests and seismic abnormalities, under land or sea.

There wasn't much to do here on this remote island, except count sheep on the way down to the nearest tavern, which was four miles away. But Brandon didn't mind. He kept the equipment in tune and reported his findings to his superior on a daily basis, which took him all of an hour if he dragged it out. The rest of the time he quite happily whiled away the hours, reading his abundant library of spy and conspiracy novels.

Lifting the coffee to his lips, he turned the page for the next chapter, when out of the blue, a loud beeper went off, jolting him out of his reverie. Surprised by the sudden burst of noise, he sat bolt upright, knocking the scalding beverage everywhere in the process. He yelped with pain as the coffee spilled over his lap and began creeping across the console desk.

As he frantically tried to clean up the mess, to stop it dripping off the edge of the desk onto the floor, he looked up at the source of the unwelcome interruption.

"What the.... This doesn't make sense!" he muttered under his breath.

Forgetting the spilt coffee for a moment, he wheeled his chair closer to get a better look. Tapping the digital gauge under the red beeping light, a deep frown creased his brow.

"This can't be right."

The readout was registering a radioactive fluctuation in the Northeast Atlantic Basin, approximately 200 miles off the Eastern coast of North America. He leaned over to the desk intercom and spoke into it.

"Sir, you better come in here and take a look at this."

Station Commander Mike Henn, strode into the room and stood by his junior's side.

"What's up son?"

Brandon pointed to the flashing light.

"See that, sir. Unless I'm very mistaken, it's registering a nuclear device arming itself, and it's come out of nowhere!"

Henn ran his finger over the readout.

"That's impossible," he argued.

Sure enough though, the digital readout was indicating a fissionable arming device, coming on line.

"I'd better report this to NDC myself," said Henn. He knew the data would have been relayed automatically to the National Data Centre in the

States, but this was something extraordinary and it had him spooked. As he reached for the phone, there was another beep, this time indicating similar activity further south but still off the coast of North America. A few seconds later there was *another* beep, then two more, this time in the Pacific Ocean off the coast of Portland, Oregon.

The two men stared dumbfounded at the array of digital readouts beeping and flashing in front of them. There were twelve now. They lit up the console like Christmas decorations.

"What the hell's going on sir?" Brandon asked.

Commander Henn had a reputation amongst his juniors as being unshakeable, not prone to fits of hysteria, nor getting rattled under any circumstances. But on this occasion the young engineer detected a hint of panic in his boss's usually monotone dialogue.

"I have no idea son, but it's not good, whatever it is. Check those outputs again and run a standard system's diagnosis for faults," he ordered.

Henn speed dialled the emergency number. As he gripped the receiver, he noticed his hand was trembling.

Mirrors In The Sky

Chapter 27

Yukon Territory, North Western Canada

Travelling at its top speed of 550 km per hour, the Osprey made it to Carmacks just as the sun was dropping below the horizon. Their exact destination would be a few miles north of the town itself.

Sam spotted the fuel truck in the distance. It was almost invisible in the fast dimming light but her sharp eyes picked it out easily amongst the background of scrubland as Ross prepared for the final descent.

Two of Paul's men waved up at them as they neared the ground, their hair and clothes billowing in the wake of the twin propellers. As soon as the plane was on the ground, they lost no time in quickly and efficiently re-fuelling it. To ensure total secrecy, dark grey tarpaulins were slung over the fuselage and the fuel truck.

Everyone alighted and stretched their legs, enjoying a brief respite from the long flight. Here they would grab a bite to eat and prepare for the final leg of their journey. The next time their feet hit solid ground there'd be no time for relaxing.

The crepuscular light added its own peculiar resonance to the surroundings. All around them stretched hundreds of miles of wasteland. To the North was the Arctic Circle. To the South was the small town of Carmacks, its lights flickering faintly in the distance. To the South West lay the Canadian / Alaskan border and a few hundred miles further on from that, Gakona and HAARP.

As the last glimmers of fading sunlight flickered away, the sky began to twinkle with stars. One at a time they appeared, till the whole heavens were ablaze with a million pinpricks of shimmering dots set into a blanket of jet black. Then, in the far distance, over the north-west horizon, a pulsating band of multi coloured lights began to grow in the sky. Everyone stopped what they were doing and looked up at the spectacular display, watching in awe, as it weaved across the heavens till half the sky was brightly lit.

"That's the Northern Lights, right Bo?" Chelsea asked.

"Yeah, kind of, Chels," Bo replied. But he knew what was really causing it. His eyes became moist as he recalled visions of Miller. He turned away, so as not to show Chelsea the grief he was suppressing.

After a makeshift meal of sardines and potato salad, served up by the two men who'd guided them in, they re-boarded the Osprey. At 11.30p.m. on the dot, they took off again and headed South West. As the plane reached its cruising height of 20,000 feet, Paul instructed them to prepare for the jump.

Chelsea strapped herself into her stealth suit and explained to Bo how he should position himself beneath her, secured by only a flimsy harness, connected to her shoulders and midriff.

Noogie did the same with Rick as Jodi looked on.

Bo reluctantly complied, while Rick tried to calm him down, assuring him that it would all go fine.

"I've practiced a dozen jumps this way with Noogie and they all went without a hitch," he said.

But despite Rick's words of reassurance, Bo was shaking with trepidation as he peered out of the window into the black void below.

"Out of the frying pan, into the fire!" he joked. But Rick could see cold sweat on his forehead and palms.

"It's okay Bo, I wont let go of ya," Chelsea said with a wink and a grin.

A few minutes later Ross appeared from the cockpit and informed them that they were approaching the jump zone.

Sam was now piloting the plane, solo.

Ross quickly donned his stealth suit and sat down next to Bo.

Jodi held on to Rick.

Rick just held her firmly in his arms and gave her a cuddle. Then he helped her limp along the cabin and sat her in the co-pilot's seat next to Sam.

"Look after my gal, Sam," he said.

"No problem, Rick. Have fun!" Sam replied.

Rick gave Jodi one last hug and then he was gone.

The cabin lights went out, replaced by two dim lantern lights, either side of the exit door. A red light shone brightly above it.

Without further ado, Paul slid the cabin door open and a blast of ice cold air surged into the cabin.

The shock of the blast made Bo freeze, and not just from the icy temperature either.

Chelsea, who was directly behind him, began to push him towards the open door but he wouldn't budge. Bo dug his heels in as she urged him on. Harnessed together, there was no way she could move without his cooperation.

Sensing the tension in Bo's eyes, Paul stood in front of him and put two fingers up in front of his face.

"Look at me Bo," he gestured. "You can do it. Just go with the flow. Once you're airborne, Chelsea will do all the work. Just let yourself go."

With those parting words, the red light turned green and Paul launched himself out through the door, followed immediately by Michelle.

Chelsea began pushing Bo further towards the door. They were next in line to jump. The biting cold blast of air streaming in caused him to lock up once more, but this time Brook and Ross took control of the situation. With a mighty shove, they pushed the two of them unceremoniously out the door.

Seconds later, Bo was enveloped in darkness and biting cold wind. His legs and arms flailed around wildly, as he realised there was nothing beneath him anymore.

Chelsea spoke through the intercom to him.

"Relax Bo, we're doing fine," she said, placing her hands over the side of his earphones to reassure him that she was indeed still there.

They were dropping like a stone at almost two hundred feet per minute.

Bo finally regained his composure and spoke into the mike.

"H-how do you know where we're g-going?" he stammered loudly.

"No need to shout Bo, I can hear you no problem," Chels replied. "Our target is programmed into the homing device on my wrist. We'll make it alright. Just don't wriggle around so much and we'll do fine."

Above them, Noogie and Rick had also jumped, immediately followed by the rest of the team.

As soon as they were all gone, Sam banked sharply to port and accelerated away. She explained to Jodi that from now and until they had accomplished their mission, there would be no radio contact with any of them. They were on their own.

Jodi peered out of the cockpit window. It was pitch black outside. She could see nothing at all.

"Where to now?" Jodi asked.

"As far away from here as possible," Sam replied. "We need to be well clear when Bo lights up that place down there. The electromagnetic pulse from the explosion he's about to create could knock out this plane's navigational and flight controls, even if we're as much as 50 kilometres away. I'm going to set down near the foothills of the Northern Mountains. We can have a chat about boys and shopping maybe."

Jodi chuckled to herself.

"That'd be nice. Something normal for a change," she said.

At 10,000 feet, Chelsea told Bo to brace as she opened the wings of their stealth suit. As she did so the wind speed around them lessened as they began to glide rather than freefall to the invisible ground, spread out somewhere in the darkness below them.

Simultaneously, the others deployed their flaps, and with the aid of their night vision goggles were soon flying side by side as they glided downwards, silently and unobserved through the night sky.

The external material of the stealth suits had been impregnated with a photo sensitive dye that was clearly visible at night, through the goggles that each of them wore. Because the suits were so good at thermally insulating the wearer, they gave off no heat externally and therefore heat sensor detection technology wouldn't work. Similar in effect to infra red, the goggles picked up the dye and showed the suits up as a bluish white against the pitch black surroundings.

The short wave radios they were using to communicate to each other had a range of only a few hundred feet. This was to ensure that their transmissions weren't picked up by any receiver on the ground.

Paul's voice crackled in their earphones.

"Height 2,000 feet. I've got visual - wind direction North Easterly. Glide round and land against it."

Each member of the team acknowledged.

Down below, the lights of HAARP became visible. They were just pinpricks, but clearly discernable amidst the surrounding darkness of the thick woods of conifers and spruce trees.

Paul's voice, crackled on the intercom again.

"Okay, here we go. Bank left and follow me in," he directed.

Chelsea manoeuvred her and Bo into formation, directly behind Paul and Michelle, who were now leading the intrepid winged invaders down towards their landing spot.

The ghostly silhouettes of Paul and Michelle dipped downwards, followed by the others

The outline of the HAARP administration building was clearly visible below them now, its lights shining bright in contrast to the wilderness surrounding it. A few hundred metres from this stood the vast expanse of the phased array antennae poles, and further on, the river glinted in the starlight like a silver serpent, as it wound its way through the Copper Valley.

Paul led them down at a steady rate of descent till they were just above the tree tops. Suddenly he pulled up and dropped. Michelle followed, with Chelsea and Bo directly behind her.

By extreme skill, and not a little luck, Chelsea avoided catching the outstretched wings on any branches as they neared the ground. Then, with a slight jolt, they landed on the snow covered ground. Bo fell forward and got a face full of the stuff as Chelsea landed on his back with a thump. She then immediately unshackled the straps securing the two of them together and quickly jumped up, pulling him up off the ground as she did so.

Behind them, muffled thuds signified the others were landing. Surrounded by the trees on all sides, it became pitch black. Bo felt something tug at his sleeve in the darkness.

"Pull down your night vision goggles," Chelsea whispered.

He reached up over his head and secured the goggles over his eyes.

Chelsea reached across and turned them on for him.

"Adjust the sensitivity knob till you get a visual on me," she whispered, again.

Bo twiddled the sensitivity control back and forth and gave her the thumbs up.

The other fliers converged in the small clearing. Rick and Noogie appeared. They were followed by

Ross, Brook, then Leigh, Ryan, and finally Paul and Michelle.

When everyone was accounted for, Paul outlined the plan of attack one more time.

"Bo, you're the only one who hasn't drilled this procedure. The rest of you should know it in your sleep but just to be sure, I'll go over it again."

They were to split into three teams. Paul, Michelle, Ryan and Ross would be team one. Brook and Leigh, team two. Rick and Bo, flanked by Noogie and Chelsea, would be team three.

Paul's team would take care of the perimeter guards. Team two, Brook and Leigh, would head for the power station and set up the polarity reversal equipment, while team three were to make it up to the control room, where Bo would do his stuff with the controls for the transmitters.

Paul's team would then mop up any stray personnel in the grounds and then move on to the administrative buildings, to locate Bo's and Millers' parents......, if they were here!

Somewhere nearby, across the expanse of trees, the electrostatic hum of the phased array transmitters hummed as they projected billions of watts of raw energy into the night sky. Above them, intermittent waves of multi coloured light coursed through the heavens, a visual manifestation of the intense electrical current being pulsed into the ionosphere.

"They're transmitting at full power," Bo explained. "God knows what damage is being caused in some part of the world right now."

The others all looked up to the sky, then back at Bo.

"Those antennae are causing that?" asked Brook.

"Yeah, but not for much longer, I hope," Bo replied.

"Okay guys, enough talking. Let's get to work," Paul ordered.

The three teams split up and headed off in their pre-determined directions.

Paul, Michelle, Ryan and Ross made off in the direction of the front entrance gate. Silently approaching the back of the sentry hut, they spied two guards inside.

"We'll take those two last," Paul said. "First, we need to locate the walkers. We'll split into two teams. Ross and Ryan, you go to the right and make your way round the boundary fences. We'll do the same, the other way. Take out any guards you come across, but remember no noise, okay? With any luck we'll meet back here in about twenty minutes or so."

They set off in different directions and were soon swallowed up in the darkness of the woods.

There were eight perimeter guards in total. All were found patrolling around the inside of the electrified laser fences - easy pickings as far as the four karate experts were concerned. Within fifteen minutes they were all expertly and silently brought down, then securely bound and gagged.

After scouring the entire perimeter, they met up again near the sentry hut. Paul and Michelle took up positions to the left of the hut door. Ryan and Ross kept to the right.

Paul pointed at the door and Michelle walked brazenly up to it then knocked loudly.

One of the guards opened the door.

"Hi there!" Michelle said, with a cheery wave.

The man did a double take.

"Who the hell are you?"

He never got the chance to find out. A split second later, he was flying backwards through the air from the force of a mai-geri front kick, courtesy of the pretty woman standing on the doorstep.

Ross and Paul shot in and grabbed the second man before he had time to realise what was happening. Before he could get his gun out of its holster, a swift jab in the solar plexus from Paul, followed by an enpi elbow strike to his upper back, sent him crashing to the floor in a crumpled heap.

"Is that *all* of 'em?" asked Ross.

"We *hope* that's all of them," Paul replied, with a smirk. "Let's get these two turkeys trussed up and then check out the main building. They're bound to have someone guarding Bo's and Millers' parents......, like I said - *if* they're here, that is."

Ross and Ryan securely bound and gagged the two guards using duct tape and rope. They then shoved them in the corner of the hut, behind the desk.

When they were satisfied the two guards would not pose any further problems, all four headed off towards the main building.

But they were not alone, for a little way behind them, two figures, darting in and out amongst the shadows, followed them up the driveway......

......And at that very moment, several thousand miles away, a very important and very worried man cursed in disbelief......

Chapter 28

Vienna, Austria

Sacre-bleu! How could this be?
Gaston Bouillard, Director General of the International Atomic Energy Agency (IAEA), sat ashen faced and bewildered as he read the report on his desk.

"Twelve armed atomic devices, strategically placed either side of the North American Continent, no more than 200 miles from the coastline!" he exclaimed, reading aloud from the page.

Only an hour earlier he had been informed of the U.S. President's decision to upgrade the national security level to DEFCON 2, the second highest level of alertness possible.

At that moment, his secretary buzzed him on the intercom.

"Sir, there is an urgent phone call for you. It's from a Mr Asimov. He says it's very important and will speak only to you."

Bouillard looked at the intercom on his desk in a daze.

Asimov?

"Not now Petra, no more calls, unless they are from category one persons."

Category one meant heads of state or members of the U.S. Chief's of staffs, and no one else.

"Yes sir, of course."

Bouillard went back to the report.

A few seconds later the intercom buzzed again.

"Sir, I'm so sorry but this Mr Asimov is very insistent. He says he *must* speak to you regarding a matter of grave urgency. Something about submerged nuclear devices. I don't really know what he's talking about?"

Bouillard's heart skipped a beat.

"The what! Put him through immediately and trace the caller's location!" he demanded, picking up the phone.

The voice coming out of the receiver was faint; British by the sound of it, but with a very faint trace of an accent that he couldn't quite place.

"Mr Bouillard. My name is Yegor Asimov," the caller began. "You don't know me, but I know of you. I have some urgent and critical information for you, regarding the nuclear devices that have been discovered in the oceans off the North American coastlines."

A moment of silence ensued as the caller's words sunk in.

A terrorist?

The director was renowned as a cool headed character. His position as figurehead of the most senior watchdog and monitoring agency, regarding all things nuclear, demanded he be so. Even so, he was rattled. Nothing on this scale had ever happened before. His anxiety grew, as he tried to formulate in his mind what he would say next.

"Tell me, Mr Asimov, what do you know of such things?" he enquired, trying to maintain a calm resolve.

"I know a great deal, sir. I was the person who oversaw their placement over forty years ago," explained the caller.

"What do you mean? Who are you, and what are these devices?"

The voice continued its monotone dialogue.

"My real name is Boris Slatovski, former naval captain of the nuclear submarine, Kosmolov, which sank with all hands bar one, in the Northeast Atlantic basin on March 12th, 1965.

Bouillard quickly typed the details onto his web browser to verify the details as he went on to question this mysterious caller further.

"You say your name is Slatovski, an ex Soviet naval submariner captain, yet my records show me that you were killed when your submarine went down and that your body was never found."

"I'm sure it does, sir. However, I am living proof that your records are incorrect," the caller replied.

Bouillard was in a quandary. Could this be a hoax call? But if so, how could this person possibly know about these nuclear devices. At present, no one but those at the highest level were aware of the reason for the American's heightened security alert. All data from the USAED stations was heavily encrypted and no one outside a very small circle of people would be privy to their content. He decided to gamble and call this man's bluff.

"Mr Asimov, er Slatovski, I have no reason to not believe your words, but what is it I can do for you?"

"It is more like, what *I* can do for you comrade."

"And that is?"

"Assist you to deactivate those devices, Mr Bouillard. Tell me, have you ever heard of the term "Psi-generator?"

Bouillard shuddered. He had indeed heard of such a device. It was a psychotronic weapon, supposedly developed by the Soviets during the cold war for use in mind control. More myth than anything else, it was supposedly a small mobile device, but no one had ever produced a working model outside of a laboratory. The nearest thing to it was the LIDA mind control machine that had also been developed by the Russians, back in the 50's.

Bouillard chose his next words carefully.

"Mr Asimov, if what you are saying is correct, how is it that you, an ex sub mariner, know so much about these devices?"

"That is a long story, comrade Director, and one which you do not have time to hear in full. Suffice to say, I do know a great deal about these devices and possibly how to deactivate them. What puzzles me most, however, is what armed them in the first place? It must be that somewhere around the world there is an Extra Low Frequency transmitter, pulsing out over 3.5 giga-watts of microwave energy in the 8Hz frequency range that has activated them. This, I would say, is the primary and critical factor to address before anything else."

Bouillard now knew this was definitely no hoax caller, but something wasn't right about what this man was saying. The dates were all wrong.

"Mr Asimov, or would you prefer to be called Mr Slatovski?" asked Bouillard.

"It matters little to me sir. I am one and the same," said the caller.

"Very well, but how can it be that these devices even existed in the mid 60's? I have never even heard of a prototype making it out of a lab, to this day, let alone fully fledged, mobile submersible units with remote activation potential, over forty years ago! This is impossible, surely?"

"There are many things that are not known by the western powers about Soviet scientific advances in the latter half of last century. They were far more advanced than anyone has ever been led to believe. Be that as it may, you must believe me when I tell you this; they did exist then, and that they currently threaten hundreds of millions of lives as we speak."

There was a short silence, as if the caller was deep in thought. Then he spoke again.

"I have spent more than four decades dreading this day would come. Now it is here, I have come to realise that I am the only one with the knowledge to do something about it. You must believe me, comrade Director. I am quite possibly the only hope you have of averting a major catastrophe of global proportions!"

The last words seemed to jump out of the earpiece at Bouillard. He suddenly realised he had to have this person here now!

"What is it? What do you fear will happen?"

There was another palpable silence on the line. Bouillard could almost hear the heavy breathing of the mysterious caller as he prepared to speak again.

"As I just mentioned, these devices have been armed by an intensely powerful ELF signal from a source unknown to me. Should they receive another similar signal, they will activate. The consequences will be devastating. And, there is something else you should know; they are not just psychotronic weapons, they are also nuclear bombs, with the explosive power of 30 megatons each. Do you understand the implications of what that could mean, comrade director?"

Bouillard could not speak for a moment. But he knew exactly what that meant. His shaking hands and the cold sweat dripping from his forehead were testimony to that fact.

"I would very much like to meet you in person Mr Asimov. Where exactly are you right now?"

"I am in West London, United Kingdom. Twickenham, to be precise," replied the Russian.

"Can you be ready to leave in thirty minutes?"

"I am ready now comrade. I have been ready for a very long time, I assure you."

"Very well. I will have a car despatched to your address, this instant. From there you will be taken to London Heathrow airport, where my private jet will be waiting to fly you to meet me in Washington. Are you ready to meet the President of the United States?"

"It would be interesting, to say the least," came the reply.

After taking Asimov's address and telephone number, Bouillard put him on hold and immediately contacted his office in London, to have his plane readied for takeoff. After that he put in a direct call to the British Foreign Secretary, who immediately despatched a high speed car and police motorcycle escort to Twickenham.

Twenty minutes after Bouillard put the phone down, the locals of Heath Road, in Twickenham didn't know what had hit them as several police motorcycles tore down the street, sirens wailing, and proceeded to close off either end of the road to oncoming traffic. Moments later, a black 7 series BMW screeched to a halt outside a little shop called "Yegor's Eatery", disgorging three burly men. One stood outside, watching the street, while the other two ran inside.

A few moments later they emerged, hurriedly escorting an old man and bundled him into the back seat as early morning passers-by gaped in awe at the spectacle. With that, the car sped off in the direction of Heathrow airport, flanked, front and rear by the wailing police motorcycles.

Less than an hour later, Boris Slatovski, a.k.a. Yegor Asimov, was peering out at the Irish coastline through the window of a private Jet, on his way to Washington.

Meanwhile, Director Bouillard had summoned his closest aides and made his way, by chauffeured limousine, to Vienna's International airport. During the flight he made contact with the U.S. President and outlined his plan of action.

At first the President had sounded sceptical. He'd asked Bouillard how one man could be responsible for such a thing, especially an ageing Russian immigrant living in England. Also, how was it that none of his intelligence networks had absolutely no prior information on these devices, laying off the coastlines of his country?

Bouillard himself, however, was in no doubt that Asimov was the genuine article. He reasoned that there was no way any ordinary man could have known about their detection by the USAED station in Northern Scotland, only hours ago. Very sophisticated equipment would be needed for this. All data feeds from these remote stations were totally secure. Also, the man was too well informed and technically savvy to be a hoaxer. Bouillard assured the President that he was certain this individual was on the level. Anyway, he reasoned, they didn't have many other options than to listen to what he had to say.

It was only when he had outlined the details of the brief conversation he'd had with Asimov regarding the nuclear explosive capability of these devices that the scepticism of the most powerful man in the world began to wane.

The plane carrying Asimov arrived in Washington thirty two minutes after Bouillard's had touched down in and the Frenchman was waiting to meet the old Russian as he alighted.

A few minutes later, they were sitting in a limousine, escorted front and back by a phalanx of siren wailing police motorcycles bound for the White House.

Chapter 29

HAARP

Rick and Bo, accompanied by Noogs and Chelsea, had already made it inside the administration building and up the stairs to the 4th floor without encountering anyone. They stopped outside the door of the control room where voices could be heard from within. There were people inside. Two men were talking and maybe a woman by the sound of it.

Bold as brass, Chelsea signalled to the others with three fingers. Then she knocked on the door.

The talking inside the room suddenly stopped.

They heard a chair being pulled back and a few seconds later, the door being unlocked.

Rick and Bo pressed themselves against the wall, either side of it and out of direct sight of anyone inside, while the two girls stood directly in front of the doorway.

The guy who opened the door couldn't have been more surprised than if he'd seen the Pope! Two extremely attractive young, blonde females, who he'd never seen before in his life, stood before him. He looked confused and yet secretly impressed at the same time.

"Hello handsome!" Chels said, with a cute smile.

He never got the opportunity to respond.

Noogies arm came up and with clinical precision, knocked him clean out with a chop to the neck. Without so much as a whimper, he flopped to the floor like a rag doll.

With the speed and agility of a startled gazelle, Chels jumped over the hapless figure and leapt at the other man, still sitting at the control panel and was on him before he had time to get out of his chair. With a deadly accurate roundhouse kick to the side of his head, he too, crashed to the floor, unconscious.

"There's another one; I heard a woman's voice too," Noogs warned, anxiously looking around her.

They darted into the adjoining room but found it empty. Looking around, they could see no other exits.

"I heard a woman's voice as well, I'm sure of it," insisted Noogs.

After another quick check, Chelsea decided that they must have been mistaken.

Bo and Rick had by now entered the room, stepping over the unconscious man in the doorway. They were looking around them in silenced awe.

"You two did this?" asked Rick, looking down at the two inert figures.

Chelsea just shrugged.

"We're going to take a look around the rest of the floor, to see if we can find anyone else," she said. "You've got the place to yourselves boys. Hurry up and get that storm brewing, Bo!"

"And tie these two goons up in case they come round," Noogie added.

With that, the two girls ran out the door and down the corridor.

Bo and Rick had the control room to themselves.

"Okay Rick, lets get to work," said Bo. "Noogie's right. You tie these guys up in case they wake up. I'm going to check the servers in the other room."

Rick nodded and dragged the inert body of the guy away from the control desk, into the middle room. Then he did the same with the other guy lying in the doorway. He sat them up with their backs against each other and tied their hands securely behind them.

Bo went into the adjoining room and opened the closet that contained the servers. He pulled the door towards him and was just about to enter when he sensed something inside. He jumped back, startled by a sudden movement and a muffled squeal. Someone was in there! The shock of it sent him reeling backwards in fright.

Then he heard a female voice.

"Who's there?" she said.

The hairs on the back of Bo's neck tingled. Something about that voice rattled him.

Whoever it was in there, her face was hidden by the shadows cast by the light in the room. All he could see was the lower half of her body. In the intense silence he could hear her breathing erratically.

He moved another two paces backwards.

"You can come out," ordered Bo. "I won't hurt you. Come out," he repeated.

He *felt*, rather than saw her stiffen involuntarily at the sound of his voice. He still couldn't see her face.

But *she* could see him.

"My god, it *is* you," she gasped, coming into the light.

Bo staggered backwards, totally stunned, for standing there in front of him was an apparition, a ghost, come back to haunt him.

"Miller! It, it can't, it can't be. You're, you're dead!" he exclaimed, hardly able to utter the words. Pictures of leaving her in the woods that fateful night and hearing the news of her death on the TV flooded back to him like a dam bursting inside his head. His legs began to go weak under him.

"No, it wasn't me, Bo. The body they found in the river - it was Coleen Jones. They killed her and made out it was me. They needed me to help them continue the ELF scans. But they had to silence you. So they made it look like *you* did it."

Tears began to stream from her eyes and were now running down her cheeks.

"They told me if I didn't cooperate, the same thing would happen to me, Bo. I had no choice."

Bo still couldn't quite come to terms with what was happening. He felt dizzy, like he'd woken up with a bad hangover. His legs were locked solid. He couldn't move. The shock of seeing Miller alive again, in the flesh and talking to him! It was too surreal. For almost a month, he'd carried on, knowing he'd never see her again, racked with guilt and grief and now here she was! Adrenaline coursed through his veins as he rushed to hold her in his arms. The feeling of having her back again was unbelievable. The smell of her hair, her soft cheeks pressed against his; he couldn't believe it.

Miller held him close to her, compulsively gripping her arms around him.

"They even kidnapped both our parents and imprisoned them in the basement. They're still down there, Bo. Clavell is insane! He said he'd kill them too, if I didn't do what he said!"

"So that's what happened. I knew it!" said Bo.

He recalled the news on the radio back in the cottage; of the plane crash and his parents' arrests.

"Don't worry Miller. We figured they were being held here. We'll get them out safely," he said.

At that moment, it was as if a huge burden had been lifted off him. A ton weight, consisting of guilt, loss and despair had suddenly dissolved into thin air.

"How did you get back in here?" she asked. Then, looking up over Bo's shoulder, Miller jumped back reactively, startled and afraid, for Rick was standing there in the doorway, with an expression of complete confusion on his face.

"Who's that?" he asked.

Bo turned around to see Rick gawping at the two of them.

"Rick, meet Miller," Bo said. "Miller, Rick."

"Miller! Your girlfriend?" Rick gawped. "I thought you said she was dead?"

"'Fraid not. At least, not yet anyway," Miller asserted. "So! This is the famous Rick, eh. How many more of you are there?" she asked.

"It's a long story," Bo replied. "Don't even begin to ask me right now. Listen, Miller, we've got some work to do. I'm going to blast this place into the history books, and I could use your help to do it."

"But what about our parents Bo, they're still down there!"

He quickly explained that Paul and the others were looking for them as he spoke and that they would be in good hands.

Miller visibly relaxed after hearing that.

Bo then explained in detail his plan to destroy the transmitters.

Miller nodded and gasped in awe at the ingenuity of it.

When he'd finished she clasped him round the face with both hands.

"Is it possible to do that, Bo?"

"I dunno, but I'm gonna give it a whirl," he said. "Now, come on. We need to move fast."

The transmitters were still online, belting out their electromagnetic mayhem into the night sky. The raw energy they were emanating was almost visible from the control room, as it blasted upwards into the fragile ionosphere.

Bo located the digital control console and tapped in a series of commands. The power output dial began to rise slowly. Reaching into his pocket he pulled out the CD he'd created back at the cabin and slotted it into the disc drive.

As he did so he noticed the power output gauge tip over the 4 giga-watts range and the needle begin to climb towards the red zone.

The hum beneath their feet began to rise in pitch as the generators were called on to pump the maximum amount of power to the antennae grids. Several hundred metres from where they stood, intermittent sparks began to fly from pole to pole, buzzing and crackling as the immense surge of electrical energy tried to find its way between the phased array dipole masts.

By this time, Brook and Leigh had made it to the power station. Brook peered inside. They were in luck! There was only one guy manning the place.

Without hesitating, Brook crept up behind the guy and knocked him clean out with a blow to the neck. The man flopped to the ground and was still.

The cacophony of the high powered generators, pounding away inside the building made it impossible for the two men to communicate verbally. They quickly located a pair of sound-deadening headsets hanging on the wall and put them on.

Brook signalled to Leigh, using sign language, to find the main breakers.

Leigh signalled compliance and disappeared behind the bulkhead of the main instrument console.

Brook then set about making up the terminal bypass assemblies. These consisted of two high tensile wire loops with quick release clamps on either end. A sturdy switched solenoid, activated by a remote control unit, completed the circuit. When the polarities were changed round, the current would reverse the transmission sequence, effectively drawing whatever electrical charge they had previously created in the sky above, down on themselves.

The two of them worked efficiently and quickly, hooking up the bypass loops onto the main breakers for each generator. There were fifteen in total, one generator supplying power to twelve antennae respectively. Each bypass loop had an integral solenoid switch built into it which was connected to a radio controlled switch. All of which could be simultaneously activated by a single remote control unit in Brook's possession.

Several minutes later, they were finished and ready to leave.

After a rapid check of all the connections, the two of them threw off their ear protectors and slipped back outside, into the night air.

After a couple of steps, Leigh grabbed Brook by the shoulder.

"That guy in there! We can't just leave him, Brook. He'll fry when that lot goes up. The power station is a long way away from the intended blast zone but it'll bear the full brunt of the explosion. That guy could be killed, or at least, badly injured," explained Leigh.

Brook hesitated for a moment.

"Okay, let's go get him," he agreed.

They rushed back in and between the two of them carted the unconscious guy off towards the entrance gate at a brisk trot.

Meanwhile, Paul, followed by Michelle, Ross and Ryan had reached the administration building and began looking for a way into the basement area. None of them knew for sure that Bo and Miller's parents were being held prisoner at HAARP but if they were, Bo was certain it would be down here.

"If they're here, they'll be in the garage underground. We need to find the entrance door," Paul ordered. "Keep an eye out for any guards," he added, signalling to Ryan and Ross to take the right side of the building, while he and Michelle went to the left.

The basement garage had two means of entrance. The sliding shutters at the front of the building obviously operated electrically, for vehicle access, while at the back there was a single doorway with a wired glass window in the upper section of it.

As Paul and Michelle searched for a manual switch for the roller shutters, Ross and Ryan located the back door. Keeping completely silent, Ross edged up to the window and peered through. The inside of the garage was dimly lit by a bulkhead lantern on the side wall. Although it was pretty dark in there, he could just make out what looked like bodies trussed up in the far corner. He crouched back down and whispered to Ryan.

"I think I see 'em. They're tied up in the far right hand corner by the looks of it."

"Anyone watching them," Ryan asked.

"Cant see," Ross replied.

"Only one way to find out then," said Ryan.

The two of them stood up and pressed themselves either side of the door with their backs to the wall. Ryan knocked loudly on the glass porthole.

Inside the garage they heard a muffled grunt, then footsteps.

"Who's that?" came a voice.

Ryan put on a deep gruff voice. "Food!" he grunted.

There was a moment's pause, then a shuffle of keys. The lock turned and the door moved inwards.

Without hesitation, Ross slammed into the door with all his might. There was a startled scream as the man inside tumbled backwards from the impact.

Ross surged forward, rolling over in a somersault as he bowled into the room.

Ryan flew in after him and immediately spied the stunned guard flailing around on the concrete floor. With lightning fast reactions, he darted towards him as he noticed the man go for his semi automatic pistol. Ryan kicked the gun from the man's wrist and engaged him in a headlock. The guard was heavyset and strong but no match for Ryan's strength and technique and a few seconds later he was unconscious.

Ross meanwhile, had quickly checked around for any other hostiles. He found none. Then he turned his attention to the motley bundle of shivering, gagged and bound individuals in the corner, who were all staring up at him, wide eyed in terror.

"Its okay folks, don't worry. We're the good guys," Ross announced casually, as he rapidly untied the hapless victims.

There were two men and two women, all of middle age and quite the worse for wear from their ordeal by the looks of it.

"You must be the Boettos and the Millers," Ross pronounced.

The first man looked up at him, even more shocked.

"You - you know who we are?" he stammered.

"Yep, and you might like to know that your son and daughter are upstairs, as we speak."

"Where, how – wha... what the hell's going on here. Who are you guys?" exclaimed Boetto Senior, now beginning to regain a little of his composure.

"No time for chit chat, folks," Ryan interjected. "We need to get you out of here first and safely away. We'll explain everything then."

Shocked and dazed as they were, Ross and Ryan managed to bundle the four hostages out through the way they had entered, and ushered them up the back steps to the front of the building outside.

Paul and Michelle were waiting for them.

"Nice work boys. Got 'em all, I see," said Paul.

Ross and Ryan nodded.

Bo's and Miller's parents just stared dumbfounded at these other two complete strangers, who also seemed to know exactly what was going on.

"Okay. Well done boys. Take them to the woods on the other side of the road and wait there," instructed Paul. "We're going up to get the others."

Ushering their bewildered entourage forward, Ross and Ryan headed off towards the main entrance.

......And at that very moment, three thousand miles away to the east, the most powerful man in the free world was about to learn a terrible truth......

Chapter 30

The White House.

The President of the United States was sitting at his desk when Bouillard and Asimov entered. Also present were four other men. Seated nearest the President's desk was the Director of the CIA, Jack Planck. Next to him were Ben Blaggit, Chief CIA technical liaison to the Whitehouse, Secretary for Defence, Tom Dillinger and a five star General, named Fred Growel.

Bouillard commenced the formalities.

"Mr President, a pleasure as always."

The two men shook hands.

"Allow me to introduce Mr Yegor Asimov," he announced, turning to present his companion.

The President eyed the old Russian with a mixture of surprise and subdued respect. From what Bouillard had told him, there was a lot more to this meek looking individual than met the eye.

"Mr Asimov. Pleased to meet you, sir," he said, offering his hand. Then he quickly introduced the other men in the room. None of them rose to greet Asimov. They just nodded in turn.

"Under the current circumstances I'm afraid I don't have time for pleasantries, so if it's okay with you I'd like to get right down to business. Sit down, both of you, please," said the President.

Yegor and Bouillard seated themselves in front of the huge desk.

All eyes were on Asimov, who seemed dwarfed by the sumptuous leather armchair in which he sat.

"Now, Mr Asimov, for the benefit of everyone present in this room, would you please explain the details of what you believe these devices are exactly?" requested the President.

Despite the auspicious surroundings and company he was in, Yegor needed no further prompting. It was as if he had waited his whole life to be able to divulge the things he was about to say. He immediately launched into his reply.

"These twelve devices are psi-generators; weapons of mass destruction. The reason I know exactly *what* they are, and *where* they are situated is because I was responsible for putting them their in the first place."

A startled murmer of shock and surprise was heard between the four men sitting opposite.

"They were developed and produced over forty years ago in the Soviet Union, under a cloak of utmost secrecy, by a technical unit that even the uppermost echelons of Soviet power were unaware of. This clandestine special unit was set up and presided over by a man named Sergei Brikhalov, the Director of the Soviet State Committee for Science and Technology.

"In fact, only three people were privy to the overall scope of this project, of which I am one. The other two are, I believe, long dead and I am almost certain now that the secret of the psi-generator program died with them.

"Technically speaking, I too am deceased. Apparently, I went down with my submarine and all my crew, during a supposed maritime accident in 1965. In truth, our vessel was sabotaged and then sunk by our own countrymen. A savage act of treachery, masterminded, I have no doubt, by Brikhalov and his secret conspirator, to bury the true nature of our mission. Fortunately, I survived. In fact I was the sole survivor.

"Had I not had the good fortune to be picked up by a Norwegian trawler and brought to England, I am certain there would now be little or no hope of averting a global catastrophe, the likes of which has never been seen before."

His audience, one and all, were captivated by his story.

"Please, go on, Mr Asimov," urged the President.

Yegor nodded politely, and continued.

"These weapons were intended to be activated, if the need ever arose, by receiving a signal from a super powerful transmitter."

At the utterance of the word "transmitter", the Director of the CIA became instantly alert. Alarm bells began ringing in the back of his mind.

"Transmitter! What kind of transmitter?" he asked, trying to contain the urgency in his voice.

"Extra Low Frequency," Yegor replied.

CIA Director, Jack Planck's black heart missed a beat. His shaking hand reached for the glass of water in front of him, as he felt his throat begin to dry out. He could think of only one word – "*HAARP!*" He shot a furtive glance at his technical advisor, Ben Blaggit.

Blaggit returned his stare, but he said nothing.

Thinking that the silence was a prompt to continue, Yegor continued his dialogue.

"As I mentioned earlier, these devices are primarily and effectively psychotronic weapons and are just as deadly as any conventional nuclear, explosive device. Human subjects exposed to the ELF transmissions they produce, will initially perceive auditory sensations, simply described as buzzing or knocking sounds, originating from within or near the back of the head. But that is only the beginning. The end product of these weapons for their victims is, I'm afraid, madness and eventually a slow, lingering death.

"The ability to remotely transmit microwave voices inside a target's head was dubbed 'Synthetic Telepathy', by Soviet scientists and was designed to drive a target crazy with voices, or deliver undetected instructions."

Everyone listening, including the President sat spellbound. No one spoke.

Yegor paused briefly and looked around, at the six pairs of intense eyes that bore into him. He took a sip of water from the glass. Then he continued.

"Pulsed microwave transmission technology was discovered by our scientists during World War II, when radar technicians found they could hear the buzz of the train of pulses being transmitted by radar equipment they were working on.

"Subsequent, detailed studies mapped out those frequencies and pulse characteristics, which were found to be optimum for generation of what was termed "microwave hearing." The first successful Soviet unclassified experiment of this kind was in 1954. The West did not even begin to discover this technology until twenty years later. By then, the Soviets had perfected it and were using it to successfully subjugate groups and individuals at great distances......

As the old Russian reeled off these technical details, Blaggit was hurriedly making notes and shaking his head, almost in disbelief, at what he was hearing.

"......These ELF waves pass through anything. Nothing can stop them. There is no conscious defence possible against this. And that gentlemen, is what you are dealing with here."

When he'd finished, Yegor sat back in his chair.

The silence in the room was palpable.

Dillinger was the first to break the spell. He was visibly seething.

"If this is for real and you knew about this, why didn't you come forward earlier and tell someone, for Christ's sake?" he yelled.

Yegor bowed his head.

"I should have sir. I realise this now. I am a fool and irresponsible in the extreme. I withheld it to protect my family. I only hope that now I can help to prevent these devices from carrying out, what I believe to be their terrible purpose."

The old man was totally genuine in his remorse.

The President interjected.

"Please, go on Mr Asimov", he urged, his eyes blazing in reproach at his Defence Secretary's bullish attitude and violent outburst.

Visibly shaken by Dillinger's reprimand, his hands quivering, Yegor continued.

For the next half hour or so, he recounted his mission briefing with Sergei Brikhalov, head of the Soviet State Committee for Science and Technologies.

He went on to detail his mission to deposit twelve identical devices on the sea beds, two hundred miles off the East and West coasts of America. He spoke in graphic detail of the final tragic episode, as he witnessed his comrades and shipmates die at the hands of his own countrymen; innocent victims of a vicious and callous treachery.

He told them of his subsequent and miraculous escape from the sinking submarine and being picked up by a Norwegian fishing trawler, after drifting for several weeks in his life raft and eventually, how he reached British soil, where, due to his excellent command of the English language, he managed to fade into obscurity, terrified that if he tried to expose what had happened, his wife and family would be arrested, tortured and killed, not to mention himself. He told of how he thereafter watched the daily news, for decades since, dreading the emergence of an event such as this, which now, tragically, was upon them.

When he'd finished, an eerie silence permeated the room as his eminent audience marvelled at such a story.

The President looked across at his technical advisor from the CIA.

"Ben, I don't profess to understand half of what Mr Asimov here just said, but is this possible?"

Blaggit shuffled uneasily in his chair. What he'd just heard not only made total sense, it explained virtually every question he'd ever had regarding the Soviets' secret cold war nuclear research and development. What didn't make any sense to him at all however, was how they could have had such advanced technology that long ago without the rest of the world knowing about it? He wasn't even born in 1965!

"Everything this man has said is possible, sir. We have been researching ELF remote transmission technology since the mid seventies, and........."

The CIA Director cut in abruptly.

"Er, Mr President! I don't think we should be discussing such things with non-security cleared persons in the room; *if* you don't mind, sir."

The President paused a moment. What he'd heard so far had chilled him to the bone, but Planck was probably right. This was classified information, though from what he'd just been witness to, it seemed this Russian knew more than the lot of them put together!

That aside however, he personally needed to get up to speed on all this techno speak and check the veracity of Asimov's data before he did anything else. He leaned forward across his desk and spoke quietly to the old Russian.

"Mr Asimov," he said, pressing the button on his intercom. "Would you leave us for a few moments while I confer with my advisors? My secretary will see that you're taken care of."

Yegor politely acquiesced, and was escorted out to the VIP room by the President's secretary.

When they were alone, the President quizzed Blaggit once more.

"What do you make of this old guy, Ben?"

"As I mentioned previously sir, I don't understand how the technology he's referring to could have been around that far back. He's talking about stuff that, in all honesty, we're only getting to grips with today!"

But there was no honesty in Blaggit's words. He was lying through his teeth and trying to keep his composure while he did it. He dare not glance sideways but he could sense the CIA Director hanging on his every word. He attempted to divert the President's attention away from the subject.

"The Soviets were always well up on nuclear testing during the 50's and 60's, Mr President. But there's no evidence to show that they had perfected deep sea, underwater remote detonation technology, especially through the use of ELF. If this is true, it must have been the best kept secret of the cold war."

The President however, was not so easily sidetracked.

"What I was referring to was this mind control gobbledegook he's talking about. What exactly do you know about that?"

Blaggit looked distinctly uncomfortable. He glanced across at his senior without making the gesture too obvious.

Planck nodded almost imperceptibly, as if to will him not to divulge anything further, his beady eyes pleading for him to not say anything else.

Blaggit got the message. He turned his attention to the President and cleared his throat.

"Well sir, the CIA *have* dabbled in mind control technology in the past, using drugs and hypnosis, with no real lasting results. MKULTRA was a resounding failure, as you most probably are aware. In essence we're still in the primary research and development stages."

Blaggit was beginning to sweat. In truth, the extent of mind control technology was, he knew, radically advanced. But the real facts were kept totally under wraps by his superiors, under pain of death. Even the President was unaware of the true scope of the CIA's programs in this area. He had to get the President's attention off the subject, and fast!

"ELF technology is only, so far as I'm aware, for communicating to deep sea submarines, but, er - I'm sure Mr Dillinger would be able to brief you more fully on that subject than myself. It is after all, a matter for homeland defence."

Mercifully, the President took the bait. He turned his attention to the Secretary for Defence.

"Tom?"

Secretary for Defence, Thomas B. Dillinger stood up and cleared his throat. He was a professional soldier by nature, having served in several major conflicts during his distinguished army career. What he didn't know about military and state security matters wasn't worth knowing. Not only that, he loved an audience. Briefing others on his extensive knowledge was his forte.

"Well sir, the U.S. Navy operates two extremely low frequency radio transmitters to communicate with its deep diving submarines. However, it couldn't have anything to do with setting these devices off. The frequencies they operate at don't come anywhere near what this Russkie's talking about."

The President was intrigued. "Go on," he urged.

"Well, the Clam Lake ELF radio station which broadcasts messages to the fleet, operates in the 40 to 50 Hz and 70 to 80 Hz bands; the same as the submarines receiver system. The same goes for our Ground Wave Emergency Network (GWEN) in Wisconsin. Those frequencies are way above what this Russian said would set these things off."

When he'd finished, he waited patiently, while his commander in chief formulated his response.

"What would be the consequences to us if we shut it down?" asked the President.

"Shut it down! Why, that's inconceivable sir. We'd have no way of alerting our subs in the event of an attack. They'd be blind and deaf and out of our control. Besides, as I just said, they operate way outside the zero to ten megahertz frequencies. If an air attack on us was successful, we wouldn't have any way to communicate with our own fleet afterwards. We'd have no means to formulate a response."

"That's as maybe, but even if there's the remotest possibility that somehow our own ELF network has caused this to happen, we have to consider it," the President proffered.

Dillinger was having none of it.

"Sir, have you considered that this might be exactly what an aggressor would want! Suppose the Russians or Koreans, or even the Chinese for that matter, wanted to attack us and incapacitate our deep sea nuclear submarines in the process? If we couldn't communicate with them to authorise counter measures they'd be sitting ducks."

The President mulled that concept over for a few moments.

"Who's the most likely candidate to try and pull off a stunt like this," he asked.

"Definitely not the Russians. We've had them in the bag for some time now. The Koreans are just not up to speed enough with their ELF or nuclear programs to be able to pull it off. Then there are the Middle Eastern factions, such as Al Qaida and Hezbollah, but in truth, sir, they're just not technically sophisticated enough to attempt something like this."

"That leaves only the Chinese," concluded the President. He turned to face the uniformed man sitting next to Dillinger. "General. What's the current status of the Chinese nuclear defence program?"

General Growel was well acquainted with this subject. He reached into his briefcase and pulled out a bulky dossier marked Top Secret.

"Well sir, unfortunately, regarding ELF transmitters, we believe they have one in use, to communicate with their deep sea subs, just as we do. However, we know little about it, where it's located, or what frequencies it operates at. One thing that strikes our intel as odd however, is the possible clandestine usage of underground tunnels the Chinese have been digging to extract coal these last few years."

"Coal! What the hell has coal got to do with nuclear proliferation in China?"

"Possibly quite a lot, sir," replied Growel. He went on to clarify.

"China's usage of coal has increased of late, from 800 million tonnes per annum to almost 1.5 million tonnes. To extract this huge amount of coal, they've had to dig deeper than ever before. The tunnels literally stretch the length and breadth of the country. Once they are exhausted of coal they are useless but these types of long underground tunnels are perfect for setting up ground wave ELF transmitters, not unlike our GWEN network. They could also hide a multitude of other sins in them, such as subterranean nuclear bunkers, nuclear waste, ad infinitum, without anyone knowing. Our spy satellites can only detect fissionable material up to 100 metres below ground, at a push, so there's no way of telling what's in them."

"Okay, that's what we *don't* know. What about what we *do*?" retorted the President.

"Well sir," Growel continued. "There has been a large build up of military facilities in the Tibetan regions over the past two decades. Our latest intelligence shows they have 17 secret radar stations, 14 military airfields, eight missile bases, at least eight ICBMs, 70 medium-range missiles and 20 intermediate range missiles in the whole of Tibet alone.

"According to various reports, a launch site for missiles, which are equivalent to Russia's CSS-2, was built in Tsaidam. These missiles, located at Large Tsaidam and Small Tsaidam, are reported to have a range of over 4,000 kilometres, placing the whole Indian sub-continent within striking distance."

"That's not a threat to us though," countered the President.

"No sir," agreed the General. "But a new nuclear missile division has also been established on the Tibetan Plateau, on the border between Qinghai and Sichuan provinces, in the Tibetan province of Amdo. Several CSS-4 missiles are deployed there, which have a range of 8,000 miles, capable of striking the United States, Europe and anywhere in Asia."

"I see. Go on, general," urged the President.

"Numerous reports have recently surfaced regarding their stockpiling of more nuclear weapons. These reports also confirmed that missile base construction work had started about 10 miles north of Nagchuka, in the East Tibet Autonomous Region and that there was a considerable build up of Chinese military personnel in the area. Missiles, possibly of a nuclear nature, are also reportedly stored in the underground rocky tunnels of Tagho Mountain."

"What about their air force?" the President enquired.

"There are three types of aircraft in China, currently available for nuclear bombing missions, sir; the Hong-6 bomber, the Hong-5 bomber, and the

Qian-5 attack jet. There are three main military airbases in Tibet, Lhasa, Chabcha and Golmud. Chabcha and Golmud airfields are used as refuelling stations. The Gongkar airfield, located 97 kilometres southwest of Lhasa, has been the main military airfield and the main supply centre for the Chinese forces in the border area. Training sites have also been observed by our spy satellites in nearby Haiyan."

"What about our friends, the Russians. Could they be in league with the Chinese, secretly?" asked the President.

General Growel raised his eyebrows.

"It is possible sir, though unlikely. However, Russia *has* sold 100 advanced artillery systems with precision guided shells to China in secret arms deals, including modern aircraft, destroyers, and other high-tech arms.

"They've also purchased some 50 SU-27 flanker warplanes from Russia, and have plans to purchase 250 more jets, apparently. The SU-27s will be fitted with AA-11 air-to-air missiles, a very effective radar guided rocket with electronic counter-measure pods.

"It's evident that China is modernising its nuclear weapons and developing multiple warhead missiles, and now have intercontinental nuclear capability. The most worrying development, according to our intel sources, and as I stated previously, is that their intercontinental ballistic missiles can now reach most of the USA. Their latest intercontinental ballistic missiles include the DF-31, a road-mobile missile with a range of more than 4,500 miles and a second new ICBM, with a range of more than 7,000 miles.

"To summarise, their total nuclear power is estimated to be 16,000 times greater than the atomic bomb dropped on Hiroshima."

With that, General Growel ended his briefing and sat down.

The President's already furrowed brow creased even further.

"Thank you, General."

The President turned his attention to the other men in the room.

"Well gentlemen, like I said, we're going to have to tread carefully with these characters. For all we know, the Chinese are gearing up for a major assault on us as we speak. If not and if they *are* transmitting with a facility similar to GWEN and Asimov is telling us the truth, then it's possible that they are the source of the problem without being aware of it. If that's the case we are going to have to get them to shut it down."

Dillinger guffawed like an old bulldog.

"I don't think the Chinese Premier is likely to comply with a request to turn off his only means of communicating with his deep sea submarines, sir, even if you ask him nicely," he retorted.

"Not if his Defence Secretary is anything like you he won't!" replied the President.

"I'll take that as a compliment, sir," said Dillinger.

Chapter 31

HAARP

In the control room on the fourth floor of the administration building, Bo put the final touches to his master plan. The transmitters were now pulsing at maximum power, directly into the sky above them and at the exact frequencies he had programmed into the computer. Thick dark storm clouds were already forming overhead with lightning bolts sparking inside them.

"We've got about another thirty minutes at best," Bo explained to the others. "After that the electrostatic energy in the storm will begin to reach a critical point. That's when the polarities need to be reversed. We need to be well out of here before that happens, or we're toast."

"What about Clavell. We need to find him and that computer of his," Rick said.

"I've got a feeling he'll find *us*," replied Bo.

As it turned out, Bo's intuition about Clavell was not too far off the mark.

At the other end of the building, Chels and Noogs had begun a systematic check of each room along the corridor, looking for any other personnel. Finding the top floor empty they made their way down the stairs at the far end of the corridor. Half way down the first flight of steps, Chels, who was in the lead, stopped suddenly and raised her arm.

"Someone's coming!" she whispered.

With supreme, soundless agility the two girls retraced their steps up to the 4th floor landing and lay in wait.

As the footsteps reached the final step, they faltered for a split second, but it was too late! Before he could react to defend himself, a perfectly aimed foot swung out from behind the wall above and struck the man in the solar plexus, followed by another one just below the throat. He keeled over and fell backwards. As he did so, Chels and Noogs grabbed him by the lapels, preventing his heavy, limp body from tumbling back down the staircase. With both arms firmly gripping their victim under his armpits they lowered him onto the landing floor.

The man was still conscious, but completely winded and unable to resist. Without hesitating, Noogs applied pressure with her thumb to the side of his neck and seconds later he was out for the count.

They dragged him away from the edge of the stairwell, then turned him over onto his back and stood over him.

"The bigger they are, the harder they fall, eh Chels?" declared Noogs.

"I wonder if this is the big cheese Bo was telling us about?" Chels pondered, rifling through his pockets for ID.

"He looks a bit like the guy, that's for sure," Noogie replied. "C'mon, let's drag him back to the ops room. The boys can keep an eye on him while we search around some more."

They both grabbed a handful of the prostrate man's clothes and dragged him down the corridor to the operations room like a sack of coal. As they shuffled the heavy, limp body in through the door Bo and Rick came out of the adjoining room. They were closely followed by a strange woman that neither of the girls had seen before.

"Who's she?" Noogs asked.

"This is Miller," Bo replied.

"Miller? But I thought ...."

"I'll explain later," said Bo.

Noogs shrugged, then pointed to the unconscious man lying at her feet.

"Is this Clavell?"

Bo recognised him immediately. He felt the back of his neck tingle as his emotions welled up inside.

"That's him alright, the scumbag! I'd like to......"

He rushed forward and aimed a kick at Clavell's ribs but Rick acted quickly, grabbing his arm and pulling him back.

"Hold it Bo! Time for that later. Let's finish what we started first, okay."

Rick had to use all his strength to hold him back. Bo was incensed.

Bo hesitated for a moment then relaxed. Rick was right. He'd have time later on to deal with this son of a bitch. He still had to reconfigure the computers and anyway, revenge wasn't one of his natural traits.

Miller however, was not so restrained. Her eyes flashed with anger and before anyone could stop her, she landed a powerful kick in Clavell's face, splitting his nose and mouth open with a sickening crunch. The big man's body shuddered with the impact of it, as a piece of his front tooth skittered across the shiny linoleum floor.

"Bastard!" she screamed, and by the contorted look on her face, she meant it too.

Rivulets of blood began to seep from the gash in Clavell's upper lip.

"There ya go Bo, I did it for you," she rasped, her breath coming hard and fast as she spoke.

Noogie just looked at Miller in amazement.

"Jesus, you sure don't like this guy do you," she exclaimed, shocked and surprised at the venom in this strange woman's voice.

"He's a murdering, conniving bastard," replied Miller, still sneering at the inert body on the floor. "You have no idea how long I've waited to do that."

"Well, I don't think he'll be getting up to murder anyone else for a while!" Noogs replied. "I take it you weren't the person Bo said they dragged out of the river, then?"

"Nope! Alive and kicking honey," Miller replied.

"Aint that the truth!" Chels cut in. "You should take up Karate, then again, maybe not!"

Bo suddenly remembered the computer.

"We have to get hold of those secret documents in Clavell's computer. Miller, take them down and find his laptop. It'll be in his office on the 3rd floor. If it's not there, look in his living quarters. I'd come with you but I've got work to do up here."

Miller nodded.

"I think I know where he keeps it," she said.

As the girls headed for the door, Bo made one last comment.

"And don't take too long either. You've got about ten minutes max. When it's time to go there won't be any coming back," he warned.

Chels and Noogs nodded in synch, checked their watches and following Miller, they disappeared down the corridor towards the stairs.

Bo looked down at Clavell's battered and bruised face.

"Couldn't have happened to a nicer guy," he sneered. "Tie him up with the others, Rick. When Paul and the guys get here we'll have to lug them all out with us. On second thoughts, maybe we'll leave *him* here."

Rick grabbed hold of Clavell's jacket and hauled him up into a sitting position. There was no rope left, so he used a reel of electrical wire he'd found in the closet to tie Clavell's hands behind his back. He slid him over to the other two and propped his back up against them.

Using copious amounts of wire, he wound it round all three, several times. When he was satisfied there was no way Clavell could get loose, he tied the wire tight and went back into the control room......

......As he did so, far away to the east, in Washington, the President of the United States pressed the intercom button on his desk......

Chapter 32

The Oval Office:

"Janet, send Mr Asimov back in, would you please," requested the President.

The old Russian was ushered back in and seated once more in the large leather armchair.

"Mr Asimov, or may I call you Yegor?" enquired the President.

"You may call me what you wish sir, it matters little to me any more."

"Very well, er, Yegor. So far I'm intrigued by your story but one thing puzzles me; exactly how is it that the Soviet Union came to be so advanced with this technology, while America did not?"

Yegor fixed his eyes on the President.

"Are you aware of the work of a certain Nicolai Tesla, sir?"

"I am indeed; a very great man by my reckoning," the President replied.

"He definitely was, and very underestimated in his day. Well, unfortunately the Soviet Union was the only country to take the work of Tesla seriously. Though he emigrated to America early on in his life, and always considered himself an American citizen, he received nothing but abuse, ridicule and scorn from your robber barons, capitalists and politicians who, rather than embrace and cultivate his genius, decided to either steal or usurp his work for their own vested interests.

"By 1937, when it was clear that war would soon break out in Europe, Tesla came up with one of his more radical inventions, his "peace beam" as he called it. He sent an elaborate technical paper, including diagrams, to a number of Allied nations. These included the United States, Canada, England, France, the Soviet Union and Yugoslavia. The paper was titled 'New Art of Projecting Concentrated Non-Dispersive Energy Through Natural Media,' and it provided the first technical description of what later became known as a "charged particle beam weapon."

"Of all the countries to receive Tesla's proposal, the greatest genuine interest, believe it or not, came from the Soviet Union. In 1937 Tesla presented a plan to the Amtorg Trading Corporation, an alleged Soviet arms front in New York City.

"Two years later, in 1939, one stage of the plan was tested in the USSR, for which Tesla received a check for $25,000. Tesla hoped that his invention would be used for purely defensive purposes and thus would become an anti-war machine. Unfortunately, the Soviets had other plans for it.

"His ideas were never taken seriously by the Western powers at the time unfortunately and he died penniless and debt-ridden in a New York hotel, in 1943. However, a prototype compact version of the peace beam generator was hidden in a trunk in the basement of his hotel and immediately after he died, a Soviet spy raided the room, as well as the safe, which contained the schematics of this device. The FBI arrived shortly thereafter but never found any of the important parts of the schematics, nor the trunk with the prototype inside, as it was already on its way to Moscow. It was these schematics which were used to develop the first ELF transmitter station on the Kola Peninsular and subsequently the psi-generators."

Ben Blaggit, who had been listening with baited breath, finally couldn't withhold himself any longer.

"Then it's true! The Soviets did have this technology way back then. But what happened to that particular transmitter station? We know it doesn't exist any more."

"You are correct, it doesn't." Yegor concurred. "As well as being the location of the transmitter station, the Kola Peninsula was also a key testing site for conventional nuclear devices and it was this fact that was to prove to be its undoing. Three civil nuclear bombs were to be detonated in the mine of Kulpor in the Khibini Mountains, fifteen kilometres east of the town of Kirovsk, to be exact, and approximately 100 kilometres from the transmitter station. The aim was to increase the amount of extracted apatite-ore for production of phosphate. Phosphate, if you didn't already know, is used for production of artificial fertiliser.

"The first bomb was detonated in 1972 and had the explosive force of approximately 1 kiloton. Unfortunately it caused a minor earthquake that shifted the tectonic plates under the transmitter plant, although this in itself did not cause too much concern at the time. But it is a little known fact, even to this day, that powerful ELF waves transmitted through the earth can also cause seismic disturbances.

"When the transmissions from the plant were stepped up in intensity a few months later, they caused exactly that phenomenon. The already weakened tectonic plates, compromised by the nuclear explosions, the same plates that sat beneath the transmitter station, underwent massive seismic shifts which devoured it wholesale. The entire facility literally disappeared into the fissures, caused by an earthquake of its own making. In the aftermath, large crevices and piles of rubble were all that was left.

"I am almost certain now that Sergei Brikhalov and the one other person who was privy to the full psi-generator program, whose identity remains unknown to me to this day, were killed in that catastrophe. I believe this because he often frequented that place and nothing was ever heard of him since that time. That is why I am almost positive that I am the only one left alive who knows the whole story."

Blaggit sat back in his chair, a look of stunned fascination on his face.

"So that's what happened! Did they build another one after that?"

"Yes, another facility was hastily put together in Kiev, but it never achieved the power outputs of the original. Its purpose was modified and it was used ostensibly as an ELF transmitter, for communicating with the Soviet navy's fleet of deep sea submarines."

"Mr Asimov, let's address the matter to hand," interjected the President. "You say these devices, these so called, psi generators, can be activated by powerful ELF waves. Is that correct?"

"Yes sir, but they would need to be *extremely powerful* ELF waves."

"Where do you assume they are coming from?"

"They could be emanating from one or more sources, however, I can only surmise as to where these might be located.

The Director of the CIA looked extremely agitated. He shot a nervous glance at Blaggit.

"Mr President, would you excuse Ben and myself for a moment? I need to talk with him in private – Agency business."

The President shot the CIA Director a pained look.

"Make it quick Jack!"

"Yes sir."

Planck cocked his head to one side, motioning towards the door.

"Ben!"

Planck and Blaggit made a hasty exit from the tense atmosphere of the Oval office and walked briskly down the corridors of power, till they came to the large French doors which opened out onto the patio.

The vast expanse of carefully manicured and trimmed lawn stretched out before them.

When they were out of sight of any prying eyes Planck spoke furtively to his partner in crime.

"Have you made contact with Clavell yet? It's taking long enough goddammit! Much more of this and I'll be pissing my pants. We've got to get HAARP's transmissions shut down, and erase all the evidence of Project Elfstorm, *now!*"

Blaggit fumbled in his pocket for his cell-phone.

"I'll give him another call, sir." He speed dialled Clavell's number once more.

The phone rang but again there was no answer.

"He's not answering. I'll check the administration building."

The phone purred in his ear but again, no answer. The consternation on his face was plain to see.

Planck was pacing around in a circle, looking extremely put out.

"There, er, doesn't seem to be any answer there either, sir," Blaggit said, a lump forming in his now dry throat.

The veins in Planck's neck began to protrude over his neck collar as he vented his ire on Blaggit.

"Listen to me, and listen good, do you realise what's going to happen to you - to me - to us if we don't get this mess under control? Here we are lying our asses off to the President, telling him that we don't have a clue what he's talking about. When, for all I know, a bunch of slant eyed terrorists are already inside HAARP, have done away with Clavell and are about to set those goddammed psi-generators off, as we speak!"

"But sir, how can you be so sure HAARP is to blame for this?" Blaggit pleaded.

"You heard what that old Russian said; *very powerful, extra low frequency waves.* Does that ring any bells, huh? Do you know of any other transmitters that push out almost 4 giga-watts of juice? No. I didn't think so."

Blaggit looked despondent.

"What's even worse, I can't let on what's been going on in that godforsaken place, or we'll both go to jail for a very long time," Planck warned.

Blaggit could only manage a weak, "Yes sir" in reply.

"Now listen to me and listen good because you're neck is on the line here along with mine. As long as the President still thinks that the GWEN network or the Chinese military are to blame, we're in the clear. I want you to get a special ops S & D team up to Gakona right away and I want to know what's going on at HAARP, seeing as no one else does," commanded Planck.

"Blaggit looked at his boss, perplexed.

"Search and Destroy, sir?"

"You heard me. And if it turns out that it's been infiltrated by terrorists or has been compromised in any way I want it destroyed; levelled, – do you hear me? No questions asked; blown to hell and everyone in it."

"But sir, there are civilian technicians in there, and Clavell, and..."

Planck's eyes narrowed. The venom in his voice put paid to any thought of further back-flash on Longley's part.

"Look, you idiot, so far, we've managed to keep the CIA's black-project-mind-control programs quiet, but at this rate it's not going to be long before they're discovered. When that happens, Project ELFSTORM will come to light. If you don't want to wake up behind bars in the morning, get to it!"

"Yes sir."

Blaggit immediately headed off, without further need for instruction.

Planck turned towards the White House building and made his way back to the Oval Office, whereupon the President's personal secretary escorted him back in.

Dillinger was quizzing Asimov further.

"How do we deactivate these monstrosities? If they're nuclear bombs they must have neutralising codes, we should be able to lift them off the seabed and....."

"NO! You must not touch them." Yegor yelled out.

The Secretary of Defence was taken aback by the Old Russian's retort.

"Why the hell not?" he demanded.

Yegor wiped the sweat that was forming on his forehead.

"Because once they are armed they are designed to detonate if moved or tampered with in any way. Sensitive trembler devices connected to the firing pin will detect any form of mechanical movement. They cannot be touched under any circumstances; not until the primary source that caused them to activate is extinguished."

"Jesus Christ! This is a nightmare!" Dillinger exclaimed. "If we can't move them, what *can* we do?"

"We must find the source of the transmissions that activated them in the first place and shut it off. It is these that are keeping the arming device live. Nothing else will work," Yegor asserted.

"This is blackmail!" Dillinger screamed at the top of his voice, turning abruptly to face the President. "I don't believe this son of a bitch, sir. He's holding us to ransom. The only ELF transmissions we put out, with anywhere near the power outputs he's talking about, are coming from our GWEN network. If we shut that down we're defenceless against external attacks. How do we know this guy isn't trying to get us to do just that?"

Yegor fixed his gaze on the President.

"Sir, I believe you to be an honest and responsible man. You must believe what I am telling you. These devices were designed to be totally controllable at the flick of a switch but only by the original source transmitter station. This, as I told you, no longer exists. We must locate the *new* source and quickly. It has been almost thirty hours since the devices were armed. If they do not receive a further signal that shuts them down, in less than seventy hours, they will begin transmitting a lethal cocktail of radioactive microwaves across the length and breadth of the North American Continent. They cannot be tampered with physically, or they will detonate, causing a tsunami, the likes of which has never been seen. Either scenario will result in hundreds of millions of deaths."

The President held his head in his hands for a moment. Looking up, he faced the Secretary of Defence.

"How long will it take to restart the GWEN system, if we shut it down, Tom?"

Dilliger's eyes, creased in disbelief.

"Sir, you can't be serious!"

"How long!" the President shouted.

"Er, a few days at least, sir. Once it's shut off, our subs will have to surface to receive radio instructions and calibrate new receiver frequencies. That will expose their positions to any foreign aggressor. Our surface to surface defences won't take as long to re-calibrate, but it's still too risky. An ICBM from Tibet or Russia could be launched and reach the United States well before we got it back on line."

"Do we have a back up defence system in place?" asked the President.

"Well, yes sir. The Nimrod, air-to-surface fleet can maintain a basic defence shield using satellites, but they'd need to be reprogrammed to allow for GWEN being off line."

"Do it!" said the President.

"What! You can't be....."

"I'm not going to say this again, Tom. Do it, *now*! That's a direct order from your commander in chief."

Dillinger glowered at the President.

"Yes *sir*," he rasped, and stormed out of the room.

At that very moment, far to the West, two menacing shapes rose into the night sky above Fairbanks, U.S. military airfield in Alaska and headed eastward. They were the advanced AH-64D Apache Longbow Gunships, equipped with the latest sensor suite and weapon systems - Jack Planck's CIA Special Ops, Search and Destroy team.

With a primary external armament of 16 laser-guided AGM-114 Hellfire anti-tank missiles, and a cannon with 1,200 rounds of ammunition, capable of firing off 650 rounds per second; these baby's packed a powerful punch.

Inside the cockpit of the lead chopper, the navigator passed on flight data to his pilot.

"Maintain altitude of 2,000 feet on a heading due east. Target acquisition in zee minus 19 minutes."

The pilot set the coordinates into his onboard computer and headed towards Gakona, followed closely by his wingman.

Checking the digital barometer, the co-pilot of the lead chopper frowned.

"The weather up there is weird?" he commented. "We got some serious electrical disturbance occurring, and get this - the pressure's dropping over the target site at a rate of five millibars per minute! That can't be right?"

"You been drinkin' on duty again, Clem? No weather fronts drop that fast. Check it again," the pilot ordered.

His co pilot did so.

"That's what it says, Vince. It's dropped 13 millibars since we took off. It's unbelievable!"

The pilot hailed the chopper behind.

"Buckle up guys. This could turn out to be a rough ride!"

Chapter 33

HAARP

"All systems go!" announced Bo.

In the sky above them a tumultuous electrical storm was now raging. Flashes of forked lightning seared across the heavens between ever increasing black, rolling clouds. The lightning flashes were followed almost instantaneously by sharp, ear splitting claps of thunder that rattled the windows of the operations room with such force that slight cracks were beginning to appear in the toughened glass.

"Let's get the hell outa Dodge," Bo declared.

"What about Clavell and the two techies?" Rick asked.

"We'll have to take them with us, I guess, though I'd still like to leave Clavell here to roast. Better get some of the other guys to help carry them down the stairs. I'm gonna make one more check on the system.

Rick left Bo alone in the control room and ran outside into the corridor. But what he saw when he got there made his blood run cold! The bound and gagged bodies were there all right, but there were only *two* of them. Clavell was missing!

"Oh shit! He must have come to and got free," Rick muttered to himself.

He ran back into the control room.

"Clavell's gone!"

The look of horror on Bo's face was genuine.

"Jeezus, that's all we need, *that* maniac on the loose," Bo groaned.

At that moment Paul and Michelle turned up.

"You guys done?" Paul asked.

"Clavell's on the loose, Paul. He got away," Rick blurted out.

"Don't worry. The others are watching the front entrance," said Paul. "If he comes out that way, they'll nab him." He looked over at Bo. "By the way, we got yours and your girlfriend's folks out. They're with Ross and Ryan."

Bo's face lit up. That was something he'd been waiting to hear for a long time.

Paul then he looked down at the two unconscious men at his feet. "What about these two characters?"

"We need to take 'em with us. Come on, give me a hand," Rick replied, leaning down to grab the first limp body.

Without further ado, the two technicians were hoisted up and sprawled over Paul's and Rick's shoulders. Then they made a hasty exit down the stairs to the front entrance. Michelle followed behind them.

Once outside, the full intensity of the storm became apparent to them all. The pressure drop was so severe it caused their ears to pop as they ran towards the main gates.

A few moments later, Bo came racing out of the front doors and caught up with them.

They were followed by a jubilant Miller, Noogie and Chels.

"We got it. We got the laptop," Chelsea shouted. In her hands she held a pc notebook.

Bo took it from her and gave it the once-over.

"That's it alright. Nice work girls." Bo said, licking his lips with anticipation. "Keep hold of it for me, will ya Chels."

"You bet!" Chels said, still grinning like a cheshire cat.

As they reached the sentry hut they were met by Brook and Leigh. Two small, scruffy looking individuals accompanied them.

"Mahgee!" shouted Bo.

He rushed forward to hug his little Indian friend.

"So, you come back after all, sky devil man." Mahgee quipped.

Brook slapped Mahgee on the back.

"Seems your little pals here came in quite useful, Bo." he said. "Ross and Ryan nearly came a cropper, while they were escorting your parents to safety. They were trounced by two guards we didn't know about. They just popped out of nowhere, bristling with semi-automatics, so Ryan says. These two little characters took em out with slingshots. Can you believe it - catapults!"

Mahgee and his brother dangled their sligshots in front of them, grinning like banshees.

"Ha, I can believe it alright," Bo laughed, remembering Mahgee's deadly accuracy while out hunting for birds with his little makeshift weapon.

"Our parents? Are they okay, Brook?" asked Bo.

"Safe and sound, pal. Ross and Ryan are looking after them, across the way," Brook said, pointing to the trees on the other side of the road.

Bo and Miller exchanged concerned glances and without another word she ran off across the road to find them.

Brook then proudly held up the remote control unit; the one that would reverse the polarities, and passed it to Bo.

"All set and ready to go," Brook said, with a grin.

Bo nodded, and thrust the remote in his pocket.

In the tumultuous skies above them, intense thunder and lightning, now only seconds apart, crashed and flashed with increasing ferocity as the small group of people ran through the entrance gates and out onto the main road.

As he slid down the embankment, Bo's parents rushed to meet him. His mother hugged him as his Dad stood by.

"Bo. Oh my god! What's all this about?" asked his mom.

"No time to explain Mom, Dad. I'm just glad you're both okay. Let's get this over and done with and I'll fill you in on everything later."

Looking back towards HAARP, Bo couldn't help thinking it resembled a scene from an old 'end of the world' B movie, as the transmitters, now at full power output, shimmied and shook under the strain. Sparks of intense electrical energy arced violently between the dipole antennae, as they pulsed out their almost visible beams of electromagnetic energy into the ever increasing cloud formations above.

"Everybody take cover behind the trees, and hold on tight!" Bo screamed at the top of his voice.

Kneeling behind a thick tree trunk, Bo reached into his coat pocket for the remote control unit and to his horror realised it wasn't there! His fingers poked frantically through a tear at the bottom of the pocket.

He locked eyes with Brook.

"Shit! I must have dropped it!"

Brook shook his head in disbelief and cursed.

"I gave it to you at the entrance gate, remember?"

Bo realised it must have fallen straight through the lining of his pocket and must be lying on the ground by the sentry hut.

"I'll get it. Hold on!"

Before anyone could stop him, Bo leapt up and running as fast as he could, made it across the road to the main gate. He reached the sentry hut and stopped, peering down at the road surface for any sign of the remote control unit. Aided by the light from the ever increasing lightning flashes, he madly scrabbled around on the ground at the point where he remembered taking it from Brook. Then he saw it! He reached out to grab it.

But then, just as his hand closed around the remote, he heard a loud whooshing sound above him. It sounded a bit like a rocket at a fireworks display.

A split second later, the sentry hut exploded in a massive fireball, the explosive force of it was such that it literally lifted him off the ground. He flew through the air and landed several metres away in the undergrowth.

Although he didn't realise it at the time, it was this that actually saved his life, for seconds later, the surface of the road where he had been kneeling, erupted from the impact of a round of high velocity bullets. Tarmac and dust spewed into the air as the barrage chewed up the surface of the road.

Then it stopped as abruptly as it had started.

Stunned with shock from the explosion and seared by the heat of the blazing inferno, where once stood the sentry hut, Bo wiped his face and tried to take stock of his surroundings.

He was laying prostrate in a gorse bush, having narrowly avoided being propelled into the trunk of a large conifer tree, just to his left.

Looking up at an awkward angle, between a break in the trees, he squinted in disbelief as he spied two menacing silhouettes, hanging in the sky. They were about a hundred feet from where he lay and resembled jet black bugs with green glowing eyes, like malevolent winged beings borne out of the darkness.

A flash of forked lightning seared across the sky, outlining the shapes more clearly. It was only then that he realised what they were.

Helicopters!

Being the first moving object to be picked out by the lead Apache's infra red scanners, he was the primary recipient of its hellish firepower.

Bo tried to make sense of what was going on. They were helicopters alright, and they definitely weren't friendly. He guessed they would almost certainly possess thermal heat imaging sensors. It would only be a matter of time before they differentiated his body heat from the blazing inferno of the sentry hut, and homed in on him with those cannon. After that he was as good as minced mutton.

He knew he was too close to the antennae array, to fully escape the blast zone, but he also knew that running back across the road would be suicide.

It was now or never!

Grabbing the remote firmly in his left hand he clicked it on.

"Here goes nuthin!" he muttered to himself.

But before he could press his thumb down on the button, there was movement to his side. Bo just had time to look sideways before his hand snapped back from a sudden impact, broken at the wrist, like balsa wood. The remote flew out of his hand and spiralled upwards, landing in the middle of the main road with a clatter.

Bo grabbed his shattered wrist with his other hand and looked up in confusion and terror.

A dark form, silhouetted by the raging inferno of the hut, lunged down and grabbed him by the throat. Through the choking smoke and blaze of fire he heard a familiar voice.

Then he recognised the face!

……And at that very moment, the President of the United States of America, seated at his desk in the Oval Office, wiped the sweat from his brow and paused for thought……

Chapter 34

The Oval Office

Here I am, the most powerful man in the free world, surrounded by a plethora of modern gadgets and surveillance devices; satellites that are capable of reading a newspaper from space and an intelligence network that spans the globe. Yet here I sit, tearing my hair out, trying to locate the switch to turn the goddamn microwave off!

It was so ridiculous it was funny, in a perverse kind of way, he thought.

The President, now at his wits end, had instructed his communications chief to set up a secure video link with his Chinese counterpart, Chairman Hoi, Premier of the Peoples Republic of China.

His communications chief's voice disturbed his thoughts.

"Sir, Chairman Hoi is coming on line now."

The digital screen flickered for a moment. Then Chairman Hoi's rotund, serious face appeared.

"Good morning Mr President," he smiled.

"Good morning, Chairman. I trust you are well?"

"Indeed I am. You however, must have a problem. Otherwise you would not be calling me at such an ungodly hour, or at such short notice. What is it I can do for you, my friend?"

The President realised that it must be around 4a.m. in Beijing. He also remembered that Chairman Hoi liked his sleep and his food and right now he was probably lacking in both. Nevertheless, he got right down to business.

"Mr Chairman, I have little time at my disposal. Therefore I am going to be totally candid with you. My country is currently under threat from a source unknown to us."

Chairman Hoi's expression darkened.

"A terrorist threat?"

"Not quite, Chairman, at least, not along the same lines as we have experienced recently. We are currently being threatened by several electromagnetic weapons that are on a countdown to self destruct in...." He checked his watch. "In approximately 35 hours."

Chairman Hoi was somewhat taken aback.

"Electromagnetic weapons! This is most unusual," he remarked.

"More so than you can imagine, Chairman. That is why I am calling you. I urgently require your assistance."

"Even *more* unusual, Mr President! This must indeed be a very serious situation. I take it that is why you have armed the 12 nuclear submarines in the Atlantic and Pacific oceans, that our spy satellites picked up recently?" replied the obviously well informed Premier of China.

"Not exactly. What you have seen are not *our* weapons being armed, they are the devices that currently *threaten* us."

There was a brief pause while the Chinese Premier digested the data he was being given.

"Not yours?" he questioned.

"No. This may come as quite a shock to you, so please bear with me, Chairman. Those devices your satellites spied are in fact nuclear powered ELF transmitters, strategically placed, so as to swathe the North American continent with powerful microwaves, capable of killing millions of innocent people."

Again, there was a brief pause at the other end while Chairman Hoi pondered the President's last words. Then, strangely, a wry smile crossed his lips and his tone softened.

"Mr President, it never ceases to amaze me how you keep your vibrant sense of humour. Most amusing; most amusing indeed. However, you should know that we are fully aware of the undersea exercises you are carrying out in the Atlantic and Pacific Oceans. As I just told you, our network of spy satellites picked up your twelve nuclear submarines as soon as they armed themselves. Quite a display, I must say, and quite unexpected. I would have at least appreciated some warning beforehand. My military aides, as you Americans say – "have been having kittens!" However, as the submarines are so close to your shoreline, we knew it must simply be a routine exercise. "The American's flexing their muscles again" as my Minister for Defence so eloquently put it."

The President of the United States was, for the second time that day, completely flummoxed.

He actually thinks they're ours, the fat idiot!

The President remembered that he was dealing with a very wily old fox here. Chairman Hoi did not suffer fools gladly and could also be extremely difficult on an empty belly and no sleep. He chose his next words carefully.

"Chairman Hoi, this is no joke. It is not an exercise either. This is a real and present danger?" he asserted.

The oriental statesman gave an inscrutable grin.

"Mr President, please do not play games with me. You know full well what you are doing with your nuclear submarine fleet. Now, what is it you really want?"

The President realised he was getting nowhere fast here, and sensed that the conversation was becoming strained. Somehow, he had to find out the truth – and fast!

"Chairman, please try and understand, I am not in the habit of phoning people up at all hours and playing jokes on them, especially not with esteemed persons such as yourself," explained the President.

Chairman Hoi's head nodded in mock acceptance of that last statement. However, his posture and facial expression remained sour and impassive.

The President continued.

"But, we are in a rather difficult situation here. These nuclear devices are not ours, chairman. They were put there by the Soviets, in 1965 to be precise!"

No sooner had he finished the sentence, than he realised how ridiculous it sounded.

Chairman Hoi sat stone faced for a moment. Then, as if he couldn't contain himself, he burst out laughing.

"The Russians! In 1965! Mr President, forgive me for appearing sceptical, but really! You expect me to believe that?" he guffawed.

The President thought about that for a moment.

"I suppose not chairman. Nevertheless, it's the truth, and we have very little time to do something about it."

"Suppose I were to believe you, Mr President. What exactly do you want *me* to do about it? Surely, you should be talking to the Russian Premiere right now. Not myself!"

"I'm afraid that's the other problem, Chairman. The Russian Premiere knows nothing of this, either. Apparently these devices were commissioned, built, and deposited off our coasts by a super secret project that not even the members of the Soviet Politburo knew about it at the time."

"If it was so secret, how come you know about it then?" Chairman Hoi enquired.

"Because I have with me here, the one and only person left alive today who knows the full story."

"Well, if that is the case. Get *him* to tell you how to deal with them."

"Unfortunately, *he* doesn't know either. He believes that these devices have been activated by a powerful burst of Extra Low Frequency microwaves, somewhere in the world."

Chairman Hoi seemed to be distracted for a moment by something off to his side. He was obviously conferring with someone. Then he spoke again.

"Even if that *were* the case, what do you want me to do about it?" he asked again.

The President decided that now was as good a time as ever to pop the question.

"Chairman Hoi. We believe that your military possess an underground ELF transmitter system, similar to our own Ground Wave Emergency Network, in order to communicate to your deep sea submarines. If this is so, we would very much like you to turn it off."

Again, the Chairman's attention was distracted by someone off to his side. When he turned his attention back to the President, he seemed slightly perturbed, agitated even.

"Mr President. I find all this very hard to understand. You phone me up out of the blue and tell me that there are a dozen or so nuclear devices sitting off you coastlines that you knew nothing about until a few hours ago. You then inform me that the Soviets put them there four decades ago, and that your great nation is in grave danger because of this. Then, you request that I simply switch off my Navy's only means of communicating with its deep sea submarines. Mr President. Have you taken leave of your senses? You must admit. This is very unusual, to say the least."

"Chairman Hoi. The only way we can be certain that your ELF transmitter system is not causing these devices to remain active, is to switch it off. I have already spoken to the Russian Premiere and he has agreed to do this with the ELF transmitters under his control. However, despite this drastic move, the devices *still* remain active. I am reliably informed that if you *do* have an ELF transmitter, and it *is* causing them to remain live, they will deactivate and the danger will be over."

Once again, Chairman Hoi was distracted by someone at his side.

This time, the President could hear raised voices, agitated voices in the background to the side.

Chairman Hoi turned his attention back to the camera again.

"I am sorry, Mr President. I cannot accede to your demands. What you are asking is impossible. Should we shut down our ELF transmitter, we will have no contact with our deep sea submarines for some time. We would be open to attack from any foreign aggressor for the time that it remains offline."

Jesus! Where have I heard that before!

"Chairman Hoi. This is a serious situation. If we don't shut these things off within two and a half days, they will activate and cause tremendous damage across the length and breadth of our country. Millions of people will die. Is that what you'd like to see, chairman - millions of people dead across the United States? - dead or dying, because you wouldn't help us in our hour of need. If nothing else, think of all the Chinese people that reside in our country. What about them?"

The President realised, after he'd finished talking that he'd gone too far. He'd let his emotions overrule his diplomacy.

Chairman Hoi's face became hard and cold. His reply mirrored his look.

"Are you blackmailing me, Mr President? From what I'm hearing, we could be putting ourselves in a very precarious position by carrying out your request. Suppose this was a ruse to weaken our defences, so that we were blind in the event of a nuclear attack. I would like to remind you, that we are fully aware of the United States' military build-up and stockpiling of missiles in Afghanistan. It would be very easy for your forces to enter our airspace and territory from there, especially with our early warning defences incapacitated."

The President sensed the conversation was reaching a critical point and he tried to appease the now irate Chinese Premier.

"Please, Chairman, don't take this the wrong......"

"No, Mr President! I will not accede to your request. Find another way to turn off your Russian doomsday machines. Thank you. Goodbye."

The screen went blank.

The President sat, looking at the dark screen for a moment, unblinking, then he turned to his Chiefs of Staff.

"Well, that went well didn't it!" he said, mockingly.

At that moment, a senior secret service agent walked over to the President and whispered in his ear.

"Sir, you have to evacuate from the White House. We have to get you to a safe and secure location immediately. Come with me please."

Less than ten minutes later, amid great commotion, Marine One, the President's personal helicopter, took off from the White House lawn and headed for Andrews air force base, carrying himself, his wife and his Chiefs of Staff.

Air Force One was waiting on the runway for them, fully fuelled and ready to take off; her blue and white livery reflecting the rays of the winter sun.

Upon his arrival, the President, holding the "football," the briefcase that holds the codes for nuclear deployment, was ushered up the unique retractable stairs of the 6 story high Boeing 747 plane, followed closely by his entourage.

When everyone was comfortably aboard, Air Force One took off, flanked by four U.S. Air Force F18 fighter jets. It would stay in the air until the danger was over.

It was now painfully clear, to not only himself, but to his Chiefs of Staffs also, that there may *not* be a way of averting a country wide catastrophe, the likes of which had never been seen before.

All U.S. controlled ELF transmitters, including GWEN and those controlled by the Russians had been shut down. But the psi-generators were *still* active. The countdown to the potential annihilation of nigh on 300 million people had begun.

In an act of total desperation, a troupe of emissaries from the U.S. had been sent to Beijing, in supersonic air force planes, to try and persuade the Chinese to accede to the Presidents previous request to shut down their ELF system, but in his onboard office, situated in the middle of the 4,000 square foot floor space of Air Force One, the President received the damning news from his attaché in Beijing. The Chinese would *not* shut down their ELF transmitter, and were at the point of cutting off all diplomatic relations with the U.S.A. to boot. Despite the American delegation's best efforts to persuade them otherwise, Chairman Hoi's administration would not accept their preposterous "story" about Soviet nuclear devices placed in the sea, over forty years ago. The more the pressure was put on them, the more they withdrew from the negotiations, now convinced that this was a ploy to gain information on their top secret ELF transmitter network. It was a stalemate.

The countdown had now reached exactly 15 hours before the psi-generators activated.

With no other options available to them, U.S. strategic command, on the President's authorisation, had begun a full scale evacuation of all coastal cities on both sides of the U.S.A. It had been unanimously decided that, if the psi generators could not be deactivated, they were to be destroyed before they began to transmit. This was considered the best solution and the one that would save the most lives.

Waiting for them to activate would spell certain doom to anyone in the path of their transmissions, and that amounted to pretty much any person currently standing on U.S. soil. There was no defence against them. The Extra Low Frequency microwave beams would go through anything, including lead walls. No one would escape their invisible fury.

The effect of 12 nuclear explosions on the sea beds of the Atlantic and Pacific oceans however, was still being predicted using computer generated models. The latest scenario indicated that the tsunami like tidal surges would hit the coastlines at a speed of approximately 500m.p.h. with a wave height of no less than 300 feet. The surge was estimated to come inland as far as Washington on the Atlantic coasts, and could possibly reach as far East as Colorado on the Pacific side.

A mass exodus was now under way to get people evacuated to high ground as soon as possible, but the reality of saving even 20% of these was unlikely, given the lack of time.

Another idea had been proposed and was being given serious consideration. This was a pre emptive strike on China's ELF underground network in an attempt to shut down their ELF transmissions. The trouble was, no one in his administration knew where the hell they were located anyway! The only sure way of putting them out of action would be to commence a full scale nuclear attack on all potential sites where the Chinese could be hiding their ELF transmitters and this just wasn't an option. He had enough to contend with, let alone starting world war three with a previously friendly nation, who were themselves armed to the teeth with nuclear weapons. He also knew that carrying out an act of aggression on this scale would only end up with more of the same result - mass murder on a global scale.

In the past twenty four hours, the Presidents hair had turned grey at the edges. Usually a man with a humorous disposition, he'd forgotten what it meant to smile and now, with only hours left to go, he reluctantly convened his staff. It was time to order the destruction of the psi-generators.

Chapter 35

HAARP

Pinned to the ground and racked with pain from his broken wrist, Bo stared up into the bloodied face of his surprise aggressor. The man's bulky frame was silhouetted against the backdrop of the burning sentry hut. It was Clavell! He cried out as a large boot slammed hard down onto his already injured wrist. The pain was excruciating.

"So, you think you got away again, eh Boetto? This time it won't be so easy, you little fuck!"

The big man ground his foot into Bo's injured hand once more.

Bo screamed out in agony.

"That's it. You scream. You'll wish you were dead before I'm finished with you. Where's my laptop you thieving little terrorist," Clavell snarled.

Completely helpless and almost on the verge of passing out, Bo looked up into the face of his demented assailant. Clavell's right eye was almost closed and badly swollen. His nose was broken and one of his front teeth was missing. All courtesy of Miller's frenzied attack on him while he lay unconscious in the control room. He looked a fiendish sight in the half-light produced by the flames.

Bo could feel himself wavering in and out of consciousness. He knew that had to get to that remote or all of this would have been for nothing but Clavell was straddled across him and had both feet plated firmly on his wrists. He couldn't move. However, his legs were free. With one last adrenaline rush, and all the strength he could muster, he brought his right knee up into Clavell's groin. There was a sickening crunch as it compacted into the big man's balls.

Clavell's eyes rolled upwards as he gasped in surprise and agony and fell forward.

Bo rolled to the left as Clavell's face hit the ground, then clawed himself away using his left arm. His right hand was useless. It felt like numb putty but he managed to push the wounded man away with his legs to get free.

Then, with superhuman resolve, Bo struggled to his feet and made a desperate dash for the road. He knew that any second, those choppers would detect his movement and body heat and when they did, they would send another deadly barrage of high velocity bullets raining down on him. But he had no choice.

The remote was dead centre in the road, about 5 metres away. He could see it laying there, its shiny white plastic surface glinting in the darkness, as it reflected the flames of the burning sentry hut.

Surging forward out of the undergrowth and running at full pelt, he reached the remote, grabbed it up with his left hand, and dived for the cover of the brush on the other side of the road.

Alerted by the sudden movement below them, both the Apache's homed in on his location.

On the other side of the road, Clavell, holding his bruised crotch, limped across in pursuit.

He never reached the other side.

Caught in the infra red targeting sights of the Apache's guns, he was literally shredded by a round of bullets from the air. His body shuddered and gyrated as the high velocity shells tore into his flesh, severing his head from the neck and tearing him limb from limb. A fountain of blood cascaded across the highway, splattering red across the snow covered road.

When the shooting stopped, there was nothing much left of Mr Jim Clavell.

Bo pulled the remote control from his pocket and clicked it on. A red light flashed on the fascia.

This time he was going to finish the job.

He pressed the button.

Nothing happened. With no way of knowing if the remote even worked any more. He nervously jammed his finger down on the button several times, but he needn't have bothered.

Inside the power station, several hundred metres from where he lay, the solenoid switches had already clicked on, causing the bypass loops to reverse the polarities of the current feeding the antennae.

For a few more seconds, Bo lay there, waiting, holding his breath, wondering if it had worked or not.

He didn't have to wait long to find out.

Several miles above the ground, the full force of trillions of volts of electro-magnetic energy, generated by the last half hour of transmissions, was inexorably drawn to its source.

The tumultuous storm clouds that had formed overhead appeared to glow and draw in on themselves.

Then, suddenly, a blast of light came out of the sky and hit the ground. With an ear splitting, sizzling explosion, the entire battery of 180 transmitters was consumed in a fireball that literally vaporised them in a split second.

A moment later the shock wave hit, bending the huge trees surrounding the blast zone to breaking point.

From the epicentre of the explosion, a huge plume of glowing, electrostatic dust rose up into the sky, resembling images Bo had seen on TV of an atomic bomb blast. The shimmering plume of smoke and ash spread out high up in the sky like a giant mushroom.

On the other side of the road, the others shielded themselves from the blast, behind the trees. It was like being caught in a hurricane and they clung on to anything they could get their hands on as the sheer force of it attempted to wrench them away.

50 metres above the ground and directly in the path of the blast wave, the two Apache gun-ships never stood a chance. They were spin-balled backwards and hurled up into the air like small toys.

The tail rotor of the lead chopper clipped the main rotors of the second, sealing their fate.

With a resounding crack a rotor blade severed off and hurtled through the air.

Hopelessly out of control, they spiralled, almost majestically, downwards to the ground, resembling giant maple seeds falling from a tree.

The first helicopter impacted into the earth nose first and erupted in a maelstrom of exploding fuel and twisted, churning metal.

The second came down about 50 metres from the first. It, too, blew up on impact, sending up a gushing fireball and smoke pall to mingle with the now receding storm clouds.

The blast wave abated as quickly as it had come.

Then it was over.

Looking out across the road, the shell shocked company of men and woman looked on aghast at the sight that met their eyes.

Where once stood a quarter of a square mile of wires, antennae pylons and netting, there was nothing but a smouldering crater, almost ten metres deep at its centre.

The trees surrounding the impact zone were flattened for a further hundred metres or so. Those that remained were black and charred, the ones closest to the blast zone resembling burnt matchsticks, with smoke streaming from their tips.

The wind carried an acrid smell of burnt metal and caustic fumes.

Several hundred metres away, the outline of the administration building glowed in the dark. It was still standing, but its roof was completely gone and every window had been blown in. It was ablaze inside with smoke and fire belching from every orifice.

All that remained of the Apache gun-ships were two burning pyres of twisted metal.

Miller screwed her eyes up, looking for Bo, but he was nowhere to be seen.

Paul and the others, especially Bo's parents, did likewise.

"Where the hell is he?" asked Paul.

Miller scrabbled to her feet and launched herself out into the road. She screamed his name as she ran.

"Bo! Bo!"

But there was no reply.

She stopped to examine the remnants of Clavell's body. There was nothing left to identify him by, really. Bits of him were splattered along the road, amidst gouges and furrows caused by the high velocity bullets that had carved him up into mincemeat.

The burning sentry hut was completely obliterated, blown clean away by the blast. All that was left standing was the mangled, twisted remnants of the metal post that once held the security gate drop bar.

"Bo, where are you!" she screamed again.

Still, there was no answer.

The others followed, hot on her heels. They too began shouting his name.

Then, a weak voice hailed them from the undergrowth.

"Over here!"

Searching frantically in the gorse and bush, next to the roadside, Miller eventually found him lying prostrate on his back, nursing his broken wrist. Paul helped her drag him out, still groaning and laid him down on the roadside. Paul quickly checked him over for other injuries. Finding none, he held his hands on his hips and looked back at the smouldering wreckage that once was HAARP.

"Well Bo, if I ever need to rewire my house, I won't be calling you in a hurry!" he quipped.

"Ha! That's funny. Jeez! those poor guys!" Bo said, still clutching his injured wrist and casting his gaze over to the burning choppers.

"Poor bastards, my arse!" said Paul. "They ejected before they hit each other. I saw them go."

"Yeah! me too; I saw their chutes open!" added Chelsea, pointing to the East. "They came down over the other side of those trees."

"Well, in that case we better not hang around," Paul warned. He turned to Ross, who was standing behind him.

"Boss-man! Radio for Sam to pick us up, pronto! I think it's time for us to make a hasty exit."

Chapter 36

Washington:

Once the news reached the President of the United States that the psi-generators had suddenly and inexplicably deactivated, it didn't take long for his security advisors to work out what had happened.

They had gone offline, date coincident with a massive explosion in a remote Ionospheric Research Observatory in Alaska, known as HAARP.

When investigators from the NSA finally tracked down who had been running the place they discovered that it was a front company, owned and financed by the CIA. After that, it was just a matter of time before all fingers began pointing to the CIA Director, Jack Planck.

Within hours, Planck and his technical liaison sidekick, Ben Blaggit, were summoned to the Whitehouse to face the music. The two men sat uneasily before the President, who was accompanied by his National Security Advisor, Henry Pratt. The

President's posture and deep frown indicated that he was not a happy man.

"Well gentlemen! I've just finished a lengthy discourse with the Chinese Premier over the secure video link and apologised profusely for virtually accusing him of gross negligence towards us. Fortunately he has a humorous disposition and accepted my apologies."

Planck cleared his throat.

"Tha – that's great, Mr President. Glad to hear it."

You may be, Jack, but I don't think you'll be glad to hear what I have to say next."

Planck reached up to loosen his tie.

"Uh huh, what would that be, sir?"

The President fixed his steely glare on his CIA Director.

"All in good time, Jack. All in good time. Firstly however, I'd like some answers to a few burning questions I have."

Planck shuffled uneasily in his chair.

"Yes sir, of course – shoot!" he bleated.

The President picked up a sheaf of papers lying on his desk blotter and put on his reading glasses.

"What exactly is Project ELFSTORM?"

Almost as if they'd been simultaneously punched in the gut, Planck and Blaggit gasped. They both sunk further into their seats.

For the next ten minutes CIA Director, Jack Planck confessed his innermost secrets on the subject of HAARP and Project ELFSTORM. He knew he was done for. Why prolong the agony?

As he spoke, he even felt a kind of relief. From the first secret funding of HAARP and its designation as a "Black Project", to the final calibration tests of potentially lethal transmission sweeps of Asia and the Middle East, he spilled the beans on all of it.

The President sat through all of it without a word. When Planck had finished he remained silent for a moment, as if contemplating what to say next.

"So, this has been going on for some time, without my knowledge, I take it?" asked the President, peering obsequiously over his gold rimmed glasses.

"Since before Desert Storm, to be precise sir." replied Planck.

The President baulked at that last statement. "Desert Storm! Since when were 'mind control' weapons used in that conflict? I never knew about this."

The CIA Director cleared his throat.

"Um, well sir. That was also designated as a Black Project. Better you didn't know. Even your predecessors were unaware of it. That way, what you don't know, can't be used against you, so to speak."

"A Black Project, huh. Anything else you wanna tell me, Jack?"

The CIA Director loosened his collar even further, looking extremely agitated.

"Not right now Mr President. I'd rather Ben filled you in on the tech specs first."

The President looked warily at him and shook his head in disgust. Then he turned his attention back to Ben.

"So in essence, what you're saying is, we've been using these machines for years, as a form of mind control on human subjects, is that correct?"

"Yes sir, that is quite correct." Ben replied.

"And the majority of them have been undertaken without my knowledge or the House of Representatives; these so called "Black Projects" as you put it?"

Planck and Blaggit looked sheepishly at one another.

"That's correct sir," they concurred, in unison.

"So you lied to me!"

"Not everything is as simple as lies and truth, Mr President."

"Is that so? Maybe you could expand on that piece of prosaic wisdom for me."

Blaggit attempted to do so.

"Well, we were planning to extend the range of this technology to envelop all peoples, all countries. This was being accomplished by utilizing several ionospheric heaters under our control, placed in strategic locations around the globe; all in the worthy cause of preventing International terrorism, of course."

The President's eyebrows raised up at that last unconvincing statement.

"How many of these damn things exist? He asked, genuinely ignorant of the scope and progress of this radical technology.

"Well, regarding those under our control, there's one in Dushanbe, Tadzhikistan. Then there's Arecibo observatory in Peurto Rico. The British have a powerful transmitter at Akrotini Salt Lake in Cyprus. In Scandinavia we have the EISCAT transmitters, located in Tromso and then, of course there was the HAARP project."

The President raised his hand to stop him.

"Hold on a moment. As far as I can see here HAARP was a research observatory for - what was it now?" The President looked down at the briefing sheet that his secretary had hastily procured for him and read from it, aloud. "Auroral and Ionospheric research; not goddammed mind control!"

The CIA Director intervened once more in an attempt to answer the President's question.

"Yes sir, it was originally intended for that purpose but we found that it was capable of much, much more as the experimentation progressed. I ordered it to be shut down as a civil research facility while we investigated its potential as an electromagnetic weapon for use against terrorism.

"We found that strong electromagnetic fields can be bounced off the ionosphere using a new technique called artificial ionospheric mirrors, or AIMs, for short. This technology was developed and greatly improved by a young Canadian civil engineer, whilst he was working there for the Raytherm Corporation - one of our front companies.

"It had the potential to affect brain patterns of individuals in locations even as far as the other side of the planet. Not only that, it could be done with pinpoint accuracy, and it worked up to depths of several kilometres underground. It was turning out to be the perfect anti terrorism weapon that could potentially stop terrorism where it begins, inside the terrorists head."

"Are we and the British the only ones with this technology?" asked the President.

Ben took over the conversation.

"No sir, the Russians still have active transmitters in Sura, Gorkity, Monchegorsk and Kiev. After the fall of the Soviet Union we discovered their technology of electromagnetic weapons research was far in advance of ours, just as the old Russian, Mr Asimov said. We managed to "borrow" some of their R & D before they got wise to us. That's where we got the idea of the phased array antenna system that comprised the HAARP transmitters in Alaska. We also gained some knowledge of their mind control capability using microwave technology."

"I see," said the President, abruptly closing the dossier in front of him and leaning back in his chair. "Well, gentlemen, it seems you've been busy little beavers in your secret underground burrows. Unfortunately, all that's going to stop, as of now."

As if on cue with those words, four armed marines strode into the room and stood to attention behind Planck and Blaggit.

The two men turned uneasily and looked behind them, unsure of what was going on.

The President lost no time in telling them.

"Jack, I'm relieving you of your post as Director of the CIA, effective immediately. These men will escort you to your cell where you'll be kept until a Judicial State Committee Board of Investigation is undertaken, to determine what criminal proceedings will be brought against you."

The two marines standing directly behind Planck grabbed him by a shoulder each, hauled him out of his chair, and marched him away. Then the President turned his attention to Blaggit.

"Ben, your complicity in this can't be overlooked either; you'll receive the same treatment."

Blaggit's face turned to cold stone.

"But sir, I was just following orders! I – I didn't mean to....."

He was still pleading his innocence as the remaining two burly marines took him by each shoulder and brusquely escorted him out the same way.

Chapter 37

Perry Ranch:

Safely back at the ranch, all thirteen members of the intrepid team were sitting in Paul's lounge recounting their adventures.

They had also just become aware, via the news networks, of the series of events over the past few days, regarding the evacuation of millions of people from their homes across the North American Continent. The media was awash with it. The official explanation given for the evacuations was that a series of earthquakes had been predicted that could possibly cause a devastating tsunami. But now, apparently, the danger was over, with everyone being told to go back to their normal lives.

"Looks like we missed out on all the fun while we were away," said Paul.

He turned his attention to Bo, Miller, Rick and Jodi.

"So what are you four musketeers going to do now?"

"Well me and Miller are going to hand ourselves in to the FBI," Bo pronounced.

"And do what?" Paul enquired.

"It's pretty simple, really." Bo explained. "Now we've got the goods on the bastards behind HAARP, and Miller is most definitely alive and kicking, it's just a matter of making sure my name is cleared and seeing to it that a monstrosity like HAARP is never resurrected."

"I can see your point about Miller. She's definitely not dead, that's for sure," Rick agreed, pinching her on the arm.

Miller jumped.

"Ouch! That hurt!" she yelled.

"Yep! She's definitely still alive alright." Rick joked. "But what makes you think they'll listen to you about HAARP?" Rick asked.

"Don't worry, they'll listen." Bo grinned, patting Clavell's laptop that sat perched on his knee. "Besides, Rick, I don't know what you're looking so smug about. You're coming in with us."

"Huh!"

FBI office, Denver, Colorado

When FBI Special Agent, Ted Palmer received the phone call that morning, he knew it had to be a hoax.

Andrew Boetto, the most wanted man in the U.S.A. and Canada, was coming in to give himself up. Just like that! He reflected on the fact that this had been a week to end all weeks. First the nationwide evacuations, and now this! He decided he was due for a vacation after this little lot. Of all the Federal offices throughout the United States, this guy was coming into his. The caller, purporting to be Boetto, had requested that he drive to downtown Denver and pick him up outside the Mall.

But it wasn't a hoax. Less than half an hour later, Bo, Miller and Rick sat in the back of an unmarked Buick, flanked by a rather confused Palmer, and his partner, Felix Spittell.

Apparently the girl with Boetto and his friend was the one he was supposed to have murdered – Karen Miller? They were taken to the FBI offices and put under armed guard in the one and only cell available.

Palmer immediately checked out their story. It transpired, through DNA testing and fingerprints that this girl actually *was* Karen Miller! The FBI man was at a loss.

But before he had time to go into more detail, Palmer received another urgent phone call. This time he got an even bigger shock. On the phone, speaking directly to *him* was none other than the Secretary of State, Edgar Mullins, himself.

Mullins' orders were clear and concise. Boetto and his associate were to be kept under wraps and were to talk to no one. He informed Palmer that two Secret Service agents were on their way from Washington and that he was to hand the two men and the girl over to them. The agents would be there in two hours!

Washington

The pretty young secretary looked extremely flustered as she stood in the doorway.

"Sir, there are two Secret Service agents, with two men and a woman to see you. They don't have an appointment but they refuse to leave. They're waiting outside, but they're not in your appointments agenda for today, sir."

Secretary for State Jack Mullins' response was short and to the point.

"It's okay, send them in Miss Jenkins, I'm expecting them," he said.

The secretary looked bewildered, but obediently complied with his request.

Bo, Miller, and Rick entered the room, flanked by their two minders, and were met with a pair of seasoned, steel blue eyes.

"Good morning, Mr Secretary, I think you probably know who I am," said Bo.

"Yes, I think I do, Mr Boetto. Pleased you could make it. I trust you and your friends had a pleasant flight?"

Bo ignored the pleasantries.

"Allow me to introduce my friend, Rick Hayden," he gestured, motioning to Rick at his side. "And this is my girlfriend, Karen Miller."

The Secretary of State just nodded blankly at Miller and Rick.

"What exactly is it I can I do for you?" Mullins enquired, with the tone of a man ordering eggs for breakfast.

Bo was distinctly unnerved by the lack of concern in the man's voice. Something was definitely wrong. He tried to keep his voice from betraying his concern.

"Well, it's quite simple really, Mr Secretary," Bo began. "To start with, I've been accused of a murder I didn't commit. That should be pretty self evident, seeing as the supposed victim of my crime is standing right next to me. The real victim was......"

......"Miss Coleen Jones" Mullins interjected. "Yes, Mr Boetto. I'm well aware of what you're about to say. We already know about Clavell and his attempts to silence you."

"You do?" Bo gasped. He was genuinely taken aback by Mullins' last remark.

But, what about.......?"

"If you'll let me finish – we know you didn't kill your girlfriend. As you say, it's pretty evident you didn't," he said, smiling at Miller. "Clavell ordered the killing of Miss Jones."

"You knew!" Bo said. "What – all along?"

"No. We only recently discovered all the gory details. Clavell's peers told me themselves, from behind the bars of the prison cells they are now languishing in. It was a foolish gesture by them in an attempt to keep you quiet and conceal their crimes. There is no question as to your innocence, none at all. As for Clavell, well, I don't think anyone will be interrogating him, now or any time in the future. Our pathologists are still scraping bits of him off of Highway 1, in Alaska." Mullins looked intently at Bo. "Now, what do you *really* want?" he asked, searchingly.

Bo was flummoxed for a moment. He hadn't expected the conversation to go this way. Regaining his composure, he pulled out a sheaf of papers from his briefcase.

"Mr Secretary, I have something here you might find interesting."

He offered the copies of the documents to the statesman.

"These are copies of a top secret project called E.L.F.S.T.O.R.M. I think you might find them a riveting read."

Mullins took the documents from Bo and leafed through them, looking up intermittently as he did so. When he'd finished, he didn't flinch. He simply raised one eyebrow, as if he were weighing up his options. Then he smiled.

"And?"

"Well, there is one other thing sir, now that you mention it," said Bo. "Cease all activities using ionospheric heaters and see to it that all other nations do the same, or else."

"The Secretary of State looked at Bo for a moment. Then he smiled again, as if he were mildly amused.

"Threats indeed! I don't need to remind you where you are right now. I could have you all arrested immediately, if I wished. I have many means at my disposal to deal with individuals who threaten the United States Government with blackmail."

Bo was ready for that one.

"Yes sir, you could. You have the power and the authority to do that. However, there's one last thing you should be aware of. Should any of us not walk out of here in the next hour, these documents will be posted automatically. In fact, should anything untoward happen to us, now or at any time in the future, they will find their way into the hands of every major newspaper editor worldwide, via the internet; and every member of the House of Representatives, with alarming speed."

"So you *are* blackmailing me?" Mullins challenged.

"If you want to put it that way sir, yes I am."

The U.S. Secretary of State turned his attention back to the documents in his hands, then back again to his three impromptu visitors.

"I see. And that's that, is it? No demands for money to be transferred to numbered Swiss bank accounts, no altruistic statement for the good of mankind?"

"Just what I said, sir," Bo asserted.

"Well then. I think we need to discuss a few things," he said, and with a nod of his head, he dismissed the two agents standing by the door.

The two men left quietly.

Mullins then walked over to his desk and pressed the intercom.

"Miss Jenkins. See that we're not disturbed would you," he ordered.

Seated comfortably in his sumptuous leather chair, he clasped his hands together. There was, however, not one iota of concern on his face.

Bo suddenly recalled the same body language exhibited by Clavell, back at HAARP. It made him shiver slightly. Goose pimples began to tingle on the back of his neck.

When Secretary Mullins spoke again, he was totally unfazed.

"I must say you characters have proved to be most resourceful. First, you manage to destroy a multi million dollar research facility, as well as two highly sophisticated Apache gun-ships into the bargain. Then you manage to get away without anyone noticing you. You steal top secret government documents then you give yourselves up and attempt to blackmail the US Government, without a qualm. I've got to hand it to you though, that's quite an achievement and takes some balls. You obviously discovered that the HAARP transmissions were harmful in some way or other and resolved to put a stop to them. Under the circumstances I suppose you had no choice but to do it this way. After all, who's going to listen to a felon on the run for murdering his girlfriend? Am I right?"

Bo began to feel queasy. He looked across at Rick, who seemed to be going green at the gills. Miller was chewing her fingernails. This wasn't going the way he had planned. This guy didn't seem in the slightest bit perturbed at his outrageous demands. To make matters even more confusing, what he was saying was right on the money! What the hell was going on here?

He didn't have to wait long to find out.

"However," Mullins continued. "There's one thing that none of you are yet aware of."

"And what's that exactly?" Bo asked.

"You may have noticed that the entire country has been under a state of national emergency these past few days, mass evacuations of millions of people from their homes, flood barriers being erected, that sort of thing. Well, you're probably not aware of it just yet, but you were responsible for averting what could have turned out to have been a very nasty situation, the very thing everyone was running from, in fact. What I mean exactly, is that we, the American Government, are extremely grateful for what you have done. You three and all your associates are in fact national heroes!"

"What are you trying to pull?" Rick snarled.

Bo cast a nervous glance over his shoulder, half expecting a posse of gun toting marines to come barging back in the room and haul them all off.

"Is this some kind of CIA mind fuck tactic?" Rick continued. My friend here wasn't joking about that Project Elfstorm document and we're not afraid to............"

Mullins' abruptly raised his hand, cutting Rick short.

"And by the way, there's something else you should know. The President of the United States is waiting to see you. He has something for you and your friends. I believe it's called the Congressional Medal of Honour."

Bo, Rick, and Miller didn't clearly recall leaving Mullins' office. Everything thereafter seemed to happen in a blur.

In the back seat of the plush limousine, surrounded by several siren wailing motorcycles, that whisked them through the heavy traffic to the White House, Mullins explained everything, from the discovery of the nuclear devices in the Atlantic and Pacific Oceans and the cataclysmic potential threat they posed... to the appearance of Yegor Asimov... his phone call to the IAEA secretariat in Vienna, and his subsequent arrival in Washington.

He then went on to explain how the entire resources of the U.S. military had drawn a blank on how to deactivate these so called psi-generators. And all the while, no one was aware that HAARP was responsible for the whole thing, because the CIA were keeping the truth from everyone, trying to cover their own backs, in an effort to conceal their little secret - Project Elfstorm.

He even told them about the President's conversation with Chairman Hoi and how it had been determined, erroneously mind you, that *their* ELF transmitter was the source of the problem. The bigger problem being that the Chinese refused to turn it off! It was only when HAARP blew up and spectacularly at that and the generators mysteriously deactivated, that they realised what had occurred. After that it was just simple detective work.

The three of them sat in stunned silence as Mullins spoke. If it weren't for the fact that they were sitting opposite the Secretary for State himself, in a limo bound for the White House, they would have thought this was all some kind of weird hallucinogenic dream. Not one of them, Bo, Rick, Miller, Paul or the rest of the Jin Sei Kai team included, *none* of them, had any idea that this was all happening concurrently with their mission to destroy HAARP. Then again, why would they.

"So that's what all the fuss was about on the news. Jesus! Just wait till Paul hears about this," exclaimed Rick.

"Paul? Paul who?" enquired Mullins.

"Oh! Just someone we know," said Bo.

"You're partner in crime perhaps?" Mullins conjectured.

"Well, he had a slight hand in it, I suppose," chuckled Rick.

Bo and Miller smiled at Rick's benign remark.

"I'd like to meet him sometime," said Mullins

"I don't think he'd go for that, Mr Secretary," Rick replied. "He doesn't like politicians very much."

"Not many people do these days, I'm afraid," said Mullins, pensively.

"Well, you can't really blame them, sir," Miller scoffed. "Look at the mess you guys created here. No disrespect to you Mr Mullins, but my mother told me about boys. She said that their toys get bigger but their brains stay small, and from what I've seen these past few weeks she was right!"

Mullins couldn't but stifle a laugh.

"Eruditely put, Miss Miller. I'll remember to tell that one to the President some time. The poor man could do with cheering up, especially after what he's been put through these past few days."

"Serves him right," she scoffed.

"So, you mean, what we did actually prevented these things, these psi-generators, from detonating?" Rick enquired.

Mullins smiled and nodded in response.

"That's about the long and short of it. Yes Rick."

"And this whole mass evacuation saga, the tsunami threat. That was all based on these things exploding under the sea?" Bo asked.

"You got it," agreed Mullins.

So, this thing with the Chinese, is that all handled now? I mean, are they still pissed with us?" piped in Miller.

"Everything's back to normal Miss Miller. At least as much as anything can be normal on this rather volatile planet," Mullins acceded.

The limo was gliding up to the front steps of the White House now. No sooner had it stopped than the door was opened for them and they were hurriedly ushered into the grand entrance hall. From there, they were led by Mullins to the Oval office, flanked on either side by armed marines.

As they entered, the President was deep in discussion with an oriental gentleman who looked incredibly like the Chinese Premiere!

In fact, it *was* the Chinese Premiere, Chairman Hoi. The two statesmen stood to greet them as they entered.

"Ah! Mr Boetto and Mr Hayden I presume?" the President said, sporting his wide trademark grin.

Rick and Bo just shook his hand and stared at the familiar face of the man standing before them.

"And you must be Miss Miller," the President effused, taking her by the hand and looking her over in a fatherly fashion. "I believe you've had a rather eventful past few weeks my dear. How are you feeling?"

"Not too worse for wear, sir. Thank you for asking," Miller replied.

The President seemed to sense the trepidation in his three guests, and politely offered them seats in front of his desk.

They declined his offer. All of them were too wired to sit down.

"I'd like you to meet President Hoi, premiere of China," said the President.

Chairman Hoi bowed and shook each of them by the hand, smiling and bobbing his head up and down uncontrollably as he did so.

"Now, I suppose you're wondering what on earth you're all doing here? The President asked, in a very matter of fact tone.

Bo spoke for the three of them.

"It *had* crossed our minds sir, yes."

"Well, I'm not going to beat about the bush. I, no, *we*" - the President motioned towards his oriental counterpart as he spoke, - "Chairman Hoi and myself are very grateful for what you have done. You and your associates have just pulled off a quite amazing feat, and narrowly averted what could have been a very nasty and, I might add, unnecessary international incident, not to mention exposing serious deficiencies in one of my Government's key foreign policy departments. I would like to take this opportunity to be the first to congratulate you on a job well done.........."

Rick's knees began to wobble uncontrollably. Just as he was about to keel over, Miller managed to slump him down in a nearby armchair.

"Oh Jeez," he exclaimed. "I need a beer!"

Mirrors In The Sky

Epilogue

Over the ensuing months, a major strategic plan was drawn up, ratified, and executed by all of the G8 countries.

All twelve psi-generators were lifted off the seabed and disassembled permanently.

Every other existing Ionospheric heater around the world was modified to restrict their power outputs to an acceptably safe level, as determined by a panel of experts. Chief consultants to this project were a certain Mr Andrew Boetto and Miss Karen Miller.

A major cleanup campaign was gotten underway, more expansive than ever before, to secure and safely dispose of the vast deposits of nuclear waste around the world.

HN51 Avian bird flu was eventually brought under control and finally eradicated under the capable auspices of the newly appointed World Health Organisation's field director, Jodi VanderWal.

Paul and Michelle continued on with their lives at Perry Ranch. They, along with the other team members received the congressional medal of honour for their valiant efforts. They sold them, and gave the money to Mahgee to help his family.

Rick was given a board member seat in the World Meteorological Association, where he put his "over qualifications" to good use, overseeing the development of a radical new piece of equipment, that accurately predicts and warns of the occurrence of earthquake tremors, up to a week before they occur. The "Hayden Oscilloscope" is still hailed as the foremost tool in saving lives in earthquake prone regions around the world.

Boris Slatovski, a.k.a. Yegor Asimov, returned to Russia, his mother country and under his real name. He was proclaimed a national hero and discovered on his return that he had two children and three grandchildren. He now lives his life a happy contented man surrounded by his family, in Murmansk.

Old Kwan continued his simple existence and passed away peacefully in his modest apartment on Yonge Street in the autumn of 2006 but not before he had once more visited his homeland, Tibet, one last time.

Bill Planck and Ben Blaggit were indicted for numerous crimes against humanity, including their involvement in the murder of Coleen Jones. They were both sent to prison. Planck received the maximum penalty of thirty years hard labour. Unfortunately for him, his cell mate was a homosexual Ahtna Indian. Blaggit got off lightly, all things considered, receiving only ten years.

HAARP was never rebuilt. All that now remains of the overgrown site is a small plaque made from the melted down remnants of the phased array antennae grids.

It simply reads:

"Play with fire - and you'll get burnt.

The End

About the author

Graham Zimmatore is 49 years old and a resident of the UK. He lives in Sussex, England with his wife and 3 younger children. He has raised 7 children in total, their ages ranging from 9 to 25.

A successful businessman and entrepreneur, he has worked as a project engineer in the construction industry, restored and sold vintage Jaguar cars abroad and has several times, flown on Concorde as an international courier. In the mid nineties, he travelled the world as a freelance marketing agent for an international publishing company, in areas as diverse as, Japan, Israel, Europe, USA and even Central Siberia. However, while working as a business consultant in Russia and after having had a few brushes with Mafia gangs in Siberia, he came to the conclusion that it would be safer working closer to home, (the mandatory "business partner fees" being a little too high for his liking).

He trained for 11 years in the martial arts. His hobbies include racing and restoring motorcycles and flying light aircraft. In short he hasn't lived a quiet life, though he would confess to having relaxed a little in recent years.

His writing career spans only two years but in that short time has managed to produce two successful novels with a third on the way. Calling on his engineering background, martial arts training, flying experience, extensive travels around the world and (some say) his vivid imagination, he produced his first novel in 2004, a fantasy thriller called Genetic Meltdown, which he self published to "cut his teeth" on the subject. His second novel, Mirrors In The Sky, is a political-cum-global conspiracy thriller set in Alaska and Canada.

His motto is *"it's a great life if you don't weaken"* - an attitude that seems to permeate throughout his written works.

GRAHAM ZIMMATORE

GENETIC MELTDOWN

Could it be possible that our entire planet is in the grip of a clandestine oligarchy, run by just a handful of individuals for their own vested interests? A power that reaches beyond Governments and Heads of State - so absolute and so secret that only the individuals within it know each others identity and guard their anonymity with an iron-clad fist.

When Damien Birch, a brilliant young geneticist, discovers something unbelievable in a priceless family heirloom, he begins to believe that it could be so.

And when he digs deeper, to a time before written records even began, he discovers something that is literally out of this world – something so fantastic that it propels him into a daring quest to unravel the mysteries of his own ancestry and with that, the fate of the human race as a whole.

OTHER BOOKS AVAILABLE FROM TL
PUBLISHERS

GRAHAM ZIMMATORE
GENETIC MELTDOWN   £8.99
GLOBAL HEIST   £8.99

All TL Publisher titles can be ordered from:

TLpubsorg@aol.com

or from your local bookshop and are also available by post from:

TLPublishers
4 Institute Walk
East Grinstead
West Sussex
RH19 3BD
Telephone: 01342 313015

Postage and packing extra.

Prices shown above were correct at the time of going to press. TL Publishers reserve the right to show new retail prices on covers which may differ from those previously advertised in the text or elsewhere.